emily and einstein

A Novel of Second Chances

linda francis lee

St. Martin's Griffin
New York

This is a work of fiction. All of the characters, organizations, and events portrayed in this novel are either products of the author's imagination or are used fictitiously.

www.stmartins.com

Design by William Ruoto

The Library of Congress has cataloged the hardcover edition as follows:

Lee, Linda Francis.
Emily and Einstein / Linda Francis Lee.—1st U.S. ed.
p. cm.
ISBN 978-0-312-38218-6
1. Husbands—Death—Fiction. 2. Dogs—Fiction. 3. Bereavement—Fiction. 4. Grief—Fiction. 5. Upper West Side (New York, N.Y.)—Fiction. 6. Love stories. gsafd I. Title.
PS3612.E225E45 2011
813'.6—dc22

2010040195

ISBN 978-0-312-38219-3 (trade paperback)

10 9 8 7 6

For the old man with the crazy clothes who appeared unexpectedly at my side so many years ago.

Thank you, wherever you are. . . .

More Praise for *Emily and Einstein*

"A comic charmer of surprising depth." —*Kirkus Reviews*

"A complex novel rich in interesting characters and subplots . . . I highly recommend *Emily and Einstein*." —Jane Bowers, *Romance Reviews Today*

"Powerful and perceptive, *Emily and Einstein* is an unconventional love story, one of those rare books that illuminate the secrets we keep from the world . . . and sometimes ourselves."
—Sarah Dunn, bestselling author of *The Big Love*

"*Emily and Einstein* is an extraordinary treat, a powerfully original novel about hope, redemption, and the possibility that love lives forever, written with grace and imagination." —Joan Johnston, *New York Times* bestselling author of *Shattered*

"A fun flight of fancy that proves there can be a happy ending, even when a man really is a dog." —Haywood Smith, *New York Times* bestselling author of *Waking Up in Dixie*

"A brilliant, compelling, thought-provoking read that moved me to tears of joy. I loved this book." —Kat Martin, *New York Times* bestselling author of *Rule's Bride*

"A really emotional and wonderful book." —*Affaire de Coeur*

"An amazing novel full of hope, redemption and wonderful characters . . . Once you pick this novel up, you won't want to do anything else but read it."
—*Chicklitclub.com*

"A story you'll remember long after you turn the last page, from a writer who understands laughter, longing, and the power of second chances."
—Lisa Wingate, national bestselling author of *Tending Roses* and *Never Say Never*

"*Emily and Einstein* is *Truly, Madly, Deeply* meets *Marley & Me*. . . . Funny, poignant, and hopeful, this tale is delightful from start to finish."
—Stacey Ballis, author of *Good Enough to Eat* and *Inappropriate Men*

"*Emily and Einstein* captured me from the first sentence. You'll find yourself glued to the couch and canceling your plans to find out Emily Portman's fate." —Lisa Patton, author of *Whistlin' Dixie in a Nor'easter*

"What Lee does best is get to the heart of the matter and make us care, all while making us laugh." —Lian Dolan, of the *Satellite Sisters* and *Oprah.com*

also by linda francis lee

The Ex-Debutante
The Devil in the Junior League
Simply Sexy
Sinfully Sexy
Suddenly Sexy
The Wedding Diaries
Looking for Lacey
The Ways of Grace
Nightingale's Gate
Swan's Grace
Dove's Way
Crimson Lace
Emerald Rain
Blue Waltz

Acknowledgments

Writing this book has been a journey and there are many people I want to thank . . .

My parents, Marilyn and Larry Francis.

My brothers and sister and their families: Rick and Ginger Francis, Brian and Andria Francis, Carilyn and Tim Johnson.

The best nieces and nephews—Lauren, Tyler, Grant, Spencer, Cameron, and Haley Grace.

My friends: Gloria Skinner, Jessica Bird, Maxine Bird, Saira Rao, John Resi, Jill Stockwell, John Caputo, Jim Farah, Ken Laughram, Parker Thompson, and August Nazareth.

As always . . .

Amy Berkower and Genevieve Gagne-Hawes, along with Liz Usuriello, Alec Shane, Maja Nikolic, and Jennifer Kelaher.

Jennifer Weis and the entire St. Martin's team, including Lisa Senz and Scott Harshbarger.

Tony Lee, for his amazing son.

And that son, Michael Lee, who makes it all worthwhile.

prologue

A week passed before I understood the enormity of my situation, a week before I realized I was dead.

It was February, a bitter cold day in New York with a gunmetal sky, the kind of storm blowing in that would make even the most stoic northeasterner dream of sun, sand, and a beach that stretched on forever. Wearing a heavy wool suit, silk tie, and overcoat, I walked into my office on the thirty-fourth floor, the view of lower Manhattan blocked out by the falling snow. My secretary was on the phone, her sharp Brooklyn accent and polyester clothes at odds with the old-world, fine wood surroundings of the reception area. She snapped at the caller, something about having to go through her to get to me—the very reason I employed the no-nonsense older woman who wasn't afraid of anyone.

She banged down the phone with a huff. "Pushy, pushy, pushy."

I struggled not to smile.

When she saw me, she didn't so much as blink. "Mr. Portman, there you are." She handed over a stack of memos, while giving me a brief, rapid-fire rundown of who had called. "And your mother stopped by earlier, said she needs to see you."

My mother, the demanding, if beautiful, Althea Portman, had a tendency to think my sole job should be dealing with her.

Without a hitch in my step, glancing through the stack as I went, I didn't bother to look up. "If she stops by again, tell her I quit. Tell her I got fired. Or better yet, tell her I've moved to Mongolia or the Australian Outback, someplace far away that with any luck isn't reachable by phone."

"Now, now, that's just plain mean. She's your mother."

"Mrs. Carmichael, my mother requires mean." I kept going, mentally itemizing which of the memos required my attention. "In fact, a woman like my mother demands mean."

"For a man who can't be more than, what, thirty-five, forty," she called after me, "you sure are cantankerous."

Just before I shut the door to my office, I glanced back, and this time I did smile. "Cantankerous? Me?"

She scoffed and turned away, though not before I caught a glimpse of her own amused smile.

"I'll need a car to take me uptown at seven," I told her.

With that, I tossed the stack of memos in the trash and shut the door.

■

An hour later I left my office at the Regal Bay investment firm. I was due to meet my wife at the Upper West Side Animal Clinic where she volunteered every Friday after work.

The first time I saw Emily I would have sworn she was born and bred in some place like Minneapolis or Milwaukee. It turned out she grew up in Manhattan, raised by a woman I'd had the good fortune never to meet. In her day, Lillian Barlow had been a noted and unfortunately vocal feminist, a woman who had taken a hard stand against what she called *That pack of misogynist men whose goal in life was to oppress women*.

One, I think her stance a sweeping generalization, not to mention melodramatic. And two, given her stance, how a woman who had burned bras and been arrested for protesting the Vietnam War raised a daughter as open and trusting as Emily was anyone's guess. How I ended up marrying the woman's daughter was an even bigger mystery. But when Emily and I met nearly four years earlier, I was on the backside of a skiing mishap that had left me with a shattered leg that surgeons had reassembled with screws and metal pins.

This shouldn't have hit me as hard as it did, but what can I say? For years I had wanted to run the New York City Marathon. I had dreamed of it. In some ways, I had counted on it. After my leg ended up on the wrong end of my unfortunate fall, I was told that my days of training for anything that put significant strain on the leg, much less running the marathon, were over.

All this to say that in my own moment of spectacularly self-indulgent melodrama, when I met Emily I'd just had my first taste of mortality along with an overlarge serving of hunger to be something more than the man I was.

Of course Emily didn't know any of that. The day I met her I was sitting in a conference room of the book publishing house, Caldecote Press, surrounded by the president, publisher, an editor, a lawyer, and Regal Bay's own consigliere who scared even me—and I didn't scare easily. We were there about a sticky issue regarding an upcoming book the publisher had on its fall list. Namely, a book about Regal Bay and some of its allegedly questionable activities. Victor Harken and I were there to make sure the book never saw the light of day. Rather than go the legal route from the onset, Victor wanted first to try and "convince" the publisher to see things our way.

Just before we began the meeting, Emily blew into the room like she was immortal, her long blond hair flowing behind her like a flag. She was delicate, not very tall, but somehow her presence filled the room. I had been half listening to Victor make small talk, but the minute I saw Emily everything else fell away.

Good news, bad news, depending on your point of view, I was nothing if not a connoisseur of women, and everything about Emily seemed a contradiction. She was as beautiful as any of the models I dated, her white blond hair long and loose, her eyes like an indigo sea. But combined with that intensity of energy and color, she wore a simple cream dress that hit barely above her knees. Not blue to highlight her eyes, or short to show off her amazing legs—like adding a constant in algebra to offset an equation. Though in math, the point is to solve for X. Emily seemed impossible to solve.

I was intrigued.

"Ah, Emily," the president said. "I was hoping you could join us."

Introductions were made and I gathered that while Emily was relatively new to the company she had already developed a reputation for problem solving. That the president thought she could solve anything with Victor Harken made me smile. Though when I think back on it now, I realize that despite the contradiction of her, or maybe because of it, everything in the room shifted the minute she blew through the door.

When Victor gestured toward me, and said, "This is—" I cut him off. "Sandy Portman," I offered with a wry smile. "Just another cog in the corporate machine."

Victor looked at me as if I had lost my mind, which perhaps I had. In actuality I was Alexander "Sandy" Vandermeer Regal Portman, a direct descendent of both the Vandermeer and Regal families, founders of Regal Bay, one of Wall Street's oldest and most prestigious investment firms. Whether it was Emily's counterbalanced elegance, or the easy confidence of someone who felt no need to impress, I'm not sure. All I knew was that for the first time in my life I didn't want someone to know who I really was.

We started in on the issue, Victor doing his best to intimidate and threaten, the president looking like he was concerned he'd end up with a horse head in his bed. But the women in the room hardly paid attention to Victor. They eyed me surreptitiously, weighing their possibilities, assessing. At least all the women did except Emily who didn't seem to notice me at all.

No question I wasn't used to disinterest, but it seemed more than that. Watching her, she seemed aware only of whoever was talking, as if she were listening in a way that most people never did.

When every idea and possibility had been suggested then discarded as not working for one or the other side, the president glanced over at her. "Emily, what do you think?"

She considered for a second, then turned to Victor like some blue-eyed David doing battle with a Bronx-born Goliath. "I'm not sure I understand what the problem is. No question you have the resources to tie Caldecote up with lawsuit paperwork for months if not longer, but eventually whatever you're trying to hide is going to come out." She tsked at Victor like he was a schoolyard bully getting caught playing rough on the playground.

I doubted Victor had ever been tsked at in his life.

"So how about a compromise?" she added, then shot him a dazzling smile.

She was either crazy or fearless. Maybe both. I knew with a fair degree of certainty that while Victor hadn't put a horse head in anyone's bed, he was known for his unorthodox means of getting what he wanted. My great-uncle Silas Regal employed him for that very reason. But the consigliere was as caught off guard by the young woman as I was as she made her case with passion and an idealistic conviction that she and her little publisher would win.

"Either way," she went on, "the fact is that while you're tying us up with legal documents, both Regal Bay and Caldecote are going to end up in publishing eNewsletters, financial blogs, even traditional press. Good for us. Bad for you." She shrugged and grimaced as if she were actually sorry.

Victor couldn't seem to speak. I nearly laughed.

By the time Emily finished laying out her plan, Victor had agreed that not only would we not "waste money pursuing futile legal action" but we would give the lowlife business-journalist-turned-author access to Regal Bay higher-ups, as Emily put it, "to tell their side of the story."

Great-uncle Silas was going to have Victor's head. I would have been amused but just then Emily looked at me, finally, and everything changed. The world slowed as she studied me for what seemed like forever, then she smiled. As crazy as it sounds, sitting there with her smiling at me, I felt as if I could achieve anything. In her eyes I saw the man I had the potential to be reflected back. Broken legs and shattered dreams were forgotten and I had the distinct thought that she could make me whole. The feeling was deep and primal, as unsettling as it was nearly godly.

I decided then and there that I would have her.

■

It is a well-documented fact that most males of the species long to be great. Isn't that why we admire superheroes when we are boys and moguls when we are men?

I was no different.

When I was young I wanted to be a basketball player, but while no one would accuse me of being short, I didn't have the tall, lean build of a real player. If I was destined to sit on the bench, why bother? A few years later, I decided on rowing. I was smart and strong, and was being groomed by my prep school coach for the important position of stroke. But after a few months of trudging uptown to practice, I decided rowing was more trouble than it was worth.

Later, during college, I decided to be an artist, someone great like Picasso or Salvador Dali, larger-than-life men with voracious appetites. But this time my mother, a woman known as a great purveyor of all things art, said Portmans sponsored artists; we didn't become them.

What most people didn't know, or perhaps didn't remember, was that my mother hadn't always been a wealthy patron of the arts. The truth was, Althea Portman was an enigma to most people who knew her, a puzzle people had tried to piece together for years. But eventually the questions had been forgotten, and I knew my mother intended for it to stay that way. I rarely gave it any thought; the disconnected pieces of her were something I took in stride.

Though every once in a while our eyes would meet and I could see the question. *Do you remember,* I knew she wanted to ask.

But I was no fool. I always turned away, as did she, the question left hanging in the air, unspoken.

Unfortunately, my mother wasn't one to hold her tongue on much of anything else, and on that unfortunate snowy February night when I left my office at Regal Bay, the night it all began, she and I had exchanged words. This time about my wife.

Frustrated in a way that only my mother could make me, I sat in the back of a Mercedes sedan, one of the firm's hired drivers taking me up Eighth Avenue in the swirling sleet and snow to meet Emily.

The drive took forever, the five lanes of traffic a sea of cabs, hired sedans, and people in SUVs from New Jersey heading north, the snowy street lined by the remnants of less glamorous Manhattan real estate now being encroached upon by the gleaming glass and steel of the midtown business district. An hour after leaving the firm, we finally arrived at the animal clinic on West Seventy-sixth, the narrow length lined with parked cars. The driver double-parked across the street, behind a utility van.

When I didn't immediately get out, he glanced at me over the seat back. "Isn't this the address you gave me, sir?"

"Yes, yes. It is."

Generally I wasn't a distracted person, but that night I felt something I didn't understand. I wrote it off as simple frustration after a long, snowy drive. I realize now that it was more than that, something more complex, less defined, a defiant and callous posturing in front of . . . what, the gods? Whatever the case, I was charging forward, full speed ahead, to my own undoing. And Emily's.

I got out of the car and buttoned my overcoat against the elements. Stepping around the front of the Mercedes, I was startled by a little wiry white-furred dog that leapt out and stood as if intentionally blocking my way. I tried to step around him but slipped on a patch of ice.

Steadying myself on the hood of the car, I shooed the dog away and kept going, snow and sleet coming down harder, the wind blowing, ice hitting my face. When I got to the right front edge of the Mercedes, a car turned onto the street, its headlights bouncing as the tires hit ruts in the freezing slush.

As the car roared closer, I saw that it was a taxi driven by someone who had lost all concern for the perils of driving in the snow. I took a step back, irritated that the cabbie planned to hurtle through the narrow space between the double-parked cars. Then just before the cab reached the Mercedes it happened. The little white dog reappeared and stepped into the street.

The cab driver hit the brakes and swerved, fishtailing back and forth, sliding this way, overcorrecting that way, until the yellow taxi careened into the back of the Mercedes. The thick, falling snow muffled the crash, making the impact feel less destructive. Then silence. There was a moment when I was certain I could hear the snow falling, feel a strange sort of peace.

All in all, the accident wouldn't have caused too much of a problem if I hadn't been standing at the front of one vehicle and an unfortunate five or so feet behind another. Something about thrust and velocity, mixed with angle of trajectory, even over relatively slow speeds and short distances, can make for a very dangerous combination. The long and short being that the cab hit the back of the Mercedes, jamming it forward into me, thrusting me down with such velocity and at such an angle that I crashed over like a domino, no time to break my fall. My head slammed against the fender of the van, traumatizing my brain so intensely and fracturing my spine so deeply that there was never a chance to recover. In seconds I was standing next to my body, no longer cold, merely stunned that the mess on the ground was actually me.

I watched in stunned paralysis as the driver dialed 911, tried to resuscitate my body, then called his dispatch who called the firm. No one called my wife.

I had never been one to panic, though I had never stood on a snowy street before watching someone work to revive my body. But when I tried to move and couldn't, panic spiked through me. I gasped for air, but couldn't do that either.

They say that when your life hangs in the balance, your past flashes before you. But it wasn't friends or events from my childhood I remembered. I didn't think of my parents. I only thought of one thing.

"Emily!"

Her name burst out of me, burst out of my mind, as if somehow she could fix this, could solve this problem. But there was no sound, nothing, as if nothing of substance was left of me to save.

I hadn't known Emily for more than a week the first time I pulled her close. With our lips nearly touching, I whispered, *"Fall in love with me. I dare you."*

She did fall for me, though since then I have wondered if it was the dare that set *me* up to fall.

emily

My mother used to tell me that life could change in an instant, a line drawn in the sand separating before from after, altering you completely. Was that really true? Could a person be changed in an instant? Or did a crack already have to exist in the ice, the beginnings of a change we simply refused to see?

—EXCERPT FROM *My Mother's Daughter*

chapter one

Everyone has a story but I was never interested in telling my own. I was an editor of books, not a writer. I loved to find sense in someone else's chaos, uncover the intent of a sentence or paragraph that only hinted at a truth. At least that was how I felt until I met Sandy Portman.

The first time I saw him my world tilted. Ridiculous, I know, but seeing him that first time jarred me so deeply that I had to turn away, like turning away from looking directly at the sun, and pretend I hadn't noticed him at all.

It had nothing to do with the fact that he was the most beautiful man I had ever seen. His face was a strike against him. I fell in love because there was something in his eyes that was at odds with his physical beauty. Sandy Portman drew me in, like the draft of a manuscript where perfectly constructed sentences hinted at but didn't yet reveal a deeper truth. And when he pulled me close and smiled at me the first time, a crooked smile on his perfect face, hinting at a bit more of his truth? Well, I was lost.

■

My name is Emily Barlow, and I had never been good at sensing trouble. I didn't need to be. I made lists, mapped out plans, then moved forward with a calm certainty that everything would work out. Unshakable faith. Bone-deep belief. Call it what you will. I stepped into any situation with the calm conviction that no matter what, I would survive.

Perhaps that was my mistake. Then again, perhaps that's what would save me.

That morning, the day everything began, I woke with what I now can only call a premonition that my world was about to shift. But I didn't recognize the feeling for what it was. I ignored it.

It had been snowing all night, snow on top of snow during one of the worst winters New York City had seen in a decade. It was Friday, and when I got to work at Caldecote Press almost no one was there, kept away by the storm, safe in houses reached only through bridges and tunnels, or in apartments on the island of Manhattan that climbed up floor after floor into the mottled gray clouds until the buildings disappeared.

At noon, I headed home. The animal clinic had closed due to the weather, and I tried calling Sandy to let him know I would meet him at the apartment. He didn't answer, and his voice mail was full. I'd left a message with his secretary for him to call me, but I never heard back.

We lived in the Dakota, a hundred-and-twenty-year-old building on the Upper West Side, and when I got home I worked, first on a manuscript that had come in early, then on the guest room I had been redoing for several weeks. I had painted the walls a pale yellow, with white crown molding, and a border of lavender, green, and blue flowers that I was painting myself, each delicate stroke like a line of a psalm as I sat at the top of the ladder, the impossibly high ceilings seeming to reach up to God.

For the last two years, I had put every extra cent I had into the apartment. While my husband had a great deal of money, I did not. But I gave that no thought, pouring my heart and soul into the old but enchanted residence that had been little more than a dusty museum when Sandy lived there alone.

I had ripped down ancient wallpaper, torn up broken bathroom tile, replaced outdated appliances, entwining myself in a place that represented everything I had been working toward my entire life. A home with a husband and children, Sunday dinners and friends. A life of work and family, the lines filled in with love, colored by years steadily passing. A life so different from the one I led with my mother where we moved from one apartment to the next, uptown, downtown, Alphabet City. We even did a stint in Chinatown, where plucked chickens and ducks hung in steamy shop windows like ornaments on a tree.

Over the years I learned to guard my heart, didn't let myself become attached to people or places despite my dream of having both. But the day I met Sandy in the Caldecote conference room, something inside me opened up. As everyone was leaving the meeting, Sandy stopped me. He didn't notice, or perhaps didn't care about, the glances others gave us. He looked only at me, his lips hiking up at one corner, turning what would have been a wicked smile into something boyish and playful. "Come away with me," he said. "Right now, before everyone gets wise to us and reminds me of schedules and broken legs and all the things you make me forget."

I must have given him a strange look because his smile widened and he added, "At least let me take you someplace for a drink. Then you can tell me all about why you downplay your amazing looks, and I'll tell you all the reasons why I'm falling for you."

He startled me, but I didn't show it. "Do lines like that really work in your world?"

He laughed out loud. "They do." Then that smile again, this time bordering on sheepish, his hazel green eyes flashing. "Hard to believe, huh?"

My guess was that it wasn't the lines that worked, but his looks, his easy charm. This was a man used to getting his way without having to bargain or even ask.

I smiled despite myself. "One, I have nothing to tell, and two, you don't know half the reasons why I'm worth falling for."

This time he was surprised, but he recovered quickly. "Then I'll take notes; you can dictate. It will give me an excuse to keep you out all afternoon and turn a drink into dinner."

I just shook my head and stepped around him. But at the door I turned back. "Dinner. *After* work. My choice of restaurant."

He cocked his head. "Ever the negotiator. But fine, I'll meet you in the lobby at seven."

"Make it seven-thirty." I started to leave.

"Emily."

I hesitated.

"Do you always win?"

My smile softened. "Does anyone?"

He studied me for a second, then told me I should have been named Diana after the Huntress or Helen after the woman from Troy. "Emily is too soft, too much like that boring cream dress you're wearing. Neither does you justice."

I raised a brow. "For someone who doesn't know the first thing about me, you have a lot of opinions."

What I didn't say was that in every woman there is an Emily just as in every woman there's a Helen of Troy. It depends on which part is nurtured. I'd had no choice but to be strong. And didn't the hardness of strength come when the softness underneath was a threat?

I would have written him off as yet another good-looking guy who used his charm to get what he wanted. But then his brow furrowed. "On second thought, I bet there's an Emily in there somewhere. You just keep her hidden."

My breathing grew shallow. Somehow this seemingly all-surface guy understood.

He walked past me through the doorway, stopping just long enough to tuck a single errant strand of hair behind my ear. "See you at seven-thirty," he said.

■

I had just finished putting the final touches on the painted border when my BlackBerry rang.

I clattered down the ladder, paintbrush still in hand, lavender paint splattered on the old shirt I wore to protect my clothes. When I glanced at the clock I was surprised to see how late it was. I'd have to hurry to get cleaned up before Sandy got home.

"Hello," I said on the fourth ring.

But it wasn't Sandy. It was Birdie Baleau, a woman who had recently moved to New York from Texas, and was like no New Yorker I had ever met. We had become fast friends almost instantly.

"Congratulations!" Birdie squealed on the phone, like we were still in middle school. "I just heard about your promotion to senior editor!"

I fell into a chair and kicked my feet up on the desk as we talked and laughed, excited over this new phase in my career. When I got off the phone, I tried my husband again, but his voice mail was still full.

I showered, then poured myself a glass of wine, found my iPod and cranked up a crazy mix as I danced through the apartment. "Wouldn't It

Be Nice" by the Beach Boys. Harry Nilsson's "The Puppy Song." Adam Lambert's "No Boundaries."

Then "Broken" by Lifehouse.

I didn't remember downloading the song to my playlist. But I closed my eyes and sang to the century-old walls, twirling, arms wide open, head thrown back. My life felt full, my career soaring, a simple happiness wrapping around me as if there could be no stopping me.

An hour later, Sandy still hadn't shown up. I told myself there was no reason to worry. He had been late before. But another hour passed, then two, and still Sandy hadn't called.

At some level had I known? Had I remembered the premonition, had I thought of the song, but refused to assign meaning to it?

Maybe, maybe not. All I know is that I danced and sang in my bright yellow room while snow came down outside the window like thick white curtains that blocked out the view.

sandy

chapter two

I might have called out to my wife, but it wasn't Emily who showed up next to me. All of a sudden I felt a touch of heat, the snow around me melting, one single feather drifting down from the sky. I watched it seesaw back and forth, and I had the distinct thought that I had a choice. Catch the feather—or not.

I hesitated, my mind cloudy with only half-realized thoughts, then just before the feather hit the ground I gasped and scooped it up. As soon as it hit my hand, the heat turned into a sizzle of what I can only call energy, then an old man appeared out of nowhere.

I stumbled back and he smiled at me, his longish white hair swept away from his forehead in a soft wave. He wore a double-breasted frock coat as if he had stepped out of Regency England, a loud, wide tie, and round tortoiseshell glasses. Everything about him seemed mismatched, as if his clothes and bearing had been collected over centuries.

He stepped closer. "I believe that's mine," he said, and plucked the feather from my fingers with the sort of kind, apologetic smile that wasn't a staple in Manhattan. After shoving it in his pocket, he looked me up and down. "Are you all right?"

I scoffed. "Apparently not." I was glad to see my dry wit was still intact even if my body was not.

He only chuckled. "It's always a shock at first, especially when it's an accident. It's easier when the person has been sick for a long time, when the pain is unbearable, and they're ready to move on. It's not even all that hard with the young ones. They are more accepting, not yet so set in their ways. The hardest are the middle-aged. They realize time has run out on achieving their dreams. They don't want to go. They want more time to live the life they have been too afraid or too weighed down by day-to-day existence to achieve. They're the ones who fight every step of the way."

"What are you talking about?"

Part of me knew exactly what he meant, but another part didn't want to know. One of my more useful traits had always been my ability to live and work happily with a narrow-eyed vision that allowed me to assume that I was right and everyone else was wrong. In this case, I had no interest in absorbing that I was dead and he was some sort of angel sent to cart me off to heaven just as in some overly trite movie I never would have bothered to see while alive.

"It's time to move on, Alexander."

No one, not even my mother, called me Alexander.

He started down Seventy-sixth toward Columbus Avenue, brownstones and low-rise apartment buildings forming a narrow snowy canyon. He walked in the street, no footprints left behind in the slush and snow. "Are you coming?"

I realized I had no idea what else to do. Just stand there? It seemed to me that arriving at heaven's gate should be easier than this. But I followed.

We walked the length of Seventy-sixth, crossing Columbus, eventually coming to Central Park. We entered the park on a footpath, taking the winding trail deeper into the snow-covered grounds, and turned south.

Hmmm. "Where are we going?"

"You'll see."

I panicked, the accident and my death finally sinking in.

"I can't do this."

I turned around and fled.

I hadn't run in years, but I started out at a good pace despite my handmade leather shoes, despite the fine wool suit, suspenders, and overcoat. Nothing obstructed me, not the layers of clothes, not my leg, as I ran toward the clinic.

Throughout my life, when my back was against the wall, I had always been able to find a way to save myself. I would save myself again. Surely my injuries weren't as catastrophic as the medics believed. It was probably a tough night; they hadn't put their all into saving me. It couldn't have been too long since the accident. Plus it was freezing cold, keeping my body temperature low. If I could get back into my body, I felt certain I could save myself once again.

I hit Seventy-sixth Street in minutes, arrived at the clinic seconds later. I had never moved so fast in all my life. It was amazing. I could do this. But when I got to the building, the odd old man was already there shaking his head. "You really can't outrun me, Alexander."

The sheer staggering force of it brought me to my knees, literally, my topcoat pooling around me in the frozen slush. "You can't do this. I have so much left to do."

"Technically, that isn't true." Yet again he looked apologetic.

My mind raced. "I have a wife. If I die it will kill her."

"I can't disagree with you there. That woman loves you. Really loves you. Too bad you didn't think of that sooner."

■

The evening I arrived in the lobby of Caldecote Press to pick up Emily that very first time, I expected her to choose some quaint restaurant on the Upper East Side. Someplace where her classically simple clothes wouldn't stand out. We did end up on the east side, but not at any place that could be considered quaint. She took me to an out-of-the-way coffee shop where the crusty old waiter knew her by name.

As soon as we were seated, the waiter handed us plastic-covered menus.

"I give you a second," the man said, his accent thick and nondescript.

To be perfectly honest, I had never been in a diner before, and the sheer number of choices was staggering, making me suspect the chef couldn't have time or fresh enough ingredients to make a single dish exceptional. Surely, though, he did one item better than the others.

When the waiter returned, I asked, "What is the chef's specialty?"

The man looked put out, scoffed as only a New York waiter could, then used his short, blunt-nosed pencil to point out a section of the menu. CHEF'S SPECIALS, it read.

"Can'ta you read?" the man demanded, then looked at Emily, his expression softening like a grandfather gazing at a beloved granddaughter. "He no good enough for you, *latria mou*."

Emily ducked her head to hide her smile, her long hair swinging forward.

After I learned that he had said something about adoring her in Greek, I was half afraid to eat the roast beef dinner he banged down in front of me.

"So, you were going to dictate a list of all the reasons you're amazing," I said.

"No, I just said you didn't know all the reasons."

"True. So I made my own list to prove you wrong." I surprised her when I reached into my suit pocket and pulled out a slip of paper. With ceremony, I read, "Emily Barlow is beautiful, smart, straightforward, not worried about what others think of her. And funny, despite the fact that she doesn't realize it."

"You actually made a list?" She gasped.

I turned the sheet toward her.

She laughed out loud when she saw that it was blank.

"Now, *your* turn to tell me about you," I said.

"Fair enough." But she didn't tell me anything about herself, at least not directly. She was editing a manuscript about great men. Philosophers, scientists, athletes. Her New York–bred reserve evaporating completely, she leaned forward with the kind of enthusiasm the women I dated refused to show, and told me about the book.

"What I'd give for ten minutes with one of those guys," she said.

Ah, a woman who was drawn to powerful men. I shouldn't have been disappointed. I was strong, I had power. But for some reason I had thought she was different.

She laughed, those blue eyes of hers dancing. "Though my sympathies to any woman who falls for a guy like that. Just show me a glimpse of his brain, how it works, that's what I want to see. Explain to me why one man is great and another isn't. Is one man so hungry to be something more than ordinary that he does whatever it takes, and another won't?"

Her question made a shiver run down my spine. "You want to know if you're born with talent or whether you develop it."

"Yes! If you hit a golf ball a hundred times and each time you shank, does that mean you're not meant to play golf? Or is there a magic number for each person, like if you hit a hundred-and-one golf balls, or a hundred-and-ten golf balls, or even *two-hundred*-and-ten golf balls, it's at *that* point that you'd start getting better? But you'll never know because you gave up."

When I first saw her, saw the way she blew into the conference room, I was taken by her presence. When she talked about greats like da Vinci as easily as she discussed Tiger Woods and the problems that had come his way, I experienced the same feeling that with her at my side I could do anything. Sitting in a cracked vinyl booth in an ancient diner, Emily Barlow eased the aching need that flowed through me like blood, the hunger I had never been able to satisfy.

When we finished dinner I was surprised at how much time had passed, how the restlessness had quieted. Emily proved to be a key to a lock on a door I had never been able to pass through. In her I found a foreign combination of desire and peace. And as soon as I put her in a cab and watched her fade away, I knew I would see her again.

■

The old man or angel or whatever he was shook his head at me.

I might have cringed. The fact was, nearly four years after we ate at that diner, I had been pulling away from Emily. Not that she understood this, especially since for more than two years we had been insanely happy. But in the last few months everything had changed. The hunger had taken me by surprise when it returned, like a thief jumping me in a dark alleyway, stealing something essential.

I had become short-tempered and impatient, at times shaking with frustration. Everything set me on edge. The palliative effect of Emily had worn off like a drug dissipating, leaving me in withdrawal for a fix I wanted but could no longer reach.

The fact was I had gone to the animal clinic so I could take Emily to dinner and tell her I wanted a divorce. And the way I saw it, it was Emily's fault.

The old man gave me a look as if he could hear every word I was thinking. "Denial. Selfish denial," he clarified. "No wonder I was sent here."

Which is when I, me, Sandy Portman, friend to a select few, charmer of many, began to understand that this wasn't going to go well.

"Please," I managed, my clothes a mess, my hair wild. "Don't do this to me."

He shook his head, then lifted his hands as if he was going to do something. Conjure up hell and damnation, make me disappear. I had no idea what exactly, but I knew it couldn't be good.

"Please, no!"

The old man hesitated.

"This is a mistake. You've got to believe me."

I was begging, I know, but pride has a way of flying out the window when you're faced with your sudden demise.

"Give me another chance!"

He dropped his arms and narrowed his eyes. "So you do understand."

The words surprised me. I had been babbling. But this tack appeared to be working. "Yes, yes, I understand."

I sort of panted the words and he looked at me hard, seeming to debate.

"No, you don't," he said. "But maybe that's okay."

I could tell he was thinking about something, as if running through a mental pros and cons list, and I knew my fate lay in his hands.

"I'll tell you what," he said. "I'll give you a second chance. But I've got to warn you, you're not going to like the terms."

I most definitely didn't like the sound of that, and old habits die hard—all those long established neural pathways sending jolts of ingrained behavior through me, like Pavlov ringing his damned bell.

"Now listen here, old man—"

"Fine, then. It's over."

He lifted his hands.

"Wait!"

He didn't stop.

"All right," I said, my voice both brave and resigned. "All right."

"You're sure you want this?"

I gave him a look. "If it's your way or it's over, I'll take your way."

"Okay. Here you go."

Then the world went black.

chapter three

I had gotten myself into more than a few jams over the years, which perhaps explained why when I came to and heard the howling I wasn't all that concerned. Irritated at the noise, yes, but not overly alarmed. Granted, confusion wracked my usually agile brain, making me undeniably slow on the uptake.

What I did know was that I hadn't a clue where I was, the sensation beneath my eyelids swollen and grainy. I couldn't open my eyes, but it seemed more a refusal to see than an inability to do so. I felt drugged, my heart fluttering. I sensed that my body hadn't the physical strength to filter drugs or alcohol or whatever was making me weak like it once had. First my leg, now the slow recovery rate of encroaching middle age. I groaned. I was thirty-eight, not fifty-eight. But the sound that hit my ears didn't sound like any groan I had ever experienced.

What was wrong with me?

Thankfully the howling had abated, making it easier to think. I began to see light coming through the thin cracks between my eyelids. Then came the stench, an earthy smell that made my stomach roil.

Had I been left in a barn? Or worse, based on the smell, had I been left in the bathroom of a country-western bar with a faint overlay of rubbing alcohol? Did they even have country-western bars in Manhattan anymore? Beyond that, how was it possible that I could distinguish all these smells?

Finally my vision cleared enough to make out the thin bars of a metal cage. Drugs, alcohol, now a cage? What kind of debauchery had I engaged in last night?

Then it hit me. The drive to the Upper West Side Animal Clinic. The snow. The taxi hitting the Mercedes. Me lying dead in the slush and snow. And the old man who said something about a second chance. Was it possible he had dropped me off in some sort of barn for alcoholics to do my penance?

I shuddered at the thought. As much as I didn't like to admit it, I carried hand wipes and tiny bottles of antibacterial solution with me. Safe to say, I definitely wouldn't be big on barns of any variety.

"Hello?" I called out, hoping the old man was nearby and could hop to and answer some questions. "Anyone there?"

A strangled series of barks echoed against the walls beyond the cage.

Panic ripped through me and I tried to sit up. But I couldn't move. I had no strength.

I groaned, which brought back the low howling sound. Was there a dog close by?

"Hello!"

The howl yelped into the space and I went very still, realizing that the sound was vibrating in my chest.

Panic surged, blood pumping through me, bringing adrenaline with it, and I was able to raise my head. That's when I saw the paws. White fur-covered paws attached to furry legs, traveling right up to the general vicinity of where I looked out.

With a jerk, I glanced at the body. The quick movement made me dizzy, and I nearly passed out at the sight of more white, wiry fur and another set of limbs. And a tail. Dear God in heaven, had the old man turned me into a dog? Was this even possible?

Frantically I used every ounce of mental energy I had to push forward, my brain telling my hand to move. But the only thing that stirred was one of those front paws.

I fell back against the floor. I sensed the heavy breathing, but heard a pant.

Pulling a deep breath, I concentrated, then yanked the body forward again. All I saw was the dog legs and cage. I tried to touch something. But the only way I could touch anything was with my face. And my face touched the leg, and the only leg getting touched was the fur-covered one.

Sweet mother in heaven, I was a dog. More specifically, I realized that somehow I was in the body of the white wiry stray who had stepped in front of the cab.

What started as a whimpering howl became manic baying. Shock shuddered through me. The noise echoed against the thin metal grating of the cage, desolate, devastated. But the despair quickly turned to anger, and on the heels of anger, fury consumed me.

I howled and growled, saliva pooling in my mouth, the thin floppy tongue lolling about without direction.

"How could you do this to me?" I cried, the sound a furious howl.

I had never felt such wretchedness. If there had been a spike or sharp object I would have thrown myself on it, impaling this awful body, putting us all out of our misery.

Eventually my howling tapered off, what little adrenaline I had managed to drum up deserting me. I fell back, a noise coming out of me like groaning hot air let out of a heavy balloon. The head—my head now—landed on wadded-up terry cloth, some cheap discarded beach towel from the looks of the thick bold stripes.

I don't know how long I lay there moaning in the semidarkness and barn stench without dying before I heard a door open.

"Einstein?"

It was a woman's voice, one I recognized.

"Einstein, is that you, boy?"

I was stunned and overjoyed when Emily appeared before the cage, her blue eyes filled with concern.

"Emily!" I cried. But the consonants and syllables wouldn't form into anything coherent. "Oh my God, Emily! It's me, Sandy!"

"There, there, boy. Don't try to get up."

She crouched down and stuck her fingers through the very lowest place in the cage. With serious effort, I managed to control the unruly tongue and stretch forward far enough to lick her. "Emily, Emily, Emily," I murmured, the sound echoing against the walls of what I now confirmed was the Upper West Side Clinic where Emily volunteered. "It's me," I whimpered.

"It's okay, Einstein. You're going to be all right."

I could tell from her voice that she was amazed that this dog was alive. More than that, she knew this dog. She loved this dog. And she was worried sick about this Einstein.

"Damn it, Emily, it's me!"

If her not recognizing me wasn't bad enough, I realized that the despicable old man had clearly thought to play a joke on me. Well, the old bastard would learn. You didn't play jokes on Alexander "Sandy" Vandermeer Regal Portman.

"Old man!" I barked. Literally, bringing back the despair.

"Oh, Einstein," Emily said, sinking to the floor beside the cage. "You're going to be okay, E."

The cadence of her voice and the touch of her fingers settled me. "Emily," I murmured, the sound a guttural moan.

When I finally calmed, she opened the cage door.

"I shouldn't be here," she said. "I should be at work getting ready for the editorial meeting, but Blue called and said you were awake and something must be wrong because you wouldn't stop howling. What is it, boy? Is the pain bad?"

"Yes!" said as a sharp bark. Though the body pain was the least of my concerns.

The greatest sense of frustration I had ever known hit me. My verbal skills had always been excellent, my quick wit and funny turns of phrase the foundation of my charm. The ratty old heart sank as my mind clarified the thought. *Sandy* was charming; *Sandy* had excellent verbal skills. Not the dog called Einstein.

Another howl echoed against the cinder block walls and cement floor.

"Oh, Einstein. I hate seeing you like this," Emily said, touching my paw.

Then of all things, she smiled at me. Granted, it was a strange yearning smile, but a smile nonetheless. She leaned close and cupped my head with her hands. "Can you believe it, E? You made it," she whispered. "You didn't die."

Her words shuddered down my spine with a clarity that I felt but didn't understand, before the sensation evaporated when something occurred to me. Sure, this dog had survived. But if I, me, Sandy Portman, hadn't survived, had died, my wife should be at home in anguish, distraught, unable to function. Hadn't she been notified yet? Good God, had my body somehow ended up in the morgue as an unidentified John Doe?

My mind staggered, emotion and canine pharmaceuticals finally too much for this dog's body. I welcomed the relief that crept around the edges of consciousness like an inky black darkness, and I went under.

■

I woke again.

I can't say how long I was out, but for the next period of time my new little dog's body and I existed in a vacuum broken up by visits from Emily, an intensity of smells that made me want to stuff cotton up my nose, and noise. Every sound from blocks away rang in my ears until I wanted to shudder against the racket. I could hear sirens and garbage trucks shifting gears, children laughing and screaming in the street. All of it was a din in this head, a quagmire of sound and smell, pain and anguish. I would have sunk back onto the unrelenting cage floor if the door hadn't opened.

"Einstein? How are you doing, boy?"

Emily again.

"I'm horrible," I snapped at her, angry, frustrated.

"Now, E, I know I promised to come back sooner. But a manuscript that was due ages ago came in and the production department needed it edited immediately. I read all afternoon and night. Hey, you didn't eat your food. Einstein, you've got to eat to get your strength back."

"Hello! Why aren't you upset over me, the man me, your husband?"

I know I snapped again, but really, I was a dog. A miserable dog.

"Einstein," she admonished me. "You're too much."

I *was* too much. This was too much. Then all of the sudden what equilibrium I had summoned deserted me and I started to cry. Me, crying.

Of course it came out as that horrid howling, painful and filled with desolation. Emily sat back on her heels, drawing in a shuddering breath.

One of the things I had always admired about her was the way she remained even-keeled, never crying. She wasn't one to fall apart. Though I didn't like it one bit now that her strength was employed in regards to me.

But then she leaned forward, coming closer. I saw beyond the encouraging smile and realized that there was a haunted look in her eyes. I could actually feel her pain, sensed tears that threatened, but she held them back, her fingers curling into the grated edge around the door.

Frustration snaked through me. When Emily finally threatened to fall apart in any way, why in the world was it because of a dog?

"Oh, Einstein," she said, her voice barely a whisper as she pressed her forehead against the cage. "I can't believe Sandy's gone."

emily

For all her life, my mother was part adult, part child; equally as determined as impetuous. She fought against men who didn't want to share rights that should have been afforded to all even as she collected those very same men, making them love her until she got bored and tossed them aside. My mother had no respect for any woman who needed a man.

—EXCERPT FROM *My Mother's Daughter*

chapter four

I dream of snow. White, blinding. When I see Sandy, he stands in the street, snow making the world around him soft, seemingly safe. He extends his hand to me, that smile of his pulling up at one corner. Then the car, swerving back and forth. Just before impact I gasp awake and scream, No.

■

My mother always said I never did anything halfway—not in school, not in life, and clearly not in love. On the night of Sandy's accident, when he still hadn't come home at midnight, I called everyone I could think of. No one had heard from him, and I'd had to leave a message on my parents-in-law's answering machine. I paced the apartment, anxiety trumping all the plausible explanations I managed to come up with. When the phone rang at one in the morning I went still, standing frozen for half a second before I grabbed up the receiver. "Sandy?" I blurted.

A startled silence followed. "Emily, this is Walter Portman."

My father-in-law's voice was brusque, intimidating. But that night his usual tone was mixed with something else. It wasn't alarm, as if I would need to come quickly. It was more resignation, as if whatever had happened was done, finished.

My breath rushed out in a silent gasp. My brain tripped and staggered, then righted itself, though only to the position of drunken soldier not in her right mind. At some level I knew what the call meant. But I didn't give my father-in-law a chance to tell me. I made small talk, asked how things were at the firm. "Can you believe this bizarre weather?" I bleated.

I heard him sigh, the sound of his leather desk chair groaning as he leaned back and said, "I'm afraid I have bad news."

Grief alters the mind, has the ability to take you places that seem normal but aren't. "This isn't a good time, Mr. Portman. Sandy should be home any minute."

He was silent then. After a long moment he started again, this time softer. "Emily."

But he didn't get a chance to finish before I heard his wife walk in.

"Did you tell her?"

He covered the mouthpiece, his voice muffled as he said something, then Althea came on the line.

"Emily, there's been an accident."

■

I had barely known Sandy for more than a few days when I invited him to dinner at my apartment. I made a meal of lamb chops with a mango curry, and we talked long into the night. His hands were strong and beautiful, always close to mine, but never touching.

For the next few evenings, he arrived at my apartment after work, and less than a week after I met him he burst through my door. "Honey, I'm home!"

I laughed before racing back to the kitchen.

He chuckled and closed the door behind him. My hands returned to the dough I was kneading, and I could see him take in the surroundings. I loved my home. It wasn't in an important building on the Upper East or Upper West Sides of town. It was a nondescript, medium-rise prewar space east of midtown, but a gem of light and high ceilings. It was on the top of the building, with gardens and a front door painted red. A secret jewel in a city of tiny spaces, filled with photos, flowers, and the first-edition children's books I had been collecting since I was a child.

After my mother died, the rent-controlled apartment was the only thing she left me, the one thing I needed the most. I might have driven her crazy with my desire for a permanence she didn't begin to understand, but without ever telling me, she had put my name on the lease and left me a home.

After years of butting heads, I vowed that somehow I would find a way to thank my mother. Somehow I would find a way to make her proud.

"This place is amazing," Sandy said.

"It's rent-controlled," I called back.

"Even more amazing. An incredible apartment you must pay next to nothing for, and which by law can't be taken away from you. You hear about these places, but there are so few left anymore."

"Which is why I'll never give it up."

I heard him hesitate before asking, "There is *nothing* that would make you give it up?"

I should have understood then that I had tempted fate.

"Absolutely nothing. This apartment gives me . . . freedom. It gives me a place where I belong, a home that I'll always be able to afford."

"Of course. You're right." He resumed his perusal of the living room, laughed when he opened an antique music box and it played.

"I'll be there in a minute," I said. "I've just about finished the dough."

"You're making homemade bread?"

"Rolls. Two batches. One for dinner, then another with cinnamon, pecans, loads of butter, and iced when they're done."

He popped his head around the door frame, his smile as wicked as it was charming. "I take it you're planning on me staying until breakfast?"

My pulse leaped but I gave him a stern look. "No, I have no intention of seducing you. Just feeding you. Dinner. Only dinner. I rarely take the time to make fresh bread, so while I was at it I figured I'd make my famous cinnamon rolls too."

"Ah, well, a man can dream." He extended the flowers.

"Peonies." I wiped my hands on a towel. "My favorites."

I took the flowers from him and found a vase.

He came up behind me, close, but still not touching me. "Will they get me a breakfast roll?"

A deep rush of longing ran along my senses, and after a second I turned to face him. When he lifted me up onto the tiny, cluttered countertop I didn't stop him. When he leaned in, our lips nearly touching, and whispered, "Fall in love with me. I dare you," I took his hand and pressed his palm to the side of my face, then kissed him.

I forgot about breakfast rolls and dinner when he pulled me closer. He smelled of a subtle mix of wind and leather, intensely masculine and compelling after growing up in a world of women, men coming and going only in the capacity of temporary diversions. It wasn't until Sandy slid his hands down my back, cupping my hips, that I broke away.

"I am not wasting that dough," I said, my breathing ragged.

I kissed him one more time, then pushed him out of the kitchen, handing him a glass and a bottle of wine.

Over dinner that night I told him about my only living relative.

"At forty-nine, when I was nine, my mother surprised us all when she got pregnant again and actually married." I smiled, though I knew there was a wry twist to it. "My little sister Jordan is everything I'm not. I write out lists and map out plans. She breaks the rules, gets into trouble, shuns good sense . . . and never failed to make our mother smile."

I felt the surprise I always did when I thought about my sister.

"You must have hated her."

My head jerked back. "Hate her? God no. She can frustrate me, make me insane with worry. But I have loved her from the minute my mother brought her home, loved every tiny finger and perfect little toe."

He considered me for a second. "Where's she now?"

"Who knows? She travels the world doing good works. She's convinced she can and will save the world."

"I'd like to meet her."

I had always kept Jordan away from the rest of my world, not because I was embarrassed of her, but because I knew she hated all things that involved deadlines and moneymaking, not to mention the sorts of people I tended to like. Having her point out all the reasons my friends and pursuits were suspect and inferior got old. Not to mention that when she said things like, *"Freaking A, Em, that guy has fat palms and tiny fingers. Imagine what his dick looks like . . . if you can find it since you know fingers like that mean his dick is really a dickette."* Followed by a snort. *"If a penis bangs around inside you like a clanger in a bell, I say why bother."*

Eventually I would have to break it off with the guy because I couldn't help grimacing whenever I looked at his hands. Needless to say, if I liked someone, I generally kept them far, far away from my sister.

It had never mattered before. It shouldn't have mattered then since I barely knew Sandy Portman. But already I knew I wanted more from him.

"I accept," I said after we finished eating.

"Accept?"

"Your dare."

His hazel eyes darkened and he reached for me. I nearly let him stay and finish what we had started on the kitchen counter. Instead, I shoved a paper bag of cinnamon rolls into his hand and pushed him out the door.

■

For hours after that early morning call from my parents-in-law, I existed in a state of numb disbelief.

Sandy couldn't be gone.

I washed his clothes. I ironed his crisp button-down shirts that didn't need ironing. Somehow it seemed that doing perfect housewife things would make him come home.

At some point, less than twenty-four hours after the call, my mother-in-law arrived and informed me that the funeral was to occur the following Friday at St. Thomas Church on Fifth Avenue. I couldn't quite absorb the insult or implications of her making the arrangements. Instead, when she told me, I had to swallow back a laugh—or was it a choke? I didn't believe any of it. None of this could be happening. I couldn't be a widow. Widows wore support hose and had gray hair. Or if they were lucky, they had laugh lines around their eyes from long years living with a man who made them smile. At any second I would wake up and Sandy would be at the breakfast table eating what he always ate. One soft-boiled egg. Two slices of nine-grain bread with red currant jam. Grapefruit juice and Elijah's Blend coffee. All from the Fairway market. Why didn't his mother know that?

Althea Portman looked at me oddly then left.

On the Monday before the service, three days after the accident, I made Sandy's breakfast without thinking. The surprise of seeing the meal sitting on the kitchen table brought me up short, and I backed into the wall. Without throwing it away or cleaning anything up, I dressed and hurried to my midtown office with its fax machines and break rooms where I couldn't fall into the trap of expecting to find Sandy.

I threw myself into a manuscript that was a mess, losing myself to the disconnected sentences and half-formed truths, anything that would consume my mind. At the end of the day, instead of going home, I went to the animal clinic where I volunteered. I was Emily Barlow. Strong, practical. I dealt with impossible situations. I could do this, I told myself. If nothing else, I was my mother's daughter.

When I walked into the clinic, I sensed something before I understood what it was. I should have been surprised when I found the white wiry dog on the verge of death, covered in tubes and bandages, but I wasn't. The staff said they had found him in the street out front, clearly a stray that had been hit by a car and left for dead. They had done what they could to revive him. Nothing had helped.

"Einstein."

I named him without thinking, gently running my palm over the tufts of white wiry fur that stood up on his head and I knew that I had to save the animal, as if by doing so I could save my husband. Not that I actually put this into words, or even fully formed the concept in my head. I just knew I had to save the dog. For reasons I couldn't explain, I couldn't lose Einstein.

I paid for expensive surgeries with money I couldn't afford to spend, praying for him to come out of the coma. When the vet had done all that he could, I sat with Einstein, waiting, stroking his fur. "Hang in there," I whispered. "I need you to not die."

They say that coincidences are God's way of remaining anonymous. But sometimes he opens his palm and hands us a gift we can't deny is his doing. By the time I was out of money and the staff said we really had to let him go, Einstein woke.

Part of me felt relief, as if somehow this meant that my plan of keeping busy and maintaining control was working. But the morning after Einstein woke, it was Friday, the day of Sandy's funeral.

I arrived at St. Thomas Church, not realizing I was wearing a navy blue dress instead of black until I hesitated on the church steps, my coat hem flapping open in the wind. Sitting in the front pew, I was only vaguely aware of the massive crowd in attendance; I studied lint on the blue jersey.

I saw no faces. No voice stood out. Not even my sister was there because she hadn't been able to get a flight back from South America in time.

Whenever the disjointed numbness started to crack and let something darker seep through, I refocused on the lint or thought about Einstein. I thought about the manuscript I was working on. I thought about anything except the mahogany casket at the front of the church. I only wanted to get back to work, back to Einstein, then back to the safety of the apartment Sandy and I had shared at the Dakota.

As soon as the service was over I turned to leave.

"Emily."

With effort, I made out my mother-in-law.

She came toward me with icy-cold correctness, her auburn hair pulled back, her green eyes closed off, the kind of eyes that didn't give anything back. She spoke with stiff enunciation of every syllable, jaw thrust forward, though I always had the feeling that her manner was an affectation born of necessity rather than a lifetime of New England nannies and Mayflower teas. It was Sandy's father who had the blond hair and faded gray eyes of an older New York, along with the ease of that world which he wrapped around himself like a king's robe, rich and important, but taken for granted.

Althea nodded to people as they passed, then said, "How are you doing, dear?"

I had the fleeting thought that this woman was kinder than I had always believed, and I started to blurt out that there was a photo of her and Sandy that I thought she might want.

She never gave me the chance to offer the picture or even answer her question. "Taylor," she called out to a man I somewhat recognized.

"Mrs. Portman," he said. "I'm so sorry."

Althea and I both said thank you, before glancing at each other.

"Yes, well," she said, as if I had no right to the name. "The two of you might as well set up a time to meet."

The man shifted uncomfortably.

"Meet?" I asked. "What for?"

"The apartment, of course."

Foreboding prickled my skin, and I felt the hazy scrim seep back into my mind.

"Althea," the man said with a scowl, "I hardly think this is the time—"

"Taylor, none of this is going to get any easier." She turned to me.

"My husband and I will give you time, but you need to start thinking about when you can move out."

I could only stare at her. "What?" I managed.

"Emily," she said carefully, "the apartment belonged to Sandy and is covered in his will. At his death, the residence at the Dakota goes into the Portman Family Trust."

"But . . . Sandy promised." I tried to make my brain work. "He said he was deeding it to me. He changed his will."

"Emily, you're confused. He didn't change anything."

"No. That's not possible." After a year of Sandy's prodding, a year after he promised me the Dakota, I had given in and given up my rent-controlled apartment, the decision tying me even more tightly to my husband. "Sandy said the Dakota was mine."

His mother looked me in the eye. "That's ridiculous."

Heat ripped through my face. *You can't do this!* But I caught myself. "I have to go," I managed, banging into people as I hurried toward the door.

"Emily!" Althea called out.

But I didn't stop. *You will not fall apart,* I told myself, needing to get away, though what I really needed was to see her son.

On the street, I hailed a cab, then pressed my head against the hard seat back, not realizing I had given the animal clinic address until we pulled up outside.

einstein

chapter five

I stared at my reflection in the stainless steel siding of some sort of medical cabinet. I could hardly believe my eyes. Where was my sandy blond hair, my sparkling hazel green eyes?

I had always been known for my charm, not to mention my dazzling good looks. Based on the image staring back at me, I would no longer dazzle anyone. As a dog, all white wiry fur standing on end with the random smudge of brown. I was decidedly ugly.

How could this be happening to me, Sandy Portman, a direct descendent of both the Vandermeer and Regal families of New York, Aspen, Biarritz, and the Hamptons?

At the thought of the Hamptons I felt a spurt of pure happiness, all that sun and sand. But my joy turned to a shudder of despair at the realization that the *man* Sandy Portman loved the Hamptons. I couldn't imagine that as a dog I'd ever get to see the Hamptons again.

The drugged feeling slowly faded, unadulterated doom replaced with determination to get this ludicrous situation resolved. I pushed my anger down, like embers lying dormant, waiting to burst back into flames. I thought I was dealing rather maturely with the bizarre predicament, waiting patiently for the old man to return so I could let him know in no uncertain terms that this was unacceptable.

Soon I started recognizing people I began to term "the staff." A ragtag assortment of miscreants and underachievers I never would have hired given the choice, but staff nonetheless. Once I started feeling better they put me on a schedule.

"Finally," I snapped at the nurse.

She gave me a wry look.

Soon the dog diapers were removed, along with the IV, and they led me to a small area behind the clinic where a volunteer looked at me expectantly. I couldn't imagine what he wanted.

"Come on, Einstein, you've got to take care of business."

I ruffed in confusion.

"You know," he prompted. "Take a piss. Pee. Whatever."

My body stiffened. Relieve myself? Here? On the cement? With him watching? He couldn't be serious.

"Old man!" I howled.

Thankfully the volunteer took pity on me and turned his back to give me some privacy. And really, I did need to "take care of business."

In addition to Nurse, there was a disreputable looking fellow who worked the night-shift named Vinny, and a multi-pierced, twenty-something female volunteer who came in twice a week. Her name was Blue, and while as a human I would have detested her, as a dog I liked her quite a lot. She was a veritable feast of smells, a living and breathing puzzle to keep my brain well occupied while she was there. The blue hair dye she used, the strange smell of her black lipstick. The vegetarian diet she ate.

There were a scattering of other volunteers who weren't regulars. Plus the vet, a nice enough guy who was amazed his handiwork had been able to save me.

The faces blurred together at times, depending on how much sleep I got or what kind of drugs they pumped into me. But the person who always stood out was Emily. She arrived regularly, on more than just the Friday evenings when she used to volunteer—thank God. I might have wanted to divorce her when I was a man, but as a dog my options for interaction were uninspiring at best. The vet was too needy, the nurse too distracted. Blue was interesting but not nearly as attentive as Emily. Vinny just wanted the paycheck, and quite frankly, was a little scary. What I came to understand was that no one wanted to get attached to any of the animals in the clinic.

As my health improved, I began to feel a fissure of concern. What would happen to me once I was able to manage on my own?

I consoled myself with the thought that I would convince the old man I had learned my lesson and he would put me back in my body.

Rolling over on my side, pawing distractedly at some simpleminded rubber toy Blue had left me, I was surprised when Vinny appeared one day and attempted to lure me out of the cage.

"Time for a bath."

Bath? Someone, namely this fellow, was going to bathe me?

While the idea of soaking in my deep porcelain tub back at the Dakota sounded like heaven, getting a dog bath didn't sound like anything I would enjoy.

"Come on, dog."

I deduced it to be well after midnight because Vinny had been there alone long enough to watch his favorite television show, mop haphazardly, watch his second favorite show, empty the trash cans, and take his late-night nip of cheap whiskey. Given that even as a dog I was no fool, I stayed where I was.

"You're taking a bath. The doc said it was time. When he shows up in the morning you've gotta be clean." His less than spring-fresh coveralls carried a host of competing odors, none of them pleasant. "We can do this the easy way or the hard way. Just so ya know, I'm partial to the hard way."

His low chuckle made me think of a B-level actor straight out a bad episode of *The Sopranos*. What was he going to do? Break my leg, stuff me in a trunk, and drive me to a New Jersey landfill? What would Nurse and Vet say when I went missing? They might not care that much, but I knew Emily would.

Amused at my analogies, and gratified that at least someone would notice if I went missing, I laughed at the thought. Unfortunately, it came out as a growl.

"Don't growl at me, mutt. I can hurt you without anyone knowing. I have ways."

He leaned close and I cringed at the wave of rotgut liquor coming out of him. Good lord, cheap whiskey, no deodorant, and a street-vendor wrap for dinner. The mix of smells was enough to make a lesser dog empty his stomach.

I rose, backing up until my hind quarters hit the metal grating. Vinny's eyes narrowed. The next thing I knew he reached in, dragged me from the cage, took out the kind of plastic bat you'd buy at a toy store for a child, and whacked me in the head. Other than surprise, I didn't feel a thing. But when I finally came to, I was surprisingly clean—and somehow I had managed to give Vinny a nasty black eye.

■

As much as I shouldn't admit it, I was rather proud of that black eye. It gave me something of a ruffian swagger, quite a different mien from the one I'd had as a man. As Sandy Portman, I never engaged in any sort of fisticuffs. I didn't have to. That charm of mine, not to mention my money, went a long way toward getting me what I wanted out of life. But the morning after Emily shoved the bag of cinnamon rolls in my hands and pushed me out the door, I realized she saw me solely as a cog in a corporate machine, no different from her. A novelty, sure, but I found myself dressing down and waving my driver away. More than ever I was reluctant to admit who I was, not because I was concerned she'd suddenly want me for my money, but because I was afraid she wouldn't want me at all.

After finishing off the cinnamon rolls the next morning, I dialed her cell.

"I'm serious this time, come away with me," I said when she answered. "We'll go to Italy or France. You name it."

She laughed. "I have a better idea. *I'll* take you away. Meet me at my apartment in an hour."

"What should I bring? An overnight bag? A steamer trunk so we can run away forever?"

"Just yourself. In casual clothes."

"France casual?"

More of her laughter, though it turned out her choice of getaways wasn't particularly funny.

"We're going to Coney Island?" I said. "On the subway?"

My tone must have hinted at my lack of enthusiasm.

"How else are we going to get there?" she asked, her tone careful.

Right then I should have told her the truth, but better sense was no competition for self-preservation. I rationalized not telling her by promising myself that I would confess that weekend. It never occurred to me she might learn the truth before Saturday was ever over.

"I can't think of a better way to get around," was all I said.

The day was perfect. Warm, not too hot, the amusement park crowded, but not insane. She pulled me from the bumper cars to the Wonder Wheel, the Cyclone roller coaster, and the big slide. At the shooting gallery she won a stuffed animal and presented it to me.

"I can't take that," I said aghast.

"Why not?"

"For starters, the man's supposed to win the prize for the girl."

She shot me a crooked smile, but I ignored it as I handed over a series of tickets until I managed to win a stuffed animal for her. "There," I said.

She looked at me as if I had given her a priceless emerald sculpture rather than a cheap green toy made in some slave-labor factory in China.

Amazingly, it was one of the best days of my life—right up until we ran into an acquaintance that was at the park with his kids.

"Sandy Portman," Barrett Higby said, slapping me on the back. "How are you? You're looking well. Though I'm surprised to see you at Coney Island. I certainly wouldn't be here if the offspring hadn't insisted. Said I *had* to bring them out to see how the other half lives—the half without money. Some new push these kids have gotten in their heads to be *real*."

One look at Emily's creased brow told me this wasn't going to go well.

The minute Barrett started to introduce himself to my date, I said it was great to see him, took Emily's arm, and headed for a food stand that promised coffee.

"What does that guy mean, *regular family*?" she asked.

There was a bite to her tone and I knew that the time had come for the truth. I half hoped the crowd of people at the food stand would distract her from fully absorbing the news.

The clerk asked what we wanted. "Two coffees," I said, then added to Emily, "I have money."

She glared at me. "Forget it. I'll pay for my own."

Even I knew that not fully absorbing was something altogether different from not understanding at all. With no help for it, I said it straight out. "Emily, I'm wealthy."

First more confusion, before her brows slammed together just as the clerk handed us our coffees. "What do you mean, you're wealthy?"

"I'm rich. My family is rich. I'm Sandy Portman," I added with emphasis. "As in the Portmans of Regal Bay."

"I thought the principals were the Regal family."

"Well, yes, they were, are. My father's mother was a Regal. Silas Regal is my great-uncle."

"You aren't struggling to make your way at the firm?"

"Struggling?" I might have shrugged. "Doesn't everyone struggle now and again? And let me just add, it's harder than you'd think to work your way up the ladder when you're related to the boss. Nepotism is such an ugly word, and quite frankly, can work against you as easily as not."

Emily poured sugar into her paper cup, more than seemed reasonable, before setting the sugar dispenser down with a little bang. "You lied to me."

I doubted she would appreciate the difference between an out-and-out lie and the obfuscation of truth by omission.

We rode home on the train in stony silence, she refusing my offer of calling the car service. Since the cat was out of the bag, I would have preferred to wait for a driver to hie us back to the city, but no way was Emily going anywhere near a hired anything, and I couldn't let her take the subway by herself. Whether she believed it or not, I was still the guy who was old-fashioned enough to spend a small fortune on tickets to win her a stuffed animal—a stuffed animal, I might add, that she crammed into the trash bin on our way out of the park.

For a week, she didn't take my calls. Good, I told myself, ignoring the desperation I felt returning, that strange hungry need Emily had put to rest for something more in life. I went out every night, drank and ate and did all the things I used to do, determined to forget Emily Barlow.

Only that was the thing. I couldn't.

For the first time in my life I gave in and sent a woman flowers with a card saying I was sorry. She sent them back. Frustrated, I did something I never would have thought I could do. I showed up at the Trigate building and waited outside like some pathetic stalker, taking her hands, bowing my head to hide what I knew were genuine tears. I told her that I missed her. She didn't relent, but she wavered.

For the next week I showed up at work every day, making my case. I was sweet and vulnerable. Surprisingly, I was sincere.

Five days into my quest, she stared at me for what felt like forever, then closed her eyes. When she opened them again I swear she wanted to reach out. But something held her back. She turned and walked away.

I told myself to leave, to move on, but I had seen that look.

The next day I showed up one last time, this time at her apartment. I didn't bring flowers or candy or any of the things that I knew wouldn't mean anything to her. She arrived at the front of her building, her arms loaded with groceries, and I held up a book.

She stared at the carefully preserved hardcover, the title in German. "An original 1812 edition of *Kinder- und Haus-Märchen,*" she said so softly I barely heard.

"More currently known as *Grimm's Fairy Tales.*"

"You noticed my collection."

"I've noticed a lot of things."

Her shoulders slumped, like something deep inside her was trying to give in. She pressed her eyes closed, then started to open the front door. When the groceries began to fall I grabbed them, along with the keys.

I followed her into the elevator and she didn't stop me. But I hadn't taken more than two steps into her apartment when she whirled back. "You lied!"

Her anger came at me in waves, all that careful control ripped away.

My first instinct was to make some glib remark. But I ignored instinct and went with something that I realized was from my gut.

"I'm an ass, a big idiotic ass that has the sense of a gnat. But a well-meaning gnat, I swear."

"Well-meaning?" she shot back.

"Face it, as Sandy Portman of the Vandermeer Regal Portman family, you, the daughter of the militant feminist, wouldn't have given me the time of day."

For a second I thought she was going to give in. "Don't turn this around and make me some sort of reverse snob," she snapped instead.

I must have looked as surprised as I felt. I hadn't been trying to manipulate anything. I wanted her back, I needed her back, needed that heady mix of peace and excitement she made me feel.

"I didn't mean it that way, Emily. I just wanted you to see me." My voice had risen, the desperation coming through my always-careful façade. "I just wanted to be the guy I saw in your eyes before you knew I had money."

Her jaw was tight as she stared at me. But this time when she started to move away, I dropped the groceries on the floor and caught her arm.

"I'm sorry for lying, Emily. I swear I am."

"Damn you," she whispered.

I turned her to me and she pounded my chest, not hard, more a testament to being torn between frustration and the desire to give in.

"Damn you," she repeated.

When I pulled her close, pressing her body to mine, she cursed me one last time before we fell together to the floor, kicking lettuce and bread and bags aside. I had the fleeting thought that she was doing more than forgiving me. Somehow she was saving me.

■

Had I known more about dogs, or dog clinics, or anything dog related, what happened next in my newfound existence as Einstein wouldn't have surprised me. As much as I'd like to say I was indifferent to being clean, I really adored it. For all Vinny's faults, he cleaned me up pretty good and for a second I felt badly for whatever I'd done to him. My wiry fur had softened, and I smelled halfway decent.

However, all thoughts of cleanliness disappeared when hours passed and Emily didn't make an appearance. She didn't show up that night either, or even the next day. Fortunately Blue was there, and she gave me my due. When she opened my cage door, I couldn't resist the need to strut out like a drum major in a marching band.

"You're so handsome." She laughed. "Whoever adopts you is going to be totally lucky."

I went stiff.

Sure, I had seen the Adopt-A-Pet programs on the local news, but I had given them no thought. If I had wanted a dog, I would have gone out and found a purebred something that cost a great deal of money. A moot point, however, since a dog never would have fit into my world. Dog hair, dog walking, and a secret love of hand wipes didn't go together. Though that was hardly my concern now. Adoption was.

Where the hell was Emily? Surely she would adopt me. She would take me home. My wife loved dogs. For God's sake, she loved Einstein.

"No, no, no!" I moaned.

My heart rate shot up and I started the wretched drooling thing. On my clean fur!

The next day I was moved up front to a long cinder block room filled with bright fluorescent lights and a long line of cages. Here they had a German shepherd, a few other dogs and cats, a guinea pig, even a rabbit at the end of the line. As it turned out, it was Wednesday, a big day for adoptions.

My scruffy neighbors posed for each person who entered the room looking for an animal to love. My mind raced. If I was adopted, would that make this insane situation real? Permanent?

I whimpered and moaned, foaming at the mouth like Old Yeller.

The rabbit went surprisingly fast, the cats snapped up in a matter of hours. Even the guinea pig found a home. At the end of the day only the shepherd and I were left. I was relieved. The shepherd was not. He sank down into his cage, muzzle on his paws, and stared off at nothing.

By the end of the week, "Shep" and I were still there. I'd had a close call when a young family showed up. But after a quick—and I thought, inspired—baring of canine teeth, the middle-class gaggle of four fled. Afterward, Nurse shook her head at me and conferred with the vet about something I couldn't make out. All I cared about was that I had averted disaster.

Emily still hadn't shown up, and only Blue seemed to notice that something was wrong with me.

"Hey, Einstein," she said, trying to calm me as I whimpered and drooled. "You miss Emily, don't you?"

My head went up, my ears perking forward.

"Yeah," she said, "I totally get it. You miss her. I called her, left messages telling her what was going on. But listen, she's got a plate load to deal with right now. Dead husband, and all. Shrew of a mother-in-law. On top of everything, I don't think she could take watching someone walk out of here with you. So she sort of went cold turkey. Nurse told me she resigned as a volunteer and isn't coming back."

Oh my God!

I was inconsolable the rest of the day. Shep tried to cheer me up, but he wasn't much better off than I was.

On Monday evening Vinny came in and opened the shepherd's cage. The proud dog scuttled backward, his giant paws churning up the towel and cushion flooring, his deep whimpering a plea. Not that this deterred Vinny. He reached in with some sort of stick and lasso, capturing Shep around the neck, yanking him out.

"Hey, where are you going?" I called out.

This wasn't part of any schedule I had been able to discern. But neither Vinny nor Shep bothered to enlighten me.

By the end of Vinny's shift, Shep hadn't returned. The next evening when Blue returned and saw the empty cage, she seemed surprised.

"Damn," she said.

Fear brought out the worst in me; it always had. I was barely nice to Blue, alternating growls with whimpers.

She looked at me. "You really have to get your act together. I know you never would have bitten that little girl, but you can't expect anyone else to know that. And you know what happens if we can't find a place for you, or worse, if they think you're a biter, right?"

I felt my strange, shaky heart skip a beat.

"You get put down."

Put down? As in put to sleep? Forever? Was that what happened to Shep?

The thoughts rose through me like stair steps leading back to panic followed quickly by something else. I barely knew the dog, but still. Shep was dead.

My throat tightened and for a moment I had to look away. "Shep," I whimpered and panted even more.

"Einstein. Don't freak out on me. You've got to calm down."

I didn't listen. Those embers of fear and anger flared to life. I started to howl again, though not intentionally. It just happened. Despair surged, crashing over me.

"Old man!" This time I shouted, the howling bark echoing against the cinder blocks and cement.

The swinging door burst open. "What's going on in here?"

It was Nurse with Vinny on her heels.

"He's upset," Blue said, "because of Otto. We know the animals sense when others have been put down."

Nurse looked resigned to the reality of it. Vinny shrugged then stepped forward. At the expression on his face and the sight of the stick-lasso thing leaning against the wall, I realized with a start that my time had come. I began to whimper again. Vinny didn't bother with the lasso; he reached for me with one of his meaty hands. This bastard who had been so horrible when he bathed me was going to kill me.

Blue turned away. Nurse frowned. Vinny gave me a look that said I was in for a bit of retribution before I met my maker.

"Old man!" I cried again, scrambling in the cage, backing away, the terry cloth towels bunching underneath my paws. "Oh, God, no. Please," I howled.

And just when Vinny grabbed me by the fur on my neck, a strange surge of heat and electricity shot through me. The room seemed to shift, and I swear even Vinny felt it. Confusion wrinkled his brow; his grip loosened and he glanced over his shoulder.

Yes, yes, I thought. The old man was going to step in and fix this.

But just as suddenly, the energy shifted even more, seemed to grow static—then disappeared altogether as if the old man had thought better of saving me.

Misery spiked. "Old man! You can't do this!"

Vinny shook himself, then jerked me from the cage. I cried and fought to get away, yelping when he yanked me off the floor and carried me dangling like a sack. My feet scrambled in the air, but my cries were cut off along with my breath because of his strangling grip. Then suddenly I heard the bang, like a shot echoing against all the metal and cinder blocks.

"What's going on here?"

Vinny jerked, swinging me around with him. Surprise as much as pain made me yelp, followed quickly by relief when I saw my wife standing in the doorway, her eyes wide. Then her brows slammed together. "Put him down."

"Emily!" I tried to bark. But Vinny hadn't given up. He swung me up into his arms.

"I said, put him down."

The man grumbled and glared at me.

Nurse glanced from me to my wife. "Emily, you know this is how it works. Einstein had his chance. No one wants him."

The words surprised me. Never in my life had no one wanted me.

A strange sort of disconnect raced down my spine. I refused to examine what the words made me feel, refused to put a name to the pressure I felt behind Einstein's eyes. My little dog's body trembled as I looked at Emily. "Please want me." It was yet another pathetic and embarrassing bout of begging. This from a man who had never been fond of sloppy displays of emotion. But I couldn't help it. "You have to want me."

My wife sighed. "This is crazy."

"Please," I murmured.

My wife pressed her eyes closed, exhaling sharply.

"Emily," Nurse said. "Don't get any ideas. You'd take every dog home if you could."

She opened her eyes slowly, looking directly at me. "This is different."

The skin beneath her eyes was shadowed with half-moon bruises as if she had been working around the clock—or been hit. She walked up and took me from Vinny. "Really," she said so softly that only I heard. "I don't know why, but Einstein is different."

Relief soared, making me weak, and for a second I leaned into her with whimpering gratitude. But when I looked back into her sad luminous eyes, my relief shifted and jarred, replaced by frustration. Sure I should have been nothing but grateful. It's easy to see that now. But in that moment I realized that despite the fact that her life was threatening to fall apart, somehow she still managed to be a warrior who I couldn't afford to admit was saving me once again.

emily

My mother was a woman with a grand appetite for the possibilities of life, if not the actual living. She was glorious and wild, demanding something from the world that it was never quite willing to give. When I was born she was certain she was a hero to women. In a time when the world didn't want to change, she fought against complacency. How could you not live in awe of this woman who was my mother?

—EXCERPT FROM *My Mother's Daughter*

chapter six

After I took care of the necessary paperwork, I walked out of the clinic with Einstein. I was stiff with shock. What had I been thinking? What in the world was I going to do with a dog? But I hadn't been able to ignore Blue's last frantic message that if I didn't save Einstein, he was going to be put down.

With Einstein at my side, we took a cab to the Dakota. My new dog stood on the seat next to me, his paws on the armrest so he could look out the window. He panted excitedly at the sight of the light brown sandstone and brick building with its high gables and deeply pitched roofs, balustrades and spandrels, the porte cochere archway leading into the inner courtyard and entrance. During the day, the old building looked almost white in the midday sun. But at night, when the hundred-year-old gaslights that lined the property came on, the bricks took on the rich hue of melting caramel.

The doorman opened the cab door.

"Whoa," Johnny said, stepping back when Einstein rocketed toward him. Thankfully, my new dog thought better of pouncing. E stopped and sat abruptly, then did the smiling thing that was like no other dog I had ever known.

Johnny laughed.

"Mrs. Portman," the man said, extending his white-gloved hand to help me out. "You got a new friend?"

"You could say that. I adopted him."

"Really? Hey, buddy." Johnny leaned down and scratched the dog behind the ears.

"His name is Einstein," I said.

"A smart one, huh?"

I glanced at the dog. "Smart enough to get me to take him home."

Einstein led the way through the portico. As New York apartment buildings went the Dakota was on a short list of the most illustrious. The grande dame had seen her share of grief and joy, and had survived, built in a square around a large, open courtyard with two massive fountains and main elevators in all four inner corners. Since it was built in the 1880s, a long line of famous people had lived there. John Lennon was probably the most famous, mostly because it was in the portico that he had been shot. But there was also Judy Garland, Boris Karloff, and Leonard Bernstein—to name a few. A mix of famous, wealthy, and regular people lived there now.

I didn't care about the famous residents. I loved the Dakota for its old-world elegance, its roots in New York's past, and for the fact that it had survived over a hundred years of history and heartache.

We took the northeast elevator up, and as soon as it opened Einstein strode out, heading straight for the fine French doors with inset stained glass of my apartment. Just when I thought Einstein was going to stop at the front door, he glanced back at me as if considering, then continued on, sniffing around the large common area, peering down the series of descending stairs to the bottom floor.

"For a second there I thought you knew exactly where I lived. Which is impossible. Right?"

I think he shrugged.

Once I opened the door, he trotted through the vestibule and stopped in the gallery with its intricately laid floor and massive light fixture of frosted glass and ornate metalwork hanging from the fourteen-foot-high ceiling. The gallery led directly into the library with its high, wide windows and rich draperies. To the left of the library, through a massive set of double doors with glass transoms, stood the master bedroom, which in turn circled back through a long hallway to the gallery.

I was seven years old when I first saw the glossy magazine photograph of the Dakota. From the beginning, I loved the building. I suspect it had something to do with the way it looked like the building where Eloise lived. The tale of a little girl with no discernable family who had the run of the Plaza Hotel had been my favorite book when I was growing up.

At eight, when my mother took me with her to the Dakota to visit some man, I was left to my own devices for the bulk of an afternoon. I climbed stairwells and rode elevators, sitting on the elevator's bench seat like a princess. When the concierge told me that the building had been designed by the same man who designed the Plaza Hotel, my love of the building was solidified. Just as Eloise belonged in the Plaza, I decided I belonged at the Dakota. That Sandy had brought me to this very building as a bride had seemed prophetic.

Einstein stood in the gallery much as I had the first time, absorbing the silence, the thick walls blocking out the city noise.

"It's beautiful, isn't it?"

Einstein jumped as if he had forgotten I was there.

"Sandy loves this place."

The little dog seemed to sigh.

My throat tightened at the memory of my husband, tears threatening to squeeze over, but I shook them away. I hadn't cried since the accident. That was how I saw it, an accident, something that could be fixed, undone, made right, like chiseling away broken bathroom tile and replacing it with perfect squares that matched the old. Which was crazy. But I ignored that too.

I headed down the main hall with the things the clinic had given me. "You'll sleep in here," I called back. "It's the kitchen, but it's a whole lot nicer than the clinic."

He didn't follow me. Instead he stayed in the gallery, glancing up the stairway that led to a separate suite of rooms on the floor above. The suite had always been Sandy's private space, especially in the last few months. I hadn't ventured up there since the accident.

"What is it, E?"

He raised his muzzle and continued past the stairs, marching down the hall toward the master bedroom.

"Hey!" I called after him. "No way, Einstein. It's too late for me to figure out how you know so much about this place, but if my mother-in-law shows up and finds you on her precious son's duvet there will be no mercy. I need that like I need a hole in my head."

I didn't add that I had been avoiding Sandy's mother and estate lawyer since the funeral, holding on to some gauzy-brained idea that maybe they would forget the apartment and go away.

Einstein stood at the foot of the huge bed Sandy loved, seeming to debate. With a huff, he turned back and retraced his footsteps down the hall.

When I got over the strangeness, I grabbed three of the fluffiest beach blankets I could find and dashed after him. My new dog had found the kitchen on his own and waited for me with impatience.

After I piled the blankets in the corner, Einstein strode past without so much as a nod, circled twice, and flopped down with an exhausted groan. I put out a bowl of water for him, waiting a second to make sure he was settled. When he didn't move a muscle, I turned off the light. "Good night, Einstein," I said. "I'm glad you're here."

Strangely, I was.

■

I had taken up residence in the yellow guest room where I had painted the wall border, the drop cloths removed, furniture put back into place, my collection of children's books returned to the tall shelves. I managed to stay in the numb, unfeeling place during the days by making a plan. Wake up, shower, find clothes, eat. I did everything in order, the same order every day.

But at night . . . I hated the nights, hated the dream that woke me up screaming, as if my subconscious played a continuous loop of what my conscious mind refused to accept. When I gasped awake, I couldn't breathe, my eyes burned, and I was unsure how to move forward. Then I would remember the plan. Get up, shower, find clothes, eat, and the day would lurch forward.

I woke the next morning and saw that it was six A.M., not two or three-thirty. With that little dog's presence, I hadn't dreamed at all.

Einstein was still asleep in the kitchen when I walked in. As quietly as I could, I put coffee on to brew but the noise woke the dog and he sat up groggily. For a second he looked confused, craning his neck to look at his paws, twitching in surprise. Then he groaned, falling back against the towels as if something about those paws upset him. Which was as odd as it was crazy.

Come on, Em, get a grip, I told myself.

From the pantry I retrieved the dog food the clinic had sent home with us. I shook the small box, but Einstein wouldn't look at me.

"You've got to be starved."

I shook it again, this time louder. After the third shake, he sighed and got up.

"You're okay, right?" I bent down to hug him. "Tell me you're all right."

Einstein stiffened. He was funny about hugs. Like my husband in the strange months before the accident—and unlike any dog I had ever known—Einstein seemed to be allowing me to hug him rather than enjoying it.

The concierge had given me the name of a dog walker who walked other dogs in the building, and she had agreed to take Einstein out when I was at work. After I managed to settle Einstein with food and water, then forced myself to close the door on his unhappy face, I squeezed myself onto the last car of the C train, grabbing a tiny handhold to keep myself upright among the swaying work-bound bodies of hardcore New Yorkers.

When word had gotten out about Sandy, Charles Tisdale, the president of Caldecote, encouraged me to take some time off. But the last thing I wanted was to be alone. At Fifty-ninth Street–Columbus Circle, I spilled out of the train and walked the two crowded blocks to my office on Broadway. I ran my Caldecote Press badge through the card reader and pushed through the turnstile. Once at my desk I listened to voice mail.

"Hey, Em!" my sister said. *"Just wanted to call and see how it's going. Everything's great with me . . . well, everything's great except my dad's wife is badmouthing me to their kids again. Hello, all I did was bring my little brother and sister presents. Whatever. Anyway, we'll talk later."*

As usual, Jordan failed to acknowledge the fact that the presents she took her grade-school-aged half siblings were anything but appropriate for anyone under the age of twenty-one.

I threw myself into work. I finished editing a manuscript, wrote jacket copy, attempted to return phone calls I had let pile up. But after no more than a handful of conversations, I stopped. Authors' and agents' well-meaning condolences reminded me of soft-boiled eggs, nine-grain bread, and the box of Sandy's perfectly folded dress shirts from the dry cleaners that I had started wearing to bed.

The morning passed in a blur of keeping busy. As soon as the clock struck noon, I heard Nate Clarkson coming down the hall. While publishing was a collaborative effort, Nate was our company's publisher and made the final decisions about book scheduling and book positioning for our list. Charles, as president, could overrule Nate's decisions, but he rarely did, concentrating instead on the overall vision for the company.

It was no surprise when Nate stopped to talk to Victoria Wentworth, another senior editor at Caldecote. Like me, Victoria was in her early thirties. She had pale white skin, long red hair, and a dusting of freckles across the bridge of her nose that tricked you into thinking she was as sweet as she looked.

Even though the president had taken me under his wing when I first signed on at Caldecote, until a year ago I had technically worked for Victoria. We only had one book left that we had worked on together—though *together* hardly covered it. While Victoria had officially bought the novel, I found *Ruth's Intention* in Victoria's slush pile of unagented submissions. From the first sentences of *Ruth,* which so beautifully brought to life the small heroic acts of a young mother determined to save her son, I had known it was a book that should be published.

Victoria had never been one to take advice, least of all from me. But I waited for just the right moment to pitch the idea, assuring her that she wouldn't have to do any of the work. She debated, but eventually gave in.

"Fine, work up an offer, then I'll get it approved and make the call," she had said. *"But after that, don't come crawling to me for help."*

While anyone with half a brain steered clear of her, Victoria dazzled our publisher. For once, with several e-mails from the man sitting unanswered in my in-box, this served me well. While Nate was preoccupied with Victoria, it gave me a chance to dash for the elevators and head out for lunch. He might see me, but he wouldn't be able to recover his wits fast enough to stop me and ask his questions in person.

After signing out of e-mail, I made it past Nate. He sort of jerked in surprise when he saw me, his smile starting to straighten. "Come on," I muttered under my breath. I might have thrown myself into work, but I was smart enough to know that my brain didn't have the ability to sort through problems, argue my point, or defend any position. "You can make it." The exit was in sight, only a couple of feet to the security doors.

"Emily!" he called out. "A minute, please."

For a second, I debated the wisdom of pretending I hadn't heard. That seeming ill-advised, I stopped, exhaled.

"I haven't heard back from you regarding any advance blurbs or reviews you've gotten for *Ruth's Intention,*" he said.

"Yes, Emily," Victoria added. "How's the book going?"

I rummaged around for a smile, only managed a grimace, and said, "I've gotten several advance quotes, all raves."

"Really?" Nate said. "Then why haven't you let the sales team know about them? Orders are extremely low."

Victoria looked at our boss with the sort of professional concern she must have practiced in front of the mirror. "Unfortunately, the orders are low because not everyone is *raving.* I told Emily she never should have bought it."

No one could blame her for distancing herself from a project that wasn't going well, especially when it wasn't her idea to take it on. But since the day I was promoted to senior editor, Victoria had seemed determined to see me take a fall.

"Victoria." The word sounded strange in my head. "One person in sales read it and loved it. The low orders have nothing to do with what people are or are not saying. The month is jammed with other titles that are getting support. If we could reallocate some money to—"

Nate cut me off. "Get more early blurbs. Tell the author to start a blog. Become someone who Tweets. Something, anything—short of spending money—to get attention."

Victoria gave me one of those fake concerned smiles, then followed him down the hall.

As soon as I made it to the elevator, my good friend Birdie Baleau came up beside me.

"Hey you," she said. "How's it going?"

Birdie was about my height, filled with energy, and close to my age, though she was only an assistant. Everyone knew she was from Texas—it was hard not to know given the accent she swore she didn't have. She was rarely found without a candy bar in hand; today it was a Milky Way.

After one look at me, she extended the chocolate. "It looks like you could use some, sweetie."

"I'm fine," I told her. I tried to sound convincing.

She scoffed and took another bite when I refused. "You are not fine. But I know you. Holding on. A pillar of strength. Not a bother to anyone. If I were you I would fall apart and scream and cry and make everyone feel sorry for me." She shrugged and swallowed. "But that's just me."

I couldn't help but laugh, relieved. "You know I love you, don't you?"

"Of course. What's not to love?"

Bundled in our coats, we rode down together and walked to lunch. Ever since Sandy's accident, I'd had the urge to eat, a lot, as if food could solve my problems. Psych 101, sure, but even knowing that I had to force myself past little food markets filled with preservative-and-fat-laden foods that beckoned to me like an apron-clad grandmother offering instant comfort.

Birdie and I made it to Whole Foods at Time Warner Center without me hijacking a hotdog stand or snatching her candy bar and making a run for it. From the wide variety of prepared foods that were more healthy than not, I got a salad. Birdie chose a slice of whole wheat pizza—grumbling that pizza and whole wheat should not be mentioned in the same sentence—soup, three tacos, some curry, a Parker House roll, and a chocolate croissant.

"I'm hungry," she stated when we stood in line.

"I didn't say anything."

"But you were thinking it."

"I wasn't thinking anything. I am intentionally *not* thinking."

"Ah, yes, I should have known. How's that working for you?" she asked with a raised brow.

"Surprisingly well."

Which made her laugh.

In the crush of people and clamor of voices against the stone floors and walls, we managed to get a booth. As soon as we sat down on the hard wooden benches, she bypassed the pizza and soup, took a bite of croissant, and asked, "So, what is really going on? I heard Victoria making noise about some book you have coming out."

I stabbed a piece of lettuce. "It's a novel. *Ruth's Intention*. It's dying a quiet death before it ever hits the shelves."

"Lord, this business is brutal. Who knew? But look, even in the short time I've been at Caldecote I've seen that books fail all the time. And tons of them are Victoria's. Her making noise about one of yours failing is like the pot calling the kettle black. Sheez, she is such a witch." Birdie chewed thoughtfully. "Is there anything you can do to save *Ruth*? Sure, it would be good for you, and yeah, even the book. But hello, save the book just to bite Victoria in the backside."

I cracked a smile. "You're bad."

She snorted. "Focus, Emily. The book. Remember. You need to save it."

"I don't know," I said, considering. "The book really is amazing."

"I assume sales knows it's amazing."

"I've forwarded them all sorts of reasons why it's amazing. But the month is swamped with other books, and sales doesn't have a lot of time to think about *Ruth*."

"Then force them to think about it."

"I can't force them to think about it."

She rolled her eyes. "Then cajole them into thinking about it."

"Birdie—"

"Don't Birdie me." She polished off the croissant and dug into the pizza. "You're the creative problem solver. Figure something out."

As we were walking back to the office, Birdie unwrapped another candy bar. It was when I nearly gave in and lunged for it that the idea hit me.

We parted ways after I stopped and made a purchase, then hurried back to my office. By the end of the day I had gathered some advance reading copies of *Ruth's Intention* and put them together with a color printout listing fabulous quotes and a letter I'd written from "Ruth." I hand delivered the books to every member of the in-house sales team along with a Baby Ruth candy bar tied on top of each with a bow.

It was a silly gesture, no question, but I prayed that if nothing else sales would get a smile out of the correlation, take pity on poor *Ruth,* and at least read the printed highlights as they ate the candy. My gut told me that if they took the book home over the weekend and read even the first sentence, they would fall in love.

As I was turning off my computer to head home, Victoria strode into my office.

"What is this I hear about you wasting everybody's time by passing out ARCs of *Ruth* along with chocolate bars?" She smirked. "It's going to take more than ninety-nine-cent bribes to get support for your little book."

"Maybe. But I looked over the pub list for the month and there's nothing on it that has the kind of media appeal *Ruth* does. I mean, it's a fictional version of what the author actually experienced saving her own son when he was dying. *Ruth* is perfect for morning news and talk shows. And I hardly think talk shows are a waste of time."

Victoria scoffed, but I didn't let her get to me. And when I got on the subway and saw one of the sales guys sitting toward the front of the car eating the Baby Ruth and opening to the first page of the ARC, I felt sure my instinct was correct.

einstein

chapter seven

As long as I lived, I wasn't sure that I would ever truly believe what had happened to me, not even when I turned back into a man.

A shiver of unease raced down my spine, and my hackles rose. Every quivering strand of this little dog's double helix DNA went still at the memory of my human body lying dead in the slush and snow. But I dismissed any hint of concern as ridiculous. There was no way I could spend the rest of my days as a dog. Things like that just didn't happen. I mean, really, was it possible anyone could actually believe that little Fido next door was harboring the soul of a man? Or Rex down the street was really a Brooklyn-born tough? No, I assured myself. Sooner or later something would happen and *poof,* this nightmare would be over and I would wake up back in my body, back in my bed, back in my life as a man who had it all.

Once I had gotten over the shock of the bizarre situation, I decided to look at my sojourn as a canine in the best possible light. I was a glass-half-full sort of fellow, after all. I might be a dog, but I wouldn't think of it that way. I would think of it as being on vacation from being a man. Like going to St. Barts in winter or the South of France in spring—only smellier. The only snag in this plan was that dogs were dependent on their humans. No wonder Lassie was loyal. What choice did she have if she wanted to eat?

Given my state of dependence, I had little choice but to depend on Emily. It's not hard to imagine that I didn't do, and had never done, dependence all that well. But rather than give in to frustration, I decided to look at her as, say, Julie on the *Love Boat,* my cruise director.

Whatever the case, I found it easy enough to get her to do what I wanted. When I didn't like the food, I refused to eat. Eventually I had her sharing her own dinner with me. When I wanted a scratch behind the ear, I nudged her hand. If I wanted a Mozart sonata played on my sound system, I trotted over to the CD changer and growled.

When I wasn't getting Emily to do my bidding I was sleeping. And when I wasn't sleeping, I was lying in the sun. All in all, it was a somewhat acceptable interim situation, at least for me. It might not have been so great for my wife, but that hardly seemed like my problem.

My head snapped back when I felt a zap to my flank. I jerked around, but no one was there. "Old man?" I growled.

But nobody answered.

Saturday morning I was pleasantly surprised when we headed across the street to Central Park, passing the line of park benches, the late winter sun catching on the small rectangular dedication plaques embedded in many of them.

Emily had pulled on sweaters and a muffler, topped with a heavy coat, mittens, and a hat. You could hardly see any of her, but her eyes looked like giant blue sapphires. Even bundled up you could tell she was beautiful, which somehow made me angry.

But we were going to the park and I wasn't going to let her good human looks ruin my day.

We walked underneath the twisting wood-and-vine-covered archway leading deeper into the park and caught sight of a group of dogs and their owners. I started to turn my nose up at the bourgeois scene, but then again, when in Rome. I tugged on the leash. Emily seemed to debate, then shrugged. As soon as she unclipped me, I walked with regal bearing over to the canine masses in the clearing.

Instantly, I was set upon. Noses up my hindquarters, muzzles in my face. Good God, almighty. "Back off," I barked.

Not that this did any good.

The dogs yelped with excitement over my arrival. And really, I might be in Einstein's body, but at some level I was still me. Sandy Portman. No wonder they were clamoring all around.

I put up with the attention as best I could until an overly amorous poodle tried to have her way with me. I had dated models more discreet than that blasted poodle. So really, what was I supposed to do?

I turned on the wench and snapped at her.

Every dog in the bunch leaped back—all except the poodle. She sidled closer like a downtown hooker with a bad perm and worse haircut who preferred playing rough.

The group of humans consisted of four women and one scrawny-looking man. Unlike my wife, the women were dressed surprisingly well for an early morning dog walk in the park. Not that I cared. What interested me was that the man had a ball thrower, and while the women started talking, the man resumed throwing a tennis ball for his schnauzer.

Hmmm. Chasing a ball seemed beneath me, but on the other hand I felt a strange urge to do just that. But just then everyone turned to welcome a newcomer and his dog.

"Hey, Max," the scrawny man said.

This Max fellow was tall and handsome, if you went for the Marlboro Man sort, in his sheepskin and shearling coat. He had the kind of simmering sex appeal that even I knew made most women do crazy things. Where I had always been a beautiful man, this guy was ruggedly handsome, nothing pretty about him. This, I realized, was why the women were overdressed for an early-morning dog outing. The only person there who didn't seem to notice him was my wife.

See, I really was impossible to forget.

When Marlboro Man came forward he noticed me right away. He crouched down. "Hey, boy," he said, scratching behind my ears.

Despite better intentions, I closed my eyes and leaned into him, my back leg thumping in pure bliss.

"No offense," one of the women said. "But your dog is the ugliest thing I've ever seen."

My eyes popped open and I looked at her. I had the urge to trot over and tear into the woman's fancy designer jeans. But then I took in the dog the woman owned—a yappy little Chihuahua that wore a rhinestone-studded hot pink coat. I looked at Emily. She shrugged as if to say, *You're going to listen to a woman who dresses her dog? In rhinestones?*

True. I turned my nose up and went to stand by my wife.

Marlboro Man joined us.

"You two been together long?" he asked.

Emily blinked. "What? Einstein and me?"

"It's rare that you see a dog and human communicate like that. Most of us have to use words like 'sit' and 'stay.' "

Emily blushed, as if she finally got what he was talking about—our silent less-than-kind, though effective, interaction over the woman and her Chihuahua.

"Don't worry; no one else noticed." The man laughed. "I'm Max Reager." He pointed out the golden retriever. "That's Beau, short for Beauregard."

Emily still didn't seem aware of him.

"Yes, well," Emily said. "Come on, E. Time to go."

She clipped on the leash and we headed out of the park.

"We're here every day," Max called after us.

Emily didn't look back.

The next day was the same, with the exception of the walk in the park, and by late Sunday evening I was bored out of my mind. The anxiety I had managed to suppress reared its ugly head. Vacation over.

"Damn it all to hell!" I barked.

The drooling thing started up again, the tongue flopping around in my mouth.

"Someone get me out of this body!"

But still no one answered.

Sinking down on my makeshift bed I realized that in all my musings about *Love Boat* Julie and enjoying myself during my vacation as a dog, I had given no thought to what would come next.

emily

My mother always said that if you didn't maintain the upper hand, a man would take advantage of you. She might believe in equal rights, but equal rights didn't and couldn't apply to men who still belonged in the Dark Ages.

—EXCERPT FROM *My Mother's Daughter*

chapter eight

Monday morning everything changed.

When I woke, my heart pounded with a vague sense of disquiet as if something was about to happen. The reprieve I'd managed to cobble together with work and Einstein was gone, as if I could only hold out against the creeping grief over my husband's accident for so long.

Although it seemed like it was something more than even that.

I had to force myself out of bed, and then couldn't remember what I was supposed to do next. Everything felt out of order, dread ticking through me. I dressed, then realized I still hadn't taken a shower. I got Einstein's leash before I put on shoes.

I closed my eyes and tried to think. Einstein. Food. Subway. Work. In that order. I could do this. I wouldn't fall apart now.

I arrived at work to a voice mail from the head of sales asking me to come to her office. She left no clue that she had good news or bad.

"Emily," the woman said when I knocked on her door. "Come in."

Mercy Gray was nothing if not sensible, practical, and good at her job. I had always liked her.

She didn't waste time with small talk. "I love *Ruth's Intention,*" she said.

My shoulders came back.

"I love it so much, in fact, that I came into the office ready to send the sales force back out to increase orders."

Hope started filling me, pushing at the unease I had woken with that morning.

"But when I talked to Nate, he had already moved another book into what you know is a crowded month." She looked me in the eyes. "I'm sorry. I want to do more. It deserves more. And I appreciate your effort to get us to notice the book. But my hands are tied."

"But . . . can't we move the book?"

"I asked. Nate said no."

Hope rushed out. The unease wrapped around me even tighter as I returned to my office. Victoria was waiting.

"Did you hear?" she practically squealed. "My little book, *The Reverend's Wife,* has been moved up a month and is being featured as nonfiction disguised as fiction!"

I knew right away which month she was talking about. *Ruth*'s month.

I didn't waste my breath on Victoria. I walked straight to Nate's office, startling him. "*Ruth's Intention* should be getting the media attention."

Victoria hurtled in behind me. Nate fumbled his pen and looked at me uncomfortably.

"*Ruth* would be good for the media?" he asked, practically squeaking.

"Yes, and you know it."

The man looked like he wanted to be anywhere but in that room. "Actually, I know no such thing," he mumbled. "And if you had bothered to let me know that, then maybe I could have done something about it. As it is now, I've already shifted support to another book."

"Victoria's," I stated.

Nate Clarkson jerked up from his chair. "As I said, had you mentioned *Ruth* in terms of the media, the support could have been yours."

He left the office. Victoria smiled like she felt badly, then followed him.

I could barely breathe as I made my way back to my office to pack up my things. I would go home. I would sleep. I would not think. But as some sort of Hail Mary pass, I packaged up one more advance copy along with the last Baby Ruth bar, and included a letter, not from me, but from "Ruth." I had nothing to lose when I sent off the package.

By the time I headed home the sky had grown ominous, the wind picking up, snow threatening. On the subway platform, I raced for a C train just as the doors slid closed in my face. The next train was packed, riders crammed together, the car thick with the smell of bodies and damp wool. When I came up the steps to Central Park West it had started to sleet.

The sidewalk was icy and I slipped, catching myself on the ornate railing that lined the perimeter of the Dakota. The unease that had been riding me all day rode harder. Johnny the doorman was on duty when I got to the entrance, and I said a prayer of thanks that he was busy directing a messenger to the service entrance. I didn't have it in me to smile and say anything polite. I was afraid if I opened my mouth at all I would scream.

But just before I could dash under the portico the doorman stopped me. "Miss Emily. This guy has a letter for you."

I blinked, then instinctively backed away.

"Miss Emily?" Johnny asked, confused.

"Ah—" I shook myself. "Yes, of course. I'll sign."

The messenger extended a Bic pen with no top then pulled out a thin manila envelope, the name of Sandy's estate lawyer bold on the masthead.

I shoved it into my satchel, shifting my purse, both seeming impossibly heavy. A gust of wind caught me from behind and pushed me through the portico, my heels echoing on the granite cobbles. I bypassed the lobby and concierge, and was buzzed through the inner gates. I half stumbled, half ran across the courtyard despite the sleet. Leaping over a puddle of slush, I headed toward the far steps leading to the northeast elevator. But before I could make it, my shoe caught on a rough spot and I tripped, flying forward onto my hands and knees.

Pain shot through me, but it was watching my leather bag flop open that hit me the hardest. The pages of an already-edited manuscript fell out and started dancing in the wind.

"No!"

Still on my knees, I grabbed at the pages, catching one, missing another.

"Let me help."

The voice barely registered as I snagged another sheet, feeling a disjointed sense of accomplishment mixed with an anger I didn't understand.

"Careful, you're going to do more damage."

I still couldn't focus on the voice. A white page fluttered in the wind, the black, typed sentences marked with my red pencil edits. *At this point, shouldn't the character of Bess be suppressing her grief, not giving in to it?* I had written. The irony of the statement made me groan.

I felt strong hands circle my arms before I saw him, felt the way he pulled me up with ease and set me back on my feet like I was an elementary school girl who'd taken a spill on the playground. When he had me upright I tipped my neck back to look into his face, all hard angles and strong planes, his longish dark hair raked back. He had dark eyes and his wide, full mouth pulled up in a friendly smile.

"Tough day?" he asked.

He seemed vaguely familiar.

"I'm Max. From the park."

He was handsome in a rugged sort of way, and tall with broad shoulders, making me feel tiny. Despite the fact that he wore jeans and a heavy coat, he had an undeniable stance or bearing that spoke of discipline and strength. It was easy to see that he was at ease in his surroundings, comfortable in his own skin, confident he could handle whatever came his way.

Odd that I sensed so much about him in such a short period of time. Perhaps it was because somehow I had become the exact opposite of everything he exuded. But more than that, I could tell he was young, at least younger than me, perhaps twenty-seven or twenty-eight.

I remembered him from the park, but I realized I had seen him before that day. He either lived or worked at the Dakota. But I couldn't place him; he didn't seem old enough to own in a building like this, but he seemed too old to be someone's son still living at home.

We gathered as much of the scattered manuscript as we could before I noticed the blood smeared across my palms.

"Come on," he said. "Let's get you cleaned up."

"I'm fine. Really."

But my voice cracked and I flinched when I clutched the manuscript with my scraped hands.

"It will just take a second."

"But—"

He cut off my protest and pulled me into the same northeast elevator I normally used. At first I assumed he was taking me to my apartment. But when the elevator opened and we found ourselves in the common area, he didn't stop at my door.

He guided me down the hall, pulling out a key to the apartment down the hall. "After you."

The golden retriever was sitting in the foyer, panting with excitement.

"Hey, Beau," Max said.

I had no business going inside. I hadn't a clue who he was, had never in the years I had lived there met the neighbors, a feat only possible in a New York City apartment building that thrived on privacy. For all I knew he was a crazed murderer. Though right that second a crazed anything sounded more appealing than having to face the letter that burned a hole in my satchel.

The thought brought me up short and I closed my eyes over a sudden bout of light-headedness.

"Careful," Max said, catching my arm. "Steady there."

Max set my things in the foyer, then guided me down a long hallway. My head cleared enough so that I began to feel a tad nervous about where exactly he was taking me. But then we stepped into a beautiful and bright kitchen filled with light, white tiles, and stainless steel. He tugged me over to a deep chef's sink and turned on the water.

"I shouldn't put you out. I can clean up at my apartment."

Not that he listened. As soon as the water hit my palms I flinched.

"Scrapes like that burn like hell," he said, grimacing along with me.

I started to pull back. "That should be good. Clean. Fine. No imminent danger of dying."

"Keep at it. And use soap," he instructed with what I can only call an amused smile, before he rummaged around in the pantry.

I had just finished soaping my palms when he returned with a bottle of rubbing alcohol, told me to open my hands, then poured.

I flinched again, though thankfully I didn't make a noise.

"So you're tougher than you look," he said.

"I prefer biting bullets over painkillers," I managed.

"I'm impressed. I prefer crying."

This made me laugh, a choked sound of more misery than amusement, since a simple look at the guy made it doubtful he had ever cried in his life.

"Liar," I said, but all I could think was that somehow I could breathe again.

Relief rushed through me as the heavy cloud pushed back completely. When he guided me to a chair at the kitchen table I went. Facing each other, he took my right hand and turned it palm up. "You're going to hurt like hell tomorrow when the adrenaline wears off."

"Are you some kind of doctor?"

"No. Not a doctor. But I've cleaned a wound or two in my day."

I didn't know who he was or anything about him. But there I sat. I remembered the thought that he could be dangerous. A murderer. Then he leaned over and pulled a box of bandages from a drawer.

"We'll put one on the worst of it," he said, then expertly dressed the deep scrape on the heel of my palm.

I raised my head to look at him with all the confusion I felt. "Hello Kitty?"

He laughed, though he sounded sheepish. "We only have two kinds of Band-Aids around here. Hello Kitty and Power Rangers."

"You have children?"

He looked startled for a second. "No, not me."

I heard the front door burst open, then feet racing toward the kitchen. "Uncle Max! Uncle Max! Where are you?"

Three young children who I might have seen before in the courtyard raced into the kitchen. The kids were clearly siblings, cute, well dressed. They looked surprisingly like their uncle. At the sight of me, they hurtled to a stop.

"Hey, guys," Max said. "We got a lady in distress here."

Eyes went wide and they came closer. The two boys, who appeared to be twins, inspected my scraped hands while the girl looked on with more than a little malice. She reminded me of Victoria.

"You live next door," the girl accused.

A nanny of some foreign descent came in behind them, setting backpacks and whatnot in an alcove.

"Hello, Mr. Max," she said. "They talk all the way home about you trip to museum."

"Yay!" they chimed.

"Museum of Natural History," Max told me with a shrug.

"To see the dinosaurs," one of the boys added.

The little girl glared at me. "You're not going, are you?"

"Katie." Max's voice was kind but stern. "Be nice."

Her lower lip slipped out.

"I shouldn't be here," I said, leaping up. "My husband—"

I cut myself off. What would I have said? My husband wouldn't approve?

"Thanks for the help," I managed, backing down the hallway, then turning and all but running to the foyer, where I gathered my things.

When I straightened, Max stood in the arching entrance. He didn't smile.

"I'm sorry about your loss," he offered. "I haven't been here that long, but my sister told me about your husband."

Vaguely I remembered a condolence note from a neighbor, the embarrassment over never having introduced myself when they moved in.

"I should have said something sooner," he said.

The sincerity on his face was genuine.

"Oh, yes, thank you," I managed.

At my door I fumbled with the lock until I crashed inside, pressing my forehead to the inset of glass. When I turned around, Einstein was there, his velvety nose twitching as he sniffed the air, before he bared his teeth.

chapter nine

Stop looking at me like that," I snapped.

He growled.

Ignoring Einstein, the guy next door already forgotten, I forced myself to open the letter. It didn't take more than a glance to confirm my suspicion. The Portmans were demanding a meeting regarding the property at One West Seventy-second Street.

I bent over, my fists braced on my knees, the letter crumpled in my hand.

"Sandy promised me this apartment," I whispered.

Einstein cocked his head.

"He did."

The dog ruffed then walked away.

My love of the apartment and my need for a place where I belonged was easy enough to understand. The piece that I couldn't explain to anyone was the persistent sense that I needed to be here because at any second my husband was going to burst through the door. *"Honey, I'm home!"* All I had to do was be here, be patient . . . which meant I had to find a way to prove what he promised.

"Okay," I told myself, "you can do this."

Earlier I had searched Sandy's desk in the library and his bed stand in our room and had found nothing pertaining to the apartment. The only place left to look was in his suite upstairs, a place I very much wanted to avoid since being there only reminded me of the reason I was now allowed access to Sandy's private space.

The hallways on the eighth floor were simpler than those on the lower levels since back in the day the upper reaches had been utilitarian. Sandy's suite consisted of four small rooms tucked into the eaves, creating a cozy office, sitting room, and library along with a bath and kitchenette which hadn't been redone in decades.

Einstein followed me up the stairs, stopping in the doorway, seeming to assess my intent. For a second I stood in the middle of the room, taking in a cashmere sweater that hung on the back of a chair, a water glass that sat on the windowsill, as if proving that Sandy had just stepped out for a second.

He's coming back, I thought as I buried my face in the soft folds of the sweater.

My eyes burned and I nearly left, but the letter from Sandy's estate lawyer made that impossible.

I got to work and went through Sandy's desk, then the nooks and crannies that had always been a mystery, looking for a new will or even scribbled notes, something, anything that proved his intent to deed me the apartment. I forgot about Einstein, forgot about order and organization and the careful sequence of measured steps that had kept me together. Something rose up in me, something dark, and I started whipping open cabinets, upending boxes. But found nothing.

"Damn it," I gasped, making Einstein yelp and leap out of the way when I knocked over a painting that leaned against the wall.

I was unprepared when I found the journals.

I had heard my mother talk about a line in the sand that separates before from after. It always seemed to me that nothing could be that definitive. Now I wasn't so sure.

Einstein and I stared at the beautiful matching volumes bound in rich blue leather. They had been carefully hidden behind the painting. When I pulled out the first journal, the dog growled. When I traced the delicate gold inlays along the edges and spine, he barked. When I started to read, he snapped at me.

Moving away from him, I lowered myself to the threadbare carpet. I delved into page after page of my husband's writings, words mixed with photos of a man I hadn't known. He wrote about his dreams, the different things he had tried to achieve in his life, all of it coming to a head when he decided to run the New York City Marathon.

Over the years, I had learned about the skiing mishap that had shattered his leg, but I had never gotten the sense that he had lost something of himself. As I read the details of how he planned to run the marathon, the daily planner of the mileage he put in toward his goal, the weight training, the meals he ate to build strength and muscle, I started sensing just how much he had believed he lost.

It was difficult putting together the man in the journals who wrote about losing a dream with the larger-than-life one I married. Was it possible that one race could mean so much? Or had he lost more than a single dream? More than that, how hadn't I known about it?

The unease I woke with that morning returned and grew as Einstein continued to pace. Foreboding began to tick inside me as I read, my chest tightening, pain starting behind my eyes. When I picked up the last journal Einstein leaped forward and tried to nose it out of my hands. I pushed him away and opened the cover, then felt the sharp sting of blood rushing to my face.

She was tall. Hot. The sex was amazing.

He wasn't writing about us.

I heard the deep moan before I realized that it came from me. I told myself to stop reading, to leave. Get up. Throw the journals away. What possible good could come from reading this now?

I turned to the next page.

The women didn't start the first year we were married, or even the next. But several months after our second anniversary everything changed.

Einstein continued his low growl. I ignored him, afraid if I moved at all I would be sick.

It wasn't the actual women my husband wrote about that hurt the most. It was the way he wrote about them. The desire. The longing. As an editor, I recognized the moment when intensity came back into his writing. For months before the women returned to his life the entries had been lifeless, colored by frustration. The women had filled his mind, the sex spelled out in simple sentences that made heat burn across my skin. But on top of embarrassment came a wracking stab of what I realized was anger that leapfrogged over all my suppressed grief.

"Bastard," I hissed, gasping for breath. I threw the journal, nearly hitting Einstein who scrambled out of the way.

"You lied!"

Screaming into my hands, I shook, before I grabbed up one of the journals and started ripping—pages, the spine, desecrating a book, someone's words, the very things that had always meant the most to me. "Damn you!" I cried.

I tore and cursed, throwing the pieces into the room, the shredded pages drifting down like confetti at a ticker-tape parade in lower Manhattan's Canyon of Heroes. But Sandy wasn't a hero, not to himself, not to me either, I realized, no matter how much he had wanted to be one. And with that thought, the anger shifted to something else.

I crumpled over onto the floor, the side of my face pressed against the worn wool rug. "I believed in you," I whispered. "I believed in us."

I stared without seeing, the shock and denial I had been living with since Sandy's accident finally ripped away. Finding the journals forced me to face what I hadn't wanted to admit. My husband was dead. He wasn't going to burst through the front door. But the truth was, my denial had been about more than my husband's death. The pages forced me to admit what deep down I had already known but had refused to see, what I had wanted most to deny. In the months before the accident, things between us had been falling apart.

How was it possible I hadn't been willing to admit that fact, even to myself? How had I, Emily Barlow, refused to accept a truth that had been staring me in the face?

But right then none of that mattered. What left me weak with defeat was that if Sandy was dead, not coming back, then I would never get the chance to fix what was wrong.

Call me foolish, call me an embarrassment to everything my mother stood for, but during the months before Sandy died, I hadn't been able to let go of the image of the man who had made love to me as if he were afraid when he opened his eyes I wouldn't be there. It was that man I loved, that man I hadn't wanted to accept was gone.

Even before he died.

einstein

chapter ten

Just so we're clear, it's not my fault that Emily Barlow, tiny warrior with a heart of gold, finally fell apart.

And even *if* I might possibly have played a minor role in her unfortunate communing with the Persian carpet in my *private* study, isn't it shallow, not to mention uncharitable, to pass out blame like single malt scotch and Cuban cigars at a private men's club?

Frustrated, I shook, my dog tags jangling. Not that Emily noticed. Gingerly, I stepped through the journals and shredded pages to get a better look at my wife who lay in a mess on the floor. She wasn't dead, I determined, but I had to admit this couldn't be good.

"Old man!"

I didn't actually expect him to show up, so when a bolt of electricity shot through me and suddenly I wasn't alone, I woofed in surprise.

"Jesus, Mary, and Joseph," I said, despite the fact that I wasn't Catholic. "You scared me to death."

The old man snorted at me. Yes, snorted.

His longish white hair was the same, but this time he wore a vest of delicately linked chain mail over a snowy white shirt with high ruffled collar and buckskin trousers. I looked him up and down then snorted right back at him. I can't swear to it, but he might have blushed.

Grumbling something under his breath, he got down on his hands and knees in front of Emily to get a better look. She stirred, her eyes opening, but I could tell she didn't see him.

"She's a wreck," he said.

"Just so we're clear, it isn't my fault."

"So you've been telling yourself."

My little body shuddered when I huffed, irritation racing down my wiry little back. "It's rude to read someone else's thoughts."

"Consider it a downside of the job."

Hmmm. "Speaking of which, what exactly is your job?"

"Think of me as . . . a triage specialist."

"Interesting. I take it you think I'm worth saving. Though really, as a dog?"

"You were a dog of a man. I thought it might do you good to reverse the situation."

I was indignant. And quite frankly, a little hurt. I knew plenty of people far more selfish than me. I dealt with them every day, and as far as I knew, none of them had been turned into a dog.

"Listen here, I've learned my lesson. Man as dog. Dog as man. Poetic justice. I get it. Now put me back in my body."

Not that he replied. Just like that, he was gone.

"Hey," I called out.

A second later I heard someone in the kitchen.

I scurried down the stairs and found him whipping up dinner. "Oh, thank you. I'm starved."

He scowled at me. "This isn't for you. It's for Emily. I'm worried about her."

Had I still been a Homo sapiens with better jaw capabilities, my mouth would have fallen open. "You're concerned about Emily when I'm the one mucking around as a canine, a half-dead one, at that? One who nearly got euthanized?"

He muttered something that sounded like a curse.

"No question about it," he said, "I completely underestimated you. It never occurred to me that you would find a way to ruin being adopted. You could have proved you were worthy by helping that family. But no, you had to go and growl at the little girl."

"You set that up?"

"Of course."

My neural pathways were firing so fast I felt dizzy. "Then how did Emily end up bringing me home if you had some other plan?"

He hesitated, looked a little peckish. "I don't really know. When things went awry, I was wracking my brain for how to get you out of that muddle. I even started to step in, but then she burst through the door. Saved your hide. Saved both our hides, truth be told." He sighed, almost dreamily, his pale gray eyes starting to shine like glitter. "What never ceases to amaze me is how it always works out, despite what I plan. Emily's the one who needs help. I should have realized that. And how better to prove you're worthy than for you to help the very woman you hurt?"

Some sort of emotion of an uncomfortable nature flared inside me. Since I wasn't one to muck about in feelings, I disregarded it. "Fine, as I said, just put me back in my body. Then I can take care of everything."

"Alexander, this is the deal you made. Before anything else happens, you have to help Emily and prove you're not completely selfish, not to mention, worthy. Even if I wanted to, I couldn't change that. You've got to see this through."

I braced my legs against the floor, my little body shaking with anger. "And if I don't?"

His eyes narrowed and his jaw set. He gave the bottom edge of the chain mail a sharp tug. "Then you'll fade away. To nothing. That's how it works."

I was outraged, incensed, and would have told him so, but suddenly his head tilted as if he heard something. "She's up." He debated the meal on the counter, seemed to think better of it, and made it disappear. "Time to go to work, Alexander."

He was gone before I could question him, and only then did I hear the commotion.

emily

My mother didn't believe in anything you couldn't see, touch, taste, hear, or smell. She was all about the five quantifiable senses. When I was little she read to me like a good mother, but she read from things like No More Miss America! *or* The Crime of Housework. *She hated fairy tales, refused to believe in magic. I wonder if she ever thought about what kind of daughter she'd end up with when she stubbornly refused to believe in miracles.*

—EXCERPT FROM *My Mother's Daughter*

chapter eleven

I came out of my stupor surrounded by proof of a husband I hadn't really known. I staggered up, slipping on glossy photos of Sandy in Paris, Sandy with his parents, Sandy with an assortment of women. Despair and rage ripped through me, and I banged into furniture in an attempt to make it to the door. I couldn't breathe. I couldn't cry. I had to get out of there. I couldn't think beyond that.

Einstein stood at the bottom of the stairs, his little eyes bugging out when I tripped down the last two steps, barely catching myself.

"Agh," I whispered, fighting back the tears that I still refused to give in to.

I crashed out the front door, having no idea where I was going, no purse, no coat, no thought beyond the hysterical edge that rode through me.

At the elevator, I pressed the button with urgency. My breath came in rapid jerks. "Hurry," I pleaded, pressing the call button again and again. If I could just get outside, I told myself, I'd be okay.

But when the door finally opened, I froze at the sight of one of the Dakota board members who had always adored Sandy but had been barely civil to me, speaking heatedly to none other than Sandy's estate lawyer.

My brain lurched. I couldn't let them see me, not now, but my feet wouldn't move. I stood there panicked, despair and the sheer weight of my life falling apart making it impossible to move. Then I saw him.

"What the h—"

Max cut himself off and leapt out from the corner of the elevator where he'd been standing, and grabbed my arm. The lawyer and board member continued whatever heated discussion was going on while Max half dragged, half carried me up the narrow stairs that led to the next floor.

I still couldn't think. I allowed him to take me wherever he wanted. On the eighth floor, he held my arm, and in some part of my brain I registered that his hand was large, strong, but gentle, and I remembered him putting the Hello Kitty bandage on my palm. In the disjointed fragments of my scattered mind I registered *safe,* nothing more.

We didn't stop until he came to a door of what I knew was one of the small, utilitarian apartments used for servants. He pulled one of those mountain-climbing clips from his pocket that held his keys, then he guided me inside. He didn't look at me until he shut the door.

"Are you all right?"

What to say? No, I'm not all right? No, I'll never be all right again?

"What happened back there?" he pressed, his forehead creased with concern.

My clouded brain tried to clear, my eyes burning with the effort.

"When the elevator opened," he explained, "you were standing there like you were . . . losing it."

I must have swayed because he grabbed me.

"Then when you saw that crazy whack-job board member freaking out on that guy, it was like you were going to crash."

"So you took action," I whispered.

He shrugged. "I figured I should get you away from them."

My throat tightened even more at the mix of kindness and strength, as if he were used to taking charge, making snap decisions, averting disaster.

"Hey," he said softly.

I covered my face with my hands, my hair swinging forward.

"Whatever it is, you'll get through it."

"You don't know that," I managed.

"Trust me, I know all about bad shit happening and surviving."

I glanced at him through the threat of tears. "How old are you?"

"Does it matter?"

"No." But somehow it seemed important.

"Twenty-seven."

Five years younger than me. Someone else might have wondered how bad things could have been for a ruggedly handsome man of twenty-seven who had a relative with three beautiful children and lived in a large apartment in the Dakota. But something in his dark eyes told me he had seen more than he should have or wanted to.

"I'll make you some tea," he said, guiding me to a chair in the tiny kitchen that was so like the one in Sandy's suite.

I pulled my knees up, hugging them to my chest, wanting a distraction. "Is this where you live?"

He glanced back at me with a lopsided grin as he tossed his coat aside. Raking his dark hair back with both hands, he shrugged, his forearms defined but not obscenely muscular. "I'm living here for now."

I had noticed that he was tall before, but now I could see he had the broad shoulders of an athlete rather than a bodybuilder, tapering down into a slim waist and hips. Yet again I had the sense that he was in control every second, exceptional in some way that made me feel he could do anything.

After having read my husband's journals, I had the distinct thought that this man was everything Sandy had wanted to be.

The idea startled me and I pushed it away.

I watched as he worked at the tea, surprised by the old-fashioned kettle and delicate china he pulled out of a small cupboard.

A smile tipped up, lopsided when he saw that I noticed. "The teacups are my sister's. This is my sister's place. Or I should say, the big place next to yours is my sister's place. She wanted me to stay downstairs with her and her husband and the kids. But," he shrugged again, "when they convinced me to come to New York for the year I said I couldn't stay with them like the little brother. When I said I'd get my own place, Melanie pulled the big-sister crap on me saying something to the effect of what was the point of me spending the year with them if I wasn't going to be close by."

"So you compromised by staying up here."

He chuckled. "Hell of a compromise. An amazing apartment at the Dakota with views of Central Park."

I started to smile, but the effort sputtered out and my stomach clenched at the thought of this guy with his family drawing him close. I knew I was feeling sorry for myself, and I tried to swallow it back, but I hated that I was losing so much. My home. My husband. My belief in our marriage. The belief that I was loved.

"Hey," he said, bringing me the cup of tea that looked so delicate in his large hand.

He didn't say anything else as he sat down in the chair next to me. I concentrated on the tea, taking the saucer. "You're a regular knight in shining armor. First you rescued me when I fell in the courtyard. Now again at the elevator."

He scoffed. "Yeah, that's me. A regular knight. Too bad I never learned the secret handshake, or," he glanced around the messy apartment, "remembered the knight classes about keeping all the knight gear ordered." He leaned forward, his forearms on his knees, and grinned. "But don't tell anyone. I'd hate to get my secret knight badge revoked."

I felt my lips tremble; something in me wanted to smile, but the effort wouldn't come together and the trembling turned to something else. My eyes burned and the control I had marshaled since Sandy's death tried to desert me. I looked away.

"Hey," Max said, touching my face with his finger, turning me back to look at him. "That was a joke. Jokes are supposed to make you laugh, not cry. See, I really am going to get my knight badge yanked."

His kindness and humor, his caring. I couldn't take it. The tears I had been holding back for the last two months spilled over and I broke.

"Ah, hell," he said.

I staggered up, intent on leaving. I couldn't manage a word, not sorry, not thanks, not even I have to go. I set the cup and saucer down and stumbled toward the door. But before I could turn the knob Max caught my hand and pulled me to him.

His arms were strong though gentle as he tucked me into his chest. The tears came in a torrent then, hard, not pretty, racking my body. I cried for Sandy, I cried for what I thought we'd had. I cried with bitterness and sadness. When I didn't calm, Max swore again and swept me up in his arms. There was nothing in the little room other than the two hard chairs and the table. He carried me into the next room, laying me down on the bed like I might break as my tears soaked the thick comforter.

I'm not sure how long I cried before I heard him sigh, then lie down beside me, sliding his arm beneath my shoulders and tucking me close again. "Let it go," he said, stroking my back. "Get it out."

He didn't cut me off or try to get me to talk. He let me cry.

My mother had always hated tears, refused to cry herself, and walked away from me the few times I broke down when I was little. Sandy hadn't liked tears any more than my mother. As I cried in Max's arms, I felt as if I were crying for a great deal more than my husband.

"You're going to be okay," Max told me softly. "Bad things happen, then you come out the other side. That's how it works. I promise."

Being touched nearly overwhelmed me. How long had it been since another person had held me? I could feel Max's heartbeat, could feel the controlled strength in his body.

It seemed forever before I finally calmed and rolled back. Max hoisted himself onto one elbow and looked down at me, his fingers brushing the hair away from my face. "See, you survived. And you do it one step at a time, one day at a time. Hell, sometimes you do it one minute at a time."

For the first time I wondered who he really was. What had he been through to be able to promise me that bad things happen then you come out the other side?

I closed my eyes and searched for calm, and when I looked at him again his smile was gone. He glanced at my lips, and I realized he was aware of me on a level beyond rescue.

When he saw that I understood what he was thinking, I expected him to move away. He only met my gaze and my heart stopped.

"You have the bluest eyes I've ever seen," he said.

My breath caught when he leaned forward. But at the last second he thought better of it.

"Hell, I'm sorry. This isn't the time."

I felt both confused and grateful. I didn't want this. I wanted my old life back. But that life had been a lie.

"I've got to go." I rolled away and leaped up, then raced for the door. At the last second I turned back.

"Thank you," I said. "Thanks for the rescue."

His smile was bold and warm, confident. "Anytime."

einstein

chapter twelve

Some amount of time passed before Emily returned from wherever it was she had hied herself off to, sans handbag or even a coat. Had I been more observant I might have noticed the strange, confused expression on her face when she came in through the front door. As it was, given my canine ability to smell, all I noted was a different sort of odor. A human smell, one I couldn't quite put a name to, though not a scent wrapped up in office-building recirculated air, subway smorgasbord, or even a bar. Not that I cared where she had been. I had bigger things on my mind. As in, how in God's name was I supposed to help her?

Did this cliché of an old man expect me to figure out a way to communicate so I could talk some sense into her? Tell her to buck up so I could get on with my life?

I doubted even I, with my superior mind, could learn how to write or speak given this dog's body had not evolved beyond marginal vision, limited memory, quadrupedal stature, and an unwieldy tongue. Moreover, I doubted a talking, writing dog was going to help anyone. I'd be turned into a freak. A circus display. While I could use a bit more attention, I had no interest in becoming a sideshow.

So I narrowed in on what exactly I had to do. Namely, help Emily so that I could live up to my end of this so-called bargain and get my body back, since let's face it, who wants to fade away to nothing?

Squinting my eyes, I tried to remember exactly what the old man had said. Fulfill bargain so I wouldn't fade away, yes? And get my body back, right?

I didn't quite remember that part, but surely that's what he meant.

Unfortunately, by the next morning when I found Emily slouched in the library window seat wearing a hideous pair of warm-ups, a cup of tea forgotten in her hand, I hadn't come up with any ideas about how to get this done. Her manic edge from yesterday was gone, but it was clear she wasn't on the verge of dashing off to Caldecote.

I managed to get her to take me out, but when I tried to pull her toward Central

Park she flatly refused. I had no interest in seeing the ill-mannered poodle, but I wouldn't have minded a few bracing gulps of fresh park air.

We returned to the building and were buzzed through the inner gate to the courtyard, my nails clicking on the paving bricks. There wasn't so much as a weed or dust ball to provide interest. I knew the staff hosed down all outdoor common space, even scrubbing the basement floor until you could practically eat off it. The Dakota reeked of history, but everything was exceedingly well-kept, making it seem like I stood in the 1880s when the building was new.

The fountains were lined with glass blocks that allowed sunlight into the basement. Once upon a time the basement had housed the stables. When you walked down and found wide open space instead of the maze of hallways and machine rooms as in most buildings, it was easy to imagine the area filled with horses and hay.

I inhaled deeply, at least for a dog, my low wide chest expanding. I had always loved this place. In a way, the Dakota had felt the same as my beginnings with Emily: both the building and this woman had had the ability to make me feel anything was possible, not just the type of things that I could make happen with the help of my money. With Emily, at the Dakota, I had *believed* I could be great.

I sat down on the cool brick paving stones, sitting with as much dignity as this body could manage, and I didn't budge. Emily looked back and just when she started to tug me, she stopped. She took me in, then glanced up and took in the high, café au lait walls overlooking the courtyard, the multipaned windows in their black casings peering down on us like windows into the past. Her head tipped back and she took in the tall rooftops and the blue sky beyond. Then she glanced back and forth from me to the building, her eyes narrowed.

"Oh, my God! Yes, yes, it's me!" I barked, leaping up like a circus performer.

A smile fluttered on her mouth, but just for a second. "I know. This place is special."

She leaned back against the wall and closed her eyes. Then she looked at me.

"This place is mine," she said softly, "Sandy promised. No matter what Althea says, I will not lose it."

I'm not sure who she was trying to convince. Me or herself.

According to the prenuptial agreement, if I died the apartment went to the Portman Family Trust. But the pesky little truth was, after we were married I *had* promised it to Emily. It had been a sentimental gesture, no question, unheard of in me. But it was during our second Christmas together, and after she had spent weeks beforehand decorating and shopping, vowing to bring together what was left of her family with mine, I had gotten swept up in the moment.

Truth was, I couldn't imagine that Christmas with our families would be anything but a disaster. While once upon a time I might have wished for an old-fashioned train set circling an old-fashioned Christmas tree, I had come around to my parents' preference for Christmas in Paris or on the high seas. More than that, from the beginning my mother had sworn Emily was not suitable to be my wife. *"She's not one of us, darling."* By that second Christmas, Althea Portman's campaign against my wife was in full, if subtle, swing, and Emily's sister and I got along about as well as partisan commentators on CNN.

Needless to say, my hopes weren't high for any sort of truce over a turkey dinner, though I felt pleased with myself for letting Emily have her way. Afterward, I reasoned, when all that mutual dislike spilled over like red wine on the fine linen tablecloth, I wouldn't gloat. I would take Emily in my arms and tell her how sorry I was that it had been a disaster.

I wondered now if I hadn't wanted it to go awry.

At the thought, my wiry head came back, my buggy little eyes narrowing. Had I wanted Emily's Christmas to fail?

I shook the thought away because quite frankly, it was ridiculous.

Christmas day had arrived, and much to my surprise, overnight Emily had put finishing touches on the apartment. There were partially eaten cookies by the tree, a half-full glass of milk. Boot steps in fake snow coming in from the chimney. And presents. Lots of presents.

That afternoon with Christmas carols playing on my sound system, my wife managed to circle her mutinous sister Jordan and my condescending parents around the massive dining table with a unity that I still find hard to believe. The meal was amazing, the conversation surprisingly plentiful. By the time my parents left with their presents "from me," I felt young again, just as I had when I met Emily.

More than that, I felt badly. The week before Christmas I had been so rushed with a deal I was trying to close that I had gotten my assistant to pick something up at Bergdorf Goodman for Emily.

The assistant had chosen an outfit from Bergdorf's trendy fifth floor, one more suited to a nightclub-going twenty-something than the wife of a Wall Street banker. I had been as surprised as everyone else when Emily pulled the skinny jeans and halter top from the tissue paper. I might have cringed when my mother gasped and my wife's mouth fell open. It felt even worse when Emily recovered and squeezed my hand. "Thank you, I love it."

Later when we were alone, Emily sat next to me on the sofa in front of the tree, feet tucked beneath her. I had never seen her so content. I took her into my arms, and kissed her with all the complicated emotions I felt for her in that moment. "You move me."

She touched my lips with her fingertips, then smiled at me with anticipation. "Close your eyes."

"There's more?"

She laughed and slipped away.

"What are you up to?" I expected some sexual romp to top off the evening. Emily dressed as one of Santa's helpers, perhaps, straddling Santa next to the Christmas tree? After all the good of the holiday, I nearly laughed out loud at the thought that Emily was going to be a little bit bad.

But as was my habit, I underestimated my wife.

I took in the scent of pine and cranberry candles. Then I heard the sound, faint at first, slowly growing distinct. A chug, then another, until the whistle blew and I opened my eyes.

Emily sat on the floor. She had removed the velvet tree skirt from around the Christmas tree, and underneath there was track waiting for her to place the train on to run.

"Do you like it?"

I could only stare.

"I got you lots more track, and a bunch of different cars. You can fill the whole library with track and train."

Still I just sat there.

"You hate it. It's childish."

I could hear the disappointment in her voice, but I was frozen.

She scrunched her shoulders. "It's just that when you told me how much you wanted a train when you were young, one around a Christmas tree . . ."

I looked at her, my throat working hard to swallow back what I hadn't at first understood. I felt choked by emotion, amazement mixed with a foreign sense of embarrassment that I had given next to no thought to my wife's Christmas gift.

We made love that night with an intensity I hadn't known existed. When she lay in my arms afterward, I stroked her hair. "You turned this apartment into a home," I said. "You belong here. It should always be yours."

"It will be," she said, kissing me. "We are going to grow old and gray here, with rocking chairs side by side."

I held her tight, something jarring me at the words. I hated the strange feeling, a strange fear of death I had always felt, but refused to examine.

"No matter what happens to me," I said, "I am deeding the apartment to you."

She went very still, then rose up on her elbow, her long hair sweeping my bare chest. "What do you mean?"

"I'm giving you the apartment."

"Sandy, you don't—"

"Shhh," I said, kissing her. "Merry Christmas, Emily. The apartment is my gift to you."

That was over two years ago now, and a lot had changed during that time. For one, I never got around to altering the deed. It was my feelings that had changed when I found I no longer wanted my wife.

I was yanked out of my reverie, literally. All of a sudden, I heard Emily gasp, then yank my leash and bolt for the door.

"What in tarnation?" I barked.

"Quick, E!"

I followed her, my little legs doing their best to keep pace, and just as we charged up the stone steps and inside, I caught the tiniest whiff of what I realized was the same human scent she had brought home with her the night before. But when I glanced back to see who it was, who she was clearly trying to avoid, the door had already swung shut.

Back in the apartment, I went straight for the kitchen and lapped up water from the bowl on the floor. It was impossible not to make a mess with the tongue flailing about. I got nearly as much water on the floor and streaming down the front of me as in my mouth. But finally I was sated. In my towel bed in the corner, all I wanted was to sleep. But then there was Emily, making no effort to go to work as she returned to her station at the window and stared out.

Heavy sigh.

I dragged myself up and went to her.

"Hey," she said, her voice strained. She sank to the floor next to me, pulling me close despite my resistance. Her breath came in deep, gasping pulls, her face buried in my collar. She wanted something from me, but I hadn't any idea what it was. Or perhaps if I am truthful, it was nothing I was willing to give.

This went on for a good three days. Surreptitious inspection of hallways and courtyard on the way out, before dashing outside for obligatory walks, followed by rote distribution of my food and water. That, or quick jaunts to the Pioneer market a block away, from which she returned with everything needed to produce a staggering assortment of baked goods as if she planned to open her very own bakery. She made fruit pies and chocolate croissants, cupcakes and layer cakes with thick buttercream icing that piled up on counters and filled the pantry faster than she could eat them. There was not even a hint that she remembered she was actually employed at Caldecote Press.

But if the days were bad, the nights were worse. When she first brought me home as Einstein, both of us had slept soundly. Since she found the journals, each night Emily woke up screaming. This was bad enough, but now something worse was happening, something harder to take.

It was the scent that hit me the first time, bringing me out of a deep, dream-filled sleep. When I opened my eyes Emily was sound asleep on the floor next to me, wrapped in a thick comforter. Unsettled by her nearness and what it made me feel, I went to the library chair and slept there.

The next night I wasn't surprised when I found her on the floor next to me sound asleep, her eyelashes and cheeks wet, her hand holding my paw as if needing physical reassurance that she wasn't alone. This time she was so close that if I had gotten up it would have woken her.

I told myself I didn't feel anything other than impatience that all the courage I admired had deserted her. Though really, whatever I felt hardly mattered. The situation gave me an idea as to how to help my wife, and in doing so, help myself.

The next morning I rubbed against her leg, gave her puppy dog eyes, and even leaned against her like a lovelorn schoolboy. "Cheer up, woman," I barked.

She gave me a smile, distant, distracted, but she made no attempt to clean up and head for the subway.

She wasn't making my job easy.

I huffed my frustration and started to leave her to her own devices, but yet again I had to ask, what good did that do me? I groaned. It was time to pull out the big guns. For all of the next day, then through the weekend, I did my best to charm her. I pranced on my hind feet, rolled over, sat close to her. But nothing helped. I even nudged her toward the kitchen counter and all those baked goods. When I turned back into a man, I still planned to divorce her. What did I care if she got fat?

Sue me.

On Monday morning, with no progress, I decided to take a different tack. I trotted into her bedroom, nosed into her closet, and started pulling out clothes. The shoes were easy; they were on the floor. The dress was harder, but after using my teeth to tug at the hem, it finally fell off the hanger.

One way or another, the woman was going back to work.

emily

We are all imprinted by our mothers, that imprint luring us in like a friend or sometimes an enemy, causing us to become a carbon copy or a determinedly made original. We either embrace or reject, though the luckiest among us never realize there is an imprint at all.

—EXCERPT FROM *My Mother's Daughter*

chapter thirteen

"What in the world?" I managed.

Einstein stood over a pile of my clothes, a pair of shoes, and my work satchel that he had dragged into the kitchen.

He barked at me.

"Go away," I told him. Not that it did any good.

With Einstein's determined nudging, I got myself showered and dressed. I even boxed up the baked goods and headed for the door. After a crisp nod as if his work here was done, Einstein trotted over to a sliver of sun and curled up with a contented sigh as I headed out.

I arrived at the Trigate building late, though it hardly mattered. I had missed four days with nothing more than an e-mail to Nate Clarkson saying I'd had an emergency. I hadn't responded to any e-mails or voice mails since.

My attire was haphazard, though I only gathered this when Wanda, the full-figured African-American security guard at the main entrance raised a brow and said, "You get dressed in the dark, girl?"

Glancing down, I tried to make sense of the bright yellow sweater over the brown-and-black floral dress, and the black loafers I normally wore with pants. I hardly remembered dressing at all, much less so badly. "It's the latest style," I said, rustling up a bag of German chocolate cupcakes and thrusting them into her hands.

"Latest style for bag ladies, maybe." She glanced inside the bag. "Though mmm-mmm, a mighty sweet bag lady."

I made it to my office without seeing anyone on my floor. After surreptitiously unloading the rest of the sweets in the break room, I tried to regain my control by diving into a manuscript. If closed doors in the workplace hadn't been weird when you weren't having a private conference or call, I would have shut mine to keep everyone out.

I should have gone for weird.

"You're back."

I glanced up and found Victoria standing in the doorway. I managed a big, if forced, smile along with a reflexive squint. "Yep, I'm back. Got the emergency dealt with."

I might be struggling, but I was no fool. Not that it looked like she believed me.

"Are you ready for the big meeting?" she asked.

Big meeting?

"You know about the big meeting, don't you?"

"Of course." Said with a scoff to cover the trepidation I felt over not having a clue.

Had she been nice at all, she would have tossed me a bone and told me where the big meeting was being held. But this was Victoria. She left without giving me a hint. Fortunately, seconds later, the mass exodus of the Caldecote staff toward the main conference room made digging around in my e-mail for the lost, missed, or discarded *big meeting* memo unnecessary.

Caldecote Press was a small publisher, more literary than mainstream in an age when mainstream was all most anyone cared about. I had always been proud of the fact that I had gotten a job with one of the few publishers who remained dedicated to books that mattered. What I frequently forgot was that Caldecote was owned by the media conglomerate, Trigate.

Charles Tisdale had never succumbed to Trigate's desire for us to publish big, commercial works of fiction or tell-all types of nonfiction. Charles had won the day by arguing that those books cost money to acquire, big money, the kind of money Trigate didn't want to spend, at least not on its little publishing business.

We had continued on our way, publishing award-winning work that got lots of attention for its importance but failed to consistently move books off store shelves. But every so often this mix produced a significant book that achieved blockbuster sales. Thankfully, the paradigm kept Caldecote out of bankruptcy, though never quite solvent.

Every chair in the conference room was taken, the rest of us crowding around the perimeter to find out what was going on. Speculation ran rampant in the group of editors who stood on either side of me.

Birdie nudged in beside me with a cupcake in her hand. "Have you tasted one of these? They are insane. Where'd they come from?"

I shrugged.

"What's up? another editor asked.

"Beats me," Birdie responded, running her finger through the icing.

Several of the younger editors looked at me. "What have you heard?"

Somehow I had turned into a den mother for the younger women. Before Sandy's death I had helped them with cover copy, letters to agents, brainstormed with them on ideas.

I was saved from having to say I hadn't heard a thing when Charles Tisdale walked in wearing his standard tweed jacket, khaki pants, and cordovan loafers. His gray hair was brushed back, his navy, burgundy, and forest green–striped bow tie perfectly tied.

The room began to quiet, though a few hushed conversations continued as he headed for the front of the room. The second an unfamiliar woman walked in behind him you could have heard a pin drop.

Birdie sucked in her breath. "Oh my God! That's Tatiana Harriman. What's she doing here?"

The woman at the front of the room was petite, made taller by four-inch heels. Her hair was shoulder length, jet black, and cut so bluntly that it looked like it could slice paper. If I recalled correctly, Tatiana Harriman was fifty. I had read an exposé of her once, had seen a photograph. In person she looked younger, with the face and body of a thirty-five-year-old.

"This can't be good," Birdie said.

Nan Beeker grabbed my arm. "The rumor must be true!"

"What rumor?"

"That we're getting sold," Lori Monroe said.

"I heard the same thing!"

They all turned to me. "Even if we get sold, everything's going to be fine, right, Emily?"

Sold? Harriman? My sluggish brain tried to catch up.

"Ladies and gentlemen," Charles said. "I have brought you here today to put rumors to rest. Many of you have heard that WorldPass Corporation has been courting Trigate."

"Yeah, for Trigate's digital content," someone muttered.

A ripple of unease ran through the room.

"Now, now," Charles added calmly. "I am here to tell you that indeed Trigate and WorldPass have merged."

Tension buzzed through the room before someone blurted, "What's going to happen to Caldecote?"

"Please, stay calm," Charles continued. "There is nothing to be concerned about. I have been assured that Caldecote Press is a priority."

"Yeah right," someone scoffed.

Tatiana Harriman glanced around the room like a teacher surveying her class, as if trying to put faces with outbursts.

"To show their commitment to Caldecote, WorldPass has brought in Tatiana Harriman to head our prestigious publishing house."

Tatiana straightened and smiled, indifferent to the mouths that dropped open at the news.

"No way," someone said.

"That's insane," another added.

"People, people," Charles said, attempting to speak over the growing cacophony of unhappy voices.

"I'm a dinosaur," he said, flashing the kind smile I had grown to love. If it hadn't been for him, I was certain I'd still be an associate editor underneath Victoria. It was Charles who had shown me the ropes, pulling me into meetings so I could learn the things Victoria refused to teach me.

"My way of publishing books is antiquated. As of today, I am stepping down as president of Caldecote Press—though I will remain on as a consultant for as long as Tatiana needs me."

From the look that crossed her face, I was sure Tatiana Harriman believed she didn't need anyone. Ever.

"And now I have the privilege to introduce you to Ms. Tatiana Harriman."

Charles pulled note cards from his breast pocket, then found his reading glasses. Not that a speech was needed. Everyone in the room already knew the legend that was the woman.

She had been the youngest editor-in-chief of the big British tabloid magazine, *Sass,* before it was gobbled up by WorldPass, who promoted her to head up *House of Mirth* magazine in the U.S. In record time she had turned the struggling monthly into a thriving must-read, before WorldPass trotted her over to their foundering *Chronicles,* the literary magazine that made no money but was often quoted by world leaders.

WorldPass contended that she saved the magazine, while the staff writers swore she ruined it. Not that it mattered. Now she was here, at Caldecote Press, and it didn't take a genius to understand that she was here with a mandate that we start making money.

I shuddered at the thought. *Ruth's Intention* was on the verge of failing. Victoria wanted me to take a fall. My mother-in-law wanted to take my home away from me. And as it turned out, my husband had been having a string of affairs before he died. Was it possible my life could get any worse?

Birdie glanced at me. "Are you all right, sweetie?"

I forced a smile. "Sure. I'm fine."

But when I straightened, Tatiana Harriman was looking right at me.

■

First thing the next morning, Victoria came into my office. Somehow I had managed to dress in a skirt and blouse that went together, and even managed to wash my hair. I hadn't baked nearly as much the night before, though *not as much* was still a lot by anyone else's standard, and I had managed to sneak most of that into the break room again.

"I adore Tatiana!" Victoria beamed.

"Tatiana?"

"Ms. Harriman to you. By the bye," she continued, "did you see the memo she sent out yesterday? The one about the importance of good health, eating well, and the mental benefits of dressing powerfully for work? The one that said that whoever was bringing all the cupcakes needed to stop?"

I must have looked as confused as I felt, not to mention a tad uncomfortable since I knew exactly who was bringing the cupcakes.

Victoria shook her head at me. "Do you even read your e-mail these days? Anyway, we're supposed to take care of ourselves, eat healthfully, and dress as befits people who work in offices, not college campus coffee shops."

"She said that?"

"I added the part about college campus coffee shops." Victoria shrugged. "I think it's a great idea. When Charles was here, everyone and their brother took Casual Fridays way beyond Friday, not to mention way beyond acceptable attire. I've never been so shocked as the day Lori Monroe pranced in here with a belly ring showing."

Victoria had no piercings, belly or otherwise. Not that I was one to cast stones. I had been as surprised as Victoria when Lori came to the office, midriff bare. But that was hardly the point. The message of Tatiana's e-mail was clear: I couldn't afford to miss any more work, I needed to stop baking, and I needed to find a way to make *Ruth's Intention* succeed.

Victoria left, and I dove into work. My voice mail was overflowing, my e-mail ready to explode. There were several messages marked urgent, including the infamous big meeting memo, though most were from the production head wanting a manuscript I'd been going through, checking the author changes.

By noon I still hadn't gotten to the end, but could think of nothing but eating. I pushed the manuscript aside and went to lunch. Healthy sounded horrible, and I gave in and went for the prefabricated food filled with preservatives at the corner market.

"Emily!"

Birdie came up behind me at the food bar. She wore a suit I had never seen before, one that registered in some part of my brain as too expensive for a publishing assistant. She bypassed the fattening foods and started loading her container with lettuce and raw vegetables.

"The woman is insane, demented, completely unfair," she said, tonging up a square of tofu with a grimace and a hiss.

Carla, another associate editor, came up behind Birdie. She was wearing a little black business suit. "This is ridiculous," she said.

Though I noticed she too loaded up on salad. She bit into a carrot stick with relish. "She can't do this. She can't dictate what we wear." She shook the carrot at me. "Or what we eat!"

Technically, Tatiana wasn't. She was providing reasonable dress guidelines and healthy tips. No corporation in the land, at least outside California, allowed bare bellies in the workplace.

Not that I said that. I turned back to the food bar and added another helping of cheddar cheese mashed potatoes to my container.

"Don't let the new boss see you eating that. I don't think cheddar mash is considered health food by anyone."

"Potatoes are a vegetable."

Birdie giggled.

Carla rolled her eyes. "One, I doubt there is a real potato anywhere in the mix—"

True.

"—and even if there was, the fake, processed, sodium and fat-filled cheese undercuts any nutritional value a starchy potato might provide." She smiled proudly. "I'm editing a diet book."

Birdie looked at me. "If we're quick, we can take Carla out back and choke her with tofu."

"I'm just saying," Carla said.

I responded by adding more potatoes for good measure.

But when I turned back, none other than Tatiana stood behind me.

"Cheddar mash?" she asked. "I take it you also subscribe to the theory of candy corn as vegetable, and strawberry jam as fruit."

Birdie and Carla snapped their plastic containers shut and bolted for the checkout line.

"You're Emily, right?" she said.

"Yes, Emily Barlow."

"Charles speaks highly of you."

"Charles has been an excellent boss."

Tatiana considered me. In her high-fashion cherry suit and black stiletto heels, she looked out of place in the cramped food market, her sharp bob, severe curtain of bangs, and small, round, black-rimmed glasses marking her as a player. I couldn't imagine what she was doing there, couldn't put together the perfect woman and her health memo with this appearance.

Then I noticed the container of fresh-squeezed orange juice. The corner market did a lot of things in a preprocessed, preservative-laden way, but it provided fresh-squeezed orange juice pretty much 24/7.

"Vitamin C," she explained, as if reading my mind.

She turned, walked directly to the front of the line, handed the clerk three dollars, didn't wait for change, then clipped out of the store without another word.

The following week, some of the younger editors at Caldecote cornered me in the women's room.

"Tatiana's unreasonable."

"She acts like it's my fault when an author doesn't deliver on time."

"I know she blames me that the cover copy for my January book was hideous."

I didn't need to ask who *she* was.

Birdie turned to the other woman. "You think you have it bad? My boss asked me to show Tatiana the cover for his next release. Tatiana looked me up and down and said, 'You're kidding, right?' It wasn't even my cover!"

Carla grimaced. "This morning I heard she told Letty Mayhew that her latest book was as inspiring as tooth rot on a dentist."

I had the disjointed thought that Sandy would have loved Tatiana Harriman.

I turned and stared at my face in the mirror, barely recognizing the woman who stared back.

"What if I get fired?" Carla said, her voice rising. "I can't get fired! I'm doing a time-share in Montauk this summer."

I heard the bathroom door open.

"Are we having a meeting no one told me about?"

Birdie, Carla, and the other editors whirled around. I didn't have to turn. I saw Tatiana's reflection in the mirror.

She stood in the doorway of the bathroom, like a heat-seeking missile, landing in the middle of us wherever we congregated. I turned away from the mirror and faced our new boss.

She looked us over with chilling disapproval. "This is not a sleepover where we freeze bras and use warm water to make sleeping girls pee."

Clearly her days of slumber parties were not of the braiding hair and singing "Kumbaya" variety.

None of my coworkers waited for more. They disappeared through the narrow doorway like a horde of scurrying mice.

I started to follow.

"You know, Emily, being a den mother to a bunch of ducklings won't get you anywhere in this business. Indiscriminate niceness won't either."

You'd think if she was going to say anything to me it would be something about books or the lousy job I was suddenly doing. A comment about being too nice threw me.

"People take advantage of nice," she said. "Survival means winning, and not necessarily being sweet while you're doing it."

"Are you implying life is a zero-sum game? Or maybe you just mean that's how life is going to be here at the *new* Caldecote Press?"

She smiled without humor. "So you're not always nice. Good. As for a zero-sum game, no. For one person to win, the other doesn't have to lose. All I'm saying is that constant niceness makes people wonder what you're trying so hard to hide." She walked over to the mirror and smoothed her already smooth hair. "What are you hiding, Emily?"

My mother had asked me the very same thing.

chapter fourteen

Since the day I cracked in Max Reager's arms, I had been avoiding him like the plague. Unfortunately, when I came up from the subway at the corner of Central Park West and Seventy-second Street, I saw Max and his niece and nephews a few yards from the front gates of the Dakota.

Katie stood on the sidewalk crying. Her twin brothers stood off to the side, each leaning against the handlebars of their scooters, looking bored—very much the mien of, "been there, done that," as if she threw fits regularly.

The girl cried enthusiastically, jerking her own scooter as Max worked calmly on something he held in his hands. He wore cargo pants and his coat, a messenger bag slung carelessly across his shoulder.

"You have to fix it," Katie wailed.

I'm not sure what Max said in response, but the girl wailed louder. Max didn't so much as blink. He continued with the same calm he had when I first saw him, seeming oblivious to her tantrum. I couldn't move.

Max handed whatever he was working on back to Katie. "That's the best it's going to get."

"No! Fix it!"

The girl's face was blotchy and tear-stained, her small hand clutching what now looked to be a pink watch.

"You're the one who broke it, Katie, not me." He turned to the boys. "Okay, dudes, ready?"

The twins perked up. Katie threw her scooter down. Max just gave her a look. "Suit yourself. Guys, I think Lupe has ice cream in the freezer."

"Yay!" they cheered, scootering the last few yards to the entrance.

Max followed, leaving Katie behind. "Pick 'em up, guys. No scootering in the building."

Katie stood for a second, fists clenched, her tears cut off like a water faucet. Then, "Wait for me!"

She raced after them, only to have Max stop. "Get your scooter."

Her face went red and I thought she'd throw another fit, but Max stood his ground. After a second, Katie ran back, grabbed her scooter. When she got back to him, he put his hand on her shoulder as they headed toward the gate together.

"How does chocolate sound?" I heard him ask.

I don't know how she responded, but she leaned into his thigh as they walked through the gate.

The gesture was so loving, so secure, that I had to turn away. I chided myself for being a sentimental fool as I retraced my steps so I could walk around to the back side of the building, giving them time to get inside and up to their own apartment. Whatever feelings I had for Max only confused me.

I went around to Seventy-third, then down the ramp to the back door. The staff buzzed me in through the mesh gates, and I took the elevator to the main lobby. Being the stealth sort I had become, I hurried down the first-floor hallway, intent on going up my usual elevator, certain that Max and company would be long gone.

But I skidded to a halt on the tile floor.

"Hey," Max said when he saw me.

The three kids looked back. The boys weren't particularly interested, but Katie's eyes narrowed.

"I haven't seen you in a while," Max said, his mouth ticking up at one corner. "If I didn't know better I'd swear you were avoiding me."

Yet again I felt something in me ease. "You know better, do you?"

He extended his arms to either side and shrugged. "Can you imagine anyone avoiding me, the sweet, kind, completely un-dangerous Max Reager?"

Despite myself, I smiled.

"Don't answer that," he said. "There's no good answer that in some way doesn't take a swipe at my manhood."

That actually made me laugh.

Katie's narrowed gaze turned into an official glare. "What's your name?" she demanded, taking Max's hand.

"Emily. Emily Barlow."

The elevator opened and I had little choice but to get on. Between all of them, their scooters, and me, it was a tight squeeze. Max and I stood on either side facing each other.

"We're going to have ice cream," one of the twins said.

I raised a brow. "Before dinner?"

"Don't tell," Max said. "Come have some with us."

"Yeah, come have some," the twins said.

Katie didn't share her brothers' enthusiasm.

"Thanks, but I can't."

Max looked at me like I was a coward.

"My dog. Einstein. I have to take him out."

Max just smiled. "Whatever you say. Come on, guys."

My heart fluttered the entire time I had Einstein outside. As usual my dog refused to use the restroom on the curb until both the doorman and I had turned our backs to give him some semblance of privacy. When he was done, I had the strange sense he was looking around for something, gingerly lifting his paws one at a time. Was he looking for hand wipes?

After a second, E hung his head and trotted back toward the gates. I had put Max firmly out of my head, but when the elevator opened, the twins were sitting Indian-style in front of my door.

"Hey," I said, surprised.

Einstein took one look at the boys and crouched down as if suspicious.

"E, these are our neighbors. Be nice."

With what I would have sworn was a bored shrug, he straightened and headed inside. The boys followed me inside without being asked.

Once Einstein was settled and ignoring all three of us, the twins took my hands. "Come on. If we don't hurry, the ice cream will be all melty."

They tugged me out of the kitchen. "I can't, really."

"You have to." They closed my door for me. "Uncle Max said we couldn't come back unless we had you with us."

"He did, did he?"

With not enough reluctance, I followed.

In the bright kitchen next door, Katie was regaling the nanny with tales of their adventures in Central Park. I doubted the little minx had mentioned the tantrum in the street.

The giant golden retriever Beau leapt up from the corner as the boys raced to the center island and climbed up on high stools.

Max was leaning against the counter, and when he saw me he smiled. "Glad you could join us."

"You didn't give me much choice."

"Yeah, bad habit of mine."

Katie continued with her stories.

"I see you have a way of getting girls to stop crying."

"Yep, that's me. Though I ask, why are so many girls crying around me these days?"

He smiled that gorgeous smile and pulled out three containers of ice cream from the freezer.

The children cheered.

"Ice cream to bribe crying girls. Sending the boys to coerce me over here. Underhanded tactics?"

"A Navy SEAL does not employ underhanded tactics," he said, scooping ice cream into six bowls. He stopped and glanced at me, scooper in hand. "We just bring whatever force necessary to the situation to get the job done."

"You're a Navy SEAL?"

His smile disappeared, the scoop filled with ice cream held suspended in the air. "I was. I'm out now."

"You mean you're not a soldier anymore?"

We looked at each other, and I saw the darkness then.

"I'm sorry," I said, though I wasn't certain why.

After a second, the darkness was gone as if it had never been there. "No apologies necessary, other than apologizing for calling me a soldier. I was Navy, ma'am, not Army."

"Ah. Forgive me."

"Anytime."

When ice cream was done, the boys insisted on dragging me to see their playroom. A glance at Max only produced a shrug. "They're the boss."

The apartment was more than twice as big as mine. Outside of the kitchen, we turned right then right again, heading down a long hallway that ran along the south side of the building. Inside the playroom I stopped. I felt the moment when Max came up behind me.

"A kid's version of nirvana," he said. "My sister can get carried away."

"Come on, Emily," the boys said.

The walls were covered with fun family photos done up in colorful frames. Coming down the hallway I had noted formal photographs in expensive frames.

When the boys caught me looking at the pictures, they raced over and proceeded to tell me who everyone was. But once Katie realized what was going on, she nudged her brothers aside and took over.

"That is not Uncle Max," she snipped. "That is Uncle Marcus."

Uncle Marcus looked a lot like Uncle Max, only older and far more respectable.

"My big brother," Max explained.

"And that's Uncle Marcus with Uncle Peter."

"Another brother?" I asked.

"Marcus's partner," Max clarified. "They live in Tribeca."

"And that's Aunt Mary and Uncle Howard."

Max followed along to explain. "Mary is my other sister. Melanie, Mary, Marcus, and me. In that order."

"Your parents like M's."

"Take it up with my mother." He peered closer at the photos as if he hadn't looked at them in a very long time. "Mary's a doctor at New York Presbyterian and Howard's a lawyer at one of those massive firms with a long list of names. They live on the Upper East Side."

Katie pointed out another photo. "That's our mom and dad."

"Melanie and Ben," Max added. "Ben's a Wall Street guy who managed not to lose his money in the crash."

I saw photos of grandparents and cousins and a wide array of extended family. The kids, with Max's help, explained them all.

In the middle of all the frames there was an old photo of a couple, the woman in a Jackie Kennedy pillbox hat, the man in full military dress.

"Your parents?"

"Kathryn and Dan."

"Are you close?"

"We're all close. All the kids are in New York, now. Our parents are a couple hours away in Pennsylvania where we grew up."

"Is your dad still in the Army?"

He smiled again. "Navy," he clarified and I could see the love in his expression. "Hell of a sailor in his day, always set a high bar for his kids."

Katie and the twins had lost interest and were playing.

"Did you resent your father's high expectations?"

He was quiet for a second. "Sure. Sometimes. But mostly I admired him. To his credit, he always made me feel that I could do anything I wanted, and was willing to support any decision I made as long as I had thought it through and could justify my reasoning."

"He sounds like an exceptional man."

"He is. He's retired now. Retired as a captain."

"Is that high up?"

"The equivalent of a colonel in any other branch."

"I take that as a yes?"

He shook his head again and smiled. "Yes."

I turned back to the photos and Max came up next to me. "I take it you don't have a lot of experience with people in the military."

"I'm from a house of women, more specifically, women who don't believe in war. Not a man in the bunch."

"What about your father?"

I hesitated. "As best I can tell, he was a one-night stand following a peace rally. My mother didn't catch his name."

I could feel his surprise. And why wouldn't he be shocked? He was a man with a family like the Waltons, big and loving. When I had compared my family situation to his before, I had felt sorry for myself. But right that second I almost hated him for what he had. I was jealous, and though I knew it was ridiculous I couldn't stop the feeling.

"My mother was important in her day." I felt a need to stand up for her. "She once wrote an article that was published in the *New York Times*."

"She was a writer?"

"Actually, no. She was a feminist. The article was about how nice girls didn't get ahead." I couldn't help but smile ruefully. "That might be old hat now, but back then it caused quite a stir. And not a good stir." I rolled my eyes. "I've never seen my mother so proud. She cut out the article. Your sister frames family photographs and hangs them on the wall. My mother framed her article. No matter where we lived, that's what she hung on the wall." I hesitated remembering. "Then one day the article came down and never went back up, not even when we finally stayed put in one place."

"Why?"

I blinked. "I have no idea." Before he could say anything else, I stepped away. "So, I've seen every single Reager since time began . . . except you. Where is Uncle Max?"

It was the kids who heard and all three pointed out a different photo. Max in formal sailor's garb. Max in combat gear. And one that surprised me: Max standing on a snow-covered peak that even I recognized.

"When did you climb Everest?" I asked.

"May."

"This past May?"

"Yeah."

"Doesn't it take years of training to climb Everest?"

"Not for a Navy SEAL."

"You and the SEAL thing."

I started to probe, but the kids broke in. "Come on, play with us!"

But Lupe had come in, announcing dinner.

"No!" they said in unison.

"Chow time, sailors," Max said.

The kids leaped into line and started to march like it was a game.

"Come on," he said to me, "while the coast is clear."

Out in the hall he walked me toward my apartment, but at the door he caught my hand. "I have something to show you."

He pulled me up the stairs and I assumed he was taking me back to his apartment. My heart started hammering in my chest in a completely inappropriate way. But he kept going until we reached a door I had never seen before. It was unlocked, which surprised me, and then the next thing I knew we were stepping out onto the roof in the growing darkness.

"John Lennon did an interview up here once. They took his photo over there," Max said, pointing to the thin railing that looked out over Central Park.

"Are we allowed up here?"

"Not sure. But hell—"

"You'd rather seek forgiveness than permission. That doesn't seem like a Navy sort of attitude."

He laughed, tugging me to the railing. "Let's just say that I've fallen off the military wagon in more ways than just leaving my room a mess."

The park spread out before us like black velvet surrounded by walls made of ornate limestone-and-sandstone apartment buildings, the lampposts that lined the roads lighting the way like diamonds.

"Up here you can forget the craziness of the city," he said, looking out.

"Sort of like being on top of a mountain."

He glanced at me, then smiled. "Yeah."

We stood for a time, a quiet peace settling between us.

"So, you're a mountain climber now?"

"No, but after I finished my last tour of duty, I needed . . . something different."

I could feel the tension that settled through him.

"I figured what the hell. I'd climb Everest. It was sort of a whim."

"Are you crazy?"

He was quiet for a second. "Probably. Which is why my family convinced me to come to New York. Spend time with the pack, then figure out what the hell I'm going to do with the rest of my life."

"Have you figured it out yet?"

"Negative."

I hardly knew him, but I realized even then that he didn't strike me as someone who would let the chips fall where they may.

"Your turn," he said.

"For what?"

"Telling me why you're having a tough time."

What amazed me was that I told him. I found myself explaining how my husband had died, about finding the journals, about how when Max found me in the courtyard I had just gotten an official letter from my husband's estate regarding ownership of my apartment.

"Sounds like you need a lawyer," he said. "I could hook you up with my sister Mary's husband. I'm sure someone at Howard's firm can help you."

"I couldn't impose."

He turned to face me, turning me with him. "Hey," he whispered, "I've strayed far enough from my SEAL days. Let me hold on to the knight gig."

I laughed, though barely, the sound cut off when his gaze drifted to my lips. I could tell he wanted to kiss me, but whether it was the knight thing or something else, he wasn't going to.

"No, really," I whispered, my fingers curling into his shirt, despite better sense. "I couldn't."

He hesitated, unsure of what I was referring to. But then I tugged harder, and he leaned down, kissing me, a deep groan escaping him.

"God, I knew you'd feel like this," he whispered against my skin. "I've wanted you from the first time I saw you."

"Since I fell in the courtyard?"

He chuckled, then traced my lips with his tongue. "Since even before I saw you in the park. You were standing on the corner, staring without seeing."

"You're attracted to demented and clearly lost older women?"

"I'd hardly call you an older woman. And never demented." He stopped kissing me and looked down into my eyes. "But lost, yes. It was like looking at someone I used to be. That's how I know you'll survive."

I could feel his hands on my back. "What did you survive, Max?"

It looked like he would let go and move away.

"Please. I shared my life with you."

After a second, he sighed. "Who the hell knows? Afghanistan? Iraq? Everyone's heard the story thousands of times, by now. And I got off easy."

"How's that?"

"I'm still alive."

When I would have questioned him more, he kissed me again. I didn't press this time.

His hands came up and framed my face, his fingers extending into my hair. His mouth lined my own, his teeth nipping. It seemed impossible for such a big man to be so gentle. I could have kissed him forever. But eventually the old me, the one who was sane, pushed away. I was a widow with more problems than I knew how to handle. I didn't need another one in the form of a man who clearly had his own stuff to deal with.

"Thanks for the offer of a lawyer. But I'll get it straightened out."

Then I slipped away, back through the door I had never seen before.

chapter fifteen

No matter where we lived, my mother loved giving parties. It didn't matter if we only had four walls and a shared bathroom down the hall. She had to have people around her.

My mother filled her parties with a menagerie of New York's offbeat and off-the-grid intellectuals. There was Willa, my mother's best friend, and an assortment of people she knew from WomenFirst, including a man Mother called the Professor because he spoke almost entirely in famous quotes. Mother teased him that he didn't have an original thought in his head. He countered by throwing more quotes at her, after which they'd argue, then end up in bed. That is, if there wasn't some other man at the party she liked better.

The revelers drank and talked about the state of the world, my mother charming them all with her alluring mix of sharp wit and wildness. For the short period of time that my mother was married to Jordan's father, the parties were tamer. But the marriage didn't last long, and soon it was just the three of us. Mother continued to fight her battles; Jordan was the precocious one; and I served as hostess for the motley assortment my mother called her friends.

One night a woman arrived that I hadn't seen in a while, a woman I had always loved. I took coats and made sure everyone had their drinks, and when I handed her a martini she looked at me closely then laughed.

"Every time I see you you're more grown up," she said, and looked around for my mother. "No wonder you don't need a husband, Lillian. You've got Emily to take care of all the things you don't like to do."

My mother looked at me across the room. I couldn't read her expression. The set of her mouth wasn't quite a frown, but it wasn't a smile either.

"Yes, she plays the perfect caretaker. But I wonder, is that what you really are, Em? Or are you hiding what you really want to be?" She paused. "Please tell me a daughter of mine wants to be more than a housewife and hostess."

Her friends laughed. "Good God, Lillian, don't ride her for being good at something you couldn't do to save your life."

Mother's features cemented. After a moment, she shrugged and then she did smile, lifting her glass in salute, though I had no idea if it was some strange acknowledgment of my success or her defeat.

■

The day after Tatiana cornered me in the ladies' room, I got a phone call from the assistant of a woman named Hedda Vendome of Vendome Children's Books. Bold, daring, loud, Hedda ruled with flare in children's publishing, a world where most people were quiet and conservative. She got away with it, no doubt, because she managed to publish more award-winning young adult and picture books than anyone else in the industry. And she wanted to have lunch with me.

I accepted more out of surprise than anything else. Back in the days of my mother's living room parties, it was Hedda who had looked at me closely when I handed her the martini.

I hadn't seen her in years, though I had seen a photograph or two in the newspaper. While I was almost certain she was sixty-five if she was a day, she swore she was only sixty and dressed like she was forty. Not that any of this mattered. But it was rare in the age of publishing conglomerates to still have people in any sector who were grander than the characters they published.

We met at Michael's on West Fifty-fifth Street. Most people in publishing had been to Michael's at one time or another; many of the movers and shakers in media ate there regularly. Hedda had her own table.

The maître d' seated me before Hedda arrived, giving me a chance to survey the crowd and attempt to put well-known names with faces.

Hedda entered with a flourish, stopping along the way to air kiss and say hello. When she got to me I swallowed back the inclination to stand and curtsy.

"My, my, my," she said, her voice gravelly from too many years of cigarettes. She was a throwback to a day long gone, her hair dyed red, her eyebrows penciled on. "You don't look a thing like your mother. Thank God."

She laughed, leaned over, and gave me a short crisp hug. "I haven't seen you since you were in school clothes serving dry martinis to your mother's cohorts. God, I miss those days. Waking up in the morning invigorated, ready to fight the good fight. And for so long your mother was on the front lines. How I admired her."

She paused, then to my surprise she cupped my cheek, looking me in the eye. "But I'm certain she was hell to live with."

My breath must have caught, and she dropped her hand away.

"But enough about me and my opinions on your mother. Let's talk about me and my opinions on everything else!"

Hedda fell into her seat with a dramatic sigh. "What I'd give for a martini and a cigarette right now. Alas, my doctor doesn't allow the gin, and the mayor doesn't allow the cigarettes. Men."

She laughed so loudly heads turned. At the sight of Hedda, many smiled. I realized quickly that you couldn't help but love Hedda Vendome.

"So tell me, darling, how are you? Tell me everything. How is your horrid job at Caldecote? What do you think about Tatiana Harriman?"

I couldn't imagine that she needed inside information from me. Hedda was known for her inside connections.

"Well—"

"Don't bother. I already know. If I were twenty years younger and had breast implants I would *be* Tatiana Harriman."

She ordered for both of us, Cobb salads with a side order of Michael's famous frites.

She talked of inconsequential things through the meal, introducing me to everyone who came over to the table.

"Lord, how I miss the early days with your mother," she said when the waiter took her plate away. "She knew how to get things done. Crafty little bird, true, but she knew what she was talking about." Hedda toyed with her water glass. "Which is why we are here."

"We're here because of my mother?"

"Indirectly. I hear you have a good eye for what works in publishing."

Clearly she hadn't heard about *Ruth's Intention*—or my recent bouts of not doing any work at all.

"I've had my moments," I said. "But I'm in adult publishing."

"Ah, but I am friendly with Libby Meeker."

"From Meeker Books?"

Over the years, I had spent more time than I should in Libby's famous children's bookstore searching for books to add to my collection.

I don't remember exactly when books became my refuge, but it was in the pages of a world created out of thin air that I began to find pieces I recognized as myself. In books I found characters so real that they were more my friends than the children with whom I went to school. In the stories I loved, I found adults wiser than the ones who laughed and argued in my mother's living room.

"Libby tells me you understand children's books. While you might not have actual experience in the area, I am willing to take that risk. I want you to come to work for me at Vendome."

Things might be dicey at Caldecote, but going into kids' books was no solution. If nothing else, I didn't have the energy to start over, especially in children's publishing, which couldn't be more different from publishing adult books.

"I'm flattered, but—"

"Don't answer me now. Of course it's a shock. But it's the right thing to do. Think about it."

An assistant raced in. "We've got to go, Ms. Vendome. The car is waiting."

All the larger-than-life airs disappeared and Hedda reached across the table. "I heard about your husband." She squeezed my hand. "I'm so very sorry."

■

I arrived back at the office in a daze. I hadn't been back long enough to set my handbag down when I was summoned by Tatiana.

"So," she said without preamble. "How was lunch?"

She knew about lunch? Though why I was surprised might have been the bigger mystery. Tatiana Harriman couldn't have gotten as far as she had without her ear to the ground.

"It was fine, thank you."

Tatiana looked me over, and proceeded slowly.

"I do not appreciate the fact that the minute I arrive you go to lunch with a competitor."

"Hedda? A competitor? She's in children's publishing."

"Then it's true. You had lunch with Hedda Vendome."

I felt like I was playing a new version of chess that didn't come with rules. "Yes. How did you know?"

"I have a friend at Random House who loves to gossip. He couldn't dial his cell phone fast enough to let me know that someone on my staff was already trying to jump ship. Though I certainly didn't expect you'd be the one who got people speculating that the troops were unhappy. The fact that Hedda is in children's publishing makes it even worse. My employees are so unhappy they're willing to jump to something so different, so beyond the scope of adult publishing . . ." The words trailed off and she pursed her lips like she was swallowing back anger.

"I'm not jumping ship. I've known Hedda since I was a child."

Which was true.

Her eyes narrowed and she tapped a bright red nail against her desk. "So you aren't considering leaving?"

"Absolutely not."

Also true.

I could tell she debated my answer.

"Tatiana, if I was looking for a new job do you really think I'd interview at Michael's—where everyone and their brother would know about it?"

"You're right. And I consider myself a good judge of character. You might be struggling right now, but you're not stupid." She nodded. "Maybe your friendship with Hedda will serve us well in the future, what with young adult novels being all the rage now." A smile pulled at her lips. "Fine. We're done here." I was dismissed.

But at the door she stopped me. "The next time Hedda calls you, I expect you to let me know."

einstein

chapter sixteen

It is said that all domestic dogs are descended from wolves. Pack animals. Brutal. I might have liked to be a wolf, though the thought of fighting for my place in the *Canis lupus* hierarchy gave me pause. If climbing the ladder in New York society was tough, in the wolf pack it could be a killer. Literally. So until I was relieved of Einstein's body, I didn't see that I had any choice but to throw in my lot with the domesticated pack I had with Emily.

During the day I came and went with the dog walker. Greta or maybe Gretchen, Grace, whatever, picked me up at noon and took me along with six other dogs to Central Park. While I had always loved the park, being there as a dog attached to a gaggle of odiferous canines and never let off-leash was a misery I cannot fully describe. But it beat spending all day alone in the apartment while Emily was at the office. At night, my wife took her determined baking to new heights and ignored the work she brought home with her. Even I couldn't deny she was breaking apart, the little pieces of her circling down the proverbial drain.

I was debating how to solve this new wrinkle in my life when disaster struck. Emily's sister arrived. And we know how I felt about Jordan Barlow. She might have hated me because of my family's wealth, but I hated her just because. Well, just because, and for the fact that whenever Jordan rolled into town she never failed to disrupt my life.

"Hello!" she called out, though I knew the doorman would have told her Emily wasn't at home. Which meant she had charmed the doorman in order to get the key. That, or Emily had added Jordan's name to the front desk's list of people who could access the apartment—something that, as Sandy, I had expressly forbidden.

"Emily?" she called again.

I stood in the shadows as she closed the front door behind her, pocketing the key. With no more than a twitch of my nose I detected the smell of some simple, lemony soap or light lemony perfume with an overlay of marijuana. She had the same white blond hair as Emily, though even longer, the ends touching the middle of her back. She wore layers of T-shirts, a long gauzy skirt, and flip-flops despite the relative cold.

I stepped out of the shadows, making my sister-in-law jump.

"Whoa, who are you?"

I growled, mostly because I could. As a man I'd had to pretend to be nice to her, even if we both knew the truth. Not that the growl intimidated her. Jordan laughed. Yes, laughed.

"Damn, you are one ugly mutt."

A lesser being would have been devastated. I turned my backside to her and headed for the library and my favorite leather chair.

"Pissy, are we?" She chuckled and tossed her duffel bag on the floor.

She passed me in the gallery doorway. Because I didn't have anything better to do, I forgot the chair and followed her into the kitchen. She went straight to the refrigerator.

"What's up with this? All Emily has in here is cake and pie. There's no real food. Emily always has real food."

In the pantry all she found was some old cereal along with cupcakes, croissants, and an assortment of oatmeal, chocolate chip, and sugar cookies.

She looked at me. "Really, what is up with Emily?"

Like she expected me to answer.

Grabbing a handful of cookies, Jordan started walking around the apartment. She made a few calls, none of them to my wife, read a bit, slept a lot, then woke up and read some more. She had fallen asleep yet again, this time on the sofa, a book open against her chest, when I heard the front door open and close.

I galloped to the gallery. Emily appeared surprised when she saw the canvas duffel on the floor, then tears started pooling in her eyes. For weeks after my accident she hadn't cried at all. Since the journals, she cried at the drop of a hat.

One more thing I refused to feel guilty about.

"Jordan?"

I heard the book flop to the floor, then the mind-numbing racket of the girl's rubber thongs slapping toward us.

"Emily!" she squealed.

At the sound of Jordan's voice, the darkness in Emily's eyes faded and for the first time in weeks I could see a spark of light.

"Jordie," Emily said, hugging her little sister. "Why didn't you tell me you were coming? I would have been here when you arrived."

"I didn't know when I'd get here. I hooked up with a flight attendant who got me on the plane with him. I pretended to be his girlfriend and rode for practically nothing."

Emily held her at arm's length and gave her a look.

"Hey, those corporate airline thieves steal from the public every day. The least they can do is help a girl who's trying to do a little good in the world get home from South America. Believe me, I don't feel guilty because I pretended to be in love with a gay guy."

Emily shook her head and smiled. "I didn't say a word."

"I saw that look."

"Jordan, I gave you no look—" Emily cut herself off. "This is no way to start. Come on, I want to hear all about Homes for Women Heroes."

I am almost certain my sister-in-law blanched. But she shook it away before my wife ever noticed.

"I'm taking a break from Heroes right now," Jordan said.

"A break? But you just started with them."

"It's no big deal. People do it all the time. I'm . . . going to talk to WomenFirst. Figured I'd give Mom's old organization a try."

"Jordan?"

I barked. "Hello. I need to take care of business." That was our schedule. Emily came home and took me out. Already Jordan was disrupting things.

"Oh, sorry, E."

"E?"

"Short for Einstein. I need to take him out."

Jordan looked at me. "I can do it. You just got home."

I couldn't have been more surprised when Emily actually let her. I growled my concern.

"Don't worry, Einstein," my sister-in-law said. "I promise to bring you back."

Though I swear she snickered.

Emily glanced from me to Jordan. "Don't tell me you and Einstein aren't getting along."

"Yeah, can you believe it? It's just like me and that dick face, Sandy."

Emily froze. Quite frankly, I froze. I knew Jordan didn't like me, but to say it out loud to her sister no more than a couple of months after I supposedly died?

"Geez, Em, I'm sorry. Who cares that I thought he was an ass? You loved him." Jordan rubbed her sister's arm. "I wasn't thinking."

As promised, Jordan didn't take me to the depths of the park, let me off the leash, and hope I ran away. I took care of business, and when we returned to the apartment Emily had called our favorite delivery place for dinner.

"How long do you plan to stay?" Emily asked.

"I'm not sure. Depends on what happens with WomenFirst. Though I better find something fast. I could use the money."

Emily stopped toying with her soup. "Is that why you're here?"

Jordan gave her a tight smile. "No, Emily. I am not here for money." Then she relaxed. "Though I was thinking, maybe I could walk Einstein for you while you're at work."

"No!" I barked.

They ignored me.

"I assume someone takes him out during the day."

Emily eyed her sister, though she didn't answer. They ate and talked about nothing of consequence—which was insane since Jordan had been out of the country for the last year and Emily had lost her husband. Seemed to me they had some things to talk about.

It was while they were cleaning up the kitchen that Emily agreed to call the dog walker and cancel.

Great. Just great.

For three days I dealt with the situation, though barely. One, Jordan was a slob of an unimaginable magnitude. After her own quick trip to the grocery store, she left glass rings on the tables, cracker crumbs on the sofa, mustard stains on my fine linen napkins. Then two, Emily alternated between a deep depression and a manic energy when she did her sneak-a-glance-out-the-door routine, then bolt to take me out in the mornings before work. And three, despite the fact that I had helped Emily, yes helped, by getting her back to work, there had been no further contact from the old man.

The panic returned, growing each day that passed with no discernable progress made toward getting me the hell out of this wiry little body. I panted, drool dripping out of my mouth unabated, making me panic even more.

With Jordan there, Emily didn't come into the kitchen at night and curl up beside me. Had my pride not still been intact, I would have crept into her bedroom and curled up next to her. Without me realizing it, she had kept my panic from getting the better of me.

On the fourth day after Jordan arrived, the panic had shifted into a sense of impending doom. Something was going to happen. I could feel it.

"Jordan," Emily called through the guest room door on her way to work. "Will you take Einstein for an extra long walk today? He seems kind of agitated. I think he needs more exercise."

"Sure, whatever," Jordan mumbled.

As soon as the front door shut behind my wife, I heard the rustle of sheets as Jordan rolled over and went back to sleep. I tried to do the same. I concentrated on breathing in and out. Everything was going to be all right, I told myself. The old man would be back. He would see that Emily was going to work regularly. Then he would fix this. He would.

I stretched out in my favorite slant of sun that came in through the east windows, but it felt too warm on my fur. Next I tried the kitchen floor, followed by the bathroom, lying on the cool tiles, smelling Emily's cheap shampoo. As a man I had detested it, but as a dog I thought it smelled like heaven.

But that morning nothing helped me go back to sleep.

By noon I needed to go out. Einstein was old, after all, and holding his bladder wasn't my strong suit. Jordan was still asleep, no sound whatsoever coming from inside her room. So I barked, then barked again.

Eventually she groaned. "Go away."

Even more barking. I added some growling and a howl for good measure. The howl was so exquisitely done that my instincts took over and made me leap when Jordan suddenly yanked open the door.

"Shut up, you freak!"

At least she was awake.

My head came back at the smell of her. With a mere twitch of my nose I determined she had been out with friends the night before . . . males . . . drinking, smoking pot, then . . . I cocked my head in analysis . . . eating cheap Mexican food in the early morning hours.

Before she could slam the door in my face, I picked up the leash in my mouth and wagged it at her.

She didn't look happy. "Jerk."

"Slut."

"Asshole."

"Harpy."

She glared at me and did a little growling of her own, but she did it while throwing on a gauzy skirt and a T-shirt.

As soon as we were out the door and down the elevator, the fresh air hitting my nose, I felt relief. I was sure I'd feel even better in the park. Jordan tended to let me off the leash. But no sooner did I take care of business then she started dragging me back inside.

"Hey!" I planted my paws on the sidewalk and tugged back toward the park.

"No way," Jordan snapped. "I am totally late."

I stared at her in incredulity. "*You* are late? What about me? What about my extra long walk?" I barked.

"Yeah, yeah, take a downer. I have better things to do than hang out in the park with you today."

I found myself back upstairs and alone, Jordan having inhaled a bowl of cereal and raced out the door with a bagel in her hand.

I couldn't get enough air into my lungs. It felt like I was suffocating. The panic surged, ticking through me like a bomb. I tried counting. I took another run at sleeping. In the gallery, I gave in to an urge I had fought since I woke up as Einstein: I chased my tail. I ran in tight, mad circles until I was so dizzy I tipped over on my side. I went to the window hoping the people below would provide a distraction. But I only saw men who were men, enjoying their day while I was stuck as a dog.

At this point I flipped.

It was strange how this dog's body could take over despite the best efforts of my superior mind. If I wasn't on constant guard the primal portion of me leapt out and took over. When one of my overactive senses was engaged, whether it was taste, smell, or the sight of anything that moved mysteriously, this old body had to leap up, investigate, bite, chew. If my mind didn't have my body under complete and firm control, I had no ability to stop myself from taking action, no ability to sit back calmly and assess.

That day the primal part took over when my wretchedly overactive nose caught a whiff of something. I scrambled into the kitchen to investigate and found a box of Lucky Charms along with a half-eaten bowl of cereal Jordan had left on the table.

Just so we are clear, as a man I detested store-bought cereal. As a dog, however, just like cheap drugstore shampoo, the sugar-filled cereal smelled like heaven. I found myself climbing up onto the kitchen chair, then struggling to get myself onto the table. Nothing was going to keep me from my prize.

Once there, I sidestepped the opened box, crouched over Jordan's forgotten bowl, and proceeded to lick it clean, lapping up the remnants of milk and the soggy rainbow of marshmallows.

Unfortunately there wasn't much left, just enough to get my senses kicked into overdrive. Much like Pavlov's dog, I started salivating, the need for more of those horrid Lucky Charms suffusing my body. So I did the only thing I could. I upended the box, cereal spilling across my fine wood table. I could hardly contain myself as I scarfed up every last puffy marshmallow and crunchy nugget.

I forgot about being a dog. I gave no thought to the elusive old man. No consideration for what the future held. I ate and ate, and when the tabletop was clear, I nosed my head into the box, inch by inch, finishing off the last few morsels.

After I licked the bottom of the box clean, I lifted my head and was startled by the unexpected darkness. I jerked my head to the right, then to the left, but still everything was dark. I yelped, my intellect shoved aside by the sheer staggering force of Einstein's baser instincts.

I scrambled to my feet on the kitchen tabletop, lost to the unwieldy darkness. I swung my head, unable to see a thing as I tried to remove what I only half understood was the box. I barked and whimpered, dancing over the table, mindless of my hard, curving nails clawing into the wood, certain the damned cartoon leprechaun was attacking me.

The bowl and spoon crashed to the floor, followed by the sugar bowl. The salt and pepper shakers went next as I growled and bucked until finally the box fell free. For reasons I can't now explain, I felt the need for retribution. I pounced on the box, chewing and ripping the cardboard and thin plastic liner like a diabolical fiend ravenously trying to satiate some hunger. My raw pulse of terror had morphed into something more insidious. I was mindless and craven, but I felt heady with power. Eventually I won, the box decimated, as much of it swallowed as shredded.

I leaped down from the table to the chair, then the floor, skidding in the spilled sugar and broken china. But I didn't miss a beat. I found my way into the open pantry and consumed whatever I could get my muzzle and paws on. Cupcakes covered in plastic wrap. Homemade cookies in pastry boxes. I fought and chewed and ripped inside the cool darkness.

It was sometime later when I heard the front door open.

"Einstein?" Emily called out. "Jordan?"

By then the battle was over and I was laid out on the kitchen floor, my stomach distended in misery. I could hardly hear much less move, certain I was dying all over again. What had I done?

My half-working senses made out the sound of Emily finding my leash in the gallery.

"Einstein? Where are you?"

Then the sound of her hurrying down the hallway.

I didn't see her enter the kitchen, but I was vaguely aware of her shoes skidding to a halt when she hit the smears of buttercream icing, melted chocolate chips, and by that point who knew what on the floor. She gasped.

Some measure of relief hit me, the idea that Emily was home, that I wasn't alone; she would take care of me. But the relief was short lived when I moved an inch and had the sudden sensation that I was going to explode.

I won't go into detail, but rest assured, everything that went in came out again from both ends of my wiry body.

"Einstein!" Emily squeaked.

I was a mess for hours. Thankfully Emily couldn't have been more efficient, a regular Florence Nightingale. If I hadn't been so miserable, I might have felt badly about the whole thing. As it was, me being a dog and all, by midnight when I finally started to recover I barely remembered the incident. Water under the bridge and all that. Emily and Jordan didn't get over it as easily.

"I told you not to leave the cereal out!"

"I didn't come here to play servant!"

"I never expected you to be a servant! I asked you to make sure you didn't leave food out. *You* asked to walk Einstein. And I'm paying you to do that! You never even bothered to ask if you could stay here. You just showed up, unannounced!"

"Oh, I see. Now I need an invitation to stay with my sister when I come to town. I knew I should have stayed with my dad."

"Then why didn't you?" Emily snapped.

Hmmm, my always-tactful wife had had it.

"What?" she continued. "Did you forget to arrive with inappropriate gifts? Is that why you stayed away from your dad's? No anatomically correct male dolls for your eight-year-old sister? Or old editions of *National Geographic* with naked tribeswomen for your thirteen-year-old brother?"

Now this was interesting.

Jordan stiffened. "I'm not fifteen anymore, Emily."

"No, you're twenty-two and last I heard you had moved on to telling them to rebel against their parents."

"I'm just trying to get them to think!"

"Sure, that's your motive. Whatever the case, even I know parents generally don't appreciate other people telling their kids how to think."

"Unless they're you, in which case it's fine to tell people how to think, right Em?"

My wife blinked then searched for calm. "I don't want to fight with you."

"Then don't."

I could practically hear my wife's teeth grind. If she was smart she would mention the pretty huge fact that since Jordan's arrival the girl hadn't cleaned up after herself, had left food out, had ruined my coffee table. And excuse me, if Jordan hadn't left the cereal and milk out I never would have gone crazy. There was only room for one person/being/dog to be waited on around here. And that would be me.

"Why didn't you stay with your dad?" Emily asked, this time with a soft sigh. "Why are you really here?"

In the past if my wife had asked Jordan this, the girl would have gotten huffy and gone on about Emily always thinking the worst of her. Of course, minutes later she generally followed up her complaints with a request for money. I expected this day to be no different. Hadn't she already said as much? But Jordan was nothing if not full of surprises.

"Well," she said, her embarrassment gone, an excited smile crossing her face, "if you really want to know, I'm writing a book!"

Emily's expression went blank. Even I knew Emily hated the myriad friends and strangers who hit her up to publish what invariably turned out to be less than literate accounts of odd personal contretemps disguised as fiction.

Jordan saw it too. "I knew it! I knew you wouldn't be happy for me!"

"Jordan, of course I'm happy for you, it's just . . ."

"It's just what?"

"Have you written the book yet?"

Scoff. "Not all of it. Do you think I'm that naïve? First, I'm going to get money for it, then write it. I'll get an advance based on my proposal."

I noticed Emily's temple started to throb.

"Good for you, Jordan. Good luck."

"That's it? Good luck? You're an editor. You're my sister. The least you could do is help me."

I watched Emily's temple, fascinated by the way I could sense blood pounding through the veins.

"Fine, write the book and then I'll tell you what I think."

"Like I said, Em, I'm not going to write the freaking thing first."

"It is rare that an unpublished author with no particular credentials gets published without first writing the book, or at least a good portion of it."

"You're just saying that so you don't have to help me. Figures. You never want to help me!"

"That isn't true."

"Then prove it. Just listen to what it's about. How hard is that?"

They stared at each other for a moment before Emily said, "All right. What's it about?"

Jordan's ire burned out as quickly as it had ignited, and her excitement rushed back. "It's about Mom!"

Even I was thrown by this. Emily rarely spoke about her infamous mother.

"What are you talking about, Jordan?"

The younger sister launched into an excited if somewhat erratic spiel about a biography/memoir of the great Lillian Barlow and what it was like to live with her. "Everyone who knows she was my mom wants to know what she was like. I'm calling it *My Mother's Daughter*. Isn't that great?"

You'd think Jordan had shot Emily between the eyes.

"I was thinking about it and it occurred to me," Jordan continued, "that it would be totally awesome if you, as her other daughter, edited it!"

Silence. Then, "I can't do that," Emily said, her voice strained.

Watching Jordan from my vantage point as an uninterested, though keen, observer brought home the fact that my sister-in-law was a living roller coaster of emotion. Up, down, zinging every which way.

"You can't or you won't?" Jordan fired back.

"It's a conflict of interest."

"Only if you want it to be. Just read what I have. It's not that long."

Emily shook herself. "No."

"I knew it! Ever since I was little you always had a book in your hand. You were always reading something. Big books, little books. Long-as-hell books! But you won't even read my short proposal!"

Emily turned away and Jordan visibly tamped down her anger.

"Aw, Em, don't be that way. Just read a little bit. It's not like it's going to take up tons of your time."

"I said no."

Emily left the room. Jordan was wise enough not to follow.

■

For two of the three days it took my stomach to recover from the unfortunate Lucky Charms episode, Emily and Jordan barely spoke. They came and went, passing carefully in the narrow hallways like ships in the Panama Canal. This would have been fine with me, but while they were ignoring each other it spilled over and they ignored me too.

During this time I became consumed by a new understanding. I had to find a way to fix my own life since clearly the old man was no help. Emily couldn't do it; she could hardly help herself. Jordan was worthless—not that I would have turned to her anyway. And even if I could figure out how to use the telephone, I doubted a call to my lawyer would produce more than a hang up.

Which left my mother. She might be a harridan of the first order, but she was a harridan who could get things done. Stat. I had no clue what exactly she could do, but it occurred to me that if anyone could solve this whole dog dilemma it was Althea Portman. She was the only person I knew who could make magic happen. Hadn't she gotten my wealthy father to marry her? Then later, the woman with virtually no art credentials had landed her very own one-woman show at one of the city's most prestigious art galleries. Wasn't that a feat worthy of a magician? If I wanted her to make some magic happen for me, I had to find a way to get her to the Dakota and make her realize Einstein was me.

Easier said than done.

But the solution came an hour later when one of the building's staff members slipped a notice under the front door. My eyes might not have been the best, but they were good enough to make out the big red block letters that spelled out LATE. The maintenance fees for my apartment hadn't been paid since my unfortunate demise.

Maintenance in Manhattan co-ops is a staggering expense. My maintenance at the Dakota was more than most people spent on their mortgage. Not that I ever gave it a thought when I was a man. My accountant took care of all that. So I couldn't understand why he had let it go now.

I went in search of more information. On the desk in Emily's room I found a letter from Gruber, Hartwell, and Macon. Through a series of eye squints, head cocks, and a basic understanding of how the Vandermeer Regal Portman world worked, I deduced that now that I, me, Sandy was dead, under the prenuptial agreement the apartment would be turned over to the Portman family estate. No news there.

I continued to snuffle through my wife's papers using my squint-and-head-cock thing until I figured out that the Portman Family Trust had advised Emily that they would not pay the maintenance on the apartment until she vacated the premises.

Hmmm. This was a dicey move, as far as I saw it. What would stop the Dakota from taking legal action against the estate for not paying?

I had never given much, if any, thought to how much Emily made working as an editor. But standing there I realized that my wife wasn't the type to let bills go unpaid and would have taken care of the fees if she'd had the money. At the back of my mind, I had a half-formed thought that she had probably spent a fortune saving me, him, Einstein, whatever. But again, I wasn't big on guilt.

What I was big on was self-preservation and I wondered what would happen if I found a way to pay the past-due bills.

If I could have I would have smiled. I had no doubt that if I foiled my mother's plan, Althea Portman would storm back over here faster than a cab speeds down Broadway in the middle of the night with no traffic. Then I would get my chance to prove my identity to my mother.

The only thing I had to do was determine how to pay the maintenance and figure out what would convince my mother that I was her son.

emily

I know my sister Emily loves me. But I also know that she believes she was the good one, the one who did everything right while I broke all the rules, disregarding everyone but myself. But life isn't as black and white as she believes. Sometimes there is more to a person's need for white picket fences than safety, just as sometimes there is more to a person's rebellion than the need to lash out against rules.

—EXCERPT FROM *My Mother's Daughter*

chapter seventeen

Einstein stood in the gallery in that odd way he had of anticipating my arrival. But this time he wasn't waiting to be taken out or given a treat. His teeth were clamped onto a maintenance fee late notice.

My own mouth fell open. "Where did you get that?"

He shook the notice at me in answer.

"I can't believe you went through my things!"

He barked, the slip falling to the ground.

I walked over and snatched up the notice. "This is none of your business."

He growled.

I glared. "So you live here too. I get that. But until you have the ability to cough up this kind of money, keep your mouth shut."

He glared right back.

Then we both jumped when someone spoke. "Uh hum."

We whirled around to find Jordan standing in the open doorway, her backpack slung over her shoulder. She glanced from me to Einstein, her face scrunched in disbelief. "I'd say you're losing it, Em, talking to a dog, and all. But I swear he's talking back. You two are way too weird for me."

With a grimace, she headed for her room.

Einstein glared at Jordan. "Brat," I'm sure he barked at her.

"Don't talk that way about my sister."

I shook myself. Jordan was right. I was talking to a dog like he was human.

"You're making me crazy," I said.

He grabbed the late notice in his mouth and shook it.

Whether Einstein understood me or not, the fact remained that the maintenance fee problem was a dark cloud hanging over my head. I knew Sandy's parents were using the mounting debt as a way to pry me out of the apartment, but I refused to give in. If I walked away, if I let the Portmans have my home, somehow it proved that everything about Sandy and me was a lie.

Now that I had accepted the reality of the journals, and even the other women, I had come back to the place I had been when I married him. I might be furious with him for his lies, but I believed he had cared for me, loved me in a way that was deeper than the surface feelings he was used to. A man who hadn't felt something intense for me would never have held me like he was afraid of what would happen if he let go. End of story. I refused to believe anything else. His promise to give me the apartment represented the truth of the connection we'd had from the beginning.

But sitting there, I couldn't deny that in all the time we had been together, he had said he wanted me, needed me. He had never said he loved me.

I felt the cracks in my foundation widen as I realized that I needed Sandy's promise to be true because I needed to believe that I hadn't given up so much—the home my mother gave me, my love, my pride—for a man who hadn't really loved me in return.

I told myself that I hadn't believed blindly. My strength wasn't an illusion. I wasn't weak. I had believed in something real. To prove that, nobody was going to take Sandy's gift away from me. Which meant I had to come up with the maintenance fee, if only to buy some time.

I tipped my head back and pressed my eyes closed. "I need a miracle."

Einstein barked.

When I didn't immediately turn to him he barked again.

"What is it, E?"

He trotted to the stairs leading up to the suite, then looked back. When he saw that I was still standing there, he barked again.

Hesitantly, I followed him to the suite, and once inside Einstein walked over to the beautiful old desk. He growled under his breath, then nudged a bottom drawer.

"What?" I asked carefully.

He barked again, nudging a second time.

It was the strangest thing. For a second I felt something I could only call otherworldly. But then it was gone and I pulled the drawer open and looked inside.

"Nothing here."

He growled his frustration before he used his muzzle to point toward the back of the drawer.

My heart started to race and I looked at the dog. Half shaking, I reached inside. At first I didn't feel anything. But then I felt a tiny groove in the wood.

Einstein came up to me holding a sharp pencil between his teeth. Feeling strangely disconnected from the real world, I took the pencil and worked it into the groove, prying until the back panel of the drawer came free. When I emptied the contents I found a savings account book.

"How did you know this was here?" I whispered.

He just barked, nudging me on.

I flipped open the leather cover, then fell back onto the floor when I saw that it was a joint account with both Sandy's and my names at the top. The account balance nearly made me pass out. There was enough money to pay the maintenance for several months and then some. If I used the money I could buy myself a temporary reprieve.

chapter eighteen

Despite my mother's feminist beliefs, and her absolute conviction that a woman should always support herself, she had a thing for men. Old ones, young ones, it didn't matter, as long as they adored her.

The summer I was eight, she took me with her to the Hamptons on Long Island. We stayed in a big cedar shingle house on the beach, a two-story fairyland owned by one of the long line of men she teased with her affection. He was letting her use the place for a month, and during that time the parties never stopped.

The Professor came out with us, along with Mother's other friends from the city. Most nights a darkly handsome man showed up for my mother's parties. He was from Italy and spoke with an accent that made familiar words sound like poetry. I knew my mother well enough to know she had found her new toy, despite the Professor, despite the fact that she was staying in a house that belonged to another man.

Mother and her group of hangers-on talked politics and glass ceilings, Karl Marx and corner offices. It was the usual suspects discussing the usual topics. One night I was half asleep on the sofa when the Italian leaned forward, taking the tips of my mother's fingers.

"You speak of a pragmatic world," he commented, "where who succeeds and who fails is determined by a finite set of rules established by opinions that are not necessarily held by all. What about the power of something beyond what you can see?" He turned her palm over and traced the very center, the others watching. I watched too, feeling hot, embarrassed. "Where I am from," he added, "we believe God looks deep inside us and determines who is worth saving."

The group was silent. My mother sat there, her martini held forgotten in her other hand.

Her friend Willa laughed uncomfortably. "That's ridiculous."

The Professor sat back and considered.

After a second, my mother smiled boldly at the Italian. "Who are you and how did you get invited to my party?"

"You invited me," he said with an undercurrent I didn't understand.

Mother laughed then. "So I did. Well, fine, God it is. Though if you're sure there is a God, then you'd do well to tell him to stop looking deep inside anyone around here and get busy working on far bigger problems than me."

I uncurled myself from the sofa, unused to talk about God. I expected everyone to laugh, tell my mother how clever she was, then move back to the kind of conversation they were used to.

The man wouldn't let it go. "But if He did look, what would He see, Lillian?"

Lillian, spoken like a one-word poem.

Mother shifted uncomfortably. Her friends murmured until Willa broke the strained moment. "Emily, sweetie, hand me that bottle of wine."

My mother blinked. "This is a ridiculous conversation. Emily, it's past midnight. Why aren't you in bed?"

She didn't look at me; she stared at the man. It was the Professor, seemingly amused, who broke the charged silence. Years later I searched until I found the exact quote he used.

> *For as bats' eyes are to daylight so is our intellectual eye to those truths which are, in their own nature, the most obvious of all.*
>
> —Aristotle, *Metaphysics,* I (Brevior) i.

As a child I hadn't understood the words, but I could tell my mother had. She set her drink down and met the Italian's eye.

"If this *God* of yours looked deep inside me, or if you did, or if even *I* looked deep inside myself, all we'd find would be me, nothing more, nothing less. I've never pretended to be anything other than who I am."

The Italian smiled then, picking up her drink and handing it back. "To a maddeningly wonderful woman who is as intelligent as she is beautiful."

All these years later, I understood that Lillian Barlow had never been a woman interested in self-reflection. Was she afraid of what she would find? Or did she already know, and didn't like what she saw?

■

For the month-long stay on Long Island, I had brought a stack of books to keep me company since none of the other adults who came and went had children. While the whole looking-deep thing had caught my attention, nothing else they talked about interested me.

I sat in the room where I was staying with its white eyelet canopy bed and miniature vanity, the ocean just beyond the dunes, sounds of water lulling me while I read. I felt like a princess, serving fake tea to the stuffed animals in someone else's room. Such a child's game when on most Saturdays at home in the city I made real tea for my mother, who remained in bed until her friends showed up in the afternoons.

I would stay in the cedar shingle house forever, I promised myself. I would sink my toes in the warm sand, build castles, and hide among the stuffed animals and dolls when my mother and her friends returned to the city.

After breakfast each morning, my mother and I went to the beach. She laid in a lounge chair, outlining an article or writing letters to editors around the country with her current list of complaints. While she worked, I read or stood at the edge of the water, looking out but never going in.

One night toward the end of the month while a party raged on, I found myself alone in my room, bored and hot. I had gotten tired of fake teas with childish toys. I had read all my books, everything from *Eloise* to a Young Reader on the ocean that my mother had bought me. Lillian Barlow thought I should learn about currents and tsunamis, but she hadn't thought to teach me how to swim.

When I left my room that night, I didn't intend to go to the beach. Dressed in my nightgown I walked downstairs, past the adults amused at "Lillian's little woman," and out the back door to get away from the noise.

The moon was high, the black sky dotted with stars. I made my way over the dunes, the still-warm sand sifting between my toes. The beach was empty, the ocean spread out before me. I looked up at the sky, thinking about the Italian's words. Lying back in the sand I wondered if God really was watching, and if He was, what did He see deep inside me.

■

When I became an editor, I was drawn toward manuscripts that stretched the mind. In college I had learned that through reading, difficult ideas and even unpalatable truths could be digested in manageable bites. When I thought about Jordan's pitch of *My Mother's Daughter,* I felt certain that no matter how she doled out the pages, they would not be manageable bites, at least for me.

Jordan and I had barely spoken since she pitched her proposal. I couldn't put into words what I felt. Threatened. Or maybe jealous. I knew her version of life with Mother would be different from mine. I loved my sister, but I didn't want to read about how great she and Mother got along.

Jordan was still asleep when I headed for work. I had the savings account book Einstein had guided me to in my purse, but I was still unsure what I was going to do with it.

On the subway I barely noticed the crush of bodies. On the street I was oblivious to how people pushed and jostled their way to work. When I arrived at Caldecote I felt disoriented, as if I hadn't slept. The dreams had returned leaving me exhausted.

When I got off the elevator, I found the office buzzing with excitement.

"What's going on?" I asked Birdie.

"I don't know. But I hear it's good news."

I followed Birdie toward the conference room, arriving just as Tatiana walked up to the head of the long table. Victoria raced in and practically threw herself in the chair next to Nate just before someone else sat down.

"Sorry," she said with that fake smile.

When Tatiana reached the front, the staff quieted. "I wanted to bring everyone together to announce a first for Caldecote Press."

The crowd's interest was piqued.

"I had dinner with a friend who works at *People* magazine. She mentioned a book to me that she received along with, of all things, a candy bar."

I went still.

"She was so intrigued by the old-fashioned means of getting attention that she actually read the book herself. As it turns out, it's one of our books. And she loved it." Tatiana paused, her sharp gaze traveling across the room. "She loved it so much, in fact, that not only is the magazine going to review the book, but they want to do a front-page feature on the author and the young son she saved as well."

The crowd cheered, even the old hands who hated all things popular.

"Which book?" someone asked.

"The title is *Ruth's Intention*."

A silent beat passed while I took in the news. I couldn't believe it. This was amazing. But my brain staggered when Victoria leaped out of her seat and cried, "Oh my God! That's my book!"

Stunned, I swiveled to face her. "Victoria—"

"Of course, Emily helped by doing some mailings and things for me. But I can't tell you what a joy it was when I was able to call the author myself and offer to buy her manuscript. *Ruth's Intention* is a book I knew we had to publish!"

Words escaped me. Shock, denial, and bone-sucking grief were gone. But nothing useful filled the space as Victoria launched into a short synopsis of the story, then went on about how we really needed to get behind the book in a big way, about her commitment to put *Ruth* on the *New York Times* Best Sellers list. I barely heard, only saw her mouth moving, the others in the room caught between rapt attention and simmering resentment. Mercy Gray from sales looked confused. Nate had his eyes fixed on his notepad, as if too busy to take notice of what was going on. But I saw that he wasn't writing anything at all.

Then there was Tatiana. She sat back in her seat, as always watching me. I had recently read an article by a former big-name New York editor who claimed that publishing's dirty little secret was that in this day and age of bottom lines and corporate conglomerates, there was no longer a collegial "team" of editors, only competition. Was Tatiana watching my reaction to someone else's success? Or was there something else below the cloudy murk of her hard gaze?

■

In the ocean, when you open your eyes underwater at night, it's impossible to see through the cloudy murk.

From the Young Reader my mother bought me, I learned that the ocean covers approximately seventy percent of the earth's surface, circling the globe in currents that travel for thousands of miles. Water that crashes onto the shores of Long Island could previously have been to Africa or South America, or possibly even Spain. Lying on the beach just beyond the cedar shingle house on Long Island, with the black sky above me, African water or maybe South American water rushed up the sand and touched my feet. Sitting, I tucked my knees inside my little girl's nightgown.

When I finally stood to go back inside, I could see the big house. Lights blazed, the crowd of men and women loud, drunk.

Not ready to face the noise, I turned back to the ocean. The waves were small, gently running up the sand. Safe. Benign in a way that they weren't during the day. I lifted my hem and tiptoed into the ocean. The water was cold, and I jumped when a wave rolled in. I laughed and danced, proud of myself for being brave.

I was surprised when the next wave hit me, knocking me over. I tried to get up, but the wave that had rushed in rushed out, the current dragging me with it. I clawed at the water, fighting to grab hold of something, but I only got pulled out farther. I wasn't as scared as I was amazed that this was happening to me.

"No!" I yelled when my head broke the surface.

Each time my head came up, I cried out again. I fought as long as I could, the nightgown sucking at my legs. When I couldn't fight anymore, I started sinking in the pull of water. I hung suspended, sinking and drifting. Then just as suddenly as the waves pulled me in, they scooped me up and tossed me back out. Sputtering and dazed, I landed on the hard wet sand, cold but barely noticing. Instead I looked up at that big black sky and wondered if it was Spanish water that had swept me up and thrown me back? African water? Or had God seen me, looked deep inside, and decided I was worth saving?

■

After Victoria took credit for *Ruth's Intention,* everyone in the room started talking at once. When I finally got my head around the need to say something—though what exactly I had no idea—Tatiana had moved on to other business.

My heart pounded hard. My cheeks felt hot when thirty minutes later I walked into Victoria's office.

"I can't believe you took credit for *Ruth* when you wanted nothing to do with the book."

My upset was disproportionate to what had happened. I should discuss, gain a better understanding of the situation, look for a solution. But I felt unhinged.

"*Ruth* is my book," I bit out.

At the very least Victoria should have looked uncomfortable. She didn't. All of her pseudo-concern and pretend smiles were gone. "You are sadly mistaken, Emily. You might have found *Ruth,* but you did it while working for me. I was the one who got the offer approved, not you. I was the one who called the author and bought the book, not you. Whether you like it or not, *Ruth's Intention* is my book. If you'd like credit for editing a book that came in nearly perfect, go right ahead. At the next meeting feel free to tell everyone that."

Standing there, the old me seemed far away and the new me didn't know how to proceed.

I had learned that God could open His palm and produce a miracle. He could put Sandy in a meeting he was never supposed to attend; He could save Einstein at the very moment I ran out of money. It was even possible He had pulled me out of the waves. But I was fast learning He could just as easily take His gifts away.

I nearly laughed at the thought that I had been tossed back into the ocean, and this time He was letting me drown.

einstein

chapter nineteen

Emily crashed into the apartment from work like a hurricane hitting shore, banging pots and pans in a way that I suspected had nothing to do with food preparation. Jordan had been out all afternoon, no doubt getting friendly with yet another male like the assortment I'd had the misfortune to smell on her every day since she arrived.

Not that I cared one whit about either of them. For twenty-four hours I had been waiting on pins and needles, not knowing if Emily had used the money to pay the maintenance fees or not. But when the doorbell rang and I caught the scent of my mother from under the door, I leaped up and barked excitedly. Finally, I was going to get something done.

The pot banging stopped abruptly, but Emily didn't appear. I sensed that my wife had frozen in the kitchen and was trying not to panic. And why wouldn't she? No one just showed up at the door unannounced in the Dakota unless they lived in the building, were on the list, or were my mother.

The bell rang again, and after a second I heard keys jangle in the lock. My mother was nothing if not ballsy.

Emily must have heard the keys, too, because she flew into the gallery just as my mother strode into the apartment like a fishwife at a street market, spitting mad and fit to be tied.

"Mrs. Portman," my wife gasped. "What are you doing here?"

There weren't many in New York who dared cross or even question Althea Portman. She had too many connections in the worlds of art and high society—many of those connections overlapping—and a ruthless willingness to use the combination to her benefit. But she hadn't always had that power . . . or even wanted it.

When Althea O'Brien married my father, Walter Vandermeer Regal Portman, she was the proverbial poor girl from the wrong side of the tracks, a starving artist who had risen above her station. In the years after I was born and before I started school she took me with her across the park to this apartment at the Dakota which she used as an art studio. Back then she wore her reddish-brown hair long, twisting it up only when she pulled out her paints and put on an oversized shirt to protect her clothes.

In the Dakota she and I painted and played. If I got paint on the floors, *No problem!* If I drew on the walls, *How lovely!*

Once I even took a black marker to one of the tall, spacious walls. My mother had been absorbed with a still life she was working on. I half wrote, half drew *I ♡ Mommy* on the bottom corner of the gallery wall.

When she saw my declaration she only laughed, sweeping me up in her arms and dancing me around the room. *"Look at all that big love."*

And it was big love. I had loved her with the intensity that only a young boy can feel for his mother.

At dinner each night, back in our east side town house just off Fifth, my very formal father asked how her painting had gone.

"Perfectly, love."

When she was with my father, my mother dressed in designer gowns and family jewels, joking that he was putting a superficial shine on his unpolished wife. She would get up from that big formal dining table, walk over to her husband and despite the cadre of servants, sit on his lap. Even as a child I could tell my father both hated and loved how my mother acted in those moments. But his fascination always won out and all too often they excused themselves from the table and I finished my meal alone. Not that I minded. My parents were happiest then; my life seemed perfect, as if nothing could hurt us.

But life has a way of turning upside down.

I was five when my mother managed to secure the show for herself at one of Manhattan's premiere art galleries. No one knew how she did it, though many assumed it was through her connection to my father. The event became the talk of the town, a huge affair since there weren't many men or women in my parents' crowd who painted, much less showed their work. Everyone who was anyone RSVPed yes and the show proved a massive success, the most important art critic in town claiming a new talent had arrived.

The day after the show, my mother and I returned to the Dakota, but this time she wore a Chanel suit instead of her gossamer dresses and fly-about hair. I was stunned when we arrived to find workmen waiting. It took hours as the place I loved was cleaned up, the furniture covered with white sheets. Just as we were leaving, I watched a man run thick glue and new wallpaper over my marker declaration, covering all my big love in fine beige stripes.

My mother never painted again. She translated her show's success into becoming a powerhouse—not as a painter, but as a woman who knew a great deal about art.

I hated the memory, hadn't thought of it in years. But sitting in the gallery as a dog, I knew that was when my life changed, my innocent past disappearing like someone had covered it with thick glue and expensive wallpaper. I never saw my mother sit in my father's lap again. In only a matter of months, the free and easy mother I loved disappeared, the important woman who everyone came to for art discussions firmly rooted in her place. It was this woman, perfectly dressed in a Chanel suit from the latest collection, who entered my apartment now, heels resounding against the hardwood, Kelly bag swinging on her wrist.

"Emily," my mother said with icy coldness. "I believe you know why I'm here."

But she wasn't looking at my wife. She glanced around the apartment, her brow furrowed, and I realized at some level that she expected to see me, or I should say, expected to see Sandy. Then she blinked, and the tightness gave way, her body sagging.

"Mrs. Portman," Emily said, her voice soft.

At the sound, my mother pulled her shoulders back. "It's time we talked."

My heart hammered in my chest and I felt like I was five years old again, desperate to feel her arms around me. If I could just get her to see me, let her know that she was right to sense I was here, then I was certain everything would be okay.

I shook my tags.

Her head came back and she turned. When she saw me her eyes went wide. She tilted her head in confusion as she looked at me, as if something deep and knowing had begun to stir. If Einstein had had the capability I would have wept.

Racing across the gallery, I jumped up on my hind legs. "Mother!" I barked. "Yes, it's me!"

The woman who had given birth to me stood very still, staring at me, one moment stretching into two, before her green eyes narrowed. "Good Lord, Emily, get that mangy dog away from me."

chapter twenty

Admit it, you're smug.

You saw my mother's reaction coming a mile off and are smirking at the thought that I could be so naïve. But I ask: If my wife at some subconscious level recognized me without even realizing it, shouldn't the woman who gave birth to me have had at least a flicker of connection with me as a dog?

"This is exactly the sort of thing I would expect from you, Emily," my mother went on. "A complete lack of understanding for everything my son really was. He never would have allowed a dog in here. Just as he never would have promised you this apartment."

Emily stood silently, her jaw tight.

"But that's beside the point. I am here because I learned that you paid the overdue apartment maintenance. Tell me, Emily, where did you get the money?"

My wife debated, and if I could have I would have shouted, *Tell her the truth!*

"Sandy had a joint account in both our names. Legally, that money is now mine, and I used it to pay the fees."

My mother's mouth set in a hard line. "If Sandy left you a joint account, why didn't you use it earlier?"

Emily shifted uncomfortably. "I just found out about it."

"You just found it?"

Yes, good, tell her how!

Emily seemed to debate, then plunged ahead like a rickety canoe going over the falls. "Actually, Einstein, the dog, found it."

Good girl!

My mother squinted at Emily. "You expect me to believe an animal found a bankbook?"

For half a second my mother softened, nearly reaching out as if to comfort a clearly unstable daughter.

"I'm telling you, Althea, it's uncanny. Einstein knew right where it was. And before that, when I put a Mozart sonata on to play, the dog curled up in the library chair just like Sandy used to do."

These two women who remained as bookends to my life stared at each other in silence. I couldn't have planned this any better. My mother's sudden softness. Emily surprisingly making my point for me.

But when I looked closer I realized my mistake.

"Good Lord, Emily. What has happened to you?" My mother shook herself, then waved the words away. "How you paid the fees hardly matters. The fact remains, the apartment is not yours. I don't know how many ways I need to tell you this before you finally accept the truth."

"This is my home," Emily said. "I have spent the last two years, not to mention my own money, replacing broken appliances and damaged wallpaper, painting, scraping, fixing. I've done whatever needed doing."

As if that gave her a claim.

Emily, Emily, Emily.

"Enough." Mother sighed wearily. "Emily, let's deal with the facts. You don't have any proof that my son promised you anything. If you did, you would have produced it by now. As to the money you've put into the place, you would have been better served if you'd put it in a savings account. It does you no good here. And let's be truthful. We both know the maintenance fee alone has to be more than you make in a month. Plain and simple: You can't afford this apartment."

My wife flinched.

"Emily, it's time you move out and get on with your life. You're still young. You'll find someone else."

I swung my head back to my mother, Einstein's ratty old heart twisting. How was it possible that she could be so detached?

"I am not giving up on this," Emily said, her tone resolute. "I will get proof."

My mother's shoulders set, her lips pressed together. "Let me get this straight. You're going up against me?"

At another time this would have been fascinating—why in the world had my wife chosen this moment to stand up to my mother?—but right then it was not fascinating because, hello, this was not about them and any petty grievance they might have harbored against one another. My mother's visit was supposed to be about me, and it was high time they knew it.

"Mother," I barked, sitting prettily in front of her.

I pulled my biggest smile, barely able to contain my need for her to recognize me.

"It's me," I barked, demanding her attention.

She ignored me, so I re-sat myself, scooting closer. The scent of her perfume nearly overwhelmed me. I felt dizzy at the smell, dizzy for the mother I had loved and lost decades ago.

"Mother, please! It's me!" I barked, shivering with pent-up emotion as I scooted even closer. Before I could think better of it I licked her on the leg.

Mother made a low noise through gritted teeth and for half a second I thought the unflaggingly proper Althea Portman would kick me in the chest.

"I'm your son!" I barked in a jumble of yelps and growls.

And unlike naïve Emily, I could prove my claim.

I raced over to the wall, skidding into the mahogany door trim with a bang. Using my sharp little teeth, I grabbed the loose corner of the wallpaper Emily had yet to replace.

"What is that dog doing?"

"Einstein!" Emily blurted.

But it was too late. I tugged and pulled, growling, throwing every ounce of energy I had into my effort.

Emily raced over to me, but before she could pull me away, or perhaps because of her added force, the paper ripped free with a start, revealing the decades-old heart and the word *Mommy* through the dried glue.

I ♡ Mommy.

My mother's face went white.

I sat as perfectly as I could next to the inscription, desperately staring at my mother, willing her to understand. But it was Emily who glanced back and forth between me and the wall.

I could see the muscles working in my mother's throat. But there were no tears, no grand recognition. "I want you out," she said with the coldness of a slowly moving glacier. "And make no mistake about it. I will ensure that you and that hideous dog are gone."

My mother left me alone with my wife, and my desperate need turned to misery. My plan had failed. My mother was never going to understand that it was me. She had no ability to believe in anything beyond the concrete world she saw and the limits of reality. She might have made magic happen by getting my father to marry her and earning her own art show, but her ability to believe in something beyond a seeable, touchable reality had very real limits. And who was I to blame her? There was no way I would have believed had I not found myself in the body of a dog.

Every ounce of hope I had held on to was gone. I was too depressed to call out to the old man. Not that it would have done any good. He came and went at his leisure. Neither my name nor my wealth mattered a bit to him. Not that I had those things anymore. I was simply Einstein the Dog. A *hideous* dog, at that.

I collapsed on the floor. My mother's inability to recognize the essence of her only child, to even be moved by my childhood scrawl underneath the wallpaper, forced me to accept what I had been denying.

This situation couldn't be fixed.

For the rest of the evening and during the long dragging hours of the night, I remained inconsolable. At noon the next day when Jordan took me out I stood at the curb, staring at all the humans walking by, the nannies and children, men and women. I hated every one of them.

Jordan tugged at my leash impatiently. How was it possible that I had fallen so low that a female I didn't respect had me on a leash?

Rage and depression simmered inside me, caged behind teeth I clenched so hard my jaw hurt. And I realized it was time to put an end to this madness.

With no time to think about consequences, I bolted, yanking the leash free from Jordan's lax hand. I flew off the curb into the street just as an M72 bus careened around the corner onto Seventy-second Street.

"Oh my God!" Jordan screamed. Others shouted. The doorman cried out. All I cared about was the grinding churn of engine as the bus bore down on me. Please, God, let this nightmare end.

But I should have known better. The guy driving was a New York City bus driver used to crazed messengers on bikes, disoriented tourists stepping off curbs, and maniac cab drivers cutting him off. He stopped that mass of rubber and steel on a dime.

When my heart started beating again, I stared up at the driver through the windshield. He hunched over the oversized steering wheel, sweat having broken out on his forehead as he stared down at me. I expected him to yell at Jordan for not controlling her dog. But I could see from the dark condemnation in his eyes that he understood I had tried to kill myself. "Screw you!" I barked. "Don't you dare judge me!"

The next day I gave it another try when Jordan took me to the park.

"Don't you go doing anything stupid," she admonished.

Like I cared what she said.

This time I went for a tree, running downhill full-force and headfirst into a two-foot wide towering oak. All I got was a headache.

When that didn't work—and I realized Jordan wasn't taking me out ever again—I decided to poison myself. I knew as Sandy I had kept painkillers in my medicine chest, but after making the precarious climb up onto the counter of my old bathroom, I found that the drugs were gone, the cabinet bare.

I howled and bayed, then fell off the counter. I lay there for a second, hoping for a broken neck. First I moved my paws, then my head. I thought I would cry in disappointment.

Emily's bathroom didn't prove any more promising, though I did find a bottle of Tylenol with codeine a doctor had given her ages ago after she'd had a wisdom tooth extracted. The bottle was full but childproof caps, I found, were dog-proof as well. Even me-proof. I had to settle for half a dozen aspirin and a prayer that acetylsalicylic acid was poisonous to dogs.

After gobbling them down, I rolled over on my back to get the feel of being dead. But after a mere thirty minutes all I felt was better. My headache was gone and I suspected that I had thinned Einstein's blood enough to give him another year or two of life.

"This is so unfair!" I howled.

Not that it was over. I had every intention of finding a way to put an end to the insanity.

emily

My mother believed in dreaming, but she only believed in my dreams when they matched hers. She hated that Emily was so fixed in beliefs so different from her own. But in truth, our mother was no different. She was captive to the narrow world of her own beliefs and dreams.

—EXCERPT FROM *My Mother's Daughter*

chapter twenty-one

Pick up the phone, Emily. If you don't it will force me to cancel the first date I've had since I moved to town and personally come over there to hand-deliver candy."

I stared at the answering machine. After a second of indecision, I picked up the receiver. "Candy isn't necessary, Birdie. I have a date, too, with Julia."

"What? You've gone gay?"

I stood in the kitchen watching butter soften in the microwave for another round of baking. If I was lucky, the radiation would kill me. That or cure me of any impending Alzheimer's.

I gave a snort of laughter. "No, I have gone cake. Again. Though this time I'm working my way through *Baking with Julia,* as in Julia Child."

"Ah, that's my girl. Doctors underestimate the medicinal power of scads of butter and even more sugar."

Since my run-ins with Victoria and Althea, anger had taken up residence in my brain like an unwelcome guest. Though when I thought about it, anger was a relief from the numb despair and insecurity.

"I saw you storm out of the office," she said. "What was that about? And I thought you said *Ruth's Intention* was your book."

"*Ruth* is my book. And you saw me storm out?"

This time she snorted.

I cringed. "Do you think anyone else saw?"

She added a scoff to the snort.

"Okay, so everyone saw me."

"Only everyone on our floor, and probably only everyone in the lobby. But more importantly, why did you let Victoria take credit for your book?"

I sighed. "What was I going to say? Technically she did buy it."

"What?" she screeched. "Where is my friend, the Emily Barlow who doesn't put up with crap from anyone?"

With the receiver tucked between my ear and shoulder, I took the softened butter out of the microwave. "I'm not sure, but her doppelganger is here getting ready for a date with an oven-roasted plum cake with chocolate sauce. Besides, Victoria is the least of my concerns. Sandy's mother is determined to evict me."

"Althea Portman should date Victoria. Witches all. When are you going to get it through your head that you need a lawyer, sweetie? Even I know that sugar can only get you so far."

"But . . ."

"No buts. You know I'm right."

Which was true, and which was how, just hours after my mother-in-law's visit, I found myself at Max's door.

I went there reluctantly, and no wonder. My mother might have complained about my lists and plans, but that hadn't stopped her from allowing me to take care of our little family. At ten years old, if Jordan was sick, I called the doctor. At eleven, when a bill came in I put it in front of my mother along with the checkbook. At twelve, I saved us both the trouble and forged her signature.

It was when Jordan was two that Mother changed all of our lives. For a short period of time, she dressed in a suit and cut her hair. She left in the morning carrying a briefcase.

"There's a new face on the women's movement," she said. *"And I'm going to show them that I can be that new face."*

But not long after she started this new phase, she came home and didn't go back. She even took down the framed article. The woman who had fought for equal rights stayed home to bake and arrange sleepovers.

Unfortunately, despite her conversion to a more traditional role, she never lost her radical leanings. She stayed home, but took to protesting whatever "injustice" she suspected at Jordan's or my school. If it wasn't a fight for better cafeteria fare, it was for better testing methods. And if the school ran out of transgressions, she turned her attention to the corner deli or dry cleaners. There wasn't a shopkeeper in our neighborhood that didn't flip over the CLOSED sign if they had the good fortune to see her coming.

Worse, she took over the bills and doctor's appointments. This would have been fine except she wasn't good at it, and she resented my attempts to help: I ended up looking rigid when I pointed out that the electricity was about to be turned off, picky when I wanted my whites washed separately from Jordan's red and orange baby clothes. I had finally gotten what I wanted, for my mother to stay home and be a regular mom. Only Lillian Barlow didn't know how to be regular.

All this to say that when I found myself standing in front of Max Reager's door, I had never learned how to ask for help.

At the last minute I nearly turned around and bolted, but just as I started to go the door opened.

Max stood there, a good foot taller than me. I had to crane my neck to look up at him. He held keys in his hand, clearly on the way out. At the sight of me he stopped abruptly, everything about him radiating a finely controlled tension, his dark eyes narrowing. Then he registered that it was me, and I could practically feel the taut coil of him ease.

"Emily. Hey." So casual, almost practiced.

But whatever I might have thought about Max and his odd reaction evaporated in the face of the woman who peeked out from around his shoulder. She was young, probably mid-twenties, gorgeous, as in model gorgeous, and she held on to Max's arm like she had a right to.

I would have thought maybe it was one of his sisters—please God let it be one of his sisters—but he'd already told me he was the youngest in his family. Not to mention she didn't look a thing like Max.

"Ah, hello," I said, feeling like a chaperone as the woman stepped around him and looked me up and down. "I've caught you at a bad time," I added.

I turned to go, thinking maybe I could outrun my humiliation if I moved fast enough.

"What is it?" Max said, catching my arm.

He didn't say anything more, but I saw that same concern he'd had when he bandaged me up and held me when I broke.

"It's nothing. Really."

"Emily." Just that.

"Well, you mentioned your brother-in-law was a lawyer and I thought perhaps I should look for one after all."

"No problem. I'll talk to him and set up a time to meet."

"Thank you."

"Max," the stunningly beautiful female whined. "We're going to be late."

"Yes, well," I mumbled, managing to stutter out my cell phone number while Ms. Beautiful all but tapped her high-heeled foot.

I turned and bolted for the stairs.

■

Needing a distraction, basically from my life, I cajoled Jordan into going to Central Park. It was Saturday, the weather finally warming up. We ended up at the Boathouse for lunch. Since Einstein was with us, we sat outside and ordered burgers and fries from the café. Jordan leaned back in her chair, her face lifted to the sun. It was good to see my sister at ease, her laughter hinting at someone I didn't really know beneath the confrontational surface.

Abruptly she leaned forward, a gleam in her eye. "Let's rent one of those boats and row out on the lake."

Central Park was a miniature world filled with wonders one would never guess could be found in a rectangle of trees and grassy lawns rolled out in the center of a city made of concrete and steel. There were the stone towers and crenellated battlements of Belvedere Castle high up on a granite hill overlooking the Turtle Pond and the open-air Delacorte Theatre that hosted Shakespeare in the Park. The lawn bowling and croquet courts. The century-old carousel. Even a meandering lake with rowboats and a gondolier.

For a second I could only stare at her. "Jordan, we have Einstein with us." Even I heard how nervous I sounded.

"So what? We take Einstein. It's just a rowboat. No big deal."

Unfortunately, I had a very long memory. While my ocean incident had happened decades earlier, I hadn't been in any body of water larger than a bathtub since.

Jordan stood, her expression devilish. "Come on, Em."

"I don't know—"

She pulled a fake sad face. "Emily, please, I'm trying here."

I had to smile.

"Fair enough." I stood, refusing to add fear to every other emotion that had rushed into my life recently. "Let's rent a boat."

Einstein didn't look any more thrilled to board the tiny vessel than I was. But Jordan picked him up, giving him little choice. I stood on the dock telling myself to stop being ridiculous. It was a small, man-made lake that couldn't be all that deep.

Jordan took the oars. I sat on the front bench, forcibly keeping my hands in my lap instead of clutching the sides. Einstein looked over the edge with a grimace of distaste.

Jordan laughed at us both.

We made our way out into the lake, the trees that were just beginning to bloom lining the shoreline like a pale green ruffle. Beyond the trees, the prewar apartment buildings on Central Park West rose up like sentinels. The Dakota, the San Remo with its twin beacons on top, and farther north just beyond the Natural History Museum, the Beresford with its three towers, standing like an emperor's castle.

With each oar stroke through the water, Einstein became more relaxed, carefully making his way over my bench to the bow of the boat. He stood at the front, his head extended as he sniffed, breathing in.

"See, even Einstein is having fun now," Jordan said, rowing.

Like my dog, I started to loosen up. "This was a good idea, Jordan."

"Thank you. I have a good one every once in a while."

I heard the sarcasm in her voice, but didn't say anything. I tried to relax completely, take in the sun after a long northeastern winter of snow and overcast skies. "This is nice."

I tipped my head back as Jordan had done at lunch, feeling the sun on my face. "How's the job hunt with WomenFirst going?" I asked for no other reason than to make conversation.

She stopped rowing. When she didn't say anything I opened my eyes.

"It's not going so great," she admitted. "Look, here's the deal, I really need to borrow some money."

I forgot about the sun and the boat, fought to keep the lid on the anger that still simmered beneath the surface.

"How much?" I asked carefully.

"A couple thousand."

"A couple thousand!"

Einstein glanced at us and seemed to roll his eyes.

"I'll pay you back! Though if you had bought my book I wouldn't be broke. Since that didn't work out I need a loan."

"Loan? You haven't repaid a dime in the four years I've been lending you money! I have tried to be patient. I have tried to be what you needed. What have I done wrong, Jordan? What can I do to make you see you've got to grow up?"

Her head fell back and she groaned up to the sky. "Nothing! There is nothing you can do because you aren't my mother! It's not your job to take care of me. It never was!"

We stared at each other in that little boat, the angry words echoing against the water as we both grew quiet.

"Someone had to," I said, the words barely heard. "Our mother certainly didn't."

After a second, her mouth opened to say something. But the words were lost when the boat suddenly rocked. I heard a splash, saw Jordan's eyes go wide.

"Freakin' A! Einstein just went over."

I leaped up from the bench, the boat heaving, and leaned over just in time to see his little head go under.

"Einstein!"

"Emily, he's a dog. He'll be fine."

"He is not fine! He's sinking!"

The boat wobbled as Jordan came forward to look over the edge. "Man, he really is."

"Help!" I yelled. But there were no other boats close by.

"Man," Jordan repeated, her voice uncertain, young.

I thought I was going to be sick. It didn't matter that it was a small lake, not deep. It didn't matter that it wasn't the ocean and that I was now an adult. I had never learned to swim.

Fear clutched at me as I lifted my legs over the side.

"What are you doing, Em?"

The boat tipped precariously as I inched my butt closer to the edge.

"Come on, Emily, you can't go in there. No telling what kind of crap is in that water. Just give E some time. He'll come back up. Remember, he's a dog! And dogs can swim!"

But I wasn't listening. I heaved my body over the side, the boat nearly capsizing, my head going under as I fought back a scream.

einstein

chapter twenty-two

A surprised woof rushed out of me as I hit the water.

On the bow, standing on a pile of extra life jackets, I had realized this was my chance. I waited, poised to leap, but I made the mistake of looking down. The water was thick with mire and no doubt crawling with germs. Vertigo hit me hard, my stomach clenched. I was too afraid to jump. Which depressed me even more, and in turn sent me over the edge. Literally.

"Damn it!" I barked on the way over the side, praying I didn't have the ability or strength to swim, at least for very long.

The bite of cold took my breath away. Surprise made me gasp, my mouth opening on a gush of water. The sting of algae burned my lungs as I choked. The instinct rose to fight, but I clamped it down and let my body sink. I sighed in relief that soon it would be over.

It didn't take long before I hit the bottom. The water was cloudy, making it hard to see more than eerie outlines of whatever lay below. My paws hit things on the bottom. Discarded rope or tree branches, I couldn't tell, though I hardly cared as my legs settled into the debris.

I heard the shouting above, muffled even to my ears, distant. Jordan angry. Emily trying not to panic. They were fighting. Always fighting. Wasn't life too short to fight? I had made mistakes in my life as Sandy, but I had never wasted time fighting with people. If I was unhappy, I didn't go to the place of anger and frustration. I walked away. When someone phoned to apologize, I didn't take their call.

That was something else I had done wrong.

The thought came out of nowhere, crystal clear, impossible to ignore.

It was too late to think about that or anything else as the soft dimness of water and a resolve to die surrounded me. But then my body twitched, something in me trying to push up from the bottom.

Don't do it, I willed myself. This was my chance.

But my body fought with my mind. Did I really want to end what was left of my life, end it in a Central Park lake steps from the home I loved?

Yes, I told myself.

But the primal part of me took over. I let out a scream, my legs and paws completely tangled. I thrashed and kicked, squirmed violently, just as I had done with the cereal box on my head. But I couldn't get free of whatever held me.

The water was even colder at the bottom, sapping whatever strength my thrashing hadn't already used up. As quickly as it started, I couldn't do it anymore. I knew I needed to keep trying, but I couldn't. My mind grew foggy, thoughts becoming disjointed. I felt more than comprehended the thrashing of someone else next to me, the screaming underwater, the struggle to pull me up. I sensed more than saw that it was Emily, fighting against the debris with everything she was worth.

When we finally broke the surface, she gasped and sobbed as other boats rowed toward us, helping us out of the water. Jordan hung over the side, grabbing onto Emily. I was upset and ashamed, and miserable over my realization.

I didn't want to die. Not as Sandy. Not even as Einstein. Though where, I wondered, did that leave me?

chapter twenty-three

The kitchen was dark, the only light streaming in from the windows overlooking the inner courtyard. I hardly remembered getting home, Emily cleaning me up, holding me tight, her face tucked into my neck as if my brush with death had broken the last of her strength.

The apartment was quiet, and after I sniffed, I knew Emily and Jordan were home and asleep. I curled back into the towels, but I yelped when that strange electricity I had come to recognize shot through me.

"It's about time you noticed I was here," the old man said, coming out of the pantry with a plate of cookies. "You sleep like the dead."

"Perhaps because *I am* dead."

"Sarcasm is unbecoming."

"So you keep saying."

"True. And truer still is the fact that you're a real pain in the backside, let me tell you."

He wore a wide-brimmed straw hat, a white suit, and carried a cane. "I've got another case going. A Southerner," he explained. "In Kentucky."

"You look like Mark Twain. Or that fried-chicken guy."

He smiled, taking a double chocolate chocolate-chip cookie and popping it in his mouth. "You've got to love such simple pleasures. Do you have any milk?"

He didn't wait for me to answer. He walked over to the refrigerator, pulled out a carton of one-percent, and found a glass in the cabinet.

I laid there for a while longer. When I couldn't stand it anymore, I said out loud what I had finally come to understand.

"It's over for me, isn't it?"

The old man glanced across the room mid-chew. "What do you mean?"

"I'm not getting my body back."

He shrugged. "Probably not."

My head swam. It didn't matter that at some level I had suspected the truth; hearing the words spoken out loud felt like a kick in the teeth. "Why didn't you tell me before?"

"You're a smart guy, Alexander, and we both know you had already figured it out. That's always the way with people—truth staring them in the face but unwilling to accept it." He ate another cookie quietly. "But," he added, "even if I had spelled it out you wouldn't have believed me. You weren't ready or willing to accept it yet. You'd just have gotten all worked up."

"Worked up!" I barked. "Of course, I'd get worked up. And since you seem to know every thought I have in this blasted head, you knew what I was thinking. You let me go on believing it was possible anyway."

He shrugged again. "Alexander, anything is possible. Miracles happen all the time. Who am I to say that you can't make it happen? Truth is, it still could happen. But *could* and *likely* are two very different kettles of fish, especially when you've proved again and again that you're as pigheaded as you are hardheaded." He snorted. "That tree incident had to hurt."

Of course he knew about that.

"Yep," he confirmed, "the bus, the tree, the pills. The boat. Though rest assured, you just might have finished the job in the lake had Emily not saved you—again, I might add—when you're the one who is supposed to be saving her." He shook his head. "Emily doesn't know how to swim. Pure adrenaline got her down there. Which was a good darned thing since neither one of us needs you killing poor old Einstein on top of everything else. Being a murderer is far worse than having mindless, and let me say, stupid, affairs."

The affairs.

I had never intended to stray. For those first two years I ignored my mother's constant case against my wife and remained charmed by Emily and everything she did. When my wife wasn't working on some publishing project that she was excited about, she worked with great care on the apartment. The place was always in some state of renovation with sawdust on the floors, paint and tile samples covering her kitchen desk.

At first I had loved that she was making us a home. But then something happened, a shift, cracks I thought I had covered over with cement opening back up.

When the first hints of my dissatisfaction surfaced, I remember walking through the front door one evening to the smell of paint, the sound of outdated '70s and '80s music, and my wife singing off-key, unworried who might hear. I realized the combination that had enchanted me before had begun to wear.

The minute she heard me, she dropped whatever she was doing and raced through the apartment, pulling off her paint smock and tossing it aside as she threw her arms around my waist, burrowing her face into my chest.

"What happened to 'Honey, I'm home'?" She laughed, tipping her head back to look at me.

I breathed a sigh of relief when her unwavering love took the edge off my dissatisfaction.

"Bad day for cogs in the wheel?" she teased, not letting go.

"Yes," I sighed, putting my arms around her, "the cogs are on the verge of revolt. I would walk out but I have no other skills. I only seem to be good at making money." That should have been a good thing, at least for my father, but I hadn't been good at finding companies to grow and make bigger, then eventually sell to even larger companies at a handsome profit. No, I was only good at searching out the entities that were failing, businesses that were susceptible to takeover, then tearing them apart and parceling them off like car parts sold out of a chop shop in a seedy section of Staten Island.

"What do you mean, Mr. Portman?" She pulled back and gave me a schoolteacher's stern look. "You're good at loving me."

Loving her. I had never been able to say the words, admit the kind of weakness that would make me vulnerable. Instead, I found myself pulling her close and kissing her with what I can only call a desperate passion, desperate to erase the niggling feeling that even Emily wasn't enough to make me whole.

It was during our third year of marriage, by then my discontent a constant and uncomfortable companion, when my father barged into my office, berating me over yet another deal that he felt was beneath the firm. Something inside me snapped. I let my father finish, then forced myself to remain calm, practically counting each step I took in order to keep my mind from circling out of control as I left the office. I had the driver take me to the garage where I kept my own car. After slamming into the BMW, I careened out to the Hamptons, that place that had always soothed me. But hunger and anger pushed me on until I nearly killed myself and a family of six I almost ran off the road.

I hadn't snapped because I desperately wanted my father's approval. I snapped because seeing my father standing in my office, having the same argument we'd had so many times before, only proved that I worked for my father in the same building he had worked in for the better part of his life, a building that his mother's father had worked in for the better part of his life, and his father before that. I felt trapped in a predetermined life, my future seen as clearly as if a gypsy had forced me to look inside a crystal ball.

I came home to Emily cooking and dancing, and I realized she was content, happy, and it had nothing to do with money or family connections. She was successful and highly thought of at work, and she had achieved it on her own. I should have been proud. Instead I felt angry. She was successful in a way I wasn't, at ease in the world in a way that I couldn't manage.

The first affair was born of a sheer unadulterated need to get away from doubt and frustration. The woman was young, pretty, with a body that begged to be touched. I didn't even know her name.

Later at a firm party, a colleague slapped me on the back. "I hear you were out with that new young thing from your firm."

It took me a second to recall who he was talking about.

"Don't play naïve with me," he added with a chuckle. "No one could believe you stayed faithful as long as you did. We had bets going. Though not a single one of us thought you'd last over two years. I guess we all go soft eventually." The man glanced at my stomach, which was no longer flat and toned.

My anger flared into fire. I was angry at Emily for tempting me with things like lasagna, angry at the home she had built for us, a place that made me want to watch DVDs and drink wine and talk late into the night instead of staying strong and lean.

When I ran into the young woman again, we ended up in a hotel room. We had hot, rough sex that numbed my mind. Afterward she wanted to curl close, go again. All I wanted was for her to be gone. The anger had shifted to the same hunger I had felt before I met Emily, now combined with a cold numbness. I felt like I was dying.

I started working out at the gym to get back in shape. Surely that would ease the hunger. But a week later I slept with another woman. Then another. Frantically, I went through women like a drunk throwing back shots. The buzz was elusive, and all I knew was that I wanted out of my life. On that snowy February day that everything went awry, my mother had called to express her disdain about something else my wife had done. After we fought I had dialed Emily, asking her to dinner so I could tell her I was divorcing her. One way or another, I was determined to put an end to the deadness.

Now here I was, really dead, living in some capacity as a dog. The irony was that I had gotten exactly what I wanted. Out of my old life.

A shiver ran down my spine.

The old man gave a firm nod, made the cookies disappear, then brushed crumbs from his hands.

"Okay," he said. "Let's look at the bright side. You've made progress."

"Wanting to put an end to this farce is progress?"

"Yes. It means you've finally accepted that more than likely your days as Sandy Portman are over."

Renewed misery hit me, and I wished I had finished things off in the lake regardless of where that would have sent me. Heaven, hell, purgatory. Because, really, what was there if I didn't get my body back?

"Alexander, stop feeling sorry for yourself. As we've established, you've made progress. Now go back to the original question: Do you want to fade away to nothing or are you finally going to help Emily? And I'm not talking about getting her dressed and back to work or throwing money at the problem. I'm talking about really helping her."

"And if I do?" I might have sounded petulant. "What do I get?"

The old man heaved a heavy sigh. "I'm not supposed to tell you any of this, but I don't see that I have a choice. If I get questioned, I'll point out what a stubborn case you are."

"Call me what you will, but deflecting blame hardly seems like perfect behavior for a triage specialist."

"Well, there is that." He shrugged, then smiled. "All I can do is my best."

"You read that in a book."

A flush slid through his cheeks. "Again, not the point. Look, this is the deal. If you don't want to fade away to nothing you've got to become greater than a mere mortal ruled by mortal desires."

I was rather fond of my mortal desires. And I had to say, the old man wasn't so far beyond them either. I wasn't the one eating cookies.

He grumbled. "We all slip up now and again." He inhaled deeply, his eyes closing as if reestablishing his strength. "I can do this. I *am* doing this. I simply have to have a positive attitude. Believing. Having faith."

"More words of wisdom from that book of yours?"

The old man muttered something. "I've got to go," he said. "But get it right this time, Alexander. Help Emily regain her footing. Help her move on. Help her find her way back to herself. Then, I promise, great things will happen for you."

He disappeared. As in, one minute he was there, the next he was gone. Like magic. And I must say, a sizzle of surprising excitement raced through my little body along with my mind. The old man had said I could be great. Really great. As in a magical kind of great. All I had to do was help Emily. Really help her this time.

If I played my cards right, I could still achieve my dream of greatness.

emily

My mother was known for her belief that "being careful" was for weak women whose need for white picket fences trumped the desire for the kind of life that was worth living. As I got older and saw how she had changed her own life after I was born, her belief struck me as odd. But the one time I asked her why she gave up her life as a crusader for women's rights, she only looked at me with a strange, yearning expression, then turned away.

—EXCERPT FROM *My Mother's Daughter*

chapter twenty-four

When I got home from work Einstein wasn't waiting for me in the gallery.

"Einstein?"

The apartment was silent.

"Jordan?"

Nothing.

"Where is everyone?"

There was a note on the gallery credenza from Jordan.

Emily, I'm meeting friends. Don't worry about me for dinner. I took E out at noon. Jordan

But still no evidence of Einstein.

I found him in the kitchen, walking back and forth in front of the center island. Had he not been a dog, I would have sworn he was pacing while trying to figure something out.

"Come on, E, let's go so you can take care of business."

When he continued to pace, I went to the pantry and pulled out his favorite treat. Generally just the sound of the snacks rattling against the box sent Einstein into a frenzy of excitement, his body quivering, his mouth salivating. This time Einstein barely afforded me a glance.

I shook the box then retrieved one of the tiny fake steaks. "Don't you want a yummy Steakin'?"

His nose twitched. Encouraged, I waved it close to his nose. Almost despite himself, he stopped and gave a halfhearted snap at the treat.

"No way. You have to go out if you want it."

I'm pretty sure if he had been able to speak he would have peppered me with some pretty colorful language.

I tugged Einstein out the door and down the elevator. After he peed at the curb, I gave him the treat. Thinking he'd want to go straight back inside, I headed to the gate. But Einstein wouldn't budge. I glanced down, saw that he stood transfixed by a small group of runners heading into Central Park.

For half a second he whined, as if wishing he were running with them. Then his spine stiffened as if something had occurred to him. With what I can only call an excited bark, he spit out the Steakin' and started scrambling down the street in the opposite direction from the park.

"What is it?"

He tugged me toward Columbus Avenue. I couldn't have been more surprised when he stopped at the closet-sized newspaper and magazine store toward the end of the block, then pulled me inside.

"What do you want, E?"

The man behind the counter looked at me oddly. Dogs might be welcome in many New York City stores, but a crazy owner who acted as if the animal was in charge of the purchases . . . well, not so much.

Einstein nosed through the magazines on the low shelves, his eyes squinting, his head cocking this way then that, before he craned his neck to look at the magazines lining the wall. His head went row by row, up and down, until he stopped and barked. His body quivered with excitement.

"What is it, E?"

He barked again, jumping slightly toward the magazines. Without thinking, I started pointing at them one by one.

"This?"

Growl.

"That?"

More growling.

I went row by row until I came to the magazine that made my dog weep with delight.

"You want *Runner's World*?"

More happy weeping.

Both the store clerk and I exchanged an incredulous glance.

"Your doggie likes to read?" he asked with a laugh, his foreign accent heavy.

"So it would seem."

Einstein turned around, facing the counter, as if ready to pay.

"But I didn't bring any money, E. These aren't free."

The clerk leaned over the counter, studying my dog. "You take," he said to me. "Bring money later."

"I can't do that."

"Your doggie wants to read." He shrugged. "So you get him magazine."

I glanced between the clerk and Einstein. "Well, thank you," I said. "I'll bring the money tomorrow."

"Yes, okay. Now out," he added, shooing us out of the tiny shop.

We left, Einstein prancing.

"Emily?"

I whipped my head up to find Tatiana walking toward us wearing skintight workout clothes, bottled water in her hand. Her dark, chin-length hair was pulled back with a sleek band, not a strand out of place. She could have been a model for a health food ad.

"Ah, hello," I said. "I didn't know you lived around here."

"At the Majestic. I'm on my way to spinning class."

The Majestic was another A building on Central Park West where both rich and famous people lived.

"Shouldn't you be busy catching up on work?" she asked.

My mouth opened and closed.

"Nothing to say for yourself?" She shook her head. "Charles was too easy on you. I'm not so easy, Emily. I have to wonder if Charles promoted you prematurely." She unscrewed the cap on the water. "Perhaps you're not ready to work on your own list."

"But I am!" I blurted.

"Well, well, there's that gumption again."

Einstein swung his head back and forth, taking in the conversation. Why I was embarrassed in front of my dog, I couldn't say.

"So tell me, Emily. What is it that you're doing while you're at the office? I hear you're behind on all your projects. And you haven't bought anything new in months."

Blood drained out of my face. Einstein seemed to notice this too and moved closer to my leg, then barked.

Tatiana paid him no mind. "How are you going to get back up to speed?"

Einstein craned his neck to look at me, then turned back to Tatiana and barked again, tugging on the leash. When Tatiana tried to say something else, he barked even louder, the sound surprisingly ferocious for such a small dog.

The new president of Caldecote Press gave him a wry smile. "Fine, Toto, take her away from the awful green witch. But you can't protect her in the office."

Tatiana continued on toward Columbus, downing the water.

"This can't be good," I said.

Einstein just looked at me, and I swear he was once again evaluating me, or the situation. Though for once, it felt like he was on my side.

■

The next morning, Jordan was home but still asleep when I left Einstein with his magazine.

"Don't eat it," I told him.

I dropped money off at the little store and caught the C train to Fifty-ninth. I was running late, and it was no surprise that my mood wasn't the best when I arrived at the Trigate building.

"Look who's here at a reasonable time for a change."

At the sound of Victoria's voice, I grimaced. She looked at me with the dewy-eyed innocence of someone who hadn't just stolen credit for a book I had slaved over.

I scowled and pushed through the revolving doors, all but running for the security turnstiles. Balancing my belongings, I dug around in my purse for my credit card–sized ID. I hit the turnstiles, zipping my card through the reader at the same time I pushed through the metal arms. But halfway through, the metal arm yanked to a halt, stopping me. A copy editor from production who had raced in behind me, slammed into my back.

Nick was a large man and I grunted. He lifted his arms and backed up fast, as if to say, "Not my fault."

I tried to move forward again, but the strap of my satchel had tangled up in the rotary arms. A line started to form.

"Come on!"

"Hurry!"

It was Tatiana who walked up, moving people aside, swiping her own card, allowing the rotary arms to turn again and release me.

As always, Tatiana could have stepped out of the pages of *Vogue*. She wore a knee-length pencil skirt, a flowing silk blouse, and a princess jacket, all in shades of brown, gold, and café au lait, with hints of violet. And, of course, painfully high heels.

Flustered, I muttered my thanks then hurried on. But Tatiana stepped into the elevator right beside me.

Standing side by side, she didn't say a word. When we got to my floor, I swallowed back my relief and jumped off. But Tatiana got off with me. Alone in the vestibule outside the security doors, I could hardly pretend I didn't see her.

"Your dog isn't here to save you. Now, I want an answer. How are you planning to catch up?"

It didn't take a genius to know that telling her I had no idea wasn't going to win me any prizes. "I should be up to speed in no time."

"No dates. No specifics. Code, I suspect, for you don't have a clue where to start."

No one said Tatiana Harriman wasn't smart.

Anger and frustration and a whole host of other emotions that I wasn't used to rode through me. But I hadn't a clue what to do about any of it.

She scowled at me and took a step closer to me. "I can feel your anger, Emily. You're miserable but you don't do anything about it. Why don't you tell me to shove it and quit? Go home, stick your head in the oven, finish yourself off? That's got to be better than this slow death you're putting us all through."

My mouth fell open.

"Don't look so surprised. I knew your mother. She might have been half visionary, half nut job, but she wasn't afraid to speak her mind. So tell me, where did you come from?"

I blinked, though I wasn't blinking back tears or even shock. I felt validated and furious in the same moment. I had never heard anyone encapsulate my mother so perfectly. And I experienced a wave of guilt for the gratitude I felt that someone understood.

When I didn't respond, her eyes narrowed, and she leaned closer.

"Damn it, fight, Emily. Fight for what is wrong. Like the fact that Victoria is taking credit for your book. Or that after losing your husband your brain is so disjointed that you're having a hard time stringing together words that make sense."

Yet again, she surprised me, and for a second I thought she would reach out, a very different Tatiana standing before me. But then her chin rose.

"The fact is I feel for you, I do, but regardless of how good you were in the past, if you don't get your head back in the game I can't keep you on."

The elevator dinged and the doors slid open. Victoria stepped out.

"Oh! Tatiana!" she said.

Tatiana didn't give her a second glance.

"I'm serious," she said to me, "you can do this." Then she turned away. "Hold the door," she called, and slipped into the elevator.

Victoria glanced back and forth between me and the closing elevator doors. "What was that about?"

"Nothing."

"Did you talk about the editorial meeting?" she persisted.

I had to swallow back a groan.

Since Tatiana joined the company, we had been inundated with meetings. Cover art meetings, sales meetings, marketing meetings. She had also instituted a new sort of brainstorming meeting that was more gladiator sport than creativity enhancer.

A little over an hour after our confab in the entry vestibule, I had no choice but to head for the conference room for one of the brainstorming sessions to pitch new proposals for books we wanted to buy. Victoria was already there with a color-coordinated folder system. I sat down across from her at the large conference table. Everyone else was busy reading through their notes. No one but Victoria appeared at ease.

Tatiana walked into the room and went to the head of the table, glaring at a science fiction editor who'd had the misfortune to take the seat next to her. When understanding finally dawned, Eric fumbled around gathering his things. "Sorry," he managed.

"Okay, people, dazzle me with your ideas. As I told you before, I want energy, I want excitement. I want to make Caldecote Press pop." She settled into her chair, her assistant poised with notepad ready. "Who wants to go first?"

Everyone except Victoria tried to look invisible. Victoria raised her hand.

Tatiana didn't exactly sneer, but it was close. "We are not in fifth grade, Ms. Wentworth."

Victoria snatched her hand back like she didn't know how it got up there. Marshalling her unruly thoughts, she pulled her shoulders back and said, "I have a fabulous idea."

"Great. Let's hear it."

Victoria launched into one of her typically long, boring explanations. It was half enthusiasm for the material, half enthusiasm for herself.

Tatiana cut her off. "What's the idea, Victoria?"

Red flashed through the editor's pale cheeks like mercury rising in a thermometer. Had I not seen it with my very own eyes I wouldn't have believed it.

"Ah, well. It's a book about a man who travels to a small town and falls in love with a married woman whose family has gone away for the weekend. I see it as a little like *The Bridges of Madison County*."

Tatiana stared at her. "That isn't 'a little like' *The Bridges of Madison County*. That *is Bridges of Madison County*."

Subdued laughter rippled through the room.

Victoria's cheeks grew brighter.

Tatiana turned away. "Who's next?"

Victoria couldn't have been more surprised had Tatiana leaped across the table and belted her. I couldn't remember the last time Victoria had a proposal turned down cold.

"Jerry?" Tatiana said.

Jerry Martin appeared surprised that the new boss not only knew he existed, but also knew his name.

"Uh, uh, I have a proposal for a book about the brain—about the difference between the amygdala and the neocortex."

Tatiana sat back and tapped her pen. "The primal part versus the more civilized portion used to reason. Hmmm."

"Wow, great that you know about it." Jerry warmed up immediately. "It could be a really cool book. I mean, who isn't interested in the brain?"

Tatiana straightened. "Not many, actually. As is, it's a no go. If you can come up with a way to make it less about science and more about the human condition, we'll revisit. Next?"

She surveyed the crowd. Whether they volunteered to present or not, everyone was asked. Each idea was met with a variety of responses.

Too boring.

Too done.

Who cares?

It all amounted to the same thing. No.

"People," she said, her jaw tight. "How many times do I have to tell you we are going for three things? Fiction with a hook. A *fresh* twist on an already-beloved theme." She glared at Victoria. "Or big names—as in, either big authors or famous people."

Everyone started closing notebooks and pushing back from the table. I started to breathe again when I realized I wouldn't have to make a pitch.

"People, we're not done."

My lungs constricted and I would have bet my pupils dilated. The primal portion of my brain told me to run like hell.

"We haven't heard from Emily."

All eyes turned in my direction.

"What do you have for us, Ms. Barlow?"

I couldn't figure out how to say nothing, zero, zip in a way that would not have Tatiana escorting me to my apartment and shoving my head in the oven for me. While few good ideas had come across the table, everyone had at least had one.

My palms grew clammy. "Ah . . ."

Victoria covered a laugh. The others squirmed uncomfortably. But more than that, I was sure Tatiana looked disappointed.

"Fine," she snapped, starting to push back her chair.

"There's this one proposal I have," I blurted.

The room went silent, Tatiana freezing in place. After a second, she nodded and reseated herself. "Let's hear it."

"It's called *My Mother's Daughter.*"

As soon as the words were out of my mouth I willed them back.

"Keep going," Tatiana said.

"On second thought, I'm sure it won't work." I was insane to have mentioned Jordan's book.

"Emily, just tell us the idea."

I pressed my lips shut before launching into the pitch. Call it insanity, call it finally leaping back onto the playing field, whatever it was I found I couldn't do anything else. "It's a memoir."

A murmur sounded through the room. The memoir had grown in popularity despite the hit the genre had taken when several famous works turned out to be more fabrication than truth.

"Whose memoir?" someone wanted to know.

I looked directly at Tatiana. "It's about Lillian Barlow."

Her eyes narrowed.

Old-school Bart stopped whatever he was writing. "The feminist?"

"Your mother?" Victoria scoffed. "You want to publish a memoir about your mother?"

"Who's the author?" Tatiana asked, sitting back and studying me.

"My sister."

Victoria slapped her notebook shut on her multicolored files. "You can't edit a book *by* your sister *about* your mother."

Which I knew. Which I agreed with. Which was the reason I deserved to be shot for mentioning it.

"Why can't she?" Tatiana asked.

"Why?" Victoria's brow creased with exasperation. "Because editing a relative's book, a sister's book, I might add, is . . . is . . . weird."

"Under normal circumstances I would agree," Tatiana said. "But this is different. Two sisters working on a book about their once-famous mother."

Half visionary, half nut job, Tatiana had said.

"It gives us multiple media angles," she continued. "Back when I was at *Chronicles* we did a piece on the feminist movement. *The Hidden Cost of Equality.* We were flooded with reader mail."

I remembered the article, remembered the controversy it spawned when modern working women started wondering if the price they were paying to have a full-time job and raise a family was worth the toll, not just on them but on their children. Looking at Tatiana, I couldn't tell if she was thinking about the possibility of a controversy that might sell books or if she was wondering about the price a daughter would have paid.

I remembered her standing coldly outside the magazine store, pushing me. Then in the vestibule, telling me she had known my mother, again somehow pushing me. Toward what? Doing my job seemed too easy.

Tatiana leaned forward. "Work with Nate on an offer. Then buy it and get a delivery date. Given your eye for books like *Ruth's Intention,* I suspect that *My Mother's Daughter* will be just as strong."

Victoria choked out an involuntary squeak.

Tatiana met her gaze, raising a brow in challenge. Victoria glanced down at her folders and didn't say a word.

Tatiana stood. "I expect more from the rest of you next time."

I sent up a silent prayer that Jordan really did have a proposal to sell.

▪

When I walked into my office, my BlackBerry rang. My heart leapt when I saw the display.

"Emily Barlow," I answered out of habit.

"Hey Emily, it's Max. I talked to Howard and he can see you during lunch today. It's short notice, but he's flying to the UK tonight and won't be back until next week. I figured you wouldn't want to wait."

He gave me an address in the Financial District. "I'll meet you in the lobby at twelve-thirty," he said, then hung up before I could tell him he didn't have to go with me.

I took the Number 1 train downtown to Wall Street, got off and walked to the address Max had given me. At twelve-twenty-five, I spun through the revolving doors of the towering office building. At exactly twelve-thirty, Max strode in.

As always, he did something to my stomach, or maybe it was my heart. I couldn't help myself when I smiled at him.

"Hey," he said softly and smiled.

He wore a white button-down shirt tucked into charcoal gray pants, and a crisp blue blazer. With his hair brushed back neatly, he seemed very different from the rugged man who had scooped me up in the courtyard.

"Come on," he said. "Let's do this."

He took my arm and guided me to the security desk where we signed in, got our photos taken, and were given visitor badges. On the sixty-fifth floor a receptionist led us back to an office with amazing views of Manhattan.

"Wow," I said.

Max looked out for a second, but didn't appear happy. He guided me to the chairs in front of a desk.

"Max," said a man who was probably in his early forties. "Hey, buddy," he added before turning to me. "I'm Howard Deitz."

We shook hands. "I'm sorry for your loss," the man added.

I liked Howard instantly. He was a little on the chubby side and not great looking, but he seemed funny and kind, and as soon as we started discussing my predicament I could tell he was smart.

I handed over my prenuptial agreement, which he scanned. "We've got a great prenup guy here, Bert Warburg, good friend of mine, who said he'd look it over." He smiled a crooked smile. "I'm a tax guy."

"I don't want to impose—"

"Forget about it. We do family stuff for each other all the time."

Family stuff.

I felt that same yearning I thought I had fixed when I married Sandy and started making a home at the Dakota.

Howard turned to Max. "So what about you?" He leaned back, putting his hands behind his head. "Have you talked to anyone at Goldman? I know they'd take you back in a second."

"Goldman?" I asked, not that it was any of my business.

"Goldman Sachs," Howard explained. "My brother-in-law was one of their top recruits out of Penn State."

Max stood, his smile strained. "Thanks for the help, Howard. And thank Bert for me."

"Hey, sorry, man. I wasn't trying to push. Hell, you're not going to tell Mary? She'll kick my butt from here to Brooklyn if she thinks I was pushing you."

"Believe me," Max said, "not a word to Mary."

We were out on the street in record time, Howard having promised that Bert would get in touch as soon as he'd had a chance to review the agreement.

The day was bright and sunny. Max's fingers circled my arm and didn't let go as we walked steadily, bypassing every subway station we came to.

"Max?"

"I just need a second."

If someone had told me when I first met him that he had worked at Goldman Sachs I would have laughed. But now, seeing him dressed in the blazer and button-down, his hair brushed back, I could see him as a hot young Wall Street investment guy.

We didn't slow down until we came to Tribeca, as if we'd crossed a line of demarcation where he could breathe again.

"Are you okay?" I asked.

"Damn," he said, then gave a huff of hollow laughter. "I haven't been down there since nine-eleven."

"What? Oh my gosh. You should have told me. You definitely didn't need to go with me."

He had slowed our pace, and he let go of my arm. I was surprised when he took my hand. "I had to go back sometime, and I guess I thought by going with you it'd be better."

Whether it was wise or not, I curled my fingers around his. "I take it that wasn't the case."

He glanced over at me as we walked along a narrow road lined with shops and restaurants. "You definitely made it easier."

"Were you working for Goldman when the planes hit the towers?"

"Yep." He squinted as if the sun's glare was too intense.

We walked another block without a word. After we crossed Canal Street, I couldn't help myself. "Were you in the office when it happened?"

For a second I didn't think he would answer, but after pulling me back when a cab cut a corner too close, he spoke. "I had just come up from the subway when all hell broke lose. People running and screaming, that cloud of ash and crap and who knows what else rushing down the street."

He hesitated again, and we made it another block. This time I didn't push.

"There was this woman," he finally said. "I don't know, middle-aged or older. Not sure. Not that it matters, she was dazed. I grabbed for her, had her hand in mine. Then that surge hit. You can't believe the force of that thing. One second I could see the woman, then I couldn't. I held on, tried to pull her to me, but I felt her let go and she slipped out of my hand. Someone else grabbed me and pulled me inside a deli."

Having lived through 9/11 in New York, I had gotten used to the numb disconnect of the way people told their stories, as if putting too much emotion into the equation would make it unbearable for those who had lived through it. Max told his story with that same numb distance, and the pieces of this man came together like hitting the right combination of a lock. "You enlisted because you felt useless and needed to help. That's how you became the Navy SEAL guy."

This promising young man had witnessed the destruction, no doubt lost friends, and had to do something about it.

"Yeah, what can I say?"

"Your father must have been proud."

He scoffed and swore. "He was furious. Tried to talk me out of it."

"The Navy captain?"

"He told me I was going off half-cocked. But I couldn't sit back and let other guys like my father do all the hard work. When he realized he couldn't talk me out of it, he talked me into the SEAL program."

Another piece fell into place.

"The day I was shipping out, he was still pissed off, could hardly speak to me. We shook hands like strangers. Mom was crying. I hated making them so unhappy. But all I could think about was that woman's hand slipping out of mine."

Max's hard jawline was taut, his control fragile. "I was going to be late if I didn't head out, so I backed away. But my dad didn't let go. My old man, military to the bone, just looked at me for a second, then yanked me close and hugged me, said all that mattered was that I come back in one piece." Max blew out a breath, the cords standing taut on his neck. "Hell."

My heart broke for him and I squeezed his hand. "But just as with people you knew and worked with on nine-eleven, not all of your friends got out or came back alive. Survivor's guilt. Easy enough to understand." This time I hesitated. "But easy to understand isn't the same as easy to deal with, though even that isn't the hardest part for you."

He glanced over at me, wary.

"You simply *having* a hard time with it makes you feel weak. And because of your dad, or because of how you were raised, or who knows what, you don't know how to deal with feeling weak."

We walked in silence, Max staring straight ahead, holding on to my hand, the cobbled street making it feel like a small European village. Then suddenly he eased, like a breath sighing out of him, and he hooked his arm over my shoulders.

"You're perceptive, I'll give you that."

"I'm a book editor. I might as well be a shrink for all the crazy agents, authors, and publicists—not to mention certain other editors—I deal with."

He laughed, finally, with that boyishly gruff sound I had grown to recognize in such a short time. When we hit Houston Street, he pulled me down into the subway. Without the rush hour crowds, the train wasn't crowded, the last car nearly empty.

We didn't talk as we headed uptown, just sat side by side, the car rocking and clattering over the tracks. When we neared the Fifty-ninth Street station, I stood. "I get out here."

When the train stopped he got up, pulling me close. "Thank you," he said against my temple.

I started to lean into him, but he pressed his lips into my hair, then gently pushed me out onto the platform as the doors slid closed.

einstein

chapter twentyfive

While Emily was doing whatever it was she did at work, I spent hours brainstorming ideas. At the end of the day, engrossed in *Runner's World,* I yelped in surprise when I heard Emily come in behind me. Based on the look of shock on her face I deduced that had she been a dog she would have yelped too.

"You were reading," she said, her tone accusing.

"Not exactly reading," I lamented.

"Or something like reading!"

As usual, she understood. I would have chuckled if I could.

"You're a dog, and dogs don't read magazines! You were turning pages. With your nose and paw. I saw it."

Since the old man's last appearance, I had finally accepted the fact that I had to get serious about helping Emily get her life back together. Really help her this time. More importantly, when I did help her I would finally move on and achieve the greatness for which I had always known I was destined.

Sure, it would have been better to be guaranteed greatness in some sort of human variety. But at this point I was willing to take what I could get. That disconcerting lake episode had turned the tide.

To that end, and not wanting another replay of the Lucky Charms Incident, I knew I had to get control of my world. After getting the copy of *Runner's World,* and after Emily had gone to work, I knew I had to come up with a schedule, a way to occupy my mind so the ridiculous animal instincts didn't have the ability to commandeer my good sense.

Once upon a time, I had worked out regularly. Now that I was in this dog's body, I realized I needed a new kind of workout routine. For cardio: march through the apartment. For the core: I invented a form of push-ups utilizing all four of my legs. But for the life of me, as Einstein, I couldn't do anything close to a sit-up. Determined, I resorted to "rollovers." Drop down, roll over, pop back up on the other side. Then repeat.

For an odd-looking old dog, I felt certain that in no time at all I would be looking better and better. I was half tempted to coerce Emily into taking me to one of those dog salons, but in the park one hears stories. The last thing I wanted was to be at the mercy of some evil dog groomer with a pair of clippers and toenail trimmers. I still had nightmares about Vinny from the clinic.

The other thing I decided would help was reading. Okay, not exactly reading, but as with the maintenance late notice, I employed my cock-and-squint maneuver for decent results. The hardest part of my venture into this quasi-literate state was getting something down on the floor to peruse. And don't get me started on how difficult it was to turn the pages. But by the time Emily arrived home that evening, I had managed a system of climbing up on tables, countertops, and bookshelves to retrieve things. The kitchen episode might have been a disaster, but it taught me how to climb. Beyond which I became something of a master of what I liked to call the "paw and muzzle manipulation." A little descriptive, a little alliteration, all and all a fine turn of phrase that, well, helped me turn the page.

But now, I'd been caught.

"Okay, this is bizarre," Emily said, closing her eyes.

When she opened them again, I could tell she expected to find me curled up asleep, the magazine closed, maybe even eaten, the books back on the shelf.

No such luck.

I tried to smile at her, tilting my head in that way that I knew made me look adorable, or more specifically, adorably ugly.

She screeched and marched straight for the refrigerator and what I knew would turn into another round of baking.

Damn it all to hell.

Another of my habits as Sandy was that I had always done my best thinking while running. I would head out to Central Park, take the bridle path around the reservoir under the canopy of trees, and somehow something that had been a muddle when I set out would become clear. It had been this line of thought that had reminded me of running, and the fact that one of the best ways to deal with whatever it was that was wrong with my wife was exercise.

As a result, I had decided I would get her to run up to the reservoir and back on the bridle path. Which, in yet another turn, had led me to the magazine store and the purchase of *Runner's World.*

Yep, I was a genius.

Granted, I had two concerns. One, the dog walker and even Jordan had kept to the paved walkways when taking me out, so I had yet to experience the wide, cinder path where horses were still allowed. Just the thought of the gigantic four-legged beasts sent a thrill of anticipation through this little dog's body. But my superior mind tamped it down, because I had bigger worries than chasing down a horse. Namely, as far as I knew, my wife had never worked out a day in her life, and more than once I had noted that she got winded taking a mere flight of stairs. I wasn't sure how she would run anywhere without dropping dead from a heart attack. Then where would I be? Certainly not with the win-win I was hoping for.

The long and short? I had to get my wife in shape.

Insane, I know. Not only was I a dog, but let's face it, my wife had recently become enamored of desserts laced with more fat and sugar than an opera singer stuffed in a cannoli shell. Not a great combination for the superior health needed by an athlete.

Given this, my first order of business should be no shocker. I had to keep her from making another cake.

I scrambled around her, planting myself in front of the refrigerator.

"Out of the way," she said.

I growled.

"Einstein, move."

She started to brush me aside, so I did the only thing I could. "Step away from the butter, fat girl," I growled.

Yes, that might have been a little much, even for me.

Her jaw dropped. "I am not fat!"

"Not yet, maybe. But at the rate you're going, sooner rather than later you're going to expand like a dirigible in the Macy's Thanksgiving Day Parade."

She gasped, and we didn't speak for the rest of the evening. But can I just say, I might not have been sweet or kind, and certainly not charming, but didn't I deserve points for keeping her from another round of baked goods?

■

After dinner, we still weren't speaking and Emily didn't bother to enlighten me as to why every time a noise sounded in the building, she leapt up and ran to the gallery. Since I couldn't seem to make myself do anything else, I scampered after her, my nails scrambling on my poor hardwood floors, barks and yelps erupting from my chest.

Once in the gallery, Emily would pause, as if waiting for the door to open. When nothing happened, she glanced into the outer hallway and sighed.

"Jordan, where are you?"

Later that night I was curled up in the kitchen trying to sleep when my sister-in-law showed up at two in the morning. She had a male with her, twenty-four, twenty-five at the oldest.

"Shh," she hushed the fellow, laughing.

It didn't take a dog's sensory abilities to know she was drunk. If the staggeringly potent smell of tequila and margarita mix hadn't given her away, the actual staggering would have.

The guy wasn't nearly as bad off. He'd been drinking . . . my nose twitched in assessment . . . beer, and several of them, and his body reeked of pheromones. Jordan's guest wanted sex, and he wanted it bad.

I snuck up on them and gave them my scariest growl.

The guy stiffened, and a spurt of fear hormones mixed with the pheromones.

"Ignore him," Jordan said, running her hands down the guy's chest.

I growled again, crouching low, my hackles rising.

The guy backed up a step. I might not be that big, but everyone knows small dogs can do some serious damage if they get their teeth into it.

"Geez, don't let him scare you. He's all bark."

"He doesn't sound like he's all bark. Look at those teeth."

I bared my less-than-pearly whites for effect. It was the most fun I'd had, well, since becoming a dog.

"Damn it, Einstein, shut up."

I growled at her.

She scoffed. "Like I care what you think of me."

"Wench," I barked.

"Ass," she retaliated.

The guy backed up another step. "This is too weird. I've gotta go."

"Good boy," I barked.

"Jordan?"

The three of us froze at the sound of Emily's voice. I could hear my wife pulling on her robe. Jordan sensed it too.

"You've got to get out of here." She pushed the guy to the door.

I pitched in and gave a fierce growl to get him going faster. Not that I didn't want Jordan to get in trouble, but why not take one last moment of pleasure in making him squirm? Who did he think he was to come into my house and have sex on one of my beds?

As soon as the door shut, Jordan bolted for her room.

"Good night, Emily!"

She careened into the guest bedroom, closing and locking the door just as Emily emerged.

"Jordan, we need to talk."

"In the morning, Em. Sorry I woke you!"

"But I have good news."

"Really, Emily, tomorrow. I'm exhausted."

And drunk, I wanted to add, not to mention smart enough to know that her big sister wouldn't take kindly to the slightest of staggers.

The sound of the shower coming on cut off whatever else Emily would have said.

"What's that smell?" she asked.

"Your drunken sister," I barked with great seriousness.

I ask, was that not helpful?

Emily glanced from the closed guest room door to me. "Don't be a tattletale."

Then she went back to her own room and shut the door on me.

Women.

■

When I woke the next morning, it was to the smell of coffee. Ah, how I missed morning coffee, the rising sun, and a crisp copy of the *New York Times.* For a second I started to feel sorry for myself again, missing my old life, but then I focused. I was going to be *great.* After which I felt the flare of excitement and anticipation. What would that greatness look like? I wondered. What form would it take? I could hardly wait to find out what this new greatness entailed. And let me just say, if I was destined to be a triage specialist, I would make a hell of a lot better one than the old man.

I opened my eyes and was surprised to find Emily sitting at the counter reading *Runner's World.*

Interesting.

Pushing myself up, I stretched, my head low over my front legs, my rump stretching up in the back, the muscles and sinew extending. When I stood, I shook, my dog tags jingling.

"Good morning," she said.

Lost in thought, she gathered the leash and took me out. Once I was done at the curb and she had cleaned up, she straightened and stared at the park. This was interesting, but I wasn't sure what she was thinking. "Use your words!" I barked.

"So you think running would help me, huh? That's why you made me get the magazine."

Am I impressive or what?

"Yes!" I barked.

Instead of returning indoors, we headed to the park, walking under the wisteria-covered arbor that arched over the entrance. While I could use a little dog group interaction, the dog group wasn't there. Besides, Emily surprised me yet again when she led us to the bridle path.

"Okay, E, you're getting what you wanted. We're going to run."

"Run? Already?" I squeaked.

Sure I wanted her to run, and no question I needed her to get into shape, but I wasn't ready to start today. I had only just started my own workout routine, and was certainly in no shape to run. But she didn't bother to ask me. She took off with me on the end of the lead.

Good God almighty. What had I been thinking when I thought running was the solution to my dilemma? As a man, yes, I had loved running. As a dog, so low to the ground and practically a hundred years old, every step was pure torture. I tried to pick my paws up high like some demented Clydesdale, because really, those cinders and rocks on my delicate pads felt . . . well, dirty. Did they even make hand wipes for dogs?

Fortunately Emily ran about as fast as a slug, and by the time we got through the rock-lined tunnel underneath Seventy-second Street, then about a third of the way to the Seventy-seventh Street tunnel—a distance of no more than a quarter mile—she was out of breath and staggered to a stop.

Thank God.

Sheer exhaustion made me forget about the dirt and gravel on the path. I collapsed with an umph and lay panting on the ground. To my left a tree-filled incline led up to the rock wall that separated the park from Central Park West. To the right the ground dipped away, down to the winding park road and the infamous lake where only days before I had tried to do away with myself. Despite that recent memory, I would have thought the scene bucolic had my lungs not been screaming for oxygen, and had Emily not been making a terrible racket of her own, bent over at the waist gasping for air.

Eventually we recovered. The minute my breathing eased, my nose had a chance to do its thing. Namely kick into gear and want to sniff. Emily had dropped the leash and as predicted I couldn't help myself. I pushed up and ran from a rock to a tree, then to a big pile of horse dung in the middle of the path. I am embarrassed to say that I felt euphoric, forgetting all about the dilemmas that riddled my life. Emily had to chase me down and practically drag me home.

We had just reached the wisteria-covered pergola when my ever-sensitive ears detected the buzz of what I barely remembered was a BlackBerry in her pocket. Emily cringed when she saw the name of whoever was calling. After a second of debate, she answered. "Tatiana?" Pause. "You're calling about the book?"

Emily tensed, though I couldn't imagine why.

"A delivery date from Jordan. Right. I'm on it."

She was buying the book from Jordan?

Now this was interesting. I wasn't convinced my sister-in-law could read any better than I could, much less string together a series of words that would form a single coherent sentence—certainly not an entire book.

"No, no, I'm not backing down. There's no problem."

Back at the apartment I had my heart set on a Steakin' as was our tradition after returning from any sort of walk. And excuse me, I needed a Steakin' more than ever after that run. But Emily bypassed the kitchen and knocked on Jordan's door. There was no answer.

"Steakin'," I barked.

"Not now."

The door was cracked and because I was really getting the hang of being helpful, I nudged it open. If this didn't get me a Steakin' I didn't know what would.

No surprise that Jordan wasn't there.

"Where is she?" Emily asked. "Did she go back out last night?"

In the kitchen, we found an empty cereal bowl and carton of milk on the kitchen table. I sat prettily in front of the pantry door and salivated. But still no Steakin' for me.

"She's already gone?" Emily asked, confused.

I expected her to say something unkind. Jordan had yet to get the hang of cleaning up after herself. I had to wonder if she did it just to irritate her sister or if her own living conditions consisted of soured milk and unwashed dishes. Had the girl never heard of salmonella?

But Emily was full of surprises that morning. She whirled around and raced out of the kitchen so fast that by the time I got up and ran after her she was already inside Jordan's room.

"Uh-oh," I ruffed. "Even I know snooping through your sister's things isn't a good idea."

"Be quiet," Emily snapped at me.

"You understand that but won't give me a Steakin'?"

Emily ignored me, so I sat back and watched. Not that there was a lot to watch. Jordan didn't have much stuff to go through. The challenge was digging through the discarded clothes and decorative pillows strewn about the floor to find anything of interest.

"There better be a book proposal in here somewhere," Emily muttered.

If I were a betting man I would put my money on no proposal at all. More than that, I guessed that while the place looked like a disaster to Emily, there was some order to Jordan's chaos, and the second she returned she would know that her sister had gone through her belongings.

"Ugh!"

My head snapped up to find Emily standing stock-still, a pair of Jockey briefs dangling from her finger. And not a pair that looked like Jordan's size.

"Where did these come from?"

From one of the young males Jordan had a habit of sneaking inside while Emily was fast asleep. Like my wife, the fellow who had departed brief-less must not have been able to make sense of the chaos and find his undergarment.

"Emily? What are you doing?"

Emily and I whipped around to find Jordan standing in the doorway. She held a Starbucks cup in her hand. I sniffed. Vanilla latte with whole milk. I licked my chops.

"Are you going through my things?" Jordan's voice was dangerously low.

"This place is a mess."

"And that gives you permission to go through my room *how*?"

Ah, the sarcasm of youth.

Jordan walked over and snatched the underwear.

"Have you had boys in here?" Emily demanded.

"Not boys. Men. I'm an adult, Emily. An adult who has sex."

My lips curled back at more information than I wanted or cared for. Not that Jordan was done. Her eyes narrowed with something like triumph, and she added, "Our mother would have been proud."

Emily took a step back as if Jordan had slapped her, then regained her footing and stood her ground. "Perhaps, but look where that got her. One daughter who dreams of a father she never knew, and another daughter who wishes the father she actually has wasn't the type who felt comfortable in a tract house on Long Island with a nine-to-five job, a wife, and two other children."

This time Jordan stepped back. "I never said that." But her voice was shaky.

"You didn't have to. You come and go without a word of warning to any of us. And let's face it, we both know why you really take those crazy gifts to his kids. It has nothing to do with making them think for themselves. You'd do anything to punish your father for leaving you and starting a new family."

Jordan backed farther away, exhaling sharply, once, twice.

Emily sighed. "Jordan, I'm sorry."

But her sister had already bolted. All we heard was a slam and the rattle of glass in my fabulous front door.

■

The next morning Jordan was still gone. She had called and left a message on the answering machine saying she needed some space and was staying with a friend for a couple of days. In typical Jordan fashion, she left no number where Emily could return the call.

My wife alternated between regret and frustration. Every time the phone rang and it was a number she didn't recognize, she grabbed it up, praying it was Jordan. And every time her BlackBerry buzzed she flinched. If the mobile device rang, she no longer answered. I half wondered if she went into work wearing a disguise. Clearly with no answer as to when Jordan would deliver this supposed manuscript, and no sign of it in the girl's messy room, my wife was avoiding her boss like the plague.

The other person she was avoiding was my mother. Over the last few days, Althea Portman had left a series of increasingly terse messages on the answering machine.

"Emily, really, you can't avoid this."

"Now seriously, Emily, this is getting very annoying."

And my personal favorite, *"Emily Barlow, I've had just about enough of this irresponsible behavior. Call me back this instant or I'm going to . . . I'm going to . . . well, just call me back."*

My mother at a loss for words. Who would have thought it possible?

To make matters worse, my estate lawyer started calling and leaving increasingly unfriendly messages. Emily became more frantic with each call, none of which, to my knowledge, she returned.

"This can't be happening," I overheard her whisper.

After the lawyer's most recent call I found my wife turning the apartment upside down.

"There have to be receipts around here someplace, proof of all the money I've put into renovations. Receipts and photographs of before and after, of me doing the work. Evidence to build a case."

In a bottom drawer in her desk, she pulled out a stack of files.

"Doctor's receipts," she said when she opened the first. But I could tell she was hopeful.

"Old checks," from another.

"Receipts!"

Even I felt my ratty old heart leap for her.

But it was from that same file that she pulled out a photo. The excitement seeped out of her, and she sank down next to me. I saw that it was a picture of Emily and me, the Sandy me, redoing the very first room, the two of us together, laughing, covered in paint, Emily holding the camera out in front of us, our heads out of proportion to our bodies because of the angle. I remembered that day clearly. How beautiful and full of life she had been. Yet another day when I had promised myself I would be true to my wife.

Why hadn't I been able to stay true to my vows?

Why had the hunger really returned?

Not that my sudden questioning made me go easy on her. My job was to help her rise from the ashes.

After that one jaunt in the park, Emily hadn't wanted to go back, forcing me to drag her out of bed and onto the bridle path. If selfishness had stood between me and salvation before, I was a little concerned that bossiness would do me in now. But good God almighty, Emily was not a particularly gifted athlete. She'd run for fifty feet then all but collapse from exhaustion. When I snapped at her butt to keep her going, she ended up sprawled out on the cinders. I was beside myself. But on the third day, my frustration turned to a bud of hope when Emily actually came out of her bedroom wearing hideous running warm-ups.

I hadn't had to drop the leash on her face or jiggle my tags. Progress. I could practically envision the old man handing me some sort of otherworldly report card with GREAT stamped across the cover.

■

Jordan didn't return for the remainder of the week. But on Friday, Emily came home from work to the smell of cleaning supplies and some exotic meal cooked up from third-world recipes.

"Jordan?"

The younger woman rushed out from the kitchen and threw her arms around Emily. "I'm sorry I flipped."

The tension that had built up in my wife evaporated, her body easing. "I'm sorry for going into your room and saying such awful things."

That was the pattern with these two. Fight, make up, laugh, cry, swear they'd never fight again—until the next time their opposite personalities clashed.

Over dinner at the kitchen table, Emily finally had the chance to present the book deal.

"You're going to buy my book?" Jordan squealed.

"Isn't it wonderful! It's going to be so much fun to work together."

I craned my neck to see if somehow a bottle of wine had been opened without my knowledge. Or maybe Jordan was passing around a joint. What else could account for this ridiculous self-delusion? Did anyone really think these two working together was a good idea, much less a fun one?

But no one asked me.

"Freakin' A! Thank you, Emily!"

"So, let me see the proposal."

Followed by what I can only call a pregnant pause.

"You want to see it?"

"Jordan? Of course I need to see it."

Honeymoon over.

"Well, it's not done yet."

Emily drew one of her deep, bracing breaths. "Okay," she said, "so it's not done. No problem. Just show me what you have."

Jordan squirmed.

"Tell me you've something written, Jordan."

"Of course I have. It's just that . . ."

"Just what?"

"It's a little rough."

More deep breathing, then, "Rough is fine."

Jordan debated before dashing to her bedroom.

"I never should have gotten involved in this," Emily said to me.

Ah, yeah.

The younger woman returned holding a spiral-bound notebook, her face red with guilt.

Emily extended her hand. "Let me see it."

From my vantage point all I could see was messy, large, looping script, and doodles up and down the margins. Emily pressed her eyes shut and I felt certain she was praying.

"I'll let you read in peace," Jordan said.

She slipped away while Emily read one page, then another. She read without stopping, Jordan peeking her head in every few minutes. When Emily didn't acknowledge her, the younger Barlow looked at me with a question in her eyes.

"Can't help you." I shrugged.

And I couldn't. I had no sense of what Emily was feeling. She put off no scent whatsoever as she read. When she came to the end of what Jordan had written, she closed the notebook and bent over the table, pressing her forehead to the front cover.

I smelled her tears before I heard her crying.

"Emily?" Jordan said, tiptoeing into the room.

Emily sat up slowly, her eyes red.

"You hate it," Jordan said.

"I don't hate it." Though she certainly didn't look like she loved it.

"Then what is it?"

Emily stood to face her sister. "I never thought about how living with our mother affected *you*."

emily

"Don't let the world force you to be someone you're not," my mother used to tell me. Little did my mother know that in her own oblique way she had forced me to be like her, and that it wasn't necessarily what I wanted. At twenty-two, I had spent my whole life trying to be who my mother wanted me to be—to be like her, not like Emily. At twenty-two, I was fighting battles, my mother's battles, as if my legacy was to carry on her dream rather than any I might have had on my own.

—EXCERPT FROM *My Mother's Daughter*

chapter twenty-six

My mother was a puzzle. Actually several puzzles whose pieces were so shuffled together that it was impossible to form a cohesive whole. Reading Jordan's pages brought that home to me more than ever.

Lillian Barlow fought for a woman's right to have a career, but she gave up her own to stay home with her daughters. She might have needed her admirers, but she didn't respect any of them as they lined up at her parties looking for a handout of her attention like beggars at a soup kitchen.

"You can toy with men," she often said, *"but you can never need them."*

If she was free with her attention, she was selfish with her affection. I had hated that fact about her.

I had spent my life wrapped up in my own problems with being my mother's daughter. With Jordan seemingly so like her, it had never occurred to me that my sister's life had been difficult as well. In hindsight, I realized I had been blind not to see it. But more than that, for the first time I understood my mother's ability to be selfish. Sitting there with Jordan's scribbled pages, I selfishly didn't want her story to see the light of day.

"You hate it!" Jordan cried. "I never should have mentioned it."

During my time in publishing, I had seen many authors expose raw nerves of insecurity about their work. But it was disconcerting to see any sort of insecurity coming from my sister, who had been traveling the world alone since she was a teenager.

"Jordan, I don't hate it."

She bit her lower lip. "Then what?"

I hesitated. "It's just that I hadn't given any thought to what this book is about. Living in the shadow of Lillian Barlow."

"But look at you, Emily. You moved out from the shadow. You created your own life."

I was equally touched and frustrated by this, because I hadn't moved out from Mother's shadow. Not really. Wasn't I trying to find a place for myself at the new Caldecote Press with a book about her? Wasn't it a very real possibility that Tatiana was in some way keeping me on because she had known my mother? Would Hedda have offered me a job had she not known Lillian Barlow? But that wasn't my biggest concern right then.

"Jordan, what is really going on with you?"

Since Jordan had appeared on my doorstep she had been acting even more combative than usual, but I had been too wrapped up in my own concerns to give it much thought.

Jordan blew out a breath.

"Talk to me, please."

After a second, my sister wrinkled her nose, then said, "I'm not exactly taking a break from Homes for Women Heroes. I got fired."

"What?"

"It wasn't my fault." Jordan scowled. "Okay, so maybe it was my fault. But, well, there was this guy. Serge. He was totally cool, or at least I thought he was. He's all into helping people, and he was completely into me."

She hesitated.

"Go on."

She raised her chin, part defiance, part anxiety. "The deal with Heroes is that you have to pledge that while you're working on an assignment you can't, well, hook up with other members of the team." She cringed. "We were sort of caught, you know, hooking up, and that ass blamed it on me! And let me tell you, it was totally a mutual thing. We got reprimanded and kicked off the project. Then he dumped me!"

I could hardly believe it when my tough little sister started to cry. But when I reached out to her, she brushed me away.

"I am not crying," she said, crying even harder. "He's a jerk. But I was really into him. Me! Me, who never gets in a twist over any guy!"

"Jordan, don't beat yourself up because you fell for someone."

"He was everything I didn't think I would ever find. So many of the guys I meet fall into nonprofit because they think they won't have to work hard, or they do it because they think it's a free pass to cool places. But

Serge believed. He believed in what we were doing. He was willing to work his butt off to make things happen.

"Plus he was good looking and massively sexy." Her voiced trailed off. "How could Lillian Barlow's daughter be one of those girls just like the rest, the pathetic loser who gets all broken up over a guy? And even if I did fall for him, how could I possibly be the kind of person who whacks out over it?"

This time when I pulled her close she didn't resist. "Oh, Jordan," I murmured. "You're only human. Everyone makes mistakes."

"Mom would be totally mortified."

I hesitated. "Mother's way isn't the only way to live."

Jordan pushed back and looked at me. "Are you happy, Em?"

"Touché."

"I didn't mean it that way. It's just that I've always thought of you as being happy despite that prick you married."

"Jordan."

"Well, it's true. But since I've been here, sorry, but you don't seem all that happy."

"I lost my husband. What do you expect?"

She didn't back down or even look contrite. "I don't know. Something different. You don't seem sad, like *grieving* sad. It's more like you're angry and . . . lost."

Jordan was like that, young and oblivious, then all of the sudden very smart. If I was truthful with myself, at first I had covered up my feelings by throwing myself into work. After the journals, I had felt more angry and lost than sad. Had those emotions gotten in the way of true grief? What would happen if I finally managed to deal with the loss of my husband, deal with the loss of the man who I had to believe once loved me, and also deal with his actual death?

I realized I was afraid to really look at what I would find. If I had patched over the loss of my mother by marrying Sandy, then patched over the loss of Sandy with Einstein and work and even anger, when I finally let go what would be left of me? Who would I be?

"You're still going to publish my book, right?"

My sister's face was earnest and for the first time in years her hard edges softened. I didn't know how to disappoint her. More than that, I didn't see how I could backtrack. What she had written was good enough that another publisher would pick it up. If I lost this book to another publisher, Tatiana would have my head. The world might not care about the life of a former women's activist, but it did care about a woman who had led an unconventional life, only to give it all up for the kind of conventional existence that she had fought so hard against.

The surprise was that my little sister had understood that about our mother when I hadn't, and had captured it on paper.

"When can you have the whole thing done?" I asked her.

She squealed, then danced me around the kitchen. She even leaned over and gave Einstein a hug. My dog looked at me in consideration. And while there was no way to turn back, I had a bad feeling that I was going to regret the day I pitched *My Mother's Daughter.*

■

It was the next morning that I began to run in earnest. Not that I realized it at the time.

With the sun not even a hint on the horizon, Einstein nudged my door open and shook his dog tags to wake me. When I grumbled and tried to shoo him away, he jumped up on the bed, dropped the leash on my face, and barked.

"Okay, okay," I muttered. "I'm awake."

As soon as he jumped down, I rolled over and burrowed deeper into the mattress.

My dog was having nothing to do with this. He clamped onto the edge of the covers with his teeth, then pulled them off me.

"It's too early to run," I complained. But by then I really was awake. I rolled out of bed, glowered at him, and pulled on shorts and running shoes. Einstein pranced ahead of me, while I grumbled the whole way.

Once on the bridle path we didn't run far, but I had to admit that by the time we staggered back to the apartment I felt a sense of hope I hadn't felt in ages. It was the end of April, flowers starting to bloom. It was that same week that Max called.

"I heard from Bert Warburg. He's gone over your prenup and wants to know when you can come in."

"As soon as he'll see me!"

"His message said that tomorrow, first thing, would work for him, or at lunch."

I told myself I wasn't disappointed that Max didn't go with me this time. I hadn't seen him since our ride uptown on the Number 1 train, and I hadn't even been trying to avoid him this time.

As it turned out, I was massively relieved he wasn't there when the lawyer gave me the news.

"This agreement is ironclad."

"But it can't be." I spread out my meager stash of apartment photos and receipts. "My husband gave me a verbal promise. And look at all this work I put into the place."

"Ms. Barlow," he said with a sigh, "I'm sure you realize that this does nothing to negate the prenuptial agreement. And having only been married three years, your chances of getting the agreement overturned are beyond slim."

He considered me for a second, tapping his pen on the blotter. "But listen, given the prominence of the family, I'm sure if we sent a letter, threatening to sue for reimbursement, while they would know the claim would never succeed in court, I feel confident the Portmans will settle for some amount of money rather than deal with any possible bad press."

I had no interest in some monetary settlement from the Portmans. Despite that, I still couldn't shake the sense that it wasn't over. Something was making me hold on to the apartment. Something I didn't understand told me that I still couldn't give up.

■

The next morning I left the Dakota with instructions for Jordan to type up the pages of *My Mother's Daughter.* When I got to the office Tatiana was waiting in the hallway talking to Nate.

"Emily," she said.

I nodded. "Tatiana. Nate."

I didn't linger. I continued into my office, flipping on the light. When I turned back Tatiana stood in the doorway. I barely swallowed back a squeak of surprise.

"Did you get the delivery date from your sister?"

"I did." Thank God. "She said she should have the whole thing done in four months."

"Good." She turned to leave then stopped. "I want to read the proposal. E-mail it to me."

"Now?"

"Yes, Emily. Now."

Before I could come up with some excuse not to send it, she was gone. Not that I could keep it from her forever. But as long as no one else saw the pages, somehow I felt I could find a way out.

By the time I got home, Jordan had managed to input the pages. She still wore the jeans and sweatshirt she had pulled on that morning. Her long hair was pulled up in a messy twist, pencils stuck into the updo at odd angles.

"I did it!"

It was the first time I had ever seen her really work, and my confidence grew over the prospect of what we were doing together. Maybe this wasn't such a bad idea.

"Good! Tatiana wants to see it."

"Tatiana? As in your boss, Tatiana?"

"The one and only."

"Cool!"

I read through the pages, was impressed, and sent the file attached to an e-mail.

The next day Einstein tried to drag me out of bed for yet another run. "You expect me to do this every day?"

He ignored me and dropped a T-shirt on my face. But when I was dressed and ready to go, he rolled over on his back.

"Oh, I get it. You're taking the day off, but not me."

He leapt back up, nodded his head, then returned to the kitchen where he curled up in his bed.

I nearly dove back under my own covers. But I was up, and what the heck.

With the sun just brightening the sky, I made my way to the bridle path with a yawn, did a halfhearted job of stretching, groaning with each movement, and started to run. Or at least I started to jog.

A few runners zipped past me, and several people walked along with coffee and a dog. I concentrated so I wouldn't trip in a rut, and this time I made it from the Seventy-second Street underpass all the way to Seventy-seventh Street without stopping. Forget the fact that I was half dead by the time I got there. I made it and it felt amazing.

Later, when I was headed for work, there was no denying that I felt I could take whatever anyone threw my way. Which turned out to be a good thing because that afternoon Tatiana called me to her office for an impromptu meeting.

"Brady," she said, turning to one of the longtime Caldecote editors. "Did you have a chance to read the proposal for *My Mother's Daughter*?"

Brady cleared his throat, looking at her over his tortoiseshell reading glasses. "I did."

My heart raced in a way that was not so different from how it felt when I got to the Seventy-seventh Street underpass.

"I must say, Tatiana, I was impressed."

"You were?" This from Victoria.

Brady didn't so much as glance at her. "I was moved by the content and was impressed with the writing. The pages had heart and were well written." He turned to me. "Your sister is quite the storyteller."

"I thought you'd love it," Tatiana stated. She turned to the art director. "Fernando, what do you have to show us?"

My brain tried to make sense of what was happening, but even when the art director pulled out a cover mock-up, I couldn't speak.

"My Mother's Daughter," he read. "*Living with Lillian Barlow.* By Jordan Barlow."

"Edited by Emily Barlow," Tatiana added.

All in an elegant typeface, printed over an old black-and-white photograph I had seen many times before.

It had been taken when I was thirteen, Jordan three, at one of my mother's parties. A photographer had been hired to capture the event. In the picture, Mother was larger than life, full of the energy that drew people to her like bees to honey, Jordan and me sitting on the floor gazing up at her, like pages to a queen. All three of us wore elegant dresses more suited to the late '50s than more modern times.

Sitting in the conference room all these years later, I was moved. "It's perfect."

Everyone in the room except Victoria started talking excitedly.

"It *is* perfect!"

"It's fabulous."

"It screams *Read me!*"

Tatiana quieted them. "We are going to publish it in time for Mother's Day next year. And we are going all-out to make *My Mother's Daughter* work. Television and print ads. A creative promotional plan. I want Jordan and Emily booked on every national talk show."

My brain struggled to catch up. "Wait. What? You want to publish next May? Isn't that pushing it? We don't yet have the book."

Generally it took a year to bring a book to the shelves. It could be done faster, though generally not when the book in question was by a first-time author who was going to get a big push. I would have even been okay with nine months for Jordan's book, but nine months after we had the completed manuscript.

"Next May is cutting it close," I said.

"Look, we'll get the manuscript at the end of August. That gives us eight months, and we can do plenty for the book before it's turned in. I want this done, Emily," Tatiana said. "I'm counting on you to deliver."

What could I say?

She sat back and considered me. "You've certainly turned things around. We have significantly increased the orders for *Ruth's Intention.* And now *My Mother's Daughter.* You went from being behind and foundering to having the potential for two very big successes."

Or two very big failures, she didn't need to add.

Victoria hadn't been pleased before, but at this news she perked up. And why not? All of a sudden I had a novel that everyone expected to be a best seller, which meant that anything less would make it a disappointment. On top of that, I now had a memoir written by my generally irresponsible sister and a tight deadline. Given the combination, Victoria might finally get her wish that I fail in a quantifiable way.

But there was something else that played in my head. A push. A big push from the beginning that wasn't a stroke of luck gained from a candy bar. A push for a book that was indisputably mine from start to finish. This was how careers were made.

I was surprised by the sudden sense of excitement I felt. For months I had faced nothing but a long stretch of emptiness lined by battles I had no idea how to fight. Now I felt almost drunk with purpose, drunk enough to push away whatever concern remained about working with Jordan.

I gathered my notepad to leave.

"And Emily," Tatiana said, stopping me. "I want you to kick things off by taking your sister to lunch at Michael's."

"Lunch? With Jordan?"

If I had to choose one person I would never willingly take to lunch at Michael's, it would be my sister. It was hard to picture her in the power setting wearing cargo pants and combat boots—or even flip-flops. I shuddered to think what Jordan would say to me if I suggested she wear something other than her normal attire.

"Yes, Emily. I want you to take her to Michael's." Enunciated with crisp, schoolmistress diction.

A heartbeat passed before I said, "Great idea. Can't wait."

chapter twenty-seven

"What do you mean we're going to lunch at some idiotic place called Michael's and you want me to 'dress up'?"

My sister paced the kitchen. "I am not going to kowtow to some stodgy establishment dress code, all because you want to parade me in front of media types to get attention for the book."

"You're right." I held my hands up in defeat. "I'll tell Tatiana that under no circumstances will you do your part to help make *your* book a success."

"Well, I hadn't thought of it that way," Jordan said.

"No problem, Jordan. Surely the book will sell on its own. It doesn't need the kind of push so few books ever get."

"Tatiana is making my book special?"

"She was. But now . . ." I let the words trail off.

"Okay," she griped. "I'll go."

But I was no dummy. "Jordan, I appreciate that. And while I wouldn't ever want you to wear some kind of little black suit, I can't take you to a place like Michael's in flip-flops. I'll tell Tatiana it isn't going to work."

My sister was no dummy either. "Buy me a new outfit, and I'll do it."

Which was how Jordan and I, Einstein in tow, ended up on the second floor of Bloomingdale's an hour later.

"I'd rather go to SoHo to shop," Jordan said.

The smile I shot her way might not have been kind.

"But hey, I can deal with this. For the book and all."

The first outfit Jordan pulled off the rack was awful, and I told her so, which made her want it all the more. Einstein growled at me.

"Okay, I won't say another word."

But Einstein did.

When Jordan pulled out a three-hundred-dollar pair of ripped cargo pants, the dog growled at *her.*

"Yeah," Jordan said, "buying a more expensive version of what I already have doesn't make sense."

He barked his approval.

Neither Jordan nor I seemed to think it strange that Einstein was giving fashion advice.

A pair of army green leggings?

Growl.

Some sort of sacklike minidress?

A woofing scoff.

An orange fedora and green blazer?

He rolled over and played dead.

"Then you pick something out!" Jordan practically barked at the dog.

Einstein seemed to consider, then trotted through the different designers' sections, settling on items from several departments. He led Jordan and me with barking commands, guiding us to pull out each of the pieces. Then he literally herded my sister back into the dressing room.

"Get out while I change," I heard her snap.

He reappeared with what I can only call a swagger.

"Yes, you're the man," I told him.

Strolling over to a black leather seating area he looked ready to jump up on the cushions.

"Hey," the salesperson said. "Don't even think about it."

Einstein seemed to debate. But she was big, outweighing him by a good two hundred pounds, and didn't look like she ascribed to animal rights. He shrugged and lowered himself onto the white shag rug instead.

The woman harrumphed and went back to working the register.

It didn't take long before Jordan emerged in the first outfit. It was a silky dress that clung to her body in all the wrong places.

Einstein lifted his head and bared his teeth.

Next she appeared in a red-and-black knee-length wrap dress that didn't do her any favors.

Einstein lowered his head to his paws and groaned.

Jordan came out in a parade of clothing. Theory, Juicy Couture, but it was a dress by someone I had never heard of that made me gasp and sent Einstein leaping to his feet, barking his approval. I was smart enough to keep my mouth closed and my approval to myself.

"What do you think?" I asked.

I had never seen my sister look dreamy, and she actually twirled around in the short dress. The bodice was sleeveless, black, and fitted, a black belt at the waist, with a full flounced skirt of green, black, and white floral ombre print, a tiny bit of black tulle revealed at the bottom, just above the knees.

She looked edgy yet sophisticated, youthful but not too young. And with that smile on her face, excitement lighting her eyes, I realized my sister was very pretty.

"I love it," she said almost shyly.

"Then it's yours."

"But it's so expensive."

I could see the militant side of her doing battle with a never-realized girly side.

"Don't worry about the price." I prayed my credit card wasn't maxed out. "It's just one dress. For a good cause. It's not like you're going to suddenly throw out all your cargo pants and join that bourgeois elite."

"You're right!"

After a quick trip to the shoe department—quick because Einstein picked out the shoes in a few seconds flat and wasn't taking any of Jordan's suggestions—we bypassed the escalator in deference to Einstein's paws and headed for the elevators.

"What are you going to wear, Em?"

Einstein practically skidded to a halt and looked at me.

"I have tons of things."

E scoffed.

"I do."

He ignored me, herding us back to the racks. When he didn't find anything on the second floor, he guided us up a level. There he found a beautifully simple Ralph Lauren dress. I loved it. But . . .

"No way," I said when I looked at the price tag.

Einstein and Jordan ignored me, pulled the dress out and herded me to the tiny dressing room in the Ralph Lauren section.

I pulled it on despite my better judgment. When I came out and looked at myself in the mirror I saw the woman I used to be. More than that, I realized something else. "You have the same exact taste as Sandy," I said to my dog.

Einstein leapt up and barked.

Jordan laughed and I smiled.

"The Barlow sisters are going to be the talk of the publishing world," Jordan said as we walked out the door.

Einstein held his head high with what I could only call a smug sort of pride. When he glanced at me, I couldn't help but smile. "Yes, you really are the man."

■

Jordan and I walked into Michael's just after twelve-thirty the next day. It was all I could do not to squeeze her hand when the room full of power players turned around to look at us.

"Here goes," I whispered.

The hostess was a tall, beautiful woman.

"I'm Emily Barlow from Caldecote Press. I have a reservation for two."

The woman looked us over, glanced down at her reservations, then considered the table options. We were led down to a table visible to just about everyone.

"They're all staring at us," Jordan noted.

"They want to know who we are."

"Creepy."

"Not creepy. This is the launch of your literary career."

A waitress took our order. A Cobb salad for me, which got a raised eyebrow from Jordan. "Dieting?" A hamburger with Gruyère cheese and fries for her. "Not dieting?" I countered.

"Life's too short," she added.

"That's probably true."

We hadn't taken more than a few bites of our meal when Hedda Vendome appeared at the entrance like a 1920s film diva stepping onto a silent stage. She wore a black suit that looked like it cost more than I made in a month and her signature heavy makeup with penciled-on eyebrows. She surveyed the room as she headed for her table, the assistant I remembered from before hurrying along in her wake.

Hedda nodded here, waved there, then stopped dead in her tracks when she saw me.

"Emily, darling!"

"Hello, Hedda. How are you?"

"I'm terrible, terrible. I just did a round of cosmetic filler, and while I look fabulous, I hurt like hell! But really, *you* look amazing. Tell me what you're doing. Dieting? Lipo? Purging?"

Jordan looked aghast. "She's running."

Hedda glanced over at my sister. "Running, bah. I say purge. It's easier on the body. You can imagine what running does to one's knees. I should know. I watch that quivering, sweating mass of humanity scurrying up First Avenue every year during that horrid New York City Marathon. You've never seen so many knee braces on gasping people too old to be wearing short shorts and tank tops. Promise me, Emily, that you are not going to turn into one of those obsessives!"

I could only smile at Hedda. "I'm hardly in shape to run any distance, much less a marathon."

Jordan considered me. "I have a friend who ran it after only three months of training. When's the race?"

"I haven't a clue, but forget it. I am not running a marathon."

I had read about Sandy's dream of running the New York City Marathon, how he started to train, running through the park, the power it made him feel. Even more than when he had started writing about other women, the writing about his running had brought him to life.

Was it possible to be more jealous of a race than the women?

Hedda's assistant paused in her typing on the BlackBerry. "You should totally do the marathon. You can't live in New York, run, and *not* do it!"

"Don't listen to her," Hedda interjected. She put her hand up to her mouth as if to tell a secret, though her voice was loud enough for just about everyone to hear. "She's a vegan." The older woman shuddered, then looked at her assistant. "What is that again?" Before the girl could answer, Hedda waved the question away.

The assistant rolled her eyes and added, "The marathon's the first Sunday in November. I'm sure you can get in using some corporate connection, and really, all you have to do is finish. Heck, Hedda could probably get you in."

Hedda scoffed at her assistant. "Go back to doing whatever it is you do on that contraption." She refocused on my sister. "So enough about you, Emily. Who is this vision sitting next to you?" She glanced between the two of us. "Don't tell me this is that squalling second child your mother gave birth to?"

My sister looked shell-shocked.

"Hedda, this is my sister, Jordan. Caldecote is publishing her book next spring."

If Tatiana wanted word out that we were publishing a book about my mother, Hedda would be a better vehicle than a full-page ad in *USA Today.*

"You are?" Hedda arched one of her penciled-on brows. "What kind of book?"

"A memoir," I said. "It's called *My Mother's Daughter.*"

She glanced from me to Jordan, then back, putting two and two together. "A book about the mother, written by one daughter, edited by the other." Her eyes narrowed in assessment. "Brilliant. As soon as you have an advance copy, I want to see it. Though remember, just because you're making even more headway in adult publishing doesn't mean that you aren't still meant to be in the children's world."

I smiled and shook my head at her.

Hedda blew air kisses my way, told Jordan it was divine to meet her, then continued on to her table.

"My burger is cold," Jordan complained.

I was too busy watching my mother's old friend stop at this table, then that. Was she spreading the news about the project?

My excitement was still there, but I was also nervous. Could I really make this work?

Sure enough, before lunch was over, more than half a dozen people stopped at our table to introduce themselves and ask about the book. Afterward, I sent Jordan home in a cab. Back at the office, I ran into Birdie outside the elevator.

"It's already all over the Internet! Lunch at Michael's. New talent.

You've got to love bloggers! At least when they're being nice." Birdie shivered with pleasure. "This is so exciting, Emily. A big book. A big push. This is going to make you famous!"

I shouldn't have gotten caught up in her excitement. There was so much work to do before the book ever saw the light of day. Nonetheless, I floated to my office and got to work in a way I hadn't in months. Without realizing what I was doing, I sorted through old e-mail, even older regular mail, and started getting a mental picture of all I had to do. When I sat back and noticed that I had written up a list without even realizing it, I couldn't help but smile. I was doing my job. It felt great. I felt great.

That evening, I surprised even myself when I tied the laces on my running shoes and headed up the bridle path without a nudge from Einstein. A sense of hope I hardly remembered pushed me on as I made it to the Seventy-seventh Street tunnel, then started up the rise to the maintenance facility. When I saw the Marionette Cottage I knew that while I hadn't run that far in the scheme of things, it was farther than I had gone before, and my excitement grew.

Hedda's assistant's words echoed in my ears, as did Jordan's story about her friend who had only trained for three months.

When I headed back to the apartment I thought maybe, just maybe, I could run the New York City Marathon.

einstein

chapter twenty-eight

After the infamous lunch at Michael's, my wife was over the moon. My sister-in-law was not nearly as excited. Not that my wife realized this. I had begun to think Emily, for all her empathy and intelligence, was somewhat blind to Jordan. She seemed to see a version of a sister she was either afraid she had or a sister she needed.

Insight from me, Alexander "Sandy" Portman.

I hung my head, and why not? Insight is overrated. Living a life of oblivion and self-centered satisfaction is far easier. But I was fast learning that as Einstein I wasn't *trying* to be insightful, I just was.

It had started out slowly without me realizing what it was, until bam, the realization that I was being suffused with deeper meaning hit me like a two-by-four to the face. I could no more turn off the trying ability than I could shed my white wiry fur on demand. Worse still, I might have come to accept my new circumstances, and I might even have looked forward to learning where all my "helping" would lead, but truth to tell, I was having a hard time staying enthused about all the work that I had to do in order to achieve this greatness. Simply put, "helping" took a lot out of me. There was all that thinking and planning, not to mention the doing. But the other option—fading away to nothing—wasn't appealing.

In the evenings after work, Emily would waltz in, give me a kiss on my muzzle, then head back to check on Jordan.

"Hey, Jordie, how's the book going?"

"Great!"

A blatant lie. I knew for a fact that no book was getting typed into a computer or written on a page. *If* there was a book, it was still in Jordan's head.

"Can I read the new pages?" Emily would ask.

"Ah, not yet. They're still really rough. But soon!"

"Okay. But remember. It has to be done at the end of August."

"Absolutely!"

My wife could be so gullible.

At dinner one evening about a month later, Emily talked incessantly, excitement coloring her voice.

Jordan's demeanor, on the other hand, screamed that she hated the entire situation. Not that she said a word to this effect. She simply oozed unhappiness. She oozed stress. I had to wonder if something that had seemed so simple in its inception was now going against everything she thought she believed in. Namely, crass commercialism butting heads with an idealist's hope that one woman's story could make a difference to other women who came after.

At one point, she even sank down on the floor in front of me. "I'm pretty much screwed, huh?"

Had I cared one whit for Jordan Barlow, I would have felt badly for her. But as has been established, I didn't like my sister-in-law, and that night I made no bones about it. I just growled and snapped at her, almost relishing her misery, not caring how Jordan's problems would affect my wife.

Which is when it began to happen in earnest. The fading.

No sooner did I turn my back on Jordan than I felt the strange fading sensation combined with a stomach-roiling dizziness, as if I'd had a bad batch of Chinese food.

Call me stubborn. I wrote it off to the flu. But I got no better and later that night I woke up confused about which I was. A dog? A man? It took a second before I remembered I was Sandy Portman in the body of Einstein the Dog.

Squeezing my eyes shut, I thought the word *Emily,* but couldn't pull up an image to match the name. When I finally managed to put it together, panic made it hard to breathe. I panted, that drool I had only recently mastered starting up again.

I was fading, I realized, to nothing, just as the old man had warned me, one memory at a time.

Old man! I wailed.

Not that he answered. Not that I thought he would. Had he popped in, I would have told him in no uncertain terms that adding Jordan to my list of concerns was beyond the call of duty, not to mention hardly worthwhile.

But even having the derogatory thought made my stomach give another shuddering heave. Jordan was Emily's sister; they were connected. I couldn't let the sister fall apart for fear of what it would do to my wife.

More insight.

I muttered something decidedly profane, then resigned myself to the reality that I had to set my thoughts to Jordan. I couldn't let myself become nothing.

The minute I made the decision to deal with the sister two things happened. First, I felt better—my thoughts cleared, my memories came back, my body felt more solid. Second, my finely tuned ears picked up a noise in the foyer.

It was the middle of the night, I'd had a rough day, and all I wanted was to sleep. I'd deal with the sister-in-law in the morning. But I was quickly learning that whoever was in charge didn't particularly care how I felt. That strange dizziness returned and made my stomach do a decidedly unpleasant dance. I glowered into the dark, then pushed up from my bed with more inventive profanity and headed toward the gallery.

No surprise when I found Jordan sneaking out of the apartment. I swallowed back the, *Be gone, scourge and pestilence, good riddance.*

For half a second I thought I must have spoken the words out loud because no sooner did I tiptoe into the gallery than she whirled around.

"Go back to bed, Einstein."

Oh, how I wish I could.

With no help for it, I walked over and stood between her and the front door. A similar tack had worked with my wife and baking.

"Move," she said.

I mustered up a halfhearted growl in response. I even managed to show some teeth.

Jordan rolled her eyes and tried to sidestep me.

Fortunately I was too fast for her. When she went right I was there. To the left, ditto. Back and forth we went, like silent dance partners in my hundred-and-twenty-year-old apartment. Only it wasn't the 1800s. It was the twenty-first century and as I thought about my sister-in-law's actions since she arrived, I had to wonder what exactly was wrong with her.

I thought about the string of one-night stands, the fight that she and Emily had over the book—the book that Jordan wasn't writing. I even thought of the story about her breakup with that Serge fellow.

While I hadn't a clue what to do about any of this, I did understand that if I didn't want to fade, I had to do my part to keep Jordan from yet another nocturnal coupling, something she was doing in a misguided attempt to . . . what?

Truthfully, even as Einstein, I wasn't smart enough to figure this one out. Why would Jordan sleep around so determinedly without seeming to enjoy it? Why was she drinking so much? Why was she hugging Emily one day, then furious at her the next?

I was so busy thinking this through that she took me by surprise, springing for the door. I had to sink my teeth into her pant's hem to keep her in place.

The commotion made her freeze.

"Stop," she hissed, shaking her leg. "Let go."

I clamped on tighter, gave a good shake of my own, and added some heartfelt growling.

"Freakin' A, E, shut up," she hissed. "You're going to wake Emily."

I did let go this time, but only because she stopping trying to escape. I could feel her trying to regain her calm. After a second, her face softened and she smiled a big fake smile at me.

"Good boy, Einstein."

Like she was one of those clueless human dog owners straight out of an episode of *The Dog Whisperer.*

Her smile remained, but her energy shifted. As the saying goes, trick me once, shame on you, trick me twice . . . well, shame on you again.

I was ready for her when she lunged. I blocked her escape, and bared my teeth. The threat did quite the job to herd her out of the gallery and down the hall. Not that this calmed her. Her frustration grew, seeming to take up the space around her until it surrounded me too.

Once corralled inside her bedroom, she started kicking the pillows and discarded clothes that littered the floor, jabbing the air as she hissed the sort of profanity one might hear in a barroom brawl. Who exactly she was fighting in that imaginary world of hers I couldn't say, but her lip quivered, veins on her temples pulsing. Had she been seventy-five and male, I might have worried. Neither as man nor beast could I have performed CPR.

Not to put too fine a point on it, while I was trying to act cool about the ordeal, the effort was exhausting, and I barely held back a shudder of relief when I felt Jordan's frustration turn to something else. Anguish, I realized.

While this new emotion was taking its toll on her, it was far less taxing on me. She made one last halfhearted kick at a pillow, got her legs snarled up in a heap of jeans and shirts, then staggered trying to right herself and tumbled to the floor.

Thank God.

Though no sooner did she land than she started fighting to untangle herself, her impatience only making it worse.

When I determined it would be a while before she was untangled, I flopped down in front of the bedroom door with a relieved sigh.

She looked over at me and glared. "Jerk."

Excuse me? What did I do?

"You don't know what it's like," she hissed. "I am trying! I am trying to get it right!"

I lay perched on my stomach, muzzle on my paws, watching her. I was no fool. If she managed to get unsnarled and made a run for it I needed to be ready. I would lie there the rest of the night if that was what it took to ensure I didn't fade away. But surely no one expected me to listen to her.

I might have yawned.

Jordan whipped her head back around. "You're just like him. Just like that dickhead Sandy. And let me tell you, he was a major jerk, especially to my sister."

Great. More about how horrible Sandy was.

She arched her back and punched one of the decorative pillows that lay scattered beside her on the floor. "But Emily loved him anyway! I don't get it. She wasn't worried about being hurt. She wasn't worried that he'd screw her."

She grabbed the pillow and hugged it to her face, screaming into it. *A little more pressure,* I wanted to instruct her, *and you just might manage to suffocate yourself.*

Instantly, my head spun like I had thrown back a double shot of poor-grade whiskey.

Great, just great. With a weary sigh, I crawled forward and tugged the pillow away from her. Sure enough, my head cleared.

However when I revealed her face I caught a glimmer of tears. Never in my life had I felt such a physical need to flee. I could take the anger. I could take the frustration. I could even take the Sandy bashing. But I wanted out before there was any serious waterworks.

I tried to get up, but for the first time since our odd coupling, I couldn't get Einstein's body to move.

"In the beginning I think Sandy really did care for her in his own way," Jordan continued, dashing at her eyes.

She started fishing around in the mess of the floor, pillows and worn jeans flying. It took a second before I realized she had unearthed a book of photos. Emily's and my wedding album.

Come on, boy, I told myself, *push up off the floor, get the hell out of Dodge. You can do it.*

Silence settled in the room and I had the fleeting hope that Jordan was done talking.

"I hated that the most."

Heavy sigh.

Jordan rolled over on her stomach and opened the thick album cover, turning to the first heavy page. There we were. Me. Emily. I was stunning, of course. But more than that, seeing the photograph made me remember how my breath had caught when Emily stepped into the church. If she was a warrior when I first met her, she was an angel when the church doors opened, golden light coming in behind her.

She had stood by herself, no one to give her away. She had no attendants, no maid of honor, just Emily standing there radiating happiness, so beautiful in a simple but elegant gown. Jordan hadn't come to the wedding, explaining that she was too busy. But I knew Jordan hadn't approved of our marriage. Not that I had cared. But I wondered now if Emily had wished she'd had family of her own that day, a mother and father, or even just her sister to be at her side. Since I had met Emily, she had done so much on her own. I hardly gave it a thought. But I wondered now what that had cost her.

More insight. I heaved a soft mewling cry and tried to cover my head with my paws.

The old-fashioned clock ticked on the bed stand near Jordan's head. My sister-in-law's emotions had run the gamut: anger, frustration, anguish. With each thick page of the wedding album she turned I began to sense an emptying. Thank God.

Quite frankly, I found the whole Jordan-talking-to-me thing a tad unnerving. It was as if at some level she too understood that it was me, and that she wanted me, Sandy Portman, to know what she had to say. Or maybe it was the old man's doing. Maybe he wanted me to hear the girl's ramblings. But hadn't I had enough for one night? Hadn't I kept her from going off with yet another guy to do who knows what? Didn't I deserve a reprieve?

"Can you believe it?" Jordan said softly. "I hated that my sister was happy."

That did it. Through sheer will I got my body up about an inch, only to start trembling before I collapsed back onto the floor.

"But don't you see, if she loved Sandy, and they were crazy happy, then that meant everything Mom had ever said about guys was wrong." She bit her lower lip as she turned another page. "My sister being happy with a man, especially someone like Sandy, undermined everything I grew up believing."

My nose twitched with smug satisfaction at my sister-in-law's acknowledgement that I wasn't all bad.

"But it turns out Mom wasn't wrong. Guys trick you." Jordan slapped the book shut, rolled over on her back, and stared up at the ceiling.

Okay, come on, good fellow, I cajoled. *Out we go.*

"They reel you in with totally fake promises of forever. Then they show their true colors."

My heart started beating hard again at the sudden difference in Jordan's voice. Instinctually I knew I wasn't going to like what was coming. I fought my body more furiously, only managing to roll over on my side.

"A few months before Sandy died, Em heard a rumor."

My little dog's body went still.

"A rumor that he was sleeping around. But since she's Emily, she didn't believe it." Jordan scoffed. "She said that she and Sandy had just hit a rough patch like tons of married people. She said that they weren't spending as much time together, so people were speculating. God, she could be so naïve. I, on the other hand, have never been naïve. The minute she told me I knew it was true. So what did I do?" Her voice was both angry and small. "I gloated. There I was on a cell phone in a Peruvian village with Emily thousands of miles away crying. My big sister crying. I didn't say I felt bad for her. I didn't say I was sure she was right, that Sandy was totally into her and wouldn't do such a thing. I told her that Mom was right and she was wrong to ever have believed in that jerk." Jordan groaned. "Of course she didn't listen. Whatever was wrong, she swore she could fix it. She could fix her marriage. She just needed the chance."

Jordan cried then, silent sobs. My breathing grew shallow. I wanted to cover my ears, but for reasons I couldn't explain I needed to hear the rest.

"I told Emily she was crazy, told her to open her eyes. Good riddance, as far as I was concerned. But she said she believed in him." Jordan pulled in a deep shuddering breath, then let it out slowly. "She believed he was struggling, that he dreamed of being great, like all these famous guys she knew about from some book she edited. But again and again something got in his way."

My breath squeezed in my chest, my pulse banging inside my skull. Emily had understood.

"Pathetic," she whispered. "Everyone knows a jerk is just a jerk, and a jerk doesn't change. Sandy Portman was never going to be great."

Heat flooded my body.

"There Emily was on the phone, so many miles away in New York, her world falling apart, and suddenly she got really quiet."

My sister-in-law rolled to her side and looked directly at me.

"She told me that *I* was going to be great too." She sucked in her breath. "God, it felt good."

I might have blinked. As much as I didn't like Jordan, I understood what I saw in her eyes: the joy of someone believing in you.

"But it only felt good for a second. I mean, really, just before Emily said that to me,

I was over the moon because it turned out she was wrong about Sandy, which proved that Mom was right, that *I* was right." Jordan tucked a strand of hair behind her ear and wiped away her tears. "But, if Emily was *wrong* about Sandy, if her judgment was off . . . didn't that mean she was wrong about me too?" She closed her eyes. "No matter how I looked at it," she said, her voice small, "one way or the other I lost."

I got it then. Jordan had been grasping at men and lashing out at her sister because she no longer knew who was right, who was wrong. She no longer knew what to believe in.

Whether motivated by Einstein or motivated by me, when Jordan drifted off into a fitful sleep I crawled closer to her, my thoughts in turmoil. When she curled toward me I crept even closer, resting my head on her shoulder, not sure who needed comfort more, her or me, because with this new, hated depth in me came the understanding that I had been lost too. But Emily had believed in me and had tried to help me find my way back to myself even up to that last night before I died.

I groaned when the memory of coming home that last night leaped out at me. I had walked into the apartment, distracted, going through the mail, having spent the afternoon in a hotel room in midtown with yet another woman whose name was already forgotten.

I had just opened an envelope, maybe a bill, maybe something else. I don't remember. But I remember that I stopped midstride when I saw the dining room table set with china and silver, candles and flowers, and my wife waiting for me.

Lost in thought, unprepared for the sight, I had no concept of time or place. I only saw Emily, the woman I had fallen for.

"Hello," she said, coming around the table.

When she stood inches from me she hesitated as if unsure. But she shook whatever it was away. "My name is Emily."

As if we could start over.

"Fall in love with me," she whispered, repeating what I had said to her so long ago. "I dare you."

At the words, everything rushed back. The women. My discontent. The impossibility of the situation.

I didn't know how to start over. But what if I could?

"Emily," I said, then nothing else before she wrapped her arms around me.

emily

"Fly, baby girl, fly," *my mother used to tell me.* "Don't let the world hold you down." *Whenever Mom said the words to me, Emily's head would pop up from whatever she was doing. From the expression on her face, I never knew if she was jealous or wistful.*

—EXCERPT FROM *My Mother's Daughter*

chapter twenty-nine

I jerked awake.

I had been dreaming of Sandy, not of the accident this time, but of the night before he died.

"Emily." One word, nothing more.

I felt disconcerted as if he had actually whispered the word in my head.

"It's just a dream," I said out loud.

Clearing my mind, I got up. Remembering that night wouldn't help anything.

I pulled on my running shoes and tiptoed out of the apartment. I hadn't looked in on Einstein, surely fast asleep in the kitchen, or Jordan in her room. It was early enough that I would be back before either of them opened an eye.

The quiet Upper West Side was just coming to life when I hit the park. Runners stretched against the benches that lined the entrance, the sky brightening just enough to make the little plaques embedded in the wooden slats shine. During the last few weeks I had slowly built up my mileage until I was running the bridle path around the reservoir regularly. That morning I planned to venture off the dirt and cinder path and run the upper park road loop that would take me to the top of the park then back to the Dakota, nearly doubling the distance I had been running.

I turned on my iPod and set off down the Seventy-second Street transverse. Shinedown's "Second Chance" played as I passed the Bethesda Fountain with its towering bronze angel. I sloped down to the east park road and turned left to Robbie William's "Millennium." Heading north I felt fine. My footfalls were steady, my breathing easy, and my thoughts drifted. But then the music shifted, and there was that song again, the one I didn't remember adding to my playlist. "Broken" by Lifehouse.

Without realizing it, the dream that woke me resurfaced, the dream of the night before Sandy died. I saw the candlelight dinner I had prepared. I saw Sandy walking into the apartment, going through the mail, then looking up and seeing me.

By then, I had heard the whispers about the other women, but like so many wives I put blinders on under the misguided belief that it couldn't possibly be true. All I needed to do was refocus on my marriage and re-create what we once had.

Sandy didn't look away from me as I went to him. Our gazes held when I leaned into him as I had done a thousand times before. He traced my face, ran his fingers over my lips, then he kissed me, long and deep. I felt his yearning, that intensity I had never quite understood when he held me. But after a long minute, he broke away, taking my hands from behind his neck, and pulling away. Without letting go, he looked at me, his brow furrowed as he exhaled sharply, then stepped back.

"I'm sorry," he said.

He retraced his steps and left the apartment. I didn't hear from him again until he left a message for me the next morning asking to take me to dinner, saying he would pick me up at the clinic. He never got any of my own messages to meet me at home.

How many times since then had I wondered what would have happened had he not gone to that snowy stretch of West Seventy-sixth Street? Had that touch, that kiss stayed with him? Would I have been able to save my marriage? Or would I have been fighting with my husband over the apartment, rather than his mother?

During the long days that I had been unable to accept Sandy's death, I'd been able to keep blinders on to the affairs by convincing myself that he had asked me to dinner so we could start over.

In the face of all evidence to the contrary, why do women try to make things right with husbands who no longer want them? And how was it possible that I, the always practical Emily Barlow, could possibly have been naïve enough to think that I could?

I staggered at the thought, my running shoe catching on the asphalt. I felt hot and cold, angry and sad. When I hit the first incline I was thankful.

When I had to tuck my chin and concentrate on my stride, I almost laughed in relief. I didn't mind that my muscles started to protest, my lungs starting to work.

Before I knew it, the memory and embarrassment of that night were gone and I found myself at the top of the first hill—Cat Hill they called it, for the sleek bronze panther that lined the way. I felt the beginnings of the runner's high I had read about starting to take hold.

I picked up the pace as I passed the Metropolitan Museum of Art, then the reservoir. I felt strong when I came to the 102nd Street transverse. I hit the North Woods at a good clip. The descent down the north side wound like a mountain road in the Rockies, and when I passed the waterfall and swimming pool I didn't think it was possible to be happier.

But no sooner had the thought flitted through my brain than I came around the lowest northern point and realized I had to go back up the other side. A shiver of concern hit me, but I brushed it off. My body felt good, adrenaline still carried me.

As with Cat Hill, I put my head down and started up. The world around me was quiet, the granite hills and cliffs and thick copse of green trees muffling the sounds of the city. I crested the first incline before I realized it. *Not bad,* I told myself. *Just keep putting one foot in front of the other. It can't be that far to the top.*

I came around a curve, hoping I was getting close—and saw that I'd barely started. *Don't freak out. You can do this.*

But when I came around another curve and saw still more hill, my adrenaline deserted me. My muscles burned, my lungs were on fire, and I staggered to a stop, bending over at the waist, trying to catch my breath. For half a second I let it get to me. Then I straightened, walked to the top, and started running down the other side.

I can do it. I just can't do it yet.

I returned to the Dakota exhausted but determined. When I walked into the apartment the smell of coffee hit me. Dripping sweat, I found Jordan sitting at the counter reading the paper, a cup of coffee in front of her, Einstein eating breakfast from his bowl in the corner.

"Hey," Jordan said. "I figured you were running, so I took E out. Then fed him."

There was no animosity in her voice, no sarcasm.

"Thanks; that's great."

I glanced at the clock, thinking that somehow it must be later than I thought for my sister to be awake. But no, it was only six-thirty in the morning.

Einstein looked up at me, gave me that smile of his, before returning to finish off his food.

If my body hadn't been riddled with endorphins, I would have given into suspicion that these two were suddenly getting along. As it was, I squinted at Jordan in concern when she got up and poured me a cup of coffee.

"What?" she said, extending the mug.

"Who are you, and what have you done with my sister?"

I took a shower and returned to find Jordan sitting on the floor with the newspaper spread around her. Einstein sat next to her squinting his eyes, cocking his head as he tried to make out whatever she was reading.

"I thought maybe we could do something today," Jordan said.

Tension flared over the book Jordan was supposed to be writing. As far as I was concerned, she had no business doing anything but sitting in front of the computer and pounding out our mother's story.

The sister in me did battle with the editor. In the end, the decision was made for me.

My BlackBerry buzzed on the counter. REAGER, MAX flashed in the readout.

My feelings must have shown because both Jordan and Einstein gave me a strange look.

"Who is it?"

"A neighbor. A guy who's been helping me with some stuff."

I said the words as casually as I could since the last thing I wanted was for anyone to know that I couldn't stop thinking about Max.

"Aren't you going to answer?" Jordan asked.

I hesitated a second more. "Hello?"

"Come to the Hamptons with me."

"The Hamptons?"

Jordan leaped up. "We're invited to the Hamptons?"

I covered the mouthpiece. "Be quiet. And no, you are not invited to the Hamptons."

"Who's that?" he asked.

"My sister. She's in town. Staying with me."

"I'd like to meet her."

"Ah, well—"

"Get her to come with us. It's just for the day. I have to leave in a few minutes, drive a bunch of stuff out to my sister's place."

"I can't really."

"Emily!" Jordan said.

"Yeah, Emily," Max repeated. "We'll drop off the stuff at Melanie's, then we'll have a picnic on the beach before we drive back."

"All in a day?"

"If we leave in the next thirty minutes, we'll beat the traffic," he said. "And coming back will be a piece of cake because no one will be returning to town this afternoon. Come on, it's Saturday. It'll be fun."

I hesitated, then walked away from my sister and my dog. "What about your girlfriend?"

"Girlfriend?"

"The woman you were with in your apartment." I felt foolish.

I swear I could feel his smile over the airwaves.

"Roni? She's a friend in town looking for an apartment with her boyfriend." I could almost hear him smile widen. "Now will you come with me?"

"But I'd feel bad leaving Einstein alone on a Saturday."

He just laughed. "Then bring him too."

■

Barely half an hour later, Einstein, Jordan, and I climbed into a shiny, four-door black Jeep in the parking garage next to the Dakota. Max shut my door then jogged around to the driver's side.

"Ready?"

He wore cargo shorts, a faded blue T-shirt, flip-flops, and sports sunglasses. His hair, barely dry from the shower, was brushed back. He was gorgeous.

Jordan and Max hit it off from the start. They laughed and talked about music and blogs and an assortment of popular culture things that I had never heard of. Why I didn't feel awkward or jealous, I couldn't say, but I didn't. I was thrilled that the two of them got along.

The only one of us in the car who was standoffish was Einstein. The minute we walked up to Max, E stiffened, his nose in the air sniffing. He swung his head back and forth between Max and me, then shook his head as if to negate whatever it was he had smelled and let Jordan pick him up when she hopped into the backseat of the Jeep.

"This is an embarrassment," Jordan announced two hours later as we turned off the Montauk Highway and headed into the Hamptons. "How did I forget what a bourgeois nightmare this place is?"

Max laughed, putting up his hand to give her a high five. "I tell my sister that all the time."

His sister's house in Southampton was a lovely two-story clapboard and cedar shingle cape on a tree-lined street. It didn't take us any time at all to unload the boxes.

"Melanie's redoing the place and didn't trust anyone else to bring these out." Max pointed to a box and grimaced. "Handblown glass."

Once the glass was packed away, we loaded back up then made our way into the heart of Southampton for a picnic lunch. With food, sodas, and water in tow, we headed down Main to Gin Lane and parked in a sprawling lot that we may or may not have been allowed to park in.

After Jordan and Einstein raced ahead, Max hung back with me. On the long sandy path that led to the ocean, I kicked off my sandals and felt the sand between my toes. Max didn't take my hand, but our arms brushed as we made our way through the low dunes and came out on the beach.

Jordan had run forward, splashing into the tide up to her knees. Einstein followed as far as the waterline, then stopped and stood there, raising his muzzle, sniffing the air, taking in the sun and ocean. In that second, he seemed at home, at peace, as if he had returned to a place that he loved. Which should have seemed ridiculous, but with Einstein strange things no longer seemed so strange.

Like Einstein, I tipped my face up to the sun, feeling as if I could fly.

"It feels good," Max said.

"Yes." Like the sand between my toes. "I can't remember feeling this . . . carefree in a long time. Thank you."

"It's the knight thing. Lancelot's got nothing on me."

When I glanced at him his smile made me laugh, out loud, with a wonderful abandon. "If you're not careful, next you're going to make me giggle."

He slanted me a wry look. "Like a schoolgirl?"

Which made me do just that.

Together we spread out the blanket he had brought, along with the lunch. It was noon and the four of us didn't waste a minute polishing off every last bite we had purchased at the sandwich shop, including the plain grilled chicken we had gotten for Einstein.

When we were done, Max pulled off his shirt. If he had been gorgeous before, he was stunning now.

"Who wants to go in?" He looked at me.

That got my attention. "No thanks."

Jordan laughed. "She's not much for the water. But I'm game."

She pulled off her own shirt. Underneath she had on a bikini. She wasn't the least bit self-conscious about her pudgy stomach or lily white skin. Max kicked off the cargo shorts and revealed very distinct gym shorts.

"Get out," Jordan said. "You're military?"

"Navy."

She debated for a second, then shrugged. "Oh well."

They ran toward the water. Einstein leaped up and raced after them, coming to a screeching halt when a wave rushed up on the beach. Frustrated, he raced back and forth, barking, then stopping, hanging his head as if he couldn't believe what he was doing, only to leap up to race again, snapping at the air.

I put the remnants of lunch away, then stretched out in the sand, closing my eyes and feeling the sun beat down on me. I don't know how much time passed, but I surfaced from my thoughts when I felt water dripping on me.

I came up on my elbows to find Max standing over me, Jordan and Einstein walking down the beach together.

"Where are they going?"

"To scope things out."

"Maybe I should get Einstein."

He chuckled. "He can take care of himself. He's one weird dog."

I opened my mouth to protest.

"But smart," he said, dropping down on his knees in front of me. "It's like he's almost human." He shook his head. "Yep, weird. But even weirder, it's like he's all about being proud and great, or something." He shook his head. "It sounds crazy."

"I know what you mean. When I first got the job at Caldecote I worked on a book about great men. Einstein has a way of making me remember it."

"Who were the great men?"

I thought back. "Da Vinci, Mozart, even Tiger Woods, which surprised me. But what was really amazing was how the author went into these other guys, contemporaries or counterpoints to the great ones."

"Like who?"

"Turns out that Botticelli apprenticed in the same workshop as Leonardo, and a guy named Salieri had a lot more opportunities than Mozart. Even Phil Mickelson, another golfer, came up through the ranks with Tiger. They are all guys who did well, even became famous to some degree. But it's da Vinci, Mozart, and probably Tiger Woods who will go down in history as the great ones. Though I guess it remains to be seen what happens with Tiger now."

Max rolled to the side and sat next to me. "It makes you wonder," he said, "why is it that Botticelli and Salieri aren't the ones who became larger than life? Were they not as good? Did they not want it as much? Or did something get in their way?"

I jerked my head around to look at him. "Exactly!"

I felt the shift in Max as he crossed his arms on his knees. We sat side by side, looking out over the water, at ease. "But what really got me," I said quietly, "was that when anyone thinks of important names in the women's movement, they think of Gloria Steinem or Betty Freidan. After I finished editing that manuscript, it was the first time I asked myself why people didn't think of my mother."

He didn't respond, just looked out. It wasn't until we were back in Manhattan, Jordan and Einstein jumping out and bolting for the curb, that Max stopped me from getting out of the Jeep.

"There are many measures of success," he said. "No question being great at something is one of them. But I've got to believe," he added, slipping his fingers around my neck, pulling me to him, "that surviving is another." Then he kissed me just as he had on the rooftop, though this time it was a kiss that promised so much more.

"Remember that," he said against my mouth.

Too soon he pulled away, then reached across me and popped my door open.

"Thanks for keeping me company today."

■

Ruth's Intention came out the following Tuesday.

Birdie wheeled into my office. "Today's the day! This is so great. I can't wait to see Victoria's face when Nate has to announce that *Ruth* hit the *Times* list!"

For a week, my stomach stayed lodged in my throat. For a week, I checked in with sales every day. For a week, I checked Amazon and BN .com rankings with a regularity that bordered on obsession. But on the following Wednesday, despite everything we had done, it was clear *Ruth's Intention* wasn't selling.

"It's a crime!" Birdie bleated.

Tatiana scowled.

Victoria smirked.

The next week, *Ruth* sold a few copies, but in bursts and spurts in odd corners around the country, not nearly enough to achieve the kind of success Tatiana had counted on. No one was happy, with the exception of Victoria who made all the right noises, but I saw her do the Rocky air pump when she thought no one was looking.

Since our drive out to Long Island, Jordan had been happy. For days I came home to find the table set and dinner ready. When I entered the kitchen Jordan held up wooden spoons filled with exotic fare she had learned to cook in the jungle. Frequently Max joined us. He never touched me in front of my sister or Einstein, but I always knew he was aware of me, and while we talked and laughed I anticipated the moment when he would tug me away from them and run his lips along my skin.

But I could hardly concentrate.

Over dinner one night I finally admitted the mess that had happened with *Ruth's Intention*. Jordan commiserated, then surprised me when she opened up about her own manuscript. She didn't let me read any of her new pages, but I contented myself with the fact that she was telling me what she was doing with the kind of excitement my sister rarely showed.

In the mornings, I rolled out of bed determined to conquer the upper park loop. If I couldn't run it without stopping, how did I ever think I had it in me to run a marathon? But each morning I couldn't make it up to the top of Heartbreak Hill.

On the following Friday I decided that this was my last chance. If I could make it to the top, it was a sign that I could run the marathon.

I felt a shiver of apprehension at the thought. I couldn't help but wonder what would happen to me if *Ruth* failed *and* I wasn't strong enough to achieve my goal of running the marathon?

You are strong, Emily, I told myself. *This is just another challenge that you'll get through.*

The sun was barely a hint when I started out, painting strokes of red and orange into the blue-black sky. I didn't take in the sights; I didn't think about work. I focused and made it up Cat Hill easily.

I kept going, aware of nothing but my footfalls, and before I knew it I hit Heartbreak Hill on the backside of the park. The initial incline wasn't bad and I made it around the first curve ignoring the tightness that started in my legs.

I continued on. But the farther I climbed, the more my muscles strained, and I had the fleeting thought that this wasn't working.

I kept going, my breathing more labored by the second as several runners passed me like they were running on the flat. A girl and guy flew by, talking about some movie they had seen the night before. My feet were barely moving.

"You can fly."

The words surprised me, but I pushed them away as I came around another curve, praying the top was near. But I knew better. There was an even steeper incline between me and the top.

By then, every inch of me cried out to stop. Suddenly it all seemed crazy and I started to rationalize. I told myself it was just a run. Not an Olympic event. No one cared if I ran or walked or staggered over to Central Park West and caught the subway home. No one knew I had any interest in running the marathon. Not even Einstein knew that I hoped to run farther than my daily reservoir jaunt.

But I knew; I would know if I quit.

Head down. Focus. But my muscles wouldn't loosen up and my lungs burned as a man of no less than seventy buzzed past me. A woman, whose legs flailed behind her, cruised by like I stood still. And when every inch of me ached to stop at the same time a mother with a jogging stroller and sleeping child went by, I couldn't do it anymore.

I staggered to a halt halfway up the hill with a curse. I closed my eyes, my fingers pressed to my lids as if I could keep emotion in check.

"Damn it!" I yelled.

"Fly, baby girl, fly!"

The memory hit hard and fast, spurred no doubt by Jordan's book, of my mother on the beach, the same water I had nearly drowned in the night before rushing around her ankles.

I hadn't told my mother what had happened to me in the ocean. When she found me in my room the next morning, I was packing my tiny suitcase. I demanded that she take me home.

"What, you're done here?" she said, half laughing, half put out.

"Yes. I want to go home."

"Why? Give me one good reason why."

I considered what to say. I didn't know any other eight-year-olds who had to present valid arguments for anything they wanted. I had seen more than one kid in my class throw a fit to get their way. I had tried that once, never again.

I opted for a piece of the truth. *"I don't like the water."*

"The water? You?" She shook her head, then smiled. *"Emily Barlow, you might make me want to pull my hair out half the time, but I've never known you to be afraid of anything. Don't tell me you're going to start now?"*

My tiny fists knotted at my sides, my face burning. *"I am brave."*

"Then prove it."

Lillian Barlow raced out of my room barefoot, her nightgown fluttering around her as she hurried down the stairs and flew out onto the beach while the rest of the world was still asleep.

"I am brave," I repeated under my breath, fear battling with something

more complex. But I followed, scampering after her. When I got to the beach, the early morning salt air hitting me in the face, she skipped around me.

"See! My daughter, Emily Barlow," she shouted up to the sky, *"is afraid of nothing!"*

Then she took my hands and twirled me in circles, laughing, dancing, as happy as I had ever seen her, until my feet came off the sand and I flew.

"Fly, baby girl, fly!"

Over the years, there hadn't been much about how I lived that she agreed with. But she had admired the fact that I was brave, that I wasn't a quitter.

And before I realized it, standing halfway up Heartbreak Hill in Central Park, I flung my head back and cried out into the early morning sky, its edges now entirely blue. Then I started to sprint. I didn't jog; I didn't run at a decent pace. I ran hard, pushing my body, making every muscle and tendon scream. When I came to the top, the skyscrapers along Fifty-ninth Street standing faintly in the distance, I looked out, my throat tight, my eyes burning, but this time with joy. I could do this. I could run the marathon.

It was a moment of pure truth that spurred another.

Sandy hadn't kept his promise. Sandy had died. And before that I had tried to win Sandy back, only to have my efforts tossed in my face. Those were the facts, facts that I realized I could live with. And when I started down the other side, headed for home, I knew exactly what I was going to do.

As soon as I got to Caldecote, I went straight to Mercy Gray's office. Without knocking, without saying hello, I said, "Something isn't right. *Ruth* shouldn't be failing."

She beat her pen on the blotter and considered me before she tossed it aside and picked up the phone. Over the course of the day, she called sales reps, who called accounts, who called bookstores. She didn't have any answers for me, but when we got the numbers the following week *Ruth* had started to sell.

In one of Tatiana's meetings, the tension around her mouth had eased. "But we're not out of the woods yet," she said.

The following week the numbers exploded. When I saw Tatiana in the hall, our eyes met, though neither of us spoke because each of us knew what the other was waiting for.

At the end of the day on Wednesday, I walked into Tatiana's office when I knew the *New York Times* list was being released. Mercy came in behind me. Tatiana didn't have to ask why we were there. We had formed a team of sorts, each of us wanting to be together when we heard the news.

Tatiana looked at us. "It didn't make it."

I gasped.

Mercy shook her head. "The *Times* list is a strange beast, part actual numbers, part voodoo. Who really knows? Let's hope *Ruth's Intention* hits enough of the other lists so that the *New York Times* has to take notice."

Sure enough, *Ruth* showed up on every major list in the country. All except the brass ring of lists.

I tuned out Tatiana's frustration. I ignored Victoria's renewed relief. I sent e-mails to the *Times* Book Review. When I wasn't trying to figure out what more I could do, or swallowing back an aching disappointment, I threw myself into rebuilding my list. I set up lunch dates with agents. I read every proposal I could get my hands on. Then on Wednesday of the following week at the end of the day, Tatiana walked into my office.

"Number seven."

"What?"

"Ruth's Intention just hit the *New York Times* Best Sellers list at number seven."

I stared at her in shock, which quickly shifted to pure unadulterated elation. Just when I stood, to hug her or dance her around the room or who knows what, Birdie raced in. "Oh, my God! Congratulations!"

Tatiana looked at me over Birdie's head. In the months Tatiana had been at Caldecote, I had never seen her smile. Today she gave me her usual crisp, no-nonsense nod. But when she turned to leave my office, I saw her pull a deep, relieved breath and I'm almost certain she smiled.

I didn't know why the book started to sell, how it bucked the normal trend with increasing rather than decreasing weekly sales. Had the boxes of books been sitting unopened in bookstore stock rooms? Had something gone wrong in shipping? Had it been shelved in the wrong sections of stores? No one had answers, at least none that they were willing to share.

All I knew was that a book that deserved to sell had. And I had made it to the top of Heartbreak Hill.

When everyone left my office, I closed the door and raised my arms in my own Rocky air pump. Max had been right. I could survive and I had.

Emily Barlow was back.

einstein

chapter thirty

Let's have a party!"

My wife wanted to have a party?

If I didn't know better, I would swear my wife was getting over me. Which was impossible. Right?

I growled at myself. Of course it was impossible. I was not one to experience doubt.

Truth to tell, I blamed my shaky feelings on that Max fellow. Had I still been a man I might not have liked that he was young, handsome if you went for that type, and clearly capable of achieving any sort of physical quest that he wanted, but I could have fallen back on my own good looks, massive amounts of money, and fine old name. As a dog, well, I had nothing on the lad. Which didn't sit well with me.

Thankfully, he was a young one and seemed a decent match for Jordan. Had he been Emily's age, I might have been concerned. But if I knew anything about my wife, it was that she wasn't the type to fall for a younger man. She was too sensible for that.

As to the party, I had always intended to entertain. Fresh out of college I held a few impromptu gatherings, more a result of late-night drinking and ending up at my apartment than planned affairs. Then I got busy at the firm, got busy training for the marathon, got married.

And then, well, I got dead.

It was the first week of August and the plan was to have a back-to-work party after Labor Day.

"It's perfect," Emily told Jordan and me. "Everyone will be back from summering here and there, and Jordan, your book will be done! It will be both a welcome back and celebration party."

I didn't really care what the reason for the party was. A party was a party. As to Jordan, I saw what I felt certain was genuine excitement on her face. I had the feeling that she had begun to think about morphing into some kind of literary star.

For half a second, Emily mumbled something about doing the cooking herself. "But who has time?" she said, looking at me. "Besides," she snorted, "all I've done recently is bake."

So she hired a caterer to take care of the food, though it turned out the woman who showed up wasn't an actual caterer.

"Thank you for letting me do this!" a woman named Birdie said.

"If your first love is cooking, why are you working at Caldecote?"

She wrinkled her pert little nose. "After I moved here it was the only company that would hire me. Though, truth to tell, I only got the job at Caldecote because of my sister."

"Why don't I know any of this?"

Birdie smiled and patted Emily's cheek. "Maybe at heart I'm not so different from you with secrets to keep, and looking for a way to start over."

The woman was cute if you went for the perky Texas type, her accent thick as bourbon laced with honey. I'd never been one for perky, but then she kneeled in front of me and exclaimed, "Look at you! Sweet as sweet can be, I just love you!"

What could I do? I wasn't one to argue with good taste, so I decided to adore her.

I sat next to Emily on the library sofa.

"How about stuffed mushrooms?" Birdie suggested.

Growl.

Emily looked at me. "Too done?"

Bark!

"You're right," Birdie said, like she had no more trouble taking advice from a dog than my wife had.

I sat back and half listened, half participated. I felt relaxed. Had I not been worried about the final destination of my soul, I realized I could have lived quite the contented life basking in the sun and indulging in Steakin's at my Dakota apartment while I waited for the grand prize of greatness that awaited me when I finished helping my wife.

Which reminded me of the apartment. My mother and even my lawyer had gone strangely silent. Just like Emily, I had come to hope that Mother was throwing in the towel. But I knew Althea Portman. She had never in her life rolled over in a fight. Which meant she was doing something to regain the apartment. We just didn't know what it was.

As has been established, I never knew how much my wife made in salary. It had had no bearing on me when I was a man. She had never once asked me for money, so I assumed she made plenty. When something needed to be done to the apartment, we split the bills, though she did the work. When she wanted to redo something, we split that too. In hindsight, I realized that as an associate editor, or even as an editor and now a senior editor, she couldn't have come close to making the kind of money I earned on Wall Street. Yet she had never complained when I asked her to pay for her share of some new addition. That sound system which I loved, for example.

Out of habit I scoffed at the thought that I should have done anything differently regarding our bills. Water under the bridge, and all that. Besides, hadn't I paid the maintenance and taxes on the apartment? And wasn't she the one who had insisted that she contribute to everything else—those equal rights, and all? What was I supposed to do, turn her money away?

The stab of nausea brought me up short. I tripped over the carpet in my study, stumbling, hitting the floor with a woof. I laid there for a second, my heart skittering. I wanted to chalk the nausea up to yet another impending case of flu, but by then I knew better. I was fading again, but this time the sensation was even stronger.

Was it possible that the old man had decided I was hopeless after all? After all this, was he giving up on me? For no good reason!

My stomach heaved.

Terror raced through me as I realized that the essence of Sandy Portman was . . . what? Being pulled out of Einstein's body?

The nausea grew. I felt a sucking burn along with a sickening light-headedness, as if I had cut myself and blood was rushing away from my heart to the wound.

Okay, okay, there was a reason for this. I needed to keep going deeper into this awful insight to figure out what had precipitated this new round of fading.

My mother not forgetting the apartment? Could that have caused this?

The party? Me wondering where Emily was getting the money for it?

The sound system?

My hackles rose as something like a shock ran along my nerve endings. Good God, I was fading over a bloody sound system?

For half a second I was incensed, and with that my vision went blurry. All I could "see" were the thoughts in my head, memories, and suddenly I saw myself standing next to Emily at the high-end electronics store, as excited as a child over a sound system that would rival a small theater's.

"We'll take it," I told the clerk without asking Emily, who was busy typing away on her BlackBerry.

My wife never stopped working. She edited manuscripts at home like an artist in a studio, lost to everything but the work. She had just been promoted for the first time and as soon as we were done at the store we were going to celebrate. Everyone I met who knew her said she was great at what she did.

When the cashier asked how I was going to pay, I said by credit card. A heartbeat passed, then I added, *"And my wife is paying half."*

The cashier, a smart-aleck girl, no doubt from Brooklyn, smirked. I ignored her. *"Emily."*

"What?" she said when I asked for her credit card.

"Oh, what for?"

"The sound system, silly."

Her head snapped up, her thumbs poised over the maddeningly small BlackBerry keyboard as she glanced from me to the cashier to the clerk who had already retrieved the boxes for us to take home in a cab.

"Oh," then *"oh,"* again.

I got the credit card statement the next month, surprised at the total for just half. I had paid no mind to the amount when I was buying the system. But at the time, I gave no thought to Emily receiving her own bill.

Pain stabbed into my blurry vision.

"Okay! Okay!" I yelped.

Perhaps I gave it a little thought.

The pain didn't abate.

I concentrated, fought with something deep inside me, fought that place where I hated to be wrong, hated to admit that I wasn't perfect, and it was as I moved even deeper that the answer came. I had wanted to hurt Emily. I had wanted to punish her for being good at her job and succeeding while I struggled to be more than someone who ripped up companies and destroyed people's lives. Just as deep down I had suspected, but refused to admit, that during that earlier Christmas I had wanted proof that how Emily lived her life with decorated fir trees and eggnog wasn't somehow better than the way I lived mine.

The fading stopped completely then, but left me weak on my fine Persian rug. Anxiety mixed with exhaustion. After Emily went to sleep, I crept into her room and curled up in the corner. I needed to be close to her. In the morning, I woke before she did and returned to the kitchen.

For the next few nights it was much the same. I snuck into Emily's room, and with each night that passed I needed to be there, close to my wife, even more. If worry about my fate seeped in and I couldn't go back to sleep, I quietly pawed and nosed one of her children's books off the shelves, doing my best to make out the illustrations. My favorite was *Eloise.* I already knew the story and didn't have to go through the laborious process of trying to make out the words.

One night Emily woke, finding me engrossed in one of Eloise's adventures, this time in Paris. Emily didn't look surprised to see me there in the semidark, seemingly reading by the faint light from the bright streets below. She just smiled sleepily and said, "That's one of my favorites too."

She rolled over and went back to sleep. When she woke again that morning I hadn't snuck out. I watched her wake, watched her face soften when she saw me. Stretching, she reached out to me. This time I went to her without a grumble or sigh, and let her scoop me up in bed and pull me close.

She had dazzled me when she took on Victor Harken, intrigued me at her apartment when she made me dinner. When she surprised me with the train at Christmas I had been willing to admit that I cared for her more than I had cared for anyone—but I understood now that it had only been with the capacity of a man who was limited in how much he could allow himself to feel.

Lying beside her now, captive in a dog's body, I knew I had begun to feel something deeper for my wife, something truer, less shallow. I curled closer and found myself praying that somehow, someway, we could stay together forever.

■

We were both surprised the next morning when she and I woke at the same moment, our heads so close together.

"Oh!" she squeaked.

"Uhff!" I barked.

Then she laughed and I inched even closer.

It was the day of the party and we were both excited.

Jordan's book was due and I expected her to be excited as well. But as Emily flew around taking care of last minute details, Jordan was irritable and agitated.

"Jordan, are you ready yet?" Emily called out as she came out of her own room.

I was floored by the sight of her.

My wife wore her hair long and flowing down her back. She had chosen a caramel-colored dress, sleeveless, hitting just above the knee, pearls around her neck, and a sleek bone shoe with three-inch, exceedingly narrow heels. I was astonished to note that her little jaunts around the reservoir had paid off in more ways than better mental health. Perhaps I shouldn't have stopped going with her on the runs. Emily's arms and calves were sleek and defined. It surprised me that such short runs could bring about such muscle definition.

I should have known then that something was off. But all I knew was that once again my wife was the fearless woman who blew into everything like she was immortal. I might have felt a twinge of jealousy, but I quickly pushed it away and beamed with pride. More progress!

And then there was me. She dressed me in a little tuxedo jacket—I kid you not. Oddly, I couldn't muster up an ounce of indignation. I felt a twinge of embarrassment, but that was it.

"You look so handsome!" she enthused.

After one look in the mirror I couldn't deny that she was right.

The apartment looked festive with candles lit, the early September sun going down in the west, turning the buildings on the opposite side of the park a sparkling red, the treetops between Fifth Avenue and Central Park West like green velvet.

It was in the minutes before the first guest arrived that we caught Jordan sneaking through the crush of waitstaff in the kitchen on her way to the service elevator.

"Jordan?" Emily said. "Why haven't you changed?"

"Ah, oh, ah . . ."

"Jordan? People should arrive any minute. You know half of them are here to see you. Celebrating your book, remember!"

Jordan cringed, then found her more familiar militant stance. "That's ridiculous. I am not going to be paraded around like a circus animal."

I felt Emily's energy take a nosedive.

"Jordan, is something wrong with the book? We agreed this morning that you would turn it over to me first thing tomorrow. Are you nervous? Is that why you're acting like this?"

"I'm not acting like anything."

Emily gave her a look.

"Okay, so maybe I'm being a little huffy, but I need to get out. I need to clear my head. Writing is hard as hell."

"But the book is ready, right?"

The sisters stood there amid the chaos of the chef and waiters scrabbling. But before Jordan could answer, the buzzer rang. The first guest had arrived.

emily

I became my mother's favorite on purpose. Emily certainly had cornered the market on frustrating Lillian Barlow. But looking back I've begun to wonder why a perfect daughter frustrated a mother while a troublesome one made her smile.

—EXCERPT FROM *My Mother's Daughter*

chapter thirty-one

From the look on my sister's face I knew something was very wrong.

"Jordan, what is going on?"

The buzzer rang again, but I ignored it.

Jordan threw up her hands. "The book isn't done, okay?"

Dots swam in front of my eyes. "But it's *due*. You said you'd turn it in tomorrow. The wheels are in motion. It's got to be done."

"I know that," Jordan snapped, before visibly calming herself. "Yeah, yeah, I know. That's why I can't do the party thing. I have to get out, get some fresh air, and get back to work. It's almost done. Really. Maybe I need until Monday."

This wouldn't be the first time an author was late with a book, but the tight publishing schedule for *My Mother's Daughter* didn't allow for delays. I still had to edit the book before we could send it out for advance quotes and long-lead magazine coverage. But what were my options?

"If you don't attend the party and you work tomorrow, work all weekend, you'll have it done on Monday?"

"Oh, yes! Yes! Monday!"

"Jordan?"

"Emily, stop pressing me! I'll get it done. You're always this way. Breathing down my neck."

I held back a cutting retort. Ever since I had bought her book Jordan had been different, better, cooking dinner, sharing the progress on her writing. She'd even been getting along with Einstein.

"You're sure everything's all right, that you'll turn in the manuscript on Monday?"

"Emily, trust me. It's all good. I'm going out to get a quick bite to eat, then I'll slip back into my room with no one the wiser, and work like crazy."

I watched her sling her tattered backpack over one shoulder and disappear out the back door. I wanted to obsess, to fix this. But the buzzer rang yet again and I knew that whatever concern I felt would have to wait until later.

■

Once the first guest arrived, the concierge had a list of everyone else attending and simply sent them up. All told, of the sixty invitations I sent out, fifty-five had RSVPed yes, many of them couples. There would easily be a hundred people in the apartment before the night was over. I had also invited Max, with his strong yet kind smiles and his touch that was growing more heated.

The young editors from work arrived first and together, each of the women dressed in short skirts and high heels. Birdie was busy with the food, in control like a general on the battlefield. Coworkers from production and publicity arrived, along with several people from sales. I had invited friends I knew from other publishing houses, including Hedda Vendome, agents I had gotten to know, and even people from industry periodicals.

The only person who gave me pause was Victoria. The minute she walked into my home with Nate, I saw the change in her eyes, the shift from superiority to awe, then awe to jealousy. If she needed any more ammunition to hate me, she'd just found it. My peers were dumfounded by the apartment, though other than Birdie, none of them knew about the precariousness of my ownership.

"It's beautiful, Emily."

"You can feel the history."

"It's so *Time and Again,*" someone said, referring to the Jack Finney novel about a modern man traveling back in time to the 1880s in the Dakota.

"Quite frankly," Victoria retorted, "I think it's more that other story set here, the horror one, *Rosemary's Baby.*"

I walked away.

The food was perfect, Birdie blushing over the compliments, the guests mostly wonderful. Hedda arrived with a flourish, along with a surprising number of the New York literary glitterati. I found myself mingling with an ease I thought I had forgotten, completely putting out of my mind the fact that Jordan had slipped out the back door. I talked and laughed, told stories and listened while the night circled around me.

A lull came when I moved between a small group of bloggers and a smaller circle from the Caldecote art department. Relishing the night, I retrieved a glass of wine and went in search of a quiet corner. With every inch of the place teeming with people, I headed back to my bedroom. Earlier I had shut the door, so I was surprised to find it ajar.

Inside, Hedda stood in front of my collection of children's books. In one hand she cupped a snifter of brandy, an unlit cigarette caught between her fingers. She looked like a glamorous movie star from the forties.

"Hedda?"

She turned without a trace of guilt. "Caught me." She held up the crystal glass and cigarette. "It's a party. I ask, how can I not have a glass of something?" Her deep laugh filled the room. "And how can I have a drink without a cigarette—even if all I do is hold it?"

"You can drink all you want," I told her. "I'm not your doctor."

"Thank God you're not. My doctor is half my age and to-die-for good looking. Oh, if I could turn back the clock a few decades . . ."

The words trailed off and she returned to my books. She didn't say anything else, but just before I would have left her she caught me off guard.

"When are you going to accept that you are meant to be in children's publishing?"

I shook my head and groaned. "Hedda—"

"I know they are completely different worlds. But look at this." She swept her hand toward the collection. "Every important children's book since the beginning of time. It makes no sense to me that you wouldn't work in my world instead of, say . . . Tatiana's."

"Don't start. It's a party."

She ignored me, studying the shelves. When she finally spoke again there was a casualness to her tone that was at odds with the intensity of her expression. "Did you know that part of the reason *I* became a children's book editor was because of this very collection?"

"What?"

"Ah, how your mother loved her parties." She shot a wry glance over her shoulder. "Not so unlike this one, I might add, only hers were smaller, with people who rejected the idea of being politically correct. They spoke their minds, debated difficult ideas. Lord, those were heady days."

She spoke more softly than I would have believed Hedda Vendome, publishing legend, possibly could.

"Your mother and I came from a time when people believed in changing the world, one march, one commune, one move back to nature at a time. But even back then, still naïve in my own way, I wondered if it was really possible to achieve what we said. Later, after I grew more jaded, after you were born and your mother refused to let go of those earlier beliefs, I would arrive at her parties, wherever she was living at the time, get bored, wander around. And always, in each apartment, one thing remained the same. Your books.

"I watched you grow up, Emily, saw what these stories meant to you . . . and I'm convinced they saved you from the madness that was your mother's life." She turned back to me, drink and unlit cigarette forgotten. "Call me clichéd or melodramatic, or any other adjective I would slash out of a manuscript, but I realized by watching you grow up that books could make a difference. More specifically, children's books could change the world."

Hedda smiled wryly. "If you tell anyone I said that, I'll deny it." Then she sighed. "But truthfully, for all my showy ways, what I still truly believe in is the power of a good story. And I'm certain you believe the same thing. You can make a difference, Emily, a real difference, alongside me at Vendome Children's Books."

I grimaced at her words. But then she placed her free hand on my forearm, surprising me even more.

"You know," she said, "it always seemed odd that your mother didn't see the same little girl I did. She saw stubborn and immovable. I saw a little girl who was caring and loving, a little girl who desperately wanted her mother to notice her." She squeezed my arm. "But sometimes we are blind to the qualities in others that we're afraid we don't possess. You had a strength even back then that your mother never had."

This time I stared at the books, unable to look at her. My throat was tight, my eyes burned. I didn't know what to make of Hedda's claim. But there was something inside me that had always wondered how strong my mother really was.

"I'm sorry if that tarnishes your view of her," she said.

"No," I managed. I hesitated then looked at her, finally willing to face the question I hadn't wanted to ask, despite how long it had been in the back of my mind. "What I don't understand is why she gave up her position in the women's movement. It defined her. It defined our life. If she was such a force, why did she leave the organization she founded?"

"Don't look at me for answers, love. I was stunned when she announced she was hanging up her marching shoes. But Lillian swore she was determined to stay home with her girls." Hedda was quiet for a moment. "Though did you know that after Jordan graduated from high school, your mother went back?"

My brow furrowed in confusion. I remembered my mother's short stint returning to work dressed up in a suit and carrying a briefcase. "You must mean when Jordan was little."

"No, later. You had just been hired at Caldecote, and Jordan had left for South America. Lillian announced it was time to get back in the game. But she didn't go to WomenFirst. Instead she went to Women in Motion. You can imagine they were thrilled to have someone of her stature show up at their door. But the world had moved on. The girls on the front lines were just that. Girls. Raised in a world your mother didn't recognize, one she no longer belonged in." Hedda looked at me with the kind of caring I had always longed for from my mother. "You don't belong in adult publishing, Emily. You belong with me at Vendome. All I ask is that you think about it."

Hedda left me surrounded by my books. I refused to believe that I didn't belong at Caldecote. *Ruth* had worked. And I would make *My Mother's Daughter* work too. I had just gotten my legs back underneath me at Caldecote. I had no intention of giving up on that now.

I don't know how long I stood there, but I was aware of nothing else until I felt someone come up behind me.

"Hey," Max said softly against my ear. "Sorry I'm late."

Without thinking, I leaned back against him. He didn't seem surprised. He wrapped his arms around me and pulled me closer.

"I vote we blow this pop stand," he said.

I smiled. "You just got here."

"I can think of better things to do than play nice with a bunch of strangers."

"Those strangers are my guests."

"They seem pretty content to me."

"You'd make a terrible host."

He turned me around to face him, my head tipping back so that I could look at him as his fingers slipped into my hair, his thumbs lining my jaw. "I want you," he said, before he brushed his lips across mine, that commanding though gentle promise of all the things he could do to me.

The truth was I wanted him too. It was more than wanting to be touched or held. I wanted this guy, no matter what. I still thought of Sandy, and I knew that there would always be at least some pain whenever I thought of him, but it was time to move on.

When Max took my hand and pulled me toward the kitchen, then out the back door, I didn't stop him. I forgot about the guests and followed him up the stairs to his little apartment, letting him undress me. When he laid me on the bed, his palm slowly skimming down the inside of my thigh, I gasped and forgot a little bit more. I forgot for hours, forgot about any and every thing until he arched over me, clinging to me in some primal way. And later, when his heartbeat slowed, he held me close. "I love you," he said. "Please don't slip away."

I held on tight and promised him I wouldn't.

einstein

chapter thirty-two

My wife was nowhere to be found.

Strange. But with the party in full swing, the place packed, it was hard for me to see anyone clearly.

My inclination as Sandy Portman was to search out a martini, extra dry, straight up, with olives. As Einstein the Dog, I opted for a place near the dining room table and the spread of food I knew wasn't good for me but made me salivate nonetheless. If anyone dropped a goat cheese and caramelized onion tart it was mine, finicky stomach be damned.

I can't say how much time passed, but eventually even the tarts couldn't hold my interest and I started weaving my way through the sea of legs—some decent, some which should have been covered up by pants. And the shoes—high heels, low heels, loafers, lace ups. There was more scuffed footwear than not. In my Sandy days, I had been meticulous about whatever I wore. As Einstein the Dog, I found it hard to care.

That was the thing about this new life. The longer I lived it the more I felt it changing me. No question I had progressed from the old Sandy. There were moments when I felt smug over the knowledge that the old man had underestimated my ability to change. But there were other moments when I felt a vague sense of concern. I couldn't put a name to it, despite my newfound insightfulness. Something was wrong, something beyond my ability to comprehend. While I had made progress, something out there was still a threat.

I needed to find Emily. I knew being close to her would calm me.

I went from gallery to library to master bedroom, working my way through the crush of people. What had started out as an interesting diversion now felt overwhelming. The noise felt deafening, the clatter of heels on hardwood, silver on china, voices of all tones. I even went upstairs to the suite hoping Emily had needed a break as much as I did. But the door was shut, and a quick sniff told me Emily was nowhere in the vicinity.

No question I wanted to be with my wife, and yes she brought me ease. But I couldn't quite let myself think about feeling anything deeper than that. I pushed away the thought that I couldn't afford to care more for her at this point. I was a dog, after all, and while Emily at some level sensed that there was more to Einstein than met the eye, I couldn't imagine that my wife could ever truly see me as anything more than a canine. And even then, if she could, how did that help either of us?

I felt more of that concern, but pushed that away too.

Like the bloodhound I wasn't, I put my nose to the ground and tried to sniff her out. But downstairs in an apartment overflowing with bodies, distinguishing Emily's scent was next to impossible.

I trotted toward the kitchen, thinking she might be in there. Halfway down the hallway, my quest was diverted when I caught sight of that lovely Victoria. Call the woman what you will, but in another life, namely as Sandy, I would have been enamored of her fiery beauty. In this incarnation, or at least in this phase of it, I saw her differently. Through clear eyes? Who knows. But I saw the shallowness of her good looks, the thinness of her smile, so different from my wife, who had depth and warmth beneath her cool beauty.

Yet more progress.

When I saw Victoria and a decidedly dorky man sneaking off toward the back bedrooms, I decided to turn my Sherlock Holmesian skills toward my wife's nemesis. I hurried after them, but when I turned down the hall they were nowhere to be seen, forcing me to go room by room to sniff them out. With my nose to the ground, I tried to catch their scent.

But I forgot about smells when something in Emily's room caught my attention.

I had determined that Victoria and the man weren't inside the room or the bathroom and turned to leave. Then I saw the bank statement from the joint account. Because of my tremendous growth, I commended myself for being concerned about how my wife was doing monetarily. I did the squint and cock thing to make sense of the numbers. It took a while, but finally an amount registered. Even after Emily paid the maintenance there should have been plenty left. But the account was nearly empty, with a large withdrawal made just last week.

At first I was shocked. Then all the goodwill I had felt began to evaporate, replaced by a growing tick of unease. What had she done with my money?

Before I could fully absorb the emotion, or even get my head around where the money could have gone, I noticed something else. A New York City Marathon registration packet.

Memories of another life hit me, a life before Emily, a life that had been taken away. I hardly knew what to think. Like a lion stalking its prey, I crept closer, then nosed through the contents. I sat down hard, my tail catching awkwardly between me and the rug. I had once received my own packet—for all the good it had done me after breaking my leg—so it didn't take much deciphering to figure out what it meant. Emily had managed to get herself into the marathon. *My* marathon.

Fueled by jealousy, the frustration over the money ignited. I felt betrayed. Whatever those emotions and traits were that had allowed me to never actually deed the apartment to Emily when I was a man flared back to life like a spark to dry kindling. Without warning, a mewling cry came from deep inside me, twisting into a mournful howl as it hit my lungs. Somehow everything that had happened hit me all at once. All the hope I felt minutes earlier crashed around me as if it had been nothing more substantial than a dyke made of sand. I had put rose-colored glasses on in my attempt to learn and grow and appease the old man. But sitting there I was confronted with the facts. Emily was living in my home, entertaining as I had hoped to, getting ready to run the race I had coveted. Emily was living the life I had dreamed about, the life that was no longer possible for me.

Anger and defeat, jealousy and something even darker mixed in my belly. I raised my head and bayed, not caring about the crowd. I wailed for a loss I realized now I hadn't completely accepted or even understood. I wailed for all that I would never do. But just as quickly as the despair hit, it was gone, shifting, morphing like a beast let out of a cage, solidifying into fury.

emily

When my mother was young she was known for her extreme views. Soon after I was born she gave up controversy, but with the success of an alcoholic giving up wine, always yearning, forcibly abstaining, good for those around her, bad for a soul that dried up when it found no other joy.

—EXCERPT FROM *My Mother's Daughter*

chapter thirty-three

I woke in the semidark and for half a second I had no idea where I was, or for that matter, how I had come to be asleep.

Then I remembered. Me. Max. Sex. In his little apartment. After we left the guests to fend for themselves.

My chest literally hurt at how irresponsible I had been.

Though when I glanced next to me and found Max lying sprawled on his stomach without so much as a sheet or blanket to cover him, his arm pinning me to the bed, I felt a soft contentment that I had never felt before in my life.

He loved me.

And amazingly, I had no doubts that he did.

As carefully as I could, I slipped out from underneath his arm. With his hair falling forward across his forehead, it took every ounce of willpower I possessed not to brush the strands back and return to his arms. But I was made of more responsible stuff than that, even if I had left my guests in the lurch.

I felt badly for slipping out of Max's bed. But I wasn't ready to face him. I had no idea what this meant, us having sex. Him loving me. I cut the thought off. I really didn't need to think about that. At least not yet. I wanted to be able to start fresh in my life, hopefully with Max, but in order to do that, first I needed to tie up loose strings. The apartment. Jordan's book. Which reminded me of something I couldn't quite shake. Hedda's words about my mother.

Now that I thought about it, if my mother really had wanted to stay home, would she have fought with teachers and dry cleaners like she was fighting for some greater cause, then gone back to work the minute after

Jordan moved out? I had long believed that Mother had given up her job and stayed home because of her devotion to Jordan. After talking to Hedda, I wasn't so sure.

I managed to dress and tiptoe out of the apartment. The building was quiet as I made my way downstairs to the servant's entrance of my own home. It was ridiculous, really. I was a grown woman with no one to answer to.

My nose wrinkled as I turned the knob, trying to be quiet. I prayed I could make it past Einstein, who at five in the morning surely would be asleep. Which was crazy, I told myself, since why would a dog care if I slept with a man?

The light was out in the kitchen. Birdie must have taken over, directing the catering staff to clean up and close down. *Thank you, Birdie.*

The door clicked shut. With high heels in hand I turned carefully.

"Oh!"

Einstein stood in the kitchen, the hackles on his back rising, his lip curled. Seeing me, he gave a deep, low growl. He crept closer, and his nose twitched as he sniffed me. For half a second he froze in shock, then he growled again. I had the startling thought that he was going to attack me.

Was it possible he was jealous over me being with another man?

I shook the thought away. Coffee. I needed coffee. Then I could think.

I walked past Einstein, not saying a word. I put on a pot and had to force myself not to stare at the dripping brew. Einstein continued watching me, as if assessing.

"Stop staring at me."

He growled.

I had just poured my first cup when I heard the front door open quietly, then click closed. Einstein and I both cocked our heads, realizing that based on the sound of tiptoeing combat boots, Jordan was trying to sneak in.

"Didn't she come home last night?" I asked.

Einstein ignored me.

I set the coffee down and counted to ten, bracing my hands against the counter. Then I left the kitchen to confront my sister, Einstein following.

"Tell me you ran over to Starbucks for a cup of coffee to keep you awake," I said.

Jordan went stiff with guilt, which was immediately replaced by her own anger. "So what if I wasn't?"

"You told me you had to lock yourself in your room so you could finish the book."

"Yeah, that's all you care about. That freaking book."

"It's your book!" I snapped before I could stop myself. I took a moment, drawing a breath. "You're the one who wanted to write it. Not me. I didn't want anything to do with this. But I did it for you."

Jordan rolled her eyes. "You did it for me, right. You did it because your ass was on the line and you didn't have anything else to pitch."

My shoulders tensed.

"That Victoria is a piece of work," she added. "Yeah, I ran into her in the lobby last night. *'You're Jordan, aren't you,'*" she mimicked. "I said no, but she only laughed, said I looked just like you. Then she asked all about the book, told me about you blurting out the idea when you were under the gun. My book saved your ass. Though you always were good at that, saving your ass."

It took me a moment to regain my composure. "If I've had to save myself it's because I didn't have a mother coming to my rescue every time I got in trouble."

"Oh, that's rich. You were so damn boring I doubt you even knew how to get in trouble. Little Miss Goodie Two Shoes. Yep, no one could ever live up to Miss Perfect. Certainly not me, Little Miss Screwup."

"If you'd ever thought about being responsible, you wouldn't . . . mess up all the time."

"Yeah, that's the answer. I could grow up to be another *you.* A rigid sap who sucks the life out of everyone around her . . . including that jerk you married. Is it really any surprise that he had affairs?"

My head snapped back as if she had slapped me. Jordan stopped, stared, the words frozen in her mouth.

"Freakin' A, I'm sorry, Emily. Again. Hell, I didn't mean it."

"Yes, you did. You've always thought of me that way."

Jordan frowned. "I'm such a bitch. I'm sorry. I just wish . . . I just wish you could love me for who I am. Just me—stupid, irresponsible Jordan. Why can't I just be me?"

"You are not stupid, Jordan. And I do love you for who you are."

"Yeah, right. You want Little Miss Organized. Just like Mom wanted me to be Little Miss Feminist."

"Jordan. That's not true."

"Isn't it? Didn't you dress me up in perfect doll clothes when I was little and curl my hair? And when did Mom brag about me to her friends? When I chained myself to the cafeteria door to protest pay discrepancies between male and female employees."

I remembered Mother having to go to Jordan's school to pick her up. *"Jordan, Jordan, Jordan,"* she had lamented. But that night over martinis, she crowed to her friends about what little Jordan had done. *"One of these days she'll be running for president of NOW. Hell, she'll probably run for president!"*

"Admit it, Emily," Jordan continued, her voice growing strained, "you wanting me to be organized isn't for my own good. It makes it easier for you."

"If I drive you so crazy, Jordan, then why are you still here? Why did you want me to publish your book?"

She scoffed. "Who knows? Obviously I was insane."

"That's it? You've got to be insane to be around me?"

"That's not what I meant."

She tried to get past me, but I caught her arm. "Why, Jordan? Why did you really come back? Why, really?"

Blood rushed into her face, her jaw suddenly clenching.

"No reason, Emily," she bit out.

She tried to pull away but I held firm. "Damn it, Jordan, why—"

"Because I needed to make sure you still loved me, okay?"

We stood inches apart in the dimly lit hallway, the anger seeping out of her. Then she hesitated in a way that wasn't like my sister at all. There it was again, the uncertainty, the vulnerability.

"Damn it, Em, I was a jerk to you on the phone when you told me you were afraid Sandy was having an affair. I know I totally don't deserve it, but I needed to make sure I still had family."

I tried to understand. "Jordan, of course you always have me. Plus regardless of what has happened in the past, you have your father and his family."

"Yeah. *His* family. Not mine." She bit her lip. "When I got back to town, I actually went out to Long Island first. I thought I could spend time with him, and you, sort of go back and forth. So I showed up there first. He and his wife stood there in that cramped foyer stuffed with all the crap she thinks makes her look classy, asking me how long I planned to stay before I even set my backpack down. When I said it might be a little while, his wife got all huffy and walked away. And you know what my dad said?"

I hurt for her before she even said the words.

"'Jordan, I'm sorry, but I don't think it's a good idea for you to stay here. You're not the best influence on my children.'"

Jordan dashed the back of her hand across her eyes. "*His* children. Like I wasn't one of them." She dropped her head back and groaned. "I'm twenty-two but I feel like I'm still fifteen.

"I know you love me, Emily, just like my dad probably loves me in his own way, but that doesn't mean you won't get tired of me, just like my dad has, just like Serge did. But I don't know how to be any other way than this. Crazy Jordan." She took a deep breath. "I'm sorry I came here and messed everything up. But if I don't have you, if you stop loving me, then I'm completely alone."

All the pieces finally came together. The heart she lost to a guy, the job she lost because of that guy, then the father she lost because he moved on without her. Our mother had left us, two girls without family, though again and again we failed to connect with each other.

"Oh, Jordan." I took her in my arms and held her close. "I do love you."

She held on tight like she was afraid to let go.

The day I read her book proposal I had realized for the first time that her life hadn't been any easier than mine. But I hadn't taken it to heart, not really. I had read the words, felt the emotions, but my core belief about my sister hadn't shifted. Standing there now in the face of her vulnerability, I realized that her life had probably been even harder than mine. She had only been eighteen when our mother died, young and scared. And I hadn't been there for her, not really. I had been too busy falling in love with Sandy in order to get away from my own pain.

"You don't want to be here, do you?" I said. "You don't want to be an author."

"No. I don't. But after losing my job, then the whole guy screwup, I tried to figure out what I could do. I'd been thinking about Mom and writing stuff down. Then I got here and I really didn't want to ask for money, not again. That's when it hit me. A book about Mom would pay. Writing could be my job. Plus it would be something cool we could do together. Maybe it would make us close. Maybe something good could come out of my screwup."

I cupped her face and smiled at her. "I love you for that. But you don't have to stay here for me to love you. I love you no matter where you are. And no matter where I am, you always have a home with me."

Jordan buried her head in my shoulder. "Then you don't care about the book," she whispered, her tone hopeful.

"Unfortunately, I do care about the book. You promised to write it. Finish it, Jordan, and I'll help you in any way I can. I'll even buy you a plane ticket so you can fly wherever you want to go when you're finished."

Jordan straightened and stared at me for a long time.

"I love you, Emily."

"I love you too."

einstein

chapter thirty-four

Give me a break.

I had never seen such sentimental crap in all my life.

"I love you, Emily."

"I love you too."

I wanted to projectile vomit every scavenged tart and cream puff right into their tearstained faces.

Emily went to one bedroom, Jordan to another. Each closed the door, and almost simultaneously I heard the showers come on. Not even the smell of strawberry shampoo consoled me. I was furious. I felt cheated. But what was I going to do about it?

My wife had slept with another man. I had figured that out before she ever snuck back into the apartment. The smell of that boy Max on her only confirmed what deep down I already knew. But more than that, there was the whole Emily living my life situation—and based on the savings account register she had gone through my stash of money like a Saudi Arabian princess. She was over me *and* living the high life with my money.

My anger grew, every ounce of the old Sandy Portman resurfacing. Right then I hated Emily. As a man I had gotten frustrated with her, bored even. But I had never hated her.

Every ounce of growth I had achieved disappeared like dog piss in a New York City street drain. I didn't care that I was being crass. I didn't care that I wished my wife ill. Nor did I try to have better thoughts. I all but prayed that something horrible would happen to make Emily's life come unhinged.

When I felt the sharp stabbing pain between my eyes, I ignored it. "Give me your best shot, old man," I taunted, enough adrenaline coursing through my body to counter the pain.

The water turned off in Jordan's bedroom sooner than in Emily's. No surprise that

Jordan was well into drying off when Emily hadn't gotten much further along than soaping up. What was a surprise was that only a few minutes after that, Jordan cracked open her door, listened for a second, then stepped out.

Her hair was still wet, but she was dressed. She carried her duffel bag at her side, backpack strapped on.

Jordan was leaving. For good.

Interesting.

When she saw me she motioned for me to be quiet. In the last few weeks I might have softened toward her, but all that was gone too. I had no intention of keeping her from leaving. Had I been able, I would have carried her bags to the curb.

When she was certain Emily was well occupied, Jordan headed for the front door, stopping at the credenza in the gallery. She glanced back one last time, and I was surprised to see the wistful look on her face.

She pulled a sheet of paper from her pocket, set it on the table.

"Bye," she whispered to me, or to the apartment, or to Emily in her own bedroom.

I had no idea what the note said, and since there were no chairs on which to crawl up to gain access, I had to content myself with waiting.

Part of me thought about ignoring the note, thereby ensuring Jordan's clean escape. But the other part of me knew the note would decimate my wife, whatever it said, since it was clear even to me that Jordan was hightailing it out of town without finishing the book. Since I had no ability to punish Emily on my own, I was more than a little pleased that I was getting my wish, even if it was by way of my sister-in-law.

I barked until Emily emerged, pulling on a robe. When she saw me sitting in the gallery she stopped.

"What it is, E? Do you need to go out? Are you hungry?"

At the simple word *hungry,* my baser instincts leaped to the forefront. I started salivating and it was all I could do not to bolt for the kitchen. But I'd had enough of Emily and Einstein and the old man and whoever else was wreaking havoc on my life. I forced myself to stay put and barked again.

"E?"

When I didn't move, Emily came down the hall toward me.

"Are you all right?" She glanced around for the leash—then saw the note on the table.

Her own baser instinct of fight or flight flooded her body; I could smell it. Her hand trembled as she picked up the piece of notebook paper Jordan had left and read it out loud, her voice strangled.

Dear Emily,

Sorry. You were right. I am irresponsible. And I can't write the book. Not that I think it shouldn't be written, just that I haven't the first damn clue how to do it. The beginning was easy, so I thought the rest would be easy too. But no. I hated every second of it. Despite what I told you, everything I have written since the beginning sucks. And believe me, I've tried. I have written and rewritten, but none of it makes any sense.

I'm headed back to South America. Whatever mistakes I made at Homes for Women Heroes notwithstanding, I'm good in that world, helping. For good or for bad, that's who I am.

I hope you can forgive me because no matter what you think of me, I love you.

Stay cool,

Jordan

A deep keening moan slowly surfaced. "No, no, no," Emily said, the note dropping from her fingers.

She raced back down the hall to the guest room. "Jordan?"

Of course there was no response.

"Jordan!"

It was like a cry from a bad movie. Not that I cared. Triumphant, I turned my back on my wife and walked out the door.

chapter thirtyfive

I had to love the girl's tactics, if not the girl.

But my spurt of pleasure over this new development dissipated the next morning when the phone started ringing. Not that anyone bothered to answer. They left messages. That twit Max. Tatiana. Birdie. But Max was the most persistent, even knocking on the door several times.

Then there was my mother, and my lawyer, returning with a vengeance, just as I suspected they would, leaving messages with increased urgency.

My adrenaline was still there fighting off the fading, but it was weakening in the face of the growing pain between my eyes. But still I was too caught up in my own shallow pettiness to care.

I made my way to the kitchen. Emily sat at the table, one of the Julia Child–inspired creations of butter, sugar, and cream she hadn't eaten in so long sitting in front of her. She was falling back into her old ways. Good.

My guess was that she would stop running, forget to go to work, get fat, and then Max wouldn't give her the time of day. Even better.

Beyond that, she would either cancel her slot in the marathon or just not show up. Either approach was fine with me.

The answering machine beeped. I heard my own voice, which never failed to surprise me, the sound so human, so rich and full of life. Then my lawyer. Again.

"Ms. Barlow, really. This is unacceptable. No one wants to throw you out on the street. But if you don't return my call, I'm afraid we are going to have to resort to extreme measures."

The next call came from Tatiana.

"Emily? Pick up. I've called your cell a hundred times. We need to talk."

Pause.

Emily didn't move to answer.

"Emily," she added with an impatient sigh. But she didn't say anything else. She hung up.

"What am I going to do now?" Emily said, more a whisper to the cake she hadn't yet touched than any attempt to talk to me.

Unfortunately for both of us, I had to go out.

With some effort, I made this clear to Emily. My wife groaned, then got the leash. In the hallway, she glanced around before we made a run for it.

Outside, she stood at the curb, staring at the cars that went by without seeing. When I finished my business we headed back to the building.

My vivid imagination flared when a strange man called out to Emily just as we entered the porte cochere; I knew something was up. I sniffed the air for the smell of a gun. What I smelled was indeed something metallic and what I suspected was a firearm.

"Emily Barlow Portman?" the man said.

Emily looked confused. "Yes?" she said.

The man pulled out some sort of badge. I barely made out the word MARSHAL on it. After the flash of his badge, he extended an official-looking envelope. As was most anyone's natural instinct, Emily reached for it.

"You have now been officially served Notice of Eviction."

Emily stiffened as she quickly scanned the contents. When she lifted her head, the marshal was already gone.

"We're being evicted," she said to me, her voice devoid of emotion. "We have until the first week of November to move out or we'll be forcibly removed from the premises. The complaint is filed by the Portman Family Trust."

She stared at the pages as if she couldn't believe it.

Believe it, I wanted to shout.

I felt the old feelings of superiority stir inside of me, feelings I clutched at like finding an old familiar blanket that made me feel safe. Whatever motivation there had been to be good, more charitable, vanished, and with that the last of my adrenaline evaporated.

Which is when the real change began.

The new sensation was different. Not the stabbing pain, dizzy feeling, or even my memory growing dim. It was beyond a physical shift. I realized with a start of surprise that the essence of me, the Sandy me, was being erased.

What amazes me, even now as I remember back on it, is that I was so small and petty that in that moment I still didn't care. As the world around me began to lose its crispness, scents diminishing, sounds muffled, all I cared about was that while I might have been swirling around the drain, I had every intention of taking Emily down with me.

emily

For years I believed my mother wore a suit of armor. As I got older I began to see a chink in the molded steel. My mother's dream was to be great, to make a difference. When I was growing up I assumed she had achieved both. Now, years after her death, I wonder if she believed she accomplished either. And I have to ask: Did she push me to pursue greatness primarily because of her own unfulfilled need to be remembered for her own accomplishments?

—EXCERPT FROM *My Mother's Daughter*

chapter thirty-six

The sound of my BlackBerry alternately ringing and buzzing woke me from a deep sleep. It was Monday morning, four days after my party. I felt as if a semi truck had run me down, a feeling no doubt caused by the sheer number of phone calls and e-mails I had been avoiding since Jordan departed. I still hadn't come up with a way to tell Tatiana that there would be no book.

I groped around in my satchel for the wireless device. Scrolling through the messages I saw several from the publisher.

From: Nate.Clarkson@caldecotepress.com
To: Emily.Barlow@caldecotepress.com
CC: Tatiana.Harriman@caldecotepress.com
Subject: Emergency
Emily:
It has come to my attention that there is a problem with the manuscript of *My Mother's Daughter.* Please see me in my office as soon as you get in.
Nate

Damn. Was it possible that Nate already knew Jordan had fled without finishing the book? Did Tatiana already know?

No way.

I calmed myself. Perhaps they were just trying to get ahold of me in order to tell me that the book had to be pushed back, or better yet, pulled altogether. I couldn't imagine that was what Nate wanted to tell me, but that didn't stop me from sending up a silent prayer.

An hour later I strode through security and went straight to Nate's office.

"You wanted to see me," I said, trying to act casual.

But whatever calm I had managed to drum up disappeared when I realized Nate wasn't alone. Tatiana stood at the window, her jaw clenched with anger. Victoria sat in one of the leather side chairs looking smug. She held up a partial manuscript with one hand. The pages flapped as she shook it.

"You call this a book?" she said to me. "This is fifty pages of garbage."

"Victoria," Tatiana snapped.

"I'm just saying, it's a mess."

Tatiana turned that glacial stare on me.

"How did this happen?" she asked.

I marshaled my thoughts. "I'd appreciate it if someone would explain what's going on."

"The manuscript that was due last Friday is a disaster," Nate said. "Many of the pages are barely coherent. Though that's the least of our concerns. Bad pages can be fixed. The missing part of the book is the bigger problem."

"How did you get that?" I asked, my tone careful.

Tatiana glanced over at Victoria, who went red.

"You said it had been turned in," Tatiana stated.

"It's Monday!" she said. "It *should* have been turned in."

"Then how did you get it?" Tatiana persisted.

Victoria huffed. "It was out on a desk in one of Emily's bedrooms, sitting there plain as day. How in the world was I supposed to overlook it?"

I had been in Jordan's room several times, and not once had she left a single page out for anyone to see. And there was no way Jordan would have willingly forked anything over to Victoria. To find the manuscript Victoria had to have searched hard.

"Let me see that."

Victoria handed it over, albeit grudgingly.

Nate raked his hand through his hair. "This is a debacle."

But I hardly heard. I flipped through the pages. The opening was there, still phenomenal. But once I got beyond that the manuscript was indeed a mess. Paragraphs filled with a garble of incomplete sentences.

Disjointed statements such as: *Insert description,* and *Figure out what the hell Mom was thinking then.* But I could still detect Jordan's voice in the words that were written.

Nate droned on in his serious way. "We never should have chased attention. Caldecote has always been known for good sense! Now we're going to be an embarrassment. We have everyone in the media talking about this book, and now, it's a disaster."

"We'll have to pull it," Victoria added, barely able to hide her pleasure. "And everyone is watching us, Tatiana. Everyone is watching *you.*"

"Enough," Tatiana said. Everything about her exuded calm, but it was like the calm before a storm.

Victoria turned smug. "I know how to fix this."

"How?" Nate asked.

"We move fast to plug the hole in the schedule with an exceptional book. A book that will make everyone forget Emily's fiasco." She paused, squared her shoulders. "I have that book. I will come to your rescue, Tatiana."

Tatiana's eyes narrowed.

"What's the book?" Nate pressed.

"It's a story of a love that can't be denied set during the Great Depression. I see it as a cross between *Doctor Zhivago* and *The Grapes of Wrath.* But this book is filled with hope and triumph. It's the kind of story that will fill readers with courage during this modern day when we are struggling with our own form of trying times. The book is based on the true story of the author's parents."

As much as I hated to admit it, the idea had merit. As I had done with *Ruth's Intention,* Victoria could play the nonfiction angle to get attention.

Unable to take any more, I left the room, Jordan's partial manuscript still in my hands.

"Emily," Tatiana said.

But I kept going. I needed time to think.

■

The next morning I woke with a start. I didn't gasp awake because I had dreamed of Sandy's accident, or even of the night before he died. Yesterday I had wanted Caldecote to pull Jordan's book just as I'd had moments when I believed it was time to pry my fingers free from this old apartment. But after a night of sleep, I realized that after I had made it this far I would hate myself if I gave up now.

I whipped back the covers, pulled on running clothes, and searched my brain for solutions.

Einstein was still in the kitchen when I entered. He blinked when he saw the running clothes, then looked at me with what I can only call astonished frustration, maybe even anger.

I squatted down in front of him, scratching his head. "You want to go for a run?"

He looked tired, though thankfully when I touched his nose he didn't have a fever.

After I took Einstein out, then returned him upstairs, I headed to the park. I didn't worry about Max and his increasingly concerned messages. I put from my mind that on the last message he had told me that clearly I wanted him to leave me alone, and he would honor that wish. I refused to think about how much I didn't want that, because the truth of the matter was whether I wanted to be with him or not, there was no future for us. He was a twenty-seven-year-old ex-Navy SEAL who loved to climb mountains and didn't know what to do with his life. I was a thirty-two-year-old widow who still hadn't completely reclaimed herself.

I went to the bridle path and headed north. I lost myself to the rhythm of the run and by the time I hit the top of the reservoir a plan began to form in my head.

An hour later when I got to Caldecote, I went straight to Tatiana's office. The publisher was there along with the heads of sales and production. It saved me the trouble of having to track everyone down.

Victoria was there as well, which neither surprised nor intimidated me.

"I have a solution," I announced.

Nate scowled. "We already have a solution."

"My book!" Victoria crowed.

Everyone ignored her, including Nate.

Tatiana considered me. "What are you thinking, Emily?"

"Give me six weeks," I said. "Six weeks and I promise *My Mother's Daughter* will be done."

"How are you going to accomplish that?"

"Your sister clearly can't write," Victoria stated.

"Look, everyone loved the opening pages. They are phenomenal. But Jordan got overwhelmed. She's never written before. If I have to I'll hire a ghostwriter for her." I didn't mention the one little snag in my plan, the fact that Jordan had already left. "One way or another, I will get the book turned in."

No one looked convinced.

"We're in a sticky spot," I said. "Enough people know about the book that if we pull it off the schedule we definitely look indecisive."

"We already look indecisive. Face it, we look bad," Victoria countered.

"No, not yet. No one but the people in this room knows the book is"—I shrugged—"less than perfect."

Victoria snorted.

I pushed ahead, all the while aware that Tatiana was studying me. "Let me fix this. No one has to know we hit a snag."

Nate looked grim. Victoria looked at me as if I were delusional.

"Whether you believe it or not, Victoria," I continued, "Tatiana looking bad, even me looking bad, doesn't help you."

"I never said—"

I cut her off. "Caldecote Press announced the mandate that it is focusing on gaining market share in the industry, which everyone knows means that our priority is making money. Even if we hadn't announced it, Tatiana being brought in says as much. And sure, *Ruth's Intention* succeeded. But as far as outsiders are concerned, that book was well underway when Tatiana got here. *My Mother's Daughter* is the first big book acquired under her watch. Announcing a screwup right out of the gate undermines Caldecote's position as a publishing company capable of redefining its position in the marketplace."

"One book isn't going to change the face of Caldecote," Victoria snapped.

"No, that takes a series of successes. But a substantial embarrassment up front prejudices industry opinions from here on out."

Nate didn't look happy, but he didn't disagree.

"Give me six weeks to help Jordan figure out how to finish it," I reiterated. "I will fix this."

Tatiana considered, then turned to the head of production. "Tell me,

Erin, if we expedite production can we get it done and have review copies for magazines ready to go out in time?"

I could see the woman doing mental calculations. "Yes, but it'll cost a fortune."

"Mercy, what do you think?" Tatiana asked.

The head of sales looked at me, considering. After a second she nodded. "I say we go for it. If anyone can get it done, it's Emily."

Nate compressed his lips. "I don't like this one bit."

Victoria's stiff shoulders sagged with relief.

"But I don't see that we have any choice," he added. "And if all goes well, you're right, Emily. It could work."

Tatiana turned to me. "Get the book done."

einstein

chapter thirty-seven

No one was more surprised than me when Emily came home from the office with a box of her belongings.

I tried to pull myself up from where I had been lying for hours—or maybe minutes. I no longer had an accurate sense of time. "Ha!" I barked, the effort making me cough. "You've been fired!"

I might have been surprised that things were going wrong for Emily so quickly, but I was bitterly pleased. And with each bitter or hateful thought, the pulling and sucking sensation increased. Yet I still found it hard to care about the disjointed feeling my mind and body had begun to experience.

"E, can you believe it?" Emily asked, her voice full of excitement.

My hackles rose, my spine going stiff. She wasn't acting like a woman who had just been fired.

"I'm working from home until Jordan's book is finished!"

"What? How did this happen?"

"I convinced them it was in the best interest of the company for me to work from home so that I can edit while Jordan is writing!"

My mouth fell open. She grimaced. Clearly, she didn't need me to remind her of the pesky little detail that Jordan was gone. But her grimace didn't last.

"I know I should have told them about Jordan, but I couldn't. Forget about me, but if this debacle hurts Caldecote because of my harebrained idea to publish this book, I wouldn't be able to live with myself."

She gave me one of those wry smiles, and I was struck with the memory of that seemingly immortal Emily. Vibrant, full of energy, a deep belief in herself. I realized with a start that despite my hope that my wife was falling apart again, I was wrong. The old Emily was back.

My anger and bitter frustration swelled.

"Besides, look at it this way," she said. "If it doesn't work out, it will be easier for them to fire me if I haven't been in the office for six weeks."

Not only wasn't she a wreck, she moved around the apartment with a barely contained energy, going through every inch of Jordan's room.

"Surely she left behind whatever else she had on the book." She swung her head around to look at me. "Do you think she took it with her to the jungle?"

Not that she waited for an answer.

"No, she wouldn't have done that. What is she going to do with computer files in the jungle without a computer?"

Like a dervish, she zipped through drawers and the closet. "Pay dirt!" she exclaimed, dancing around the room like Rocky at the top of that ridiculous Philadelphia staircase. It was as if this potential career catastrophe had finally snapped her into full gear.

She had found an outline of sorts, along with pages of barely legible notes. Not that this cramped Emily's style. She shoved every scrap of paper into her box of office things. Next, she turned on the computer. As soon as the machine booted up, she went straight for the *My Mother's Daughter* folder. Sitting behind Emily, panting with effort, I barely made out a listing of chapters. She opened each one. "Not much, but that's okay. There's enough here for me to get started."

She turned the computer off.

That was it? She spends two seconds going over the files, then shuts down? Not exactly the way I would have gone about thoroughly assessing the situation, but heck, the worse she did, the happier it made me. So fumble away!

It turned out, however, that she wasn't done. As soon as the machine powered down, Emily unplugged it and disconnected the monitor, keyboard, mouse, and hard drive.

Suspicious, I followed her down the hall toward the library.

"You can't clutter up my five-thousand-dollar desk!" I barked.

"Don't worry. I'm not going to work in the library."

During the next hour, she did far worse. She transported every piece of computer equipment and scrap of paper upstairs to the suite. My private suite.

My apartment, my money, my marathon, my life. Now this? I was incensed and I let her know it.

"Calm down, E. It's just for six weeks. I need a private place to do this."

Like we were overrun with guests. I snorted.

"I need a place that's just for writing." She glanced down at me. "*I* am going to be the ghostwriter for Jordan. I'm going to write her book, and I'm going to write it from her point of view."

Oh, yeah, that'll work.

"I know, it'll be hard to see the story through her lens, but that's what I'm excited about. I'm excited to tell my mother's and my sister's stories. Quite frankly, I'm excited to *learn* my mother's and sister's stories."

Spare me.

Emily didn't waste a second. No sooner had she set up her command center than she got to work. She used Jordan's erratic outline and notes to create a real outline, each chapter of the book detailed. I had never seen my wife at work, nor had I been interested in listening to her talk about her job, but even I was impressed with her sheer dedication once she got started.

Interestingly, though, she didn't start to write. She made calls and set up interviews, coming home from each with pages full of notes about her mother.

This went on for days, and during that time I hit a sort of reprieve from the fading. I didn't get better, but I didn't get worse, and I had the distinct thought that the old man was waiting for something.

Once Emily finished the research, she worked at all hours, never seeming to stop. Early, late. It would be two A.M. and I'd hear her get out of bed and go upstairs. I'd hear the suite door squeak open, the light switch flip, then the computer whirring to life, always followed by the tap, tap, tap of the keyboard.

For the next four weeks Emily wrote. She also made time to go to some lawyer about the apartment. When she returned I knew she had gotten bad news. But she only nodded with determination.

"I believe it's going to work out."

Emily and her faith.

If she thought to win me over with her impassioned declaration she was mistaken. I dragged myself up off the floor and walked out on her.

■

The only other thing Emily did besides work on that book was run. Always with the running. That, and I have to admit, she continued to love me.

When she finally realized that my energy wasn't getting better, she took me to the vet. When the doctor said there was nothing wrong with me, then took her aside and told her he thought I was depressed, she brought me home and showered me with even more love and praise despite my ill-mannered attempts to make her miserable. If I was unpleasant before, I became horrible to Emily over the next few weeks.

I growled, I nipped at fingers. If she left something out, I destroyed it. Her favorite shoes. Ruined. Pages left on the floor. Ripped to shreds. When she lost herself to the words, I launched into a round of barking. I even peed on my precious floors.

No matter what I did, she hugged me every morning, and kissed me on the forehead before going to bed every night, as if the sheer determination of her love could pull me out of the supposed depression. But I was immune to her charm. I was progressing, but not to something greater. I had progressed from hating her to loathing her. I loathed her vitality, despised her ability to come and go, linger in a bath or talk on the phone.

I hated that despite the stress of writing Jordan's book, and being on the verge of losing her home, she was happy. I hated that most of all.

■

Finally the day came when I heard her whoop. "It's done!"

Despite myself, I felt a sizzle of excitement, not that it helped get me up the stairs. By this time I no longer even tried to make it to the suite. She came flying down, falling to her knees in front of me and hugging me tight.

"We did it, E! We did it!"

As it turned out, everyone back at Caldecote, at least the ones who mattered, were excited too. It didn't take long before Emily heard that they loved the manuscript. I determined this based on the congratulatory notes, candy, and flowers that arrived. Tatiana sent a bottle of Dom Perignon. The card read, *"To Jordan, for a fabulous book. And to Emily, for saving the day."*

Excuse me, I wanted to shout. *Emily was the one who got you in that mess in the first place.*

I left my wife to her celebration, heading to the master bedroom to curl up with what had become the continuous loop of my discontent. Whether I liked it or not, Emily was saved. Whether I cared or not, Emily had saved herself. I had done very little to help.

To add insult to injury, the marathon was right around the corner.

My mother had moved on months ago, and now my wife was as well. Not only had Emily been able to succeed at work, now she was going to run, building a new life, while Sandy Portman was in the process of becoming nothing and being forgotten altogether.

chapter thirty-eight

With the manuscript turned in, Emily was able to devote herself full time to training. I thought it odd that she hadn't gone back to the office, that she was still working upstairs in my suite. Strangest of all, some sort of reporter came by the apartment.

She showed him around. He asked about pictures he saw of me, the Sandy me, showed interest in photos of Jordan and Lillian Barlow, before they left together.

Tatiana called repeatedly, even came by one evening without warning.

"Finally," the woman said when she walked into the gallery like she owned the place. "You are trying my patience, Emily. You did a great job. Now it's time to come back."

My wife wasn't cowed. "I'm working on something," she said, her excitement making Tatiana eye her with speculation. "And it's not like I have a bunch of things going on at the office."

"And you won't have anything going on at the office until you get back there to start filling your pipeline with potential product."

Emily cringed. "You make it sound so sterile."

"Fine, let me rephrase. You have to get back to the office so you can start developing your list of literature that will inspire the masses. Better?"

Emily chuckled. "Yeah, that's better, but the marathon is on Sunday. I'm dealing with some things on that end. Let me get through that. I'll come in on Monday."

■

The day of the race, in the wee hours of the morning before she had to head off to Staten Island and the starting line, Emily turned on the television for me.

"I thought you might like to watch," she said.

Despite everything, I *did* want to watch.

On her way out the door, she kneeled in front of me, concern dark in her eyes.

"You're going to be okay, E," she said, though I could see she was worried.

Good. I hoped it ruined her race.

Coverage of the event began a couple hours later as the sun was coming up. My stomach churned with jealous misery at the sight of the tens of thousands of runners getting ready to run through the five boroughs of New York City. But whatever jealousy I felt tightened in a knot of surprise when a picture of Emily appeared on the screen.

"There are literally thousands of stories to be told," a reporter began, the reporter I had seen at the apartment, *"of the many men and women who come from all over the globe to run what is thought to be one of the greatest marathons in the world. Emily Barlow Portman is just one of those runners, but hers is a story that will stick with you long after the race is over."*

The program shifted to a taped piece.

"When Emily Barlow started to run, she had no plans to run the marathon."

"I got a dog," Emily said with a laugh. *"Einstein got me walking, then running. To be honest, at first I hated every minute of it. The walking was okay, but the running?"* She grimaced. *"Then something happened, and I found myself looking forward to getting out there. Clearing my head, finding peace."*

"What Emily didn't mention was that three months before she started running, she lost her husband."

"At thirty-eight," Emily added, her voice tight with emotion, *"Sandy Portman was too young to go. He was smart and funny, and we all lost a great deal when he died."*

I stared at the television in shock. A photo of me that came up on the screen made me weep. How beautiful I was. How very much alive.

The taped piece shifted to the Dakota, Emily walking out of the front gates, Johnny tipping his hat to her.

How had I not realized this was going on?

"I run in the park six days a week, generally in the mornings before work, with long runs on the weekends."

In this segment of the taped piece, the reporter now wore running clothes and walked with her to the park. When Emily started to run, the reporter ran with her on the bridle path, the cameraman doing a remarkable job of keeping the picture steady.

"My husband wanted to run the New York City Marathon, but never got the chance. I'm running this race in memory of Sandy, who didn't have the chance to realize his dream, and for my dog Einstein, who saved me when I didn't think I could get over the loss."

I couldn't believe it. She was doing this for me? Both as a man, and as a dog?

The taped piece ended, coming back live.

"People run for many reasons," the reporter said, crowds of spectators milling around him. *"Emily Barlow runs for a man she loved and a dog she says saved her. She might not place with the top finishers, but I'd like to think that by the sheer act of being here today she has already won a great deal more than a simple medal."*

After that, I sat unable to move and watched, riveted, as hour after hour of coverage unfolded. They showed Emily throughout the race. At the starting line, at mile six, at ten. And each time she looked good. She looked strong. I was surprised at myself when I couldn't help but smile.

At mile fifteen she looked directly into the camera and waved. "Hi, Einstein!"

I felt certain the masses loved this story. The woman who lost her husband, got into shape, and realized *his* dream. Even I was moved.

But just past mile twenty, everything changed. Mile twenty is the proverbial wall for many runners, that place where one hits a limit. But I could tell it hit Emily especially hard.

The question at mile twenty is: Can you run through your limit? Can you keep going? Can you reach deeper and find a reservoir of strength you didn't know you had?

I could see from the expression on my wife's face that she had hit the wall and when she dug deep she found nothing to help her.

"Come on, Emily!" I found myself barking at the screen.

But she didn't hear. She sat on the curb hunched over, her forearms on her knees, her head in her hands. I could see that her body was cramping, her energy drained, her blood chemistry off.

I was surprised when not even a part of me was happy. I felt a deep need to help, but I didn't know how. Adrenaline got me up off the floor and I willed whatever energy I had left to her, but she didn't move off the curb.

The reporter who had been interviewing her off and on along the course appeared and hunched down next to her. *"How're you hangin', Emily?"*

I growled at the screen. "Not great, you moron!"

I saw then that Emily had tears streaming down her cheeks.

"I thought I could do it. I thought if I could, if I could do this for Sandy and Einstein, then I could move on. Not just survive but move on." She glanced up, blinked, seeming to realize the camera was on her. *"Sorry,"* she whispered.

"You can do it!" I barked. "Get up! Walk if you have to! Just get up!"

But pain darkened her blue eyes. During my own training I had never gotten to the point of being able to run as far as she had now, but I had read that if you settled down, if you relaxed your mind, most of the time you could run through the pain and find your way out the other side. Though there was no way I could share that with her now.

Then it hit me. I could share it with her. I could help my wife.

I went very still, closing my eyes and concentrating. I didn't yell this time, didn't bellow.

"Old man," I practically whispered, "help her. Please."

But nothing happened. The energy around me stayed the same.

I drew a deep breath, refusing to give up. "Please, help her."

I kept my eyes closed, silently praying. Then I felt my world shift. I opened my eyes and watched the television screen in a sort of knowing surprise as Emily's body stirred. She sat up straighter, tears streaking her face, her brow creased as if she were confused.

"Come on, Emily, you can do this," I whispered.

Other runners ran past the camera, people calling out to her, cheering her on. But still she sat there lost to her misery.

Then I watched as the old man walked up and sat down next to her on the curb.

emily

Lillian Barlow was a mystery to many, including myself. It wasn't until I dug below the surface that I learned the truth. My mother hadn't stayed home to raise her girls because she suddenly wanted to bake cupcakes. She stopped working because she was pushed out of a movement that believed her wildness overshadowed the good she had done. What had been amusing antics in a carefree young woman became unattractive carelessness in someone who was old enough to know better. And when she put on a suit and carried a briefcase, no one believed that a brash woman who had been as free with her body as she was with her opinions could change her ways. Lillian Barlow had believed she was held in high regard, only to learn she was infamous instead of famous, the good she had done negated. That, as it turned out, proved to be the one thing she couldn't survive.

—EXCERPT FROM *My Mother's Daughter*

chapter thirtynine

I had never felt such pain in my life. But it was more than physical. After finishing Jordan's book, during the time I trained to run the race, I believed I had reconnected with my old self. Running through Central Park, I had thought about my job, about life, happiness. I was sure I would be able to move on completely once I crossed the finish line. But sitting on the curb I felt as if my physical inability to keep going was symbolic of something greater.

Perhaps because I was exhausted, my defenses down, I thought of my mother. In the beginning, I believed I understood her motivation. But I was wrong. If I hadn't written my sister's book I'm not sure I ever would have understood that Lillian Barlow had dreams she hadn't been able to realize. She founded an organization that didn't find prominence until she was pushed out the door—partly because she wanted the world to be different from what it was, partly because there was a restlessness inside her that men, children, even causes couldn't ease. My mother had spent more time frustrated with the world for being unfair than she'd spent being content that she was doing what she could to change it.

A futile way to live.

What was it in some people that made them, or allowed them, to go on, to endure under extreme circumstances, when others burned up or gave in? Why had I picked myself up again and again as a child, but now since Sandy's death, I couldn't truly pull myself back together? And even if I wasn't able to finish the race, why did it matter so much?

My circling thoughts cut off or eased, and I felt someone sit down next to me.

You have strength.

A sense of warmth surrounded me, and thinking a volunteer was there to help, I lifted my head. But no one was there other than the thousands of other runners streaming by.

When you didn't think you'd ever make it to the top of the hill, you did. You didn't think you'd ever return to the beach after nearly drowning, but the very next morning you went back.

Air rushed out of my lungs as my eyes narrowed in confusion.

Or even your attempts to save your marriage rather than give up on it. Every time you've hit a bump, you picked yourself up and persevered.

I listened to the words, or sensed them. I wasn't sure.

The real question isn't, why aren't you strong enough? It's, why do you keep doubting that you already are?

I tried to make sense of what was happening. I tried to make sense of the words.

It's because you want life to be something that it isn't.

Just like my mother. Fighting battles she couldn't win, like Don Quixote tilting at windmills.

I dropped my head into my hands, recognizing the truth regardless of where it came from. I had wanted a mother who matched the other mothers at my school. I had wanted a father and a white picket fence even though my mother didn't know who my father was and Manhattan didn't have white picket anything, much less fences. I wanted Jordan to be sweet and responsible instead of rebellious and wild. And I had held on to Sandy, had blinded myself to reality, because I wanted to be his passion. I had dreamed of a man who would love me forever. I had wanted my storybook world so badly that I hadn't been able to see the truth. Sure, I was angry at Victoria and Tatiana and even myself, but I hadn't wanted to admit that I was angry at my mother, angry at Sandy, not because they were selfish or cheated on me, but because neither of them had loved me enough to complete the dream I had in my head. Whether I finished the marathon or not wasn't going to change any of that.

Tatiana had asked me what I was hiding, just as my mother had asked. Sitting on the curb, I realized I hadn't been hiding some truth from others. I had been hiding the truth from myself—that my perfectly constructed world was really just a house of cards. My lists or even my plans couldn't save me. Only by accepting the messy complications of life could I really live.

I felt the warmth on my shoulders, as if someone held me tight, and I started to cry, really cry. Twenty miles into a twenty-six-point-two-mile race, I cried for my mother, cried for Sandy, cried for the little girl who had wasted thirty-two years wishing for something that didn't exist.

I don't know how long I sat there, but I began to feel a shift, the anger and sadness dissolving, replaced with the determination that I now recognized had gotten me through the difficult times in my life. I could do this. I could finish this race, for my mother, for Sandy, and most importantly, I could finish it for me.

A sense of being lifted came over me and I stood. Energy flooded my muscles and I shook out my legs. When I started to run again, the crowds that lined the road erupted in a cheer.

I emptied my mind, feeling my body, the rest of the world fading away. At first I barely moved. But as I made my way through the remainder of the Bronx, then ran over the final bridge into Manhattan, my pace picked up. When I hit Fifth Avenue, excitement carried me along, and with the turn into Central Park on the east side, I felt as if I were floating.

The trees were magnificent; the leaves changing colors. I was buoyant as I made my way back out of the park, then headed west on Central Park South, turning back into the park at Columbus Circle for the final stretch. The roar of the crowd that lined the way was deafening, the energy of the people wrapped in coats and mufflers carrying the runners along. And when I passed through the finish line I was euphoric, like a phoenix rising from the ashes.

The reporter hurried over to me. "You did it!" he cheered, hugging me. "You did it!"

I laughed, exhaustion and euphoria dancing through me. I had done it; I had gone the distance in more ways than he realized.

He stepped back to make room as the cameraman hurried up to us. When the camera started rolling, the reporter asked about the race, my fears, falling apart and pulling it back together again. Then he straightened and became very formal. "We understand that you have purchased a memorial plaque for one of the park benches along the finish line," he reported.

"Oh, yes!" In the stress of the run, I had forgotten about how I had used the last of Sandy's money from the joint bank account.

The reporter led me through the crush of runners and volunteers, camera following, and pointed to the small plaque attached to the green bench, the brushed stainless steel catching the sun.

"In memory of Alexander "Sandy" Portman, beloved husband, son, and friend. He will always be missed," he read.

I had made sure *My Mother's Daughter* was written to honor my mother, my way to ensure that the world would always remember that Lillian Barlow had been more than brashness and affairs. The marathon and the park bench along the race's finish line was my way to make sure that Sandy was never forgotten either.

I couldn't say why, but I turned and looked directly into the camera. "I love you, Sandy. You will always be remembered. Maybe now we can both find peace."

einstein

chapter forty

I sat in front of the television long after my wife dedicated the bench in my honor, trying to understand the change I felt deep in what I knew must be my soul. As the minutes ticked by everything came clear. I hadn't simply wanted to punish Emily for living the life I had dreamed of, or even succeeding at her own. I had wanted to punish her for going for what she wanted regardless of the cost to herself. I had punished her first by getting her to give up her rent-controlled apartment and not deeding her mine, then by making her pay for things she couldn't afford—as if somehow she would prove to be just as ordinary as I was and break under the weight. I had been shallow, childish, cavalier with her security. With her heart. I had squandered everything Emily had been willing to give me.

More than that, I had been jealous of the faith she had in something beyond what I had the ability to see.

Watching Emily sit on that curb in the Bronx, I realized that even though she was afraid she couldn't go any farther, she had gotten to that point. The truth was, by watching Emily live her life day after day, I had been forced to see that even as a man I had always given up at the slightest discomfort. As Sandy Portman, if I hadn't broken my leg, I would have given up long before I reached the starting line of the marathon. When the training had gotten too hard to keep going, I would have replaced that dream with another.

That, I realized, had been my way. It didn't matter what it was—art, rowing, running, even following in my father's footsteps at the firm—I had wanted it to be easy. And when it wasn't, I quit.

Sitting there staring at the screen, I wondered if I wouldn't have been better served if this God of hers had given me perseverance and drive along with the dreams . . . or not given me any dreams at all.

It's always someone else's fault, not mine.

I shut my eyes tightly at the thought and I began to understand that that too had been my weakness, just as the old man had tried to point out. I always found a way to blame everyone for my shortcomings. I wanted everything handed to me on a silver platter, and when I reached a limit, I pulled back. In life. In work. In running. With Emily when I was a man. And with Emily while I was a dog.

I managed to get myself from in front of the television to the gallery so I would be there when Emily got home. By the time she arrived, every inch of me hurt. This was beyond the sense of losing myself. Both my body and my mind ached.

She walked in, one of the shiny, paper-thin Mylar blankets they hand out at the end of the race wrapped around her shoulders, her hair a mess, her running clothes disheveled from dried sweat, a finisher's medal around her neck. She had never looked more beautiful.

"Did you see me on TV?" she asked, that smile of hers lighting her face. "I couldn't believe it when Hedda called to tell me she had arranged for the interview."

"Yes!" I gave one staccato bark.

"Did you see the dedication to Sandy?"

"Yes!"

After those simple, exuberant barks, whatever energy I'd had left drained out of me and I realized with a start that it was time.

My stomach twisted with both fear and resignation. Emily had been saved. Had the help I provided her with today been enough to move me on to a higher place? Or had I still not done enough?

The building's house phone rang, and I was vaguely aware that someone was coming up. When Emily opened the front door, my drifting thoughts cleared long enough to witness my wife being issued the final eviction notice.

Since Emily had not solved the ownership issue in the time she had been given by the earlier notice, now she had three days before being forcibly removed from the premises.

Emily read the notice once, then again. She came over to where I lay, sinking down onto the floor, her back against the wall, and touched my head like some sort of talisman. "You know what? It's okay, E. We'll be all right."

"You're giving up the apartment?"

As always, somehow she understood me.

"Let's face it, E, it's over. But just because Sandy didn't live up to his promise doesn't mean he didn't . . . care for me. I refuse to believe anything else."

She tipped over on the floor and pulled in a deep shuddering breath, but I realized she wasn't falling apart. I struggled to get closer until we lay face to face on the floor, only inches apart. She smiled at me. "Who needs a fabulous, classic six apartment overlooking Central Park anyway?"

I strained forward and licked her cheek, kissing her in the only way I could.

We lay that way for seconds, or maybe it was hours. All I knew was that since I had woken up all those months ago in Einstein's body, a veil had slowly been stripped away until I could see the reality of Sandy Portman. After a lifetime wasted living without truth, it had taken becoming a dog to understand I had lived without honor.

I also knew that it was time I saved my wife, give her what she had always wanted. A home. Security. I had to give her what I had promised.

The truth was I had known all along how to accomplish this feat. Since the day I found myself in Einstein's body, I'd had the power to force my mother to give Emily the apartment. I'd had the ability to save Emily since the beginning.

All I had to do was share my mother's secret.

chapter forty-one

A shot of strength got me up from the floor. I managed to bark at Emily, getting her to follow me up to the suite at the top of the stairs, she helping me along as I led her to the last of my hiding places. She had gotten used to me guiding her to nooks and crannies, and she followed without question.

"What is it, E?"

Suddenly I was unsure. I hesitated in front of the floorboard under which I had hidden my last and oldest journal.

I thought of my early years. My mother and her laughter, the paint and canvases. To this day the smell of linseed oil makes me yearn for something long vanished.

Back when I was young, my mother had been proud of being *in* my father's world but not being *of* it. After their wedding she continued her art, shunned the society women and traditional duties my father's world expected her to take on. And somehow his world found her quaint and original. She became known as the artist, and the most important people in town vied to be included in her dinner parties. But no one had ever seen her art.

Isn't that the way? What you can make others envision in their heads can prove far greater than the reality of what you can possibly produce.

My mother didn't know this, got caught up in the wave of her newfound popularity. And when she determined that she could solidify her reputation by gaining a showing of her work in one of downtown's most prestigious galleries, she moved mountains to get it done, ignoring the whispers that she had gotten the show because of her husband's name, not because of talent.

She painted for weeks, setting me up on the hardwood floors at the Dakota with picnic lunches and paints of my own. She played Mozart and Mahler, followed by pulsing rock and the blues. The walls vibrated with sound. My father would show up unexpectedly, and they would disappear into a back bedroom. When they emerged, my mother's hair even messier, he would kiss me on the forehead and leave us to our world.

My father went to great lengths to make sure the art showing would be a great success. He was proud of his wife. He loved that she was more than the narrow people with whom he had grown up.

A week before the event my mother's mood changed. An art professor from NYU asked to see a preview of her work. Lying on the floor in the Dakota, my colored markers forgotten, I heard words like *amateur, paint by numbers, no better than a business major needing an arts credit to graduate.* After that, there was a long pause, no one talking, before my mother laughed and said, *"Oh, silly, these aren't the paintings I plan to show! I just wanted to see how smart you really are!"*

I couldn't imagine what other paintings she could be talking about, but I didn't mention it and the professor didn't ask.

For the days leading up to the show Mother and I didn't take a car across the park to the Dakota. She dressed up in fancy clothes then vanished for hours, leaving me at home. At the end of each of those dwindling days before the big event she returned, tired and smelling of paint and turpentine, but without the telltale traces that she had been doing any painting herself.

She was nervous the night of the show, my father presenting her with stunning emerald earrings that dripped like pieces of a crystal chandelier and matched her eyes. *"Diamonds are too ordinary for my wife."*

She had fidgeted, not laughing, not kissing him as I expected her to do.

The show was declared an unmitigated success. The crowds were wowed, even the critics praised her work as far above what they expected from a rich man's wife. Standing in front of the canvases in my tiny suit and bow tie, my eyes narrowed in surprise. The paintings on the wall weren't my mother's.

I don't know where she got the work, probably from some struggling artist who had reached the end of his rope and was willing to sell his soul for the money my mother was willing to pay. The day after the show, my father confronted her about an unexplained expenditure of fifty thousand dollars. She had gone on about starting a new life, needing new clothes. Father and I looked at her in confusion, but only I knew the truth. My mother didn't have a single new dress in her massive closet.

Within days, my mother "retired," explaining that it was time to devote herself to helping those in need make their way in the world of art. The lightness left my mother, hardness rushing in to fill the void. Althea Portman became the most important benefactor of the New York art scene, a woman who served on boards, loaned out her "expertise" like a fairy godmother to the rich who wanted to build their collections. I've often thought that she had lived her fraudulent talent for so long that she actually came to believe it.

In the scheme of things, all these years later, I didn't think society would do much more than sneer at her if they found out the truth. But I knew a sneer was more than my mother was willing to risk. She wouldn't jeopardize the reputation on which she had built her life, certainly not over an apartment that mattered little to her. I had always gambled on that, held the information close in case my mother had been tempted to use her self-serving ways against me.

But another realization came on the heels of the first. The hope and excitement I felt froze. If I showed Emily the journal where I detailed the information about my mother, yet again I would be acting without honor.

The thought had never entered my mind when I gathered the information as a man. As I had already come to understand, honor had never mattered to me before.

The walls around me seemed to shudder in a sigh of disappointment. And why not, I thought. I hadn't been able to come up with a way to save my wife, at least not honorably. I had failed. If I used the information, acted yet again without honor, I would lose all chance of moving on to something great.

My thoughts raced. But I couldn't come up with any other means to help my wife. My breathing grew more labored, and I understood that I was fast running out of time. If I wanted to give my wife the apartment, the journal was the only way.

I waited for anger to hit me, waited to cry and curse at the unfairness of my life. But the anger didn't come.

Standing in front of the worn wooden floorboard, I was amazed to realize that what happened to me no longer mattered. The telling of my mother's secret would ruin me by proving that I had never had and still didn't have the ability to achieve a goal with honor. But I would do it to give Emily what she deserved.

I guided her to the floorboard in the far left-hand corner of the main room. She didn't look at me oddly. She figured it out easily, prying the board free.

emily

My sister Emily relied on hard work and faith. I relied on having fun and using my quick thinking to get out of trouble. How was it possible our mother could raise two such different daughters?

—EXCERPT FROM *My Mother's Daughter*

chapter forty-two

I read everything in Sandy's journal. When I came to the end, I knew that I had finally found the way to keep the apartment.

By Monday afternoon, I had worked hard to wrap up all that I needed to do. I had promised Tatiana I would come into the office that day. But first I had to see Sandy's mother.

It was after four when I rang the bell. At first the uniformed maid said the lady of the house was unavailable.

"Tell her that I have something she needs to see. Something of her son's."

Minutes later, the maid guided me to Althea's study on the third floor where my mother-in-law looked out into the private gardens below. Even without seeing her face, I sensed that something about her was different. For the first time since I had known Althea Portman, she seemed old.

"On Sunday," she said without preamble, without turning around to face me, "a friend called and told me to turn on the television. I saw the interview. I saw the plaque. *Beloved husband, son, and friend.*" She hesitated. "That was generous of you to include me and Sandy's father."

"I know you loved your son."

"I wonder if he knew that." I heard the sadness in her voice, almost defeat, before she turned to me abruptly. "What is it you want? I take it you received the final eviction notice."

"I did."

"Will you be out before the deputies are forced to remove you?"

I didn't respond and Althea's eyes narrowed in confusion when I extended the formal blue-leather volume.

"What is that?"

"Sandy kept a journal."

She didn't move. Somewhere in the distance a grandfather clock tolled the half hour. Four-thirty. I needed to get to Caldecote soon.

"There are several journals, actually. But I think you should see this one."

Althea seemed to debate, but in the end she walked over to me and took it. With perfectly manicured hands, she opened to the first page. I watched as a series of emotions fluttered across her face while she read page after page. Uncomfortable, I turned away.

"I always wondered if he knew the truth," she finally said.

When I turned back she was sitting in the chair at her desk. She looked even older than she had when I arrived.

"I take it you've brought this here today in order to force me to give you the apartment. I'm surprised, Emily. You've never struck me as the type who would resort to blackmail. But fine. I'll make this easy. It's yours."

"You misunderstand. I don't want it. I brought the journal so you'd have it in your possession when I move out."

"What?"

"I have no intention of doing anything with the information. Just give me time to find someplace else to live. I'll need more than the three days the final notice gave me. But I'll be out by the end of the month."

She sat there stiff and unmoving, suspicious. "After all this you don't want the apartment?"

I smiled at her, feeling a profound peace. "I don't want it this way, not by blackmailing you into handing it over. Besides"—I shrugged, finally willing to accept what we both knew was true—"we both know I can't afford it." And I understood as well that I no longer needed it. I had dreamed of living in the Dakota, and I had done that. Just as with my mother and my husband, I couldn't expect an apartment to complete the fairy-tale world of which I had dreamed.

Althea didn't argue the point, not that I expected or even wanted her to. For the first time in months, if not years, I felt free.

I smiled and started to leave, but at the door Althea stopped me.

"Emily."

She started to speak, then stopped.

"Is something wrong?" I asked.

"No, no." She flipped her hand, as if waving something away. "Send me the bill for your move. And perhaps we can come up with some sort of monetary settlement . . . for all you put into the apartment."

Her tone was brusque, as if she hated that she was offering but somehow felt she owed me something for the journal. I knew my mother-in-law would never want to be beholden to me.

"Thank you, but I'll manage."

I started out again.

"The dog," she blurted. "Einstein. You once mentioned that he loved Mozart."

"Yes," I said carefully.

"And tell me, how did you find this journal?"

My eyes narrowed, trying to put the two together. "Einstein led me to it."

"Just as he showed me the child's scrawl behind the wallpaper."

"Right. I forgot about that."

"Oddly, I haven't been able to."

"What are you thinking, Althea?"

She flipped mindlessly through the journal. Then she shook herself and closed the volume with a snap.

"Nothing. He's a smart dog. Smarter than most."

I smiled. "Smart, yes, and charming when he wants to be."

Her next words surprised me. "Do you feel that Sandy's dead?"

"What?"

She pursed her lips, but the strange look in her eyes didn't abate as she ran her finger along the gold inlays on the cover. "It's nothing. I guess I'm just missing my son. Thank you for bringing the journal to me, Emily. Take as long as you need to move out."

■

I felt excited and nervous at the same time when I turned the corner onto Fifth Avenue and pulled out my BlackBerry, punching in a number I thought I would never use.

"Hedda Vendome, please."

"She's in a meeting. Can I tell her who's calling?"

"Tell her it's Emily Barlow."

I was put on hold and half expected to be forced to leave a message.

"Emily, darling. I saw the interview on television."

"Thank you for setting it up."

"I am nothing if not a master at getting attention. And let me just say, everyone has seen the interview. My assistant even found clips of it on that ridiculous but surprisingly addictive YouTube. You are something of a star!"

Cars rushed by, buses making it difficult to hear as I leaned back against the limestone façade of an elegant prewar building. The subtle heat of the late fall sun that had beat against the stone all afternoon seeped into my spine.

"An absolute star, I tell you! And why not, you were fabulous. Kind, determined, and that whole meltdown on the curb. Inspired! Too bad you didn't time it closer to your mother's book release." She laughed, not lowering her voice. "A little bird told me your sister went AWOL. I'm guessing that you single-handedly saved that book."

"Who told you that?" I didn't want anyone to know that Jordan hadn't written *My Mother's Daughter.* I had gone to great lengths to write it from her perspective, wanted her to be the star of the story.

"Not to worry. I won't tell anyone. But really, when are you coming to work for me?"

"Actually, I wondered if we could meet for lunch. Tomorrow, if you can."

"Ha! I knew you'd come around. We'll meet at Michael's. Part negotiation, part celebration."

"Not Michael's. Let's meet at the Westside Diner on Broadway and Sixty-ninth."

"Good God! You're taking me to a diner?"

I smiled into the phone. "I'm expecting you to pay, Hedda."

She laughed loudly. "Tomorrow at twelve-thirty. I'll be there."

I disconnected, then hailed a cab. Next stop, Caldecote Press.

chapter forty-three

You can wait in Ms. Harriman's office. She'll be right in."

Entering Tatiana's corner suite, I walked over to the wall of windows, looking out at the towers of glass and steel that filled midtown Manhattan. Two blocks north, I could see slices of Central Park through the other buildings.

"This is a surprise." Tatiana stood in the doorway and crossed her arms.

"I told you I'd come in today."

"I expected you first thing this morning, at your desk, fast at work scouring the world for the perfect manuscript that would set the world on fire." She stepped forward, studying me. Before I could reply, she said, "Instead, you've come to quit."

I had to smile. "I have."

She didn't look happy. "I knew this would happen. I knew once you found your footing again you'd want to move on. But to work for Hedda?"

"Where did you hear that?"

"Do you really think I could possibly let Hedda be the only one in town who knows everything that's going on?"

I laughed and shook my head. "I suspect not. But just so you know, that isn't my plan."

This surprised her, but after a few seconds a smile cracked on her mouth. "I'm guessing Hedda doesn't know that."

"Not yet, but she will. Tomorrow. She was a friend of my mother's. I want to tell her my plans in person. The truth is, I want to start over and see where that takes me. Though don't worry; Jordan will still promote *My Mother's Daughter.* I'll see to it. But it needs to be Jordan's book, not mine. As the editor, I will talk to anyone you want me to. But I have to move on."

She didn't say anything, just stood there.

"Thank you, Tatiana. Thank you for putting up with me, for pushing me."

Still nothing, so I nodded and started to leave. But then I stopped. "There's something I need to know."

She got that suspicious look on her face, one brow lifting.

"Why *did* you push me?" I asked.

She dismissed it with a wave. "It was nothing, I didn't have anything better to do."

"We both know that isn't true."

"See, you're more straightforward than I believed."

"Which leads me to my second question," I said.

"Can't we just hug, or something?"

"And braid hair?"

She laughed. "Fine, what is it?"

"Why did you give me a chance to publish my sister's book in the first place, then give me the time to fix it once it turned into a disaster?"

"Caldecote Press couldn't afford—"

"Tatiana, please. Why really?"

She narrowed her eyes. "I told you. I knew your mother."

"There has to be more to it than that."

She debated, then after a moment she shrugged. "When I was twenty-one, I was your mother's assistant at WomenFirst."

I had expected many things, but not this. "You?"

"Yes, me. I was like so many young women straight out of college, wanting to make a difference. I was going to be a new era's Gloria Steinem. And let me tell you, I was damned good at my job."

"No surprise there."

She smiled for a second, then grew serious. "I should clarify. I was good at my job when I wasn't falling apart over some guy." She scowled. "I was a walking cliché, a slave to a series of bad boyfriends. Then one day your mother took me aside and told me I had everything it took to be successful, everything but belief in myself." She shook her head. "Saying it out loud now makes it sound so kind of her, so helpful. But she ended by telling me to buck up, stop selling myself short. Quite frankly, I was angry and I quit, dismissing her as an old woman who didn't know the first thing about being young and living in the city. Then one day I found myself between jobs and boyfriends, sitting on a bench in the Village, lost, with no idea what I was going to do next, and I remembered what she said."

Tatiana walked to the window, looking out over a world she had since conquered. "I got my act together, and now here I am." She turned to face me. "I hadn't thought of your mother in years, not until Charles Tisdale was giving me a rundown of everyone at the company, telling me who was doing what, the potential each person had. He told me you had been a rising star, but hadn't been able to recover after your husband's death. He said you were circling down the drain. His words, not mine."

I grimaced, but Tatiana didn't let up.

"When I walked into that deli and saw you with a plastic container filled with mashed potatoes, your clothes a mess, your hair worse, I realized you were me when I was sitting on that park bench." She shrugged. "Since I'm not one for mothering, I settled on pushing you. When you pitched *My Mother's Daughter,* you handed me the perfect means to help you . . . and in a strange twist of fate, to thank your mother for what she had done for me."

We stood for a second, and this time I really did feel like hugging her.

"Don't you dare," she said, though she smiled. "Any more questions?"

"No. Thank you for telling me."

"You're welcome."

I started to leave.

"And Emily."

I looked back.

"I have no doubt that whatever you decide to do you will make your mother proud."

I practically flew out of the offices of Caldecote Press understanding that my mother had done the best she could with her life, living in a world not quite at ease with her, or she with it. She had tried to do something important, but in the end felt she had failed. She hadn't gotten to see what she had achieved, the lasting effect, but I had. I had seen it in Hedda wanting to make a difference through books; in Tatiana, whom Lillian Barlow had helped become more than a young woman living at the whim of men;

in Jordan's desire to tell the story of what she had accomplished; even in myself. None of us had given in to an ordinary world. We all, in our own ways, had tried to be extraordinary. Lillian Barlow had made a difference in the world.

Now I would use the strength she had always seen in me and start over.

■

When I got home, Einstein was lying in the gallery, panting hard.

"E?"

Kneeling next to him I stroked his fur. "What's wrong, boy?"

He groaned, trying to get up. Since he had come home with me, he had been bossy and energetic, commanding. It had been easy to forget that when I found him at the clinic he had been old, tired, more dead than alive.

"You're going to be okay, E. *We're* going to be okay. I'm going to find us a perfect apartment. No stairs, close to the park. You'll love it, I promise."

He went stiff, a moan rumbling low.

"I know, I know. It won't be the Dakota. But no way was I going to use that journal to blackmail Althea. I'm plenty young enough to start over."

I sank down beside him, smiling ruefully. "Okay, so I'm thirty-two. But it's never too late. You and me, buddy. Emily and Einstein. You've just got to hang in there."

sandy

chapter forty-four

It is regret that kills, the if onlys that leave the mortal wounds.

If only I had seen myself clearly while I was still a man.

If only I had learned back then what I know now about how to live a life worth living.

If only I had understood that my wife couldn't accept the apartment before I revealed my mother's secret.

I experienced a moment of frustration that I had proven my lack of honor, all for naught. But the feeling didn't last. I hardly recognized the thought that it had happened as it should. I had done everything I could to help Emily, and with each shuddering breath I took I felt my body diminish. I didn't panic. I accepted that this was the end. And for once in my life I was ready to face the consequences of my actions.

At some point, the sounds of the city blocked out by the thick apartment walls, Emily and I were surprised when my mother arrived unannounced.

"Mrs. Portman?" Emily said when she pulled open the door.

"Emily."

My mother walked in without being asked. She stopped when she saw me lying on the floor.

"Einstein," she said simply.

I managed to lift my head and sniff. My eyesight was nearly gone, my sense of smell barely there. But I recognized the French milled soap she preferred, and I found comfort in that too. When I couldn't hold my head up any longer, she walked over and squatted in front of me.

She looked at me, her eyes narrowing as she stared into mine. She didn't pet me or say anything else. After a moment, she glanced up at Emily.

"Just so you know, I didn't buy those paintings to save myself," my mother said.

Emily looked confused.

"The paintings that I showed, the ones that weren't mine."

"Althea, you don't need to explain."

"But I do." She stood and faced my wife. "Believe it or not, I didn't do it because I refused to be embarrassed. I bought them so my husband wouldn't be mortified when the critics annihilated the woman he had defended to his friends and family. I did it because I loved my husband and my son. But in doing so, I made a deal with the devil. The only way I could live with what I had done was to give up the thing that had made me who I was, my art." She hesitated, her green eyes bright with emotion. "And that made me cold, unrelenting. I know that."

Emily took a step toward her, but my mother quickly raised her chin. "Not that I think you care why I did it, or even that you should. But . . ." She nodded. "I wanted to explain."

She reached into her handbag and pulled out some papers. "Here," she said, extending them to Emily.

"What's this?"

"Just read it."

While Emily glanced through the papers, my mother turned back to where I lay panting on the floor.

"Einstein," she said again.

It wasn't a call to me, it wasn't a question. It was some sort of mantra, a word spoken repeatedly to find a way into deeper meaning.

I heard Emily gasp. "You're deeding me the suite upstairs?"

A jolt of adrenaline ran through me, enough that I was able to pick my head up off the floor.

"Yes," Mother said.

"I don't understand. I would never tell anyone about what's in the journal. Why would you do this?"

"To be perfectly honest, I'm not sure. But if there is any truth to what you say, about Sandy making that promise . . ."

My shaky heart sputtered as my mother never took her gaze away from me, her words trailing off.

"You're a strange old dog, Einstein," my mother said, her voice soft, crouching down again. "I don't know what to make of you." She reached out, touching the very tip of my paw with her perfectly manicured hand. "But you make me feel the need to honor what perhaps really was my son's wish. The suite is something that Emily can afford."

As soon as she said the words aloud, she went bright red and stood.

"This whole situation has me acting daft. Take the apartment, Emily. Move your things upstairs and let's be done with this. I'll pay to have the apartments separated as they were originally."

She left as quickly as she came, unable to deal with something beyond her understanding. Emily and I were in shock. But more than that I felt an even deeper peace. At some level my mother had recognized me, and had attempted to do the right thing in my honor.

I could feel Emily's shock turn into amazement, and I tried to get up to show Emily how happy I was. But the stronger she became, the weaker Einstein grew. My body trembled from hackles to paw, like life passing through me, my breath coming out in a shuddering gasp.

"Oh, E," she breathed. "You can't go. Not now." She leapt away. "I'm calling the vet."

With what little strength I had left, I latched onto her pant leg with my teeth.

"No," I managed to growl.

"You can't give up, E."

But I didn't let go, not until I sensed her understanding.

Her breath sighed out of her as she lay down next to me on the floor. Tears welled up, spilling over. I strained to get closer.

"Please, Einstein. Let me get you to the vet."

There was no need. Deep down, she knew it. I knew it.

Emily cupped my head in her hand. "I love you, E."

And she did, always had.

That's when I understood I had one last thing to do before I left this body.

It took every ounce of willpower I had to fight the fading. By the time I heard the sound in the outer vestibule, every inch of me was strained. But at the sound, I gathered my remaining strength and let out an anguished howl.

"Einstein," Emily gasped.

I howled again and seconds later we heard the banging on the front door. My wife scrambled up and whipped open the door.

"Are you okay?" I heard Max ask.

"Oh, God, it's Einstein."

Max came over to where I lay and placed his hand on me as if assessing. He looked startled when our eyes met, though I suspect from the instant settling that he had seen something of death and the silent messages of the soul.

When I licked his fingers, he leaned forward. "It's okay. I'll take care of her."

I had done everything I could for my wife, and in that moment Einstein and I began to part in earnest.

There was no pain now, just a growing sense of loss, a gentle pureness that I had not fully appreciated stripping away from me. When the separation was nearly complete I shuddered at the realization that by living as Einstein I had developed a theory. In order to live a life truly worth living you had to have strength in the face of adversity, patience when confronted with challenge, and bravery in the face of fear. As Sandy Portman I had used arrogance in the face of fear, disdain in the face of challenge, and selfishness in the face of adversity.

Emily had been my biggest victim, not because of horrible things I did, but because I had dared her to love me, and when she did I was unprepared for the enormity of that love, the responsibility—something that deep down I had known I didn't know how to give back. But I had taken it anyway, handling it without care.

The fact was I had married her because in her eyes I saw the man I could be. I ended up wanting a divorce because living with her every day was forcing me to see myself for who I really was, a man who didn't have the strength to work hard and persevere and do what it took to be something beyond ordinary.

Finally, I understood.

I felt Einstein's heart beat erratically, and a sense of forgiveness washed over me, forgiveness for who I had been.

I started to shake as if I was cold.

"I'll get some blankets," I heard Max say.

I didn't need blankets, though I was happy for one last minute alone with my wife. I felt her hand stroke my side, felt her bury her face in my neck. I breathed her in one last time, and when I exhaled I left Einstein's body.

I ceased to see and smell. I became blind to the world, but I didn't panic, I waited. Eventually my senses began to return—different, more acute, but softer at the same time, as if I had entered an easier place.

Once we had separated completely, Einstein died.

"Good-bye, E," Emily whispered into the little dog's fur. "Good-bye, Sandy," she added softly.

My mother might have suspected it was me. But somehow Emily knew for sure.

The old man arrived then. With his appearance this time, every uncomfortable feeling I'd ever had, both as Sandy and as Einstein, disappeared completely.

"So, you managed to get it right," he said. "I'm impressed."

I brushed away what I sensed were my own tears, laughing in relief. "I take it I'm not fading away to nothing."

The old man snorted. "No, not that you didn't get closer than I've ever seen any soul get and still make it back."

Joy surged, but there were still traces of the old me left. "Lucky for you, I saved your backside, and you know it."

"Well, there is that."

We both laughed before I saw flashes of my life. Sandy Portman as a child with colored markers drawing in the Dakota. Sandy Portman as a young man moving into the Dakota. Sandy Portman carrying Emily over the threshold on our wedding day. Again and again a lifetime of potential had spilled out before me. Again and again I had squandered it. But I no longer felt anger or regret. I simply had a sense that I would miss this place. I would miss my life.

"You'll like where you're going even better," the old man said.

I had no fear, no trepidation. I felt comforted, optimistic. Amazingly, I was ready to go.

The hologram of me moved away from Emily. When she tensed with loss I realized that she sensed I was there. Since the day I met her I had desired her in some elemental way. I had wanted her, had needed her even. But now, I understood, after all we had been through, I had fallen utterly and completely in love with my wife.

Kneeling in front of her, I reached out and pulled her close until our lips nearly touched. "I love you, Emily. Love you forever."

She drew a deep breath and smiled through her tears, leaning into me. "I know."

I saw it then, a single feather drifting down, and I was sure Emily somehow sensed it too. This time I didn't hesitate. I plucked it from the air.

I glanced over at the old man in question. He just smiled. "Yep, that one's for you."

I looked back only once, saw Emily on the floor of the high-ceilinged gallery, tears of peace and sadness on her face, Max sitting next to her with Einstein held secure in the blanket. Then everything about me lifted, seeming to fly as the old man and I disappeared through the wall.

I didn't get to go back and relive my life as Sandy Portman; I didn't get my body back. But I did get to make things right for Emily. And by becoming a dog I had finally, for once in my life, acted as a true man.

emily

I understand now that by allowing her daughters to witness her own joys and mistakes, my mother gave Emily and me the tools to make our own way, to create our own blueprint. I always believed that Emily and I had nothing in common. But I've learned that while we're different, there is no denying we are sisters. We will always be there for each other, because at the end of the day, no matter what, we are both our mother's daughter.

—EXCERPT FROM *My Mother's Daughter*

epilogue

It seems impossible that a year has gone by since I lost Einstein, a year since I truly said good-bye to Sandy.

Yes, I found myself again, but in many ways I'm different now, someone beyond the daughter who was forced to grow up too fast, different from the girl who both loved and was jealous of a younger sister, changed from a wife who fell apart because of a husband's betrayal. My strength is no longer banked or dependent on a scaffolding of lists and plans.

I still run almost every morning along the bridle path or upper park loop. I even bake some, cupcakes and cookies and chocolate croissants, but in more reasonable quantities. And I go to work in the suite above Sandy's old apartment. In summer I fill the rooms with peonies, and in the fall I pull together an assortment of autumn flowers, then winter greens. My new home is small, but perfect for the life I have created on my own.

It was this, I now understand, that I saw in my dream, me high up in the grand old building.

The Portmans closed up the original apartment, putting sheets over the furniture. I rarely see Althea. She, like my mother, gave up pieces of herself in an attempt to fit into a world that didn't accept her as she was, remaking herself into something she never wanted to be. The difference was that Althea found a place for herself that she could live with. My mother wasn't as fortunate. I'm not sure if I admire Althea for that, or hate her just a little bit more because she survived when my mother didn't.

Whatever the case, while Althea and I never got along, we now share something in common: the knowledge that we were given a second chance with her son. It makes things both easier and more strained since she still has a difficult time accepting something that seems impossible.

But I understand. It's hard to believe in miracles until you've seen one happen. But once you've seen, well, life alters and you can never look at the world around you the way you once did.

■

I walk into Meeker Books on Columbus Avenue. At the front of the store stands a sign with my photo on it.

Reading & Book Signing
with Emily Barlow
Author of
The Adventures of Einstein:
A Dastardly Dog's Life at the Dakota

I never wanted to write, still have no interest in writing books for adults. But after finding a box of unused, beautiful blue journals with finely wrought blank pages that my husband left behind, I realized that creating picture books for children, more specifically children's stories about Einstein, felt right. I am compelled to write about my dog, about his adventures in a home that was Sandy's gift to me. Telling Einstein's stories is a gift I have given myself.

I hold a published copy of the large, thin children's book in my arms. With the tips of my fingers, I trace the cover image—a little white dog watching a single feather float down. The pages are filled with my words and the illustrations I have found the ability to draw. Is this another gift from Sandy, or perhaps from my mother, or another miracle given to me by a hand that I can't see? I don't know, and it doesn't matter. I found a way to reenter life on my own terms, with strength I earned through events I survived. And this time I step forward with a man I love in simple pureness.

Joy surges through me, then grows deeper when I see him. Max.

He stands by the sign. When he sees me, he doesn't say a word, simply walks over to where I stand and pulls me close.

"There you are. I've been waiting for you."

He has waited, patiently, kindly, despite the fact that for a few months

I slipped away. He has given me the space I needed to sort out my life, but he's been there whenever I needed him.

Max has found his way back to himself as well. He has returned to Wall Street, working for a fund that invests in start-up companies determined to make a difference. When we aren't working or meeting deadlines, he teaches me to climb mountains, and I share with him the simple pleasure of reading a good book in a quiet café. I don't know exactly what is in store for us, but I'm excited about the possibilities.

He takes my hand and we weave through the quaint shop. The event area in back is already overflowing with people. Young readers and their parents fill the seats; reporters and publishing types stand around the perimeter. Dear, sweet Birdie with her Southern charm has brought cupcakes and cookies, Birdie who is the one meant to bake, and love, and sort through her Texas-sized secrets in the apartment she lives in not far from me.

No one has seen me yet, but I see through the crowd to the front table where hundreds of my books wait.

When I met Hedda at the diner and proposed the idea of writing a series of children's books about my dog, Einstein, she was stunned. Her surprise was followed quickly by those gears in her brain clicking into place.

"It's genius! Of course you should be writing stories for children! Like Eloise in the Plaza! Only yours will be Einstein at the Dakota. I love it!"

Hedda sent me a copy of the book as soon as it came off the press, but seeing the book in stores never fails to move me.

Jordan's book hit the best-seller lists the first week out. She flew back to the States without a bit of resistance to tour for *My Mother's Daughter.* I shouldn't have been surprised that my sister loved every second of the attention. And I shouldn't have been surprised when she donated every cent of the profits to women in need. I had never loved her more.

When asked what was on tap for book two she said there would be no book two, at least not from her. I laughed and hugged her tight.

And Sandy?

I feel him every day, watching over me. *"I love you, Emily. Love you forever."*

I wasn't wrong to believe in him. And I understand now that I don't feel alone because I'm not. No matter what happens in my life, I am certain that somehow he is there.

The crowd sees I've arrived, the children circling around me, wanting to know all about Einstein and his adventures in the nooks and crannies of a grand old building that is more real in their imaginations than the actual structure which stands only a few blocks away.

These children and the world have fallen in love with a wiry little dog who acts just like a snob of a man.

"Who would've ever believed?" I whisper.

I'm almost certain I hear Sandy laugh.

1. Emily and Jordan are opposites; Jordan was their mother's favorite, and Emily always knew this. Does your personality in some way balance or counterbalance your sibling's personality? Your parent's? While being the less favorite child can be difficult, are there any advantages? Disadvantages to being the favorite?

2. Sandy Portman was a dog of a man while he was living, and he had to become a dog in order to learn how to be a true man. Do you agree with Sandy's ultimate fate at the end of the book? Do you think Einstein/Sandy changes gradually over the course of book, or just in the end? How so?

3. Emily says: "[Althea], like my mother, gave up pieces of herself in an attempt to fit into a world that didn't accept her as she was. . . ." Both Sandy's and Emily's mothers came of age during the birth of modern feminism, and each tried to lead a life that was true to who she wanted to be—ultimately paying a price for her choices. Do you feel women in this day and age can really have it all, dreams, work, and family? Do you think you see or saw your parents clearly, for who they are rather than who you want them to be?

4. Max is younger than Emily by a few years, but in many ways feels older. What made him wiser than his years? Compare Max and Sandy—how were they different? Similar? What did Emily see and need in both of them?

5. In many ways, it seems that Emily is more devastated about Sandy's cheating than by his death. Why is this? Do you think it's true to how people feel? How did Einstein help Emily recover from both—Sandy's death and his cheating—in different ways?

6. When Emily was a child, she almost drowned in the ocean, but was washed up on the beach at the last moment; she wondered then if God had looked inside her and considered her "worth saving." The idea of saving others or being saved is an important part of Emily and Sandy/Einstein's stories; Sandy feels that Emily saved him when he first met her and then she saves him again from being killed as a dog. Discuss what saving or rescuing means for these characters. How does it play into and define each of their lives? Do you feel that you've ever been rescued? Or rescued someone?

Discussion Questions

St. Martin's Griffin

7. Emily thought she knew her husband, Sandy, but didn't fully. Do you feel it's possible to truly know a spouse or significant other? Do you think you know yours? Does he or she ever surprise you? Tell you a story about their past that you didn't realize had occurred?
8. Second chances are an important theme in *Emily and Einstein;* each character goes through a transformation of some sort, and feels the need for a new start. Describe these moments for each of them. If you were given a chance to look back on your life and do something over, would you? What might you notice about yourself and your choices that you wouldn't otherwise?
9. Emily runs the New York City marathon in order to find herself after the shock of losing her husband—and to honor Sandy. How is this decision representative of her story as a whole? Do you think it's possible to truly shake the past free or come to terms with it in order to move forward? Have you ever done something drastic, like run a marathon, with the same goal in mind?
10. Consider Einstein's line toward the end: "I had wanted to punish her for going for what she wanted regardless of the cost to herself." He says that he was jealous of her faith in something beyond what he could see. What do you think this means? How does it fit into the larger themes of the book? Do you think this difference of perception might be the reason Sandy and Emily were together, or the reason their relationship failed—or both?
11. Do you think that Emily makes the right career decision at the end of the book? Why or why not?
12. "Home" plays a central role in this story—ideas of the perfect home, the homes we make for ourselves, or the ones we're given. What do you think "home" means to Emily? To Sandy? To Jordan? Do their different needs or opinions clash? What does "home" mean to you?

The award-winning novels of

LINDA FRANCIS LEE

will win your heart!

"An utter triumph all the way around, simply spectacular!"

—J. R. WARD, *NEW YORK TIMES* BESTSELLING AUTHOR

"Lee once again demonstrates her trademark wit in this hilarious, fast-paced romp."

—*BOOKLIST*

"Fresh and funny, original and outrageous, this novel is fabulous from start to finish."

—KRISTIN HANNAH, *NEW YORK TIMES* BESTSELLING AUTHOR

St. Martin's Griffin